Praise for the Damned Emperors series

'In *Caligula*, Turney uses fiction to challenge some of [the] lies that masquerade under the name of "history" ... [His narrator, Livilla] provides an energetic and intelligent eyewitness view of the imperial court and of the gradual decline of Caligula's rule ... A satisfyingly alternative look at Caligula, something perhaps better done in fiction than in academic history ... Great and enjoyable'
  Mary Beard, *TLS*

'Caligula is a monster we all know and love to hate. Turney's novel challenges our prejudice, and sketches a more understanding view of the Roman Emperor ... Turney's version is an entirely plausible take on the sources. We pity the boy, even as we deplore the insane violence of the man. *Caligula* is an engrossing new spin on a well-known tale'
  Antonia Senior, *The Times*

'Turney's masterful, persuasive writing makes you start to question everything you have ever read about Rome's most tyrannical ruler ... Finding humanity and redeeming qualities in one of history's most reviled villains is a bold move, but in Turney's hands, it pays off'
  Helena Gumley-Mason, *The Lady*

'Enthralling and original, brutal and lyrical by turns. With powerful imagery and carefully considered history Turney provides a credible alternative to the Caligula myth that will have the reader questioning everything they believe they know about the period'
  Anthony Riches, author of the Empire series

'Inspired ... a mesmerising, haunting and disturbing portrait of Caligula'
  Kate Atherton, *Sunday Express S Mag*

'*Commodus* combines thrilling Roman spectacle, star-crossed young lovers, and poisonous palace intrigue into a compulsively readable

drama … A tense, taut, thrilling character study of one of Rome's most maligned rulers, transformed here into tragic hero'
Kate Quinn, author of *The Alice Network*

'Brilliant … a gripping gallop of a read, impeccably researched, beautifully written, impossible to put down'
Angus Donald, author of the Outlaw Chronicles

'Gripping, emotional and authentic. The best Roman novel I've read in a long time. Turney is one of the best historical novelists out there'
Christian Cameron, author of *Killer of Men*

'Turney masterfully gives readers a new and illuminating look at Emperor Commodus, but also introduces us to the clever freedwoman who should have been his empress. Seeing imperial Rome through Marcia's eyes is a delight not to be missed, and Turney is at the top of his game'
Stephanie Dray, author of *Lady of the Nile*

'Commodus, son of Marcus Aurelius: mad, bad and dangerous to stand too close to according to history. Turney, however, does here what he did in *Caligula* – puts some humanity back in the beast of Rome. Warm and well written'
Robert Low, author of the Oathsworn series

'This exuberant take on one of the great monsters of history is exhilarating in its revisionist energy; Turney is a truly cherishable talent'
Barry Forshaw on *Caligula*

'Superbly researched and elegantly written. A powerful and original narrative'
Nick Brown, author of *Agent of Rome* on *Caligula*

Caracalla

S.J.A. Turney is an author of Roman and medieval historical fiction, gritty historical fantasy and rollicking Roman children's books. He lives with his family and extended menagerie of pets in rural North Yorkshire.

Also by S.J.A. Turney

The Ottoman Cycle

The Thief's Tale
The Priest's Tale
The Assassin's Tale
The Pasha's Tale

The Knights Templar

Daughter of War
The Last Emir
City of God
The Winter Knight
The Crescent and the Cross
The Last Crusade

Wolves of Odin

Blood Feud
The Bear of Byzantium
Iron and Gold
Wolves Around the Throne

The Damned Emperors series

Caligula
Commodus
Domitian
Caracalla

S.J.A. TURNEY

CARACALLA

CANELO

First published in the United Kingdom in 2023 by

Canelo
Unit 9, 5th Floor
Cargo Works, 1-2 Hatfields
London SE1 9PG
United Kingdom

A CIP catalogue record for this book is available from the British Library.

Print ISBN 978 1 80032 934 8
Ebook ISBN 978 1 80032 673 6

All images in the *Historical Note* are from the author's own collection, except the 'Severan Tondo' image © José Luiz Bernardes Ribeiro, reproduced under Creative Commons licence BY-SA 4.0 International.

Cover design by Sarah Whittaker

Look for more great books at www.canelo.co

Printed and bound in Great Britain by Clays Ltd, Elcograf S.p.A.

I

For Suzy. Thank you for the unsurpassed gifts of knowledge and understanding that you have given to my children.

Their lives will be richer for your teachings.

Damnatio Memoriae

Upon the death of an emperor, it became practice for the senate to confer apotheosis upon his name, granting him divine status and a cult of his own. If the emperor had been despised, however, the senate could choose the precise opposite and vilify rather than deify him – *damnatio memoriae* (a modern term) would occur. Without hesitation or ceremony, the emperor's name was erased from all public inscriptions (a process known as *abolition nominis*), his image would be scratched from frescoes, his statues smashed. Sometimes, even coins bearing his image would be defaced. The damned emperor was not only denied an ascent to heaven, but wiped from history. Such was the fate of the wicked, the unpopular, or the unfortunate.

Prologue

Sword into flesh.

Blood.

Screaming. His. Hers. Mine.

And there… the twin spectres of a father and son, reaching, faces twisting with fury.

I wake in a sweat, the nightmares assailing me even as light streams in through the shutters, forcing me to blink repeatedly, motes of dust dancing before my eyes. I am shivering, despite the summer heat, and the bed sheet is wrapped and twisted into knots, soaked.

Must it be like this?

May I never rest?

I know that what I have done is unforgivable, and yet could I have done any different?

I rub the sweat from my eyes and focus, the world coalescing around me.

I clench my teeth and pull on the façade of imperium. I will have called out in my sleep, and slaves will be running to check on me, even though they know there is nothing wrong, for this is common to them. I cannot let them see a hollow man. They must not see a murderer.

They must see Marcus Aurelius Antoninus, emperor of Rome.

The good of the Empire comes above all.

Part One – Dynasty

'Paucos uiros fortes natura procreat; bona institutione plures reddit industria'

Few men are born brave; many become so through care and force of discipline

—Publius Flavius Vegetius Renatus

I

By the Gods and by Fate

Sicily, Summer AD 189

My earliest memory, oddly, is of him. A fascination at what he was.

We were on board a fast and light *liburnian*, bound for Syracusae, where my father, Septimius Severus, Propraetorian governor of Sicilia, was due to take up his lucrative and impressive posting. My mother, Julia Domna, never liked sea travel, but she put a brave face on it all, for the sake of the baby.

Geta, my mewling baby brother, was swaddled in Mother's arms as we cut our way across the waves.

On one level, I perceived him as a threat, I will admit. I had been the only child in our world, and while I was still the elder, now I would have to share that attention with another person. I looked at Mother, smiling and cooing at the squirming, crying infant, putting on a brave face for him despite her own fears. My own smile faltered. She was not *my* real mother, or so I had been told.

The woman who gave birth to *me*, Paccia Marciana, had died the day I was born, in a blood-soaked bed in Lugdunum, on a stormy spring morning, as Vulcan's hammer pounded the world and the rains washed away hope and despair alike. They had even washed away grief for my father, apparently, for barely had my mother been rendered down to ash, before he was looking at a new wife. I do not remember the journey east to meet her, nor the brief betrothal and wedding. I was barely a year old when I gained a new mother, having never met the old one, so there was no bitterness there. Indeed, from Julia I received all the love and care of mother for son, and so I had never felt out of place. Though there was a nagging discomfort lurking beneath the surface that I later understood came from the fact that though I was the eldest brother, unlike Geta I was not Julia's natural son.

At the time, though, I was excited. I had a brother! Someone to play with, to learn with, to share with, to be close to. He was little more than a crying bundle so far, but I had an inkling of what having a sibling could mean, for my father and his own brother, who Geta had been named after, were very close, supporting one another in a world that had become increasingly difficult under the unpredictable emperor Commodus and his court of serpents.

As the ship lurched from wave to wave, every jarring contact threatening to send us to our knees, every soul aboard gripping a rail to stay afoot, the baby seemed to do nothing but wail. Mother's face was filled with warmth, but also with weariness.

'I fear I shall miss Antiope,' she sighed at my father, playing with the folds of the wrapped bundle in her arms. My father simply mumbled something noncommittal.

We had let Antiope, my own nurse, go when we left Lugdunum, and there would be a new one for Geta when we settled into Sicilia. But in these days in between, all the work came down to Mother.

'I barely have the time to be seasick,' she added, with a slight hint of admonishment at Father for his lack of involvement. Still, she attacked the job like a centurion, strong in both body and will, a *propraetor* in her own little world.

'Soon, Julia,' Father replied, not taking his eyes from the sea. 'Soon you will have all the help you need.'

She nodded. Even she, powerful, glorious Julia Domna, was becoming exhausted, but she would not allow it to consume her. She was ever a match for Father. My gaze slipped to him, standing at the rail near the front of the ship, watching the walls of Syracusae approach, the vessel lurching and bouncing over the waves. Lucius Septimius Severus, son of Africa, praetor of Rome, was the most imposing man I ever met. A bear in human guise. At that tender age I was in awe of the man, as most boys are, but I never lost that sense of wonder and respect. He had climbed the ladder of posts at an astonishing rate, for Rome had found herself short of capable men after the Antonine Plague. He had cut his teeth in the campaign against the Mauri in his native Africa in the wake of their attempted invasion of Hispania. Some six feet tall, swarthy, and with thick, curly black hair that was beginning to show patches of grey, he was impressive to behold.

A cry of alarm drew my attention, and I turned to see a sailor who was doing something obscurely maritime with a rope slip with one bouncing wave and hurtle towards the rail. My heart lurched, for the man was clearly doomed, the momentum carrying him over the edge, where he would plunge into the waters beside the speeding ship, probably to die against the heavy, bouncing hull, battered into the drowning black.

None of the other sailors or protective marines were close enough to help, though they ran to try as the man scrabbled desperately at the rail, trying to hold on to the slippery timbers, his weight pulling him away. They would not have time.

Then, suddenly, Father was there, his arm shooting forth like a striking cobra and gripping the hapless sailor's arm. He was immensely strong, and the sailor clung, whimpering, to the powerful fist that held him aloft, as Father hauled him back over the rail to safety.

The man fell to his knees, weeping with relief, then realised what had happened and looked up at the man who had saved his life, a proconsular governor, a man more powerful than most bar the emperor himself. His shock was visible, and he quivered as he fawned over Father, thanking him over and over. I watched, a sense of pride growing in me. That was something of a defining moment in my admiration for Father, for most men of his rank would not have risked their own comfort, let alone their safety, for a lowly sailor.

–

We entered the city harbour shortly after, and the waters calmed, the ship moving steadily to the dock, and finally we disembarked. Father was the first to reach land, preceded only by his *lictors*, an announcement of his rank, as well as protection from any potential danger. I followed after, with my favoured slave, and stood beside Father as everything else was organised.

Father's secretary, one of the few men who felt confident in speaking to him almost as an equal, pulled him aside. I was nearby, and could just overhear their conversation.

'Should you have done that?'

'What?' Father asked.

'Saved the sailor.'

'He would have died.'

'It demeans the dignity of your rank to risk your own life to save a nobody's.'

Father turned and fixed the man with a direct and very pointed look. 'Every great man can look back down his lineage and find a "nobody" at its root. That sailor is a free man of Rome, and every free man of Rome has a value beyond estimation.'

Father turned, and saw me looking at him. He smiled, dropped to a crouch, and rested his big, powerful hand on my shoulders. I looked into his dark, wise eyes.

'There is something to be learned here, my boy. Even at your age it is important to learn such lessons, for one day you will climb the *cursus honorum* yourself as the master of our house. See the sailor?'

He indicated the man who was now leaning on the rail, still a little shaky, but recovering. I nodded.

'He is no consul, or tribune, or senator, or even a citizen, probably. He will be a free man of low birth from the provinces. A nobody, perhaps. But see the muscles in his arms? It is those muscles that steered our ship from Ostia to this island. It is muscles like those that drive the empire. Some will tell you that the empire functions because men in togas with broad stripes make proclamations. That the empire only works because its top men make the right decisions. They are wrong.'

I looked at the sailor. I could see nothing impressive about him.

Father cupped my chin in his hand and turned my face back to his. 'When your time in power comes, remember this day. Hold the respect of those broad-stripe senators and the great and the rich, but remember that the empire relies upon men many think to be of no consequence. The soldier, the sailor, the farmer, the carpenter. Without these men, fat senators would have no seat to sit in, no food to eat, and no empire to govern. The powerful always think that the empire works from the top down, but you need to have seen both ends to know the truth: the empire works from the bottom up.'

Mother disembarked then and joined us, carrying the baby, who had finally settled when the ship had done the same. Father switched back from Latin to Greek, for she knew only the tongue of the East in those days, as he explained what would happen next.

8

My memories of the following few months are rather vague and confused. I wish, in hindsight, I had paid more attention to Father's activities, though my time was rather taken up by a combination of lessons with tutors, helping Mother with Geta because the new nurse was taking time settling in, and exploring what I could of the island.

Father began to spend much of his time involved in affairs of state, managing the province, for he was new to Sicilia and had much to learn. I was not aware, at the time, of the fact that he had also spent much time in close conference with priests and augurs. It came to a head one night that winter when we had just finished the evening meal. Father dismissed us. Mother took Geta and his nurse, bidding me with a kindly tone to entertain myself for an hour or two. She was learning Latin fast that year, though she still struggled with some of the words and dropped into Greek. Fortunately, I had been raised in both languages from birth, and could follow her meaning.

So Father disappeared off into his office, the women took my brother elsewhere and I was left alone to lament the fact that Geta was not yet old enough to play with me. The evening darkness had already rolled in during the meal; the shutters were closed, the doors locked and guards in place around the estate, so any adventuring beyond our own gardens was impossible. Faced with boredom and solitude, I did what all four-year-olds do: I resorted to mischief.

I sneaked around the villa, finding any door I had not yet opened and testing it. I came across several new rooms, though the only one of interest was in the kitchens, which led to the room where the slaves stored all the ingredients for baking. Moving on with a handful of tasty loot, I was still stuffing my mouth with almonds when I found myself outside Mother's window, and could hear the low murmur of conversation.

I am not one for subterfuge. Never have been. I like my friends and enemies, often the same people, I have found, to be in my line of sight and with their intentions writ upon their face. Likewise I myself have always tended, even as a boy, to speak my mind with little care for the consequences. Still, I was in a mischievous mood that night, and so I listened in.

The conversation was troublesome and stilted, for the nurse knew only Latin, while Mother still favoured Greek, floundering for an explanation. As such I had plenty of time to digest it all as Mother made her feelings known. In retrospect, perhaps it was odd that she, a noblewoman of the East and wife of a propraetor, would confide so deeply in a mere nurse. Yet it may be that the nurse was the only woman in this new land with whom she could share her thoughts. And, knowing Mother, who was strong, fierce and clever, and no shrinking flower, it is likely that she always had it in mind that if the nurse betrayed her confidence she could have the woman killed and replaced in a trice. Whatever her reasons, she would be proved foolish in her openness.

Again, excuse my paraphrasing. The precise words of that conversation were said decades ago, and I was young. But I remember the meaning well, and the foreboding they carried.

'I am frightened for him, Mita.'

'It is neither unknown, Domina, nor inappropriate for a man to consult auspices and the gods on a matter.'

Mother's voice lowered and paused periodically then as she sought the words she needed in her new language. 'It... is not the priests I worry about. He... speaks to magicians.'

'This is not so common, but hardly a reason to fear.'

'Mita, he speaks to astrologers and seers, and I know it cannot be with regard to his own future, for Lucius has always had his life mapped out by such men, and has consulted over his destiny since childhood. So if it is not his own horoscope he is interested in...'

They went quiet then, and when conversation resumed they had moved somewhere further away and spoke in even quieter voices, and I could no longer hear them. Interested, though, I hurried across the gardens to the wall of Father's office and there crouched behind the oleander, below his shuttered window. The murmur of conversation there was a great deal harder to hear, and what I did hear I really could not follow. I was rather disappointed, having expected something exciting, and after a while, I became bored. I played with a stick for a time, then dipped my hand in the fishpond and chased the small gleaming forms around with questing fingers until finally I'd had about all I could take of gardens, and went back inside.

I happened to walk into the atrium at the same time as Father's office door opened, and I ducked behind a pillar. I'm not sure why, really. I had every reason and right to be there, and my presence was purely coincidental, despite my mischievous spirit. It was instinct, and it probably saved me a slap or a tongue-lashing.

The men who emerged from Father's office were strange. One wore a long white robe with all the signs of the Zodiac stitched into it in black and gold. He wore wispy grey hair and a long beard in the manner of a philosopher, and his face was wizened and screwed up, as though he had sucked something distasteful. The second was dressed in a flowing dark blue robe, his head and face shaved clean and shiny. The third interested me in how little I could see of him. He wore a long, hooded cloak that enveloped him and hid his features. Gaining the impression immediately that these three men were involved in some sort of subterfuge with Father, and that they were the men about whom Mother had worried, it struck me that the third was the bright one for favouring a garment that hid everything, from his features and his nature to his intentions. They left, and Father escorted them out. I had no idea what storm they heralded.

That storm broke two months later, some time in Martius, if I remember correctly. I was busy with learning some tedious lesson with a gangly tutor I hated when there came such a hammering on the front door I thought it could have been a battering ram. While my tutor searched his collection for some scroll or other, I stepped out of the room and hurried to the atrium, where I could just see the front door. Father was already there, stomping across the marble like a legionary on the march, bellowing to the slaves and pointing imperiously.

The slave opened our door, and I paled at what happened next.

Soldiers invaded our home!

They actually marched in, pushing the doorman aside with their gazes fixed on Father. I was surprised that he seemed to adopt a position almost of deference, given that I knew he had commanded soldiers, and as governor should outrank them. I know now that they were men of the Praetorian Guard, although at the time I did not recognise their uniforms and insignia. I did know they looked impressive and remarkably unhappy, and were led by a man with the tallest, bushiest white plume I had ever seen. He was a tribune, I later understood, which made their presence here all the more important, for such a senior officer to have been sent so far from Rome.

'What is the meaning of this?' Father demanded, but his tone was reasonable and non-provocative, with none of the defiance, accusation and hauteur one might have expected. Of course, in the days of the height of Cleander's power, it was prudent to be cautious when dealing with Praetorians.

'It has been reported to the emperor that you have...' the tribune began, unfolding a parchment to read the rest directly, '...consorted with seers, astrologers and other sorcerers concerning the wellbeing of the emperor and the future of his reign. This is an affront to the imperial dignity, and may lead to further counts of treason under the *Lex Maiestatis*. Your tenure in Sicilia is hereby cancelled, and you are ordered to return to Rome immediately to face charges. You have until one hour past dawn to board the *trireme* in the harbour and accompany us. If you are not present at that time, you will be deemed guilty, declared a fugitive and hunted down. Do you understand?'

Without a hint of panic or anger, or even a change in his expression, Father nodded at the tribune. 'I understand perfectly. I will present myself at dawn.'

The soldiers left then without a backward glance. When the doors shut after the men, Father turned. He saw my shocked face, but spoke first to the doorman and the major domo.

'No one is to be admitted or to leave without my express permission,' he said, pointing at the doorman. Then to the head of the household staff, 'Have everyone roused. I want the entire villa packed and ready to move one hour before dawn. Send my secretary to the port. Have the authorities dragged from their beds if necessary, but I want my family and the entire household booked on ships that sail for Rome tomorrow. And good, trustworthy ships, mind you. I must accompany the tribune, but I want my family just a mile behind me all the way.'

At this point I realised that Mother had arrived and was standing in another doorway, her face as white as a senator's toga. 'What have you done, Lucius?' she said.

'Nothing that will cause us any real trouble. This is all a misunderstanding. The emperor fears for his safety in a world where too many people already hate him, blinded to those of us who remain loyal by that snake, Cleander.'

Cleander, commander of the Praetorian Guard, the most powerful man in Rome, after the emperor, and a villain with eyes, ears, and knives, everywhere.

'But loyalty, Lucius? You consult magicians about the emperor's future?'

Father fixed her with a look. 'I do not seek the emperor's fall, my love. But any man with a modicum of sense can see that the emperor has no heir, and with things moving the way they are, if he does not either secure the succession or heal his rift with the senate soon, there will be another civil war. I seek only to learn what will be, and how to navigate it successfully, Julia. I know the emperor. When he hears this, he will understand. And I have heard it foretold that something like this would happen and that I would weather the storm.'

'But Cleander holds no love for you, and that man is poison. If he has turned the emperor against you, who else has he set in opposition? Who can you turn to for support?'

'Do not worry yourself, my love. I have consulted augurs, seers, gods… Every power from Apollo to Zeus and every letter in between. All the omens are good. There are still sensible men in Rome, old friends of mine.'

'I hope you are right, husband.'

That night I got as little sleep as anyone in the villa. The metaphorical storm having already broken, the literal one followed then, crashing thunder and pounding rain. Mother continually worried about the omen in that as she worked to pack the household, though Father assured all that this was no poor omen, for he had already given much in the way of devotions to Jove and Vulcan, and the priests of both had confirmed their favour.

I was exhausted as I watched Father depart as the very first glow of dawn lit the east that morning. He rode to the port with his head held high and an escort of lictors, servants and slaves. He may have been summoned by Praetorians, but until he left the island he was still a Roman governor, and he would not allow them to strip him of his dignity in the process.

The rest of the family followed and took the ship that afternoon. We were all worried as we reached the port. It so happened that three *triremes* of the Misenum fleet were anchored that day, escorting a grain shipment, and my father's authority was sufficient to have commandeered one of them, so we made our way back to Rome at reasonable speed and in fair comfort, close behind Father.

The journey took six days: five along the coast of Italia, and most of the last up the Tiber. Each night we pulled into a harbour, we could see the trireme that bore Father already docked, but he remained aboard with the military escort. He was, after all, now just a private citizen once more; his lictors had been stripped from him, and only a small core of attendants had been permitted. Every morning we set off an hour after that Praetorian ship, following it up the coast like a nervous shadow.

We were a family on the edge. Imagine, if you can, how we felt in those days of true political danger, when good men were falling to the executioner's blade for nothing more than being in the wrong place at the wrong time. Imagine the tension and anguish. Mother must have been clinging to sanity by the hem of its tunic.

Our ship pulled up at the *navalia*, the military dock of the Tiber, on the city side at the Campus Martius. Seven other great warships were in dock there, including the one that had conveyed our imprisoned father from Sicilia. We could hardly bear to look. There have been stories of men accused by Cleander not even managing to set foot on the city's soil before death found them.

I resolved that I could bear anything more than not knowing, and broke from Mother's protective embrace as the ship pulled up to the dock. I ran to the rail and looked out over the navalia, half-expecting to see Father's body quivering in a lake of blood and the animal Cleander, whom I had never met, standing over it with a blade in his hand.

I stared, eyes wide, in shock at what I saw.

Serried ranks of Praetorians waited on the dock. Then I realised that what I was seeing was not the arrest it should have been. My father was standing in front of them, hands on his hips in a somewhat military stance… with a grin plastered across his face.

I called Mother over. She came, nervously, slowly, then frowned in incomprehension as she joined me at the rail. Father looked up from the men surrounding him, seemingly unsurprised to discover that we had docked just after him.

'Lucius?' Mother called.

'What did I tell you, my love? The gods favour me. The omens were right.'

'But Cleander?'

'Dead! He fell a few days ago. He has been replaced in the Guard by Gratus Julianus and Gaius Regilius, both friends. The accusations against me were overturned before I even arrived. There was never anything to fear.'

Mother blinked away tears of relief.

'So we brought all our things from Sicilia for nothing?' she said, with mock admonition.

'Hardly. I have been vouchsafed the suffect consulship, my dear. I am to be consul. And you know what that means? A *real* province. Somewhere important. Somewhere with a future. You know my rise was calculated by astrologers long ago. Come, my love. Let us have the furnaces lit in the city domus. We are back in Rome for the year.'

'Oh *good*,' she said, a touch of irony in her tone.

'We must endure the heat of the city, my love.' Father smiled. 'A consul must make his presence felt. Then, soon, we will have a new province to govern.'

These are my earliest memories. Geta spending most of his time crying, Father suffering a baseless accusation, and our future being decided by the gods and by fate, for the man who would see us fall had fallen before us. Finally, of the steel in my mother, for she knew that only one person could have leaked the information about the seers and magicians back to Rome.

Within the hour, Geta's nurse was crucified on the sea-shore.

II

Like Caesar of Old

Carnuntum, Summer AD 193

The few years following our brief sojourn in Sicilia were tumultuous.

Having been graced with a consulship as promised, Father was granted the province of Pannonia Superior on the Danubius River, one of the most important in the empire, host to three of Rome's most fearsome veteran legions. We moved as a family to the great fortress city of Carnuntum, where Father set about the business of governance with aplomb.

Looking back, I can see that those last days of Commodus' reign were unstable and dangerous, and I know that a number of powerful men had secured positions in the empire's more wealthy and powerful provinces, preparing for the power vacuum that would follow the emperor's downfall, which all could see coming by then. Father was no different. Indeed, driven by the belief that he was destined for *imperium*, based on predictions, omens and horoscopes, he was more prepared than most, I suspect.

When disaster finally struck back in Rome, the emperor Commodus brutally murdered in his bath, that vacuum opened up. A new emperor, Pertinax, was raised in his place, only to fall shortly afterwards, murdered by the very imperial guards who had raised him. A third bought the throne from greedy Praetorians, seeking the bonus Pertinax had promised. Still, Father did not make his move, and the reason for that took the form of an old family friend, Gaius Fulvius Plautianus.

He was a distant cousin but a close friend of my father's. They both hailed from Leptis Magna in Africa and had been childhood companions. Plautianus had served a governorship at the time Father was consul, and so was enduring the obligatory two fallow years before he could secure a new position. He lived in a townhouse in Rome, but made the journey to visit us in Pannonia every few months. I never questioned why. It seems clear now that he spent those turbulent years keeping a close eye on developments in the city and passing information to Father, who would decide how to act upon it.

When Commodus died, Plautianus urged him to stake his claim to the throne, and Father must have been ready. The omens were not, though, and Father was ever a man to trust such things. A hawk broke its neck flying into a door in Carnuntum, and a soothsayer assured Father that it was a clear warning against interfering in the current political upheaval. And so, we remained loyal to the new emperor, Pertinax, steadfast in control of Pannonia. Pertinax lasted a grand total of eighty-seven days, bearing out the prediction of that auspex in Carnuntum. Father's name could so easily have appeared on the list of victims that year had he moved too soon.

His successor, Didius Julianus, was a fool who threw money at the army to secure his accession. Barely had his backside warmed the throne before the people were calling for his end, and for a series of powerful names in the provinces to come and save Rome. Three men rose to the apex of power in that time: Clodius Albinus, over in chilly Britannia, Pescennius Niger in Syria, and Father, Lucius Septimius Severus. Plautianus spent most of his time then plotting with Father and planning their campaign. Albinus was bought off with offers of shared power, removing him from the race. Niger was far away in the east. Letters were carried by Plautianus and other trusted men, quietly securing the support of other governors. Even when Father knew he had the edge over Niger, he refused to move until the day his favourite auspex observed an eagle circling Carnuntum and then swooping off in the direction of Rome. The omens being clear, Father made his bid for the throne.

I recount such momentous events in brief for they were beyond my ken at the time, but they are pertinent for the involvement of Plautianus.

I came to hate the man.

I had probably met him once or twice when I was a baby or a toddler, but I had no recollection of him the day he first arrived in Pannonia to visit Father. I was with my tutor, enduring a horribly dry lecture on the legal activity of Domitian, something a five-year-old couldn't give two shits about, when the doorman announced the visitor's arrival.

Plautianus was a tall man with an angular face, and hair and beard that were black and shiny, oiled and curled expertly despite his travel-worn appearance. He was a striking figure, and, like Father, he favoured a military tunic and belt for his everyday dress, regardless of his current position. He entered the house as though he owned it, and embraced Father as they met in the atrium as though they were long-lost brothers. My feelings towards him were defined in that room at that very moment, and they never changed. I turned from my tutor in our little room to one side of the atrium, interested in the visitor. On the far side, across the small pool with its gurgling dolphin fountain, Mother sat with my brother, who was in the process of learning to walk, which meant falling over and crying a great deal.

Plautianus and Father clasped one another for a time, then stepped back, their hands on one another's shoulders, both grinning.

'You will have much news, Gaius,' Father said.

'The most incredible,' the man replied, 'but not for every set of ears.'

He turned, then, conspiratorial, looking to see who was listening. His eyes fell upon me, where I looked across with interest at this impressive stranger. His gaze slid away from me as though I were but a cracked floor tile, and then across to the room at the far end.

'This must be your boy,' he said.

There. A statement. I was nothing. Geta was Father's son, I was nothing. I know now that there was some shared history between Plautianus and my birth mother, Paccia Marciana, for all of them had been childhood friends in Leptis, and something had soured sufficiently for the man to write me off as the child of a dead woman he loathed. Geta, on the other hand, was the son of his oldest friend and a glorious noblewoman from a royal line in Emesa. At the time, all I knew was that for some reason Father's oldest friend disliked me. Plautianus raised his standard in my brother's camp from the start.

Over the next year and a half, as Rome underwent political upheaval and Plautianus brought news and ran errands for Father, he visited often as Geta and I grew. As the boy started to talk, to learn and to change, so my own attitude towards him evolved. I had been hopeful that he and I would be constant companions, bosom friends in the manner of Father and his own brother, currently governing Moesia.

That hope died with the visits of Plautianus. Each time, Geta was brought gifts and showered with praise, while I was largely ignored.

I will own up now to the fact that I was intensely jealous. Who was this little child to receive such attention? *I* was the older brother. I was Father's heir regardless of who my mother had been. I began to resent my brother during those days in Carnuntum.

On one such visit, the dreadful man announced that he wanted to take Geta for his first visit to the games. Mother was dubious.

'He is a little young for such violence, Gaius,' she said.

'Your husband and I were his age when we saw our first games in Leptis,' Plautianus answered, somewhat dismissively.

'Still, I worry for him.'

Father shook his head, leaning on the balustrade. 'He will be fine. If we are to reach for the greatest power in the world, we will face much. The boys need toughening up for what is to come. I have too much to do, but Gaius does not leave until tomorrow. Let him take them.'

'Them?' Plautianus said in surprise.

'Take them both. Neither of them have been to the games yet.' Clearly Father was strangely oblivious to the heavy favour Plautianus placed upon Geta.

My heart leapt at the sudden inclusion and my father's care for me. Plautianus' gaze slipped my way, and I caught his eyes in the moment. They betrayed his thoughts before he shielded them. He regarded me coldly for a moment, with disdain, as though he were being asked to do something distasteful. The look was there for but a moment before it was replaced with a warm smile, as though he had always intended to include me, and that I was the brightest thing in his day. It was utterly false, yet very convincing, and had I not seen the truth in that moment before, I might have thought he had changed his manner towards me. I was, instead, baffled and hurt by his apparent off-handedness.

'Of course, the boy must come. Both of them.' He reached down to me and gripped my upper arms. I flinched, but he didn't seem to notice. 'You have reached such an age without watching a *retiarius* swing his net, or a *myrmidon* battling his opponent? That is too much. Come. We will go early so that we can buy some sweet treats for the entertainment.'

I wanted to argue. I did not want to go with him. But then I also did not want him to take Geta without me, and how could I tell Father that this man was a snake who hated me? He was so damned good at hiding his true nature that even I had almost fallen for it. We left almost immediately. To my relief, Mother came with us, unwilling to let her youngest out of her sight at such an event. We took with us a small entourage of slaves and guards, for the *forum* of Carnuntum can be busy and even dangerous for the unwary, especially on games day.

Plautianus kept up that genial façade throughout the day. He bought treats for us all, enough that a slave carried an armful in our wake, and was full of beaming smiles and snippets of gossip and interesting facts. He laughed with Mother, told jokes, and acted towards me as though he were a beloved uncle. Yet I remembered that look back at the house, and my uneasiness remained. The look that he saved for Geta, though, I'm sure was genuine.

We were shown to our seats, the best in that great arena, which were always reserved for the governor, his family and guests. As such, I had an unparalleled view. Plautianus sat in Father's seat, as though that were natural, and then Geta beside him, the toddler flanked by Mother, with me on her far side. It was hard not to note that this positioning had put the man beside Geta and as far from me as possible without being directly insulting.

I began to feel a little happier as the amphitheatre filled with an excited crowd. I was positively vibrating with energy as the priests came out and sacrificed, announcing it to be a good day for the events. I watched as the parade came across the sand, including exotic animals I had never seen before, and all the gleaming, impressive gladiators that would grace the arena later that day. I was beginning to think that this was the best thing ever. I was, remember, still very young. I was about to turn six, in fact, that month.

Then the real show began. Four men were escorted in, their wrists bound, and were led by soldiers to the centre of the arena where an iron hoop was driven into the ground. With a little work they were attached to the hoop with chains some ten feet long. I frowned, unsure of what this was. I was expecting glorious gladiators leaping and parrying. When Geta burbled something about it, Plautianus explained.

'Condemned men. Criminals. These four were bandits that harried the road to Sirmium.'

I knew then that something unpleasant was about to happen. Sure enough, the soldiers left the arena, their charges now tethered to the ring at the centre, alone, terrified and wailing. The games' *editor* stood and announced the names and crimes of the accused, pronouncing their sentence in the name of the governor, my father. Then, when he sat once more, two gates opened, and into the arena raced a score of dogs. They were, each and every one, enormous and fierce specimens, and all had been starved to within an inch of torture. The result was predictable.

The crowd oohed and aahed with malicious glee as the prisoners fought and pushed and lurched to get out of the way of the savage animals, pushing their friends in front to save themselves, which only delayed the inevitable. The chains became tangled amid the blood and frenzied killing, the dogs tearing the flesh from their prey with the desperation of the starved.

I did not watch. It is not that I am frightened of blood, and wasn't even then, and I can hardly claim to shun cruelty. Yet I looked away. This was not sport, but public murder.

Geta did *not* look away, but I suspect that is because he was still too young to understand what he was seeing.

Mother watched it all with a carefully blank expression.

Plautianus enjoyed himself. He cheered and nudged Mother, pointing things out. Then he noticed me.

'Are you afraid, boy?' he asked.

'It's not nice.' I meant so much more than that, but forming my opinion of such things into words at that age was difficult.

'It's not meant to be *nice*. It serves a purpose.'

'A sword would do the same job,' I grumbled, 'and quicker.' That was closer to what I'd meant, at least.

'And would not make the same point,' Plautianus replied airily. 'Mercy is a thing to be rationed carefully in this world, boy.'

I disagreed, on this occasion. Death has its place, and the execution of criminals is one such place. But death should not be entertainment, it should be quick and efficient. I could not wait for it to be over. The event put a pall over the whole day for me. I watched the beast hunts and then the matches of fighters, and I could probably have enjoyed them for the skill and excitement they exhibited, but the day had been soured for me by watching those four men torn apart by dogs.

Plautianus left the next day, taking instructions to my uncle in Moesia. I cannot say I was sad to see him go.

–

His visits went on as Geta and I learned and grew, and after two years in Carnuntum, finally the omens were apparently right, and Father made his move. Leaving a small border force to control the lands of Thrace and Moesia against any move from Niger, Father gathered his legions and his supporters and marched on Rome like Caesar of old. Plautianus was with him again, then. Mother, Geta and I were taken along in the wake of that vast army, lurching and bouncing along in a carriage with poor suspension.

It was a weird journey, for though the goal was of vast importance, an army moves slowly, and the feeble emperor in Rome, Didius Julianus, continually sent agents against the approaching force in attempts to kill Father. Each failed, none of them getting anywhere near the powerful governor who had claimed the purple.

My distrust and dislike of Plautianus blossomed into true hatred on that journey, too. As though every mile we moved towards Rome made it all the more important that Father paid more attention to Geta, Plautianus seemed to engage in a campaign on behalf of my brother. Every night's stop brought fresh insults laid subtly and carefully against me, while praise was poured into Geta's ears, and those of Father on his behalf. Any complaint I issued innocently about the roughness of the journey was turned into an accusation of my coddled weakness. Any determination I showed was presented as an example of my exceeding the authority of my years. And all that time, Geta's own complaints were raised as concerns to be looked into, his rare moments of strength as 'character.' And somehow Father seemed to completely miss this, such was Plautianus' subtlety.

I considered bringing the matter to Mother's attention, but as the journey went on, I began to see a change involving her, too. Plautianus cleaved all the more to Father, brushing her aside in practise, while lauding her to her husband. She had not failed to spot the change, and she became of necessity more withdrawn as we travelled.

Still, I laboured under the impression that my brother was innocent, twisted by the words of his new friend, until I saw the look he cast at me one night. If ever one look could convey suspicion, wicked intent, and oily subversion, that was it. Indeed, it reminded me so much of Plautianus, that I began to see almost a reflection of the man in his protégé. Father's old friend was turning my brother against me, and far from resisting it, my brother was *embracing* the change, relishing it. He was, in many ways, already more of a son of Plautianus than of Severus, which only enhanced my own pride in my superiority as elder sibling. I was, of course, still too young to understand why all this was happening, but I was certainly old enough to see what it was that was happening.

As we neared our goal, I tried twice, finally, to bring the matter to an open conclusion, once with each parent.

'Father. Why does Plautianus hate me?'

My father simply frowned. I tried to explain, though my youth and nerves jumbled my words and made the meaning rather convoluted. He brushed it off, telling me that I was imagining things.

I tried, then, to speak to Mother.

'Plautianus doesn't like me. Why does he like Geta?'

Mother at least listened to me, though she wore a troubled look. 'Your father has known Plautianus since they were boys. The man's opinion holds much weight with him. I do not know their past, but he had a history with the woman who sired you. Would that you had come from my womb, Marcus, though it seems he holds me in no greater favour than you. Your father's mind is hard to change when he has it set. We will not persuade him of any wrong in Plautianus. We must simply be the best we can be, and show your father that we are better than him. As for your brother, he is too young to bear you ill-will, Marcus. I am sure when Plautianus' influence is removed, he will warm to you once more.'

Somehow I doubted that. I had seen my brother slowly turning into his mentor since Carnuntum. But I was out of arguments, and so I resolved to do as she advised and simply rise above, being the best son a man could wish for.

The garrisons Julianus put in our way fell one after another, usually without a fight. By the time we reached Rome, it was over. The Senate and the Praetorians and the urban cohorts had all gone over to Father, confirming him as emperor and condemning the panicked Didius Julianus to death. He was murdered in his bed while we were still miles from the city. The coup was over. Father was emperor. The enormity of that did not hit me for some time.

–

I was seven now, and starting to grow into myself. I was beginning to become stronger, and Father, approving, moved my tutor onto dealing with Geta, while I was given new teachers, including one with a remit to train me with a sword. Finally spending time learning alongside others, I made my first true friend in those months. Titus Flavius Herodius had had, like me, something of a solitary upbringing, though for different reasons. I had been tutored alone because we were usually somewhere in the provinces, and my brother had been too young to be a companion. Herodius had been raised and taught in the great city, but though he claimed a good Roman lineage, he also carried the blood of the Herodian line from Judea, through the infamous Berenice, lover of the emperor Titus. As such, other boys his age never really trusted him.

I did. I liked him. He was shrewd, bright, funny and straight-talking. I always knew where I was with Herodius. And, of course, because I was the emperor's son and I liked him, he suddenly became a lot more popular with the other boys at court, of whom there were now many.

Father had reorganised the administration in Rome, disbanding the Praetorians who'd been so instrumental in making and breaking emperors, and replacing them with a fresh Guard drawn from his loyal Pannonian veterans. Plautianus was made the prefect of the city watch. Everyone who could not be trusted was removed and replaced, or encouraged to be loyal. And that was where the children came from.

Not every governor takes their family with them when they take up office, and often the children remain in Rome for their education. As such, I suddenly found myself surrounded by the worried sons of governors across the empire, hostages held in the city to ensure the ongoing support of their fathers. I realise this might sound callous, but it is also a prudent thing to do, and I approve of Father's decision. At the time, all I really thought was how lucky I was. After years of being schooled alone in our villas and townhouses, I was now being schooled alongside other boys, some older, some younger, but all from important Roman families. Moreover, they were an exotic gathering.

I suppose, looking back on it, that many of the boys were really less than happy with me, trapped as they were, hostages of my father, playing the companion because I was the son of the new emperor. To me, it still felt good.

I knew little of the Jews in those days, and so events that summer came as a surprise. Herodius was absent from our lessons for three days, and I began to worry about him. Then he returned, walking oddly. When we questioned him, he replied rather evasively that he'd had some sort of procedure. I had no idea what he meant, and when some of the older boys worked it out, I was still baffled until they explained it to me.

I was shocked.

The Jews cut their manhood in some way as part of their religion. The practice had been banned by Hadrian a century ago, but it was generally understood that it still happened among their people, just quietly and secretly. I had already known that Herodius was of their blood. The fact was writ in his features and plainly displayed in his name. But it had never occurred to me that he might follow their traditions.

The older boys shunned him immediately, and others acted oddly around him. I hesitated myself, I admit, unsure of how I felt about it all. It was only when he grinned at me and said, 'now my cock will be smaller, like theirs,' thumbing over his shoulder at the others, that I laughed and realised that he was still the same boy I had befriended. Things went along then, peacefully, for another month, until it all came to a head.

Herodius' father had given up his posting, accepting some role from my father back in Rome, and had returned to the city. His boy would remain in the group, for it was still my father's position that wherever they might serve, men were more loyal with their family at stake, but father and son were reunited.

I then witnessed what, to this day, I consider to be the most vivid example of a dysfunctional family I have ever seen. His father showed up unexpectedly when we were finishing a lesson. Herodius turned, and his face broke into the widest smile I had ever seen. He had not seen his father for a year or more. He broke into a run, arms out. I grinned for only a moment until my eyes fell on his father. The man was not waiting, open-armed. In fact, he was standing with his arms folded, his face a thunderous mass of anger. Herodius faltered and stumbled to a halt.

'Father?'

'What have you done, boy?'

'Done, Father?'

'You have maimed yourself. Broken the law. Defied the emperor!'

He stormed forward and pulled Herodius' belt away, then gripped the boy's tunic, wrenching it up and off him, over his head. My friend stood there, terrified, in shock, naked but for the subligaculum wound around his modesty.

'Show me,' snapped his father.

'Father, I...'

The man, still furious, reached down and pulled Herodius' underwear away, revealing the mark of the boy's religion. There was a shocked silence from all the boys now, as tears welled up in my friend's eyes. 'Mother said...'

'Your mother should know better. I thought she was done with all of this. I will have her out of my house and gone for this. And she can take you with her. You're spoiled goods, boy. No Roman, now. A criminal.'

'Father, no.'

But his father was not done. His fury had only just peaked, and he reached out a hand, palm open. One of the attendants accompanying him slapped a birch switch into his hand, and there, in front of the assembled scions of Rome, the man proceeded to scourge his own naked son. I watched. I could do nothing to stop it. In fact, I threw up as I watched, for he did not stop at the first drawing of blood, and only let Herodius go when he was little more than a quivering, naked, bloody heap on the ground. With a last look at the son he'd disowned, the man spat on the floor, threw down the bloody switch, and marched away to divorce his wife.

Even the boys who'd shunned Herodius and taunted him looked on now in silent horror at what they had witnessed.

Lessons clearly abandoned for the day, I promised Herodius I would be back, as the palace slaves ran over to pick him up and minister to his injuries, and then I marched off, determined, to find my father. In fact, that took some doing. The Palatine was already a maze of palaces, all of which were in use for various purposes. When I *did* finally locate him, in one of the private offices, guided there by one of the freedmen of the palace, there were two grim-looking Pannonian Praetorians at the door, who looked at me with interest. It took some persuading for them to interrupt their emperor on my behalf, but finally they did, and I was admitted, the door closing behind me.

Father was sitting opposite Plautianus, the two men sharing wine. They were involved in a conversation, and Father held up a hand in a signal for me to wait.

'I had toyed with the idea of making the boy Caesar,' he said to Plautianus, indicating me, which brought an odd thrill. 'But I think seven is still too young. The army will not respect him until he can wield a sword.'

'And fuck a woman,' snorted Plautianus. 'Besides, you have two sons. You cannot make an heir of one, for that will disinherit the other.'

The bastard. I knew he favoured Geta, but this was blatant. Father had considered making me his heir already, now that he had secured the throne, and Plautianus was talking him out of it.

'I decided against it, anyway,' Father said. 'The senate may have ratified me, and the army is largely mine, but there will still be war. Clodius Albinus lurks in Britannia, claiming the purple, as does Pescennius Niger in Syria. If I march to Britannia, I open the door to Rome for Niger, and so he has to be dealt with first, but to go east and deal with him I will need Albinus to remain on side. I have promised him a share of power, and it's prudent for the time being to reinforce that promise. I will have the documents drafted up conferring the title of Caesar upon Albinus. He will be my second and my heir in name alone. There will be no real power. Then, when we have dealt with Niger, I can strip him of the title and deal with him in turn.'

'Very neat.'

My father's eyes caught mine, and he gave an odd little smile. 'And perhaps by then you'll be old enough to take the title yourself, my boy. What did you want?'

I had almost forgotten why I was there, with the revelations in that room, and I took a moment to recover my wits. 'You know my friend Herodius, Father?'

He nodded. 'Yes.'

'His father scourged him. In front of us all! It was horrible.'

Severus frowned. 'What? Why?'

'Because he's chosen to be a Jew.'

My father's eyes narrowed then. 'Do you mean that he… mutilated himself?'

I nodded, weakly.

'Then his father was in the right. Let that be an end to it.'

I blinked in surprise. 'But Father, he nearly *died*.'

'He is lucky he didn't, then. Son, the practice has been banned for a hundred years. The Jews denied our emperors' godhood, remember? I won't scold a man for upholding the law. Forget about this.'

I couldn't, of course. I simply glared at my father, unable to believe that the man I had always so respected could agree to such a thing.

'I am going to change his name,' he said to Plautianus, but indicating me. I frowned now.

'Sensible. Sever his ties to that woman.'

That woman. My mother.

'Have a care, Gaius. She was my wife, remember, and I loved Paccia.' He straightened. 'No, it is a political statement. Lucius Septimius Bassianus connects him to the family, and I have taken Pertinax into my own name, for the people need to see the line unbroken from the last good emperor. But we need more. For legitimacy, we need to go back to the best of names. I will connect the boy to the greatest houses of Rome. He will be Marcus Aurelius Antoninus. I will have the records amended straight away. Then, when we have dealt with Niger and Albinus, I can make him Caesar, and his name will be a byword for all that is good in Roman memory.'

And that was that. In but a short space of time I'd had the promise of Caesar dangled before me, then removed, been chastised and overruled by my own father, had my name changed to something utterly alien, and then had that Caesar promised me once again.

'The boy is weak,' Plautianus said, surprisingly bluntly.

'He will grow strong,' Father replied, giving me a look up and down. 'I will take him with me against Niger. Let him with his new name be *forged* anew in the crucible of war.'

III

Caracallus

Syria, AD 194

'I've found another three.'

I didn't look round this time. I'd seen enough heads. Heads on decaying bodies, heads on spikes, heads on their own, heads everywhere.

Can a boy become an adult at eight years? I think perhaps I did. I have known boys that were clearly far from adult, even years after taking the *toga virilis* and coming of age, so is it so unlikely that a boy could be ready for adulthood five years early?

'This one's still got the eyes in... *and* a silver ring,' the soldier said with glee.

I had, I think, aged six years in one. Father had been absolutely right about what the 'crucible of war' can do to forge a man. But more than merely leaving behind childish notions and seeing the world for what it truly was, I also learned more in that year than I had from half a decade of tutors. I was beginning to understand rudimentary tactics, was becoming competent with a sword, could ride a horse without falling off, and so on. But I think all that I learned paled into insignificance when placed against the one pearl of wisdom I had gleaned over a season of campaigning, and which defined my own military career. That nugget came from my father's most capable general in the field, Anullinus.

After months of fighting across the East, we reached the Taurus mountains where, in the failing days of autumn we encountered the first real obstacle. We'd fought vicious battles at Cyzicus and Nicaea, though when I say we, I mean Father's army under the generals Anullinus and Candidus, and we'd taken every Pescennian outpost across Asia and into the hinterlands of Cappadocia, but now we had to secure the passes of the Taurus mountains in order to bear down on Niger's fortress at Antioch. The man had been wily, though. While he had thrown men in our way and tried to hold various lines for a while, he had been buying time to fortify the Taurus. When we reached the place, it was all but impassable.

The pass through the Taurus range is known as the Cilician Gates, and it has been a fortified pass since days of old, the site of many famous battles. No conflict ever fought trying to take the pass had ended well, Ventidius Bassus holding the heights against the Parthian Empire two centuries ago. Niger knew its value, and he had used it to full effect, sealing the pass against us. He had built new walls and fortifications and garrisoned it with his best men, including plenty of missile troops to shower us with death should we attempt to approach the pass.

There was a massive discussion in the command tent the first night we arrived. Candidus was the most senior of Father's generals, and the one with the best record of service and of victories. He also personally led a specially formed unit of Illyrian troops Father had handpicked from his Pannonian Legions. Candidus had looked up at the pass, sighed, and noted that there was nothing for it but a direct assault. His second, Anullinus, was of a different mind.

'We will lose half the army taking this pass, and that is only if we succeed. Find another way.'

Candidus rounded on his companion. 'Easy enough to say, man, but every day Niger gathers more soldiers from the East, raises levies, and even sends requests to the powers of the East. Do we really want to sit here, scratching our arses while half of Parthia comes to the pass to face us?'

Father, I noted from my seat in the corner, where I took everything in, listened carefully to both his generals, nodding at what they were saying.

'If you assault the pass,' Anullinus pressed, 'we will not have the forces left afterwards to face anything Niger throws at us. Then he will have the freedom to push us back across Asia. I counsel patience. Winter is coming, and winter in these mountains can change everything.'

'We could retreat west and then seek the coast and come around it, circling around the entire range,' another officer put in.

To this, both Candidus and Anullinus shook their heads. 'That would take far too long, require the rearrangement of our supply lines, and put us on a narrow approach. Niger's navy controls the waters in the region. We would be running a gauntlet between his armies in the mountains and his warships along the coast. That is not a pleasant prospect.'

'But we cannot wait,' Candidus sighed.

'And we cannot simply charge,' Anullinus repeated.

There was silence for a time, then, and finally Father sat up. 'We must try something, but I agree that a full assault is too dangerous. Candidus, take the *Exercitus Illyricus* and probe the pass. Do it carefully and subtly. Do not waste men, but try and find us a weak spot we can exploit.'

The senior man saluted, left the tent and began to organise things, most of the officers nodding to Father and following suit. Soon only Father, Anullinus and myself remained. I had been given a number of wooden models of soldiers that were used for marking positions on a map, expecting me to play with them, but I had merely positioned them on the table beside me in the formation in which our army was camped while I listened.

'This is a mistake, Lucius,' Anullinus said quietly, one of few men close enough to Father to address him so.

'Perhaps. But Candidus is right that we cannot wait. I have sought the will of the gods, had animals cut open and had auspices read the signs. None of them tell me that some miracle will happen if we just wait.'

'Sometimes,' his general said quietly, 'it is nature that answers, not the gods, Lucius. Give it time.'

Father shook his head in answer, announced that he needed a bath, and rose, striding out of the tent. I realised I had been left alone with the general. He rose and crossed the tent to me, and I watched with trepidation. I was fairly confident as eight-year-olds go, and becoming more so with every battle I witnessed, but I was still in awe of certain great men. At least Plautianus was back in Rome and I didn't need to worry about him.

'You have arranged our army,' Anullinus said, gesturing to the wooden soldiers.

'I didn't have enough to place the enemy, too.'

'What would *you* do, young Marcus?'

I frowned. 'I don't know. I listened and it sounded like there was no right answer.'

'Often there is no right answer, and you have to go with your gut feeling. My gut feeling is that Niger has wagered everything on holding this pass, and we will struggle to take it, even if we succeed. But I also know that his defences are untested, his constructions quick and urgent, his men largely native levies and auxiliaries, and they lack certain skills a true legion can bring when it comes to construction and fortification. I think winter will change everything here. It is my gut feeling, but it is also based on certain logics.'

'What do you mean?'

He fixed me with a look. 'One day, Marcus, it will be you in that chair, listening to your generals. Now is the time to learn, for then it will be too late. And one thing I have learned over many years of campaigns is that the best fight is one you don't have to fight at all. Sometimes, patience and forethought can win you a victory without the need for steel and blood. Do you understand?'

I nodded. I sort of did, though I had yet to see his opinion borne out.

I did not have to wait long. The next morning, Candidus took the very best of the army and attempted to find a weakness in the pass. We watched from a lofty viewpoint as the disaster unfolded. It became clear after half an hour that the place was unassailable. Anullinus was right. An assault on the pass would halve the army at least. Walls were held on every ridge, and arrows, darts, bolts and stones came down like autumn rain, falling into the units attacking up the pass, killing men in droves. Within half an hour the vultures were circling overhead eagerly, waiting for the fighting to stop so the feasting could begin. And it was not merely missile defences. At one point Father pointed excitedly, suggesting that perhaps Candidus had found his weakness. Then the enemy sprung their trap. They had dammed and diverted an impressive waterfall, leaving a passage clear. Two score of the empire's best men moved up it, unseen by the soldiers on the nearest walls. They were too far in, with no hope of retreat, when the enemy opened their new sluice gate and let the waterfall free once more. Two dozen battered and bloated bodies washed down towards the camp over the remainder of the day.

It was evening before Candidus returned, ashen-faced and with a bleak expression. He had lost the lion's share of that veteran unit, the best in the army, and had achieved nothing.

Father was angry that night. He stripped Candidus of overall command, settling him into a secondary role, somewhat unfairly, I thought, given that he'd only been following Father's orders. Anullinus was given command, and Father sagged back into his chair. 'All right. What do we do?'

'We consolidate and lay siege. Wait and see.'

And that is what we did.

For a month and a half we held our place at the northern entrance to the pass. Gradually, the weather turned, and winter in that region can be a truly terrible thing. We endured storms and torrential rain, and the temperature dropped, turning the rain to sleet and then to snow. It was a hard time for us, though we were consoled that it was just as hard a time for Niger's men in the pass.

We almost withdrew the campaign.

Another meeting, the latest of many, saw Candidus and Anullinus at one another's throats, for they were becoming strongly opposed in every opinion.

'We must withdraw. We cannot spend the rest of the winter here. Sickness is rife, our supplies are being interrupted by the weather and conditions, and still we are no closer to success.'

Anullinus shook his head. 'Wait. The time will come. Trust me.'

The argument raged for the evening with no real conclusion. Father had his *haruspex* read whatever signs they could find and even they could not provide more than uncertainty. He finally decreed that we would sit it out until the *kalends* of next month, and if there was no advance we would withdraw and seek a new path.

It happened the next night.

The snow and rain had been bad at our camp, for the pass is high and bleak, but it had been so much worse up in the high mountains. It began as a rumble on one particularly rainy night. If all the gods had picked up drums and hammered on them with their divine might, it might have sounded like what we heard. The entire army awoke and stepped out of their tents to see what was happening. Many men were making warding signs, promising altars to gods and generally panicking, for it was a truly terrifying noise.

And then the flood came.

The build-up of snow in the heights had been substantial, and finally it had broken several of the many dams the enemy had constructed to divert the waters and allow them to garrison the pass. The torrents came from a hundred places in the mountains. We stood, in awe of nature and the will of the gods, as entire strong rivers formed, washing down the slopes. Walls were simply smashed asunder, whole units of men sent screaming into the abyss. Even in battle I have never seen so many people die so fast.

We were, ridiculously, safe. We had pitched our camps on the high ground, and seasonal river valleys abounded, which took away the floodwater as it descended from the pass, running safely past us without interruption.

In the end we just retreated to our tents. In the morning it was over. The day was an overcast steely grey, half a dozen new rivers flowing nearby, and the pass clear. Bodies lay strewn everywhere, bloated and grey, though oddly there was little blood, thanks to the torrents. Many of the walls had gone entirely, and all were ruined. The dam at the waterfall had gone, too.

The Cilician Gates were open.

Anullinus was gracious in his success, another sign of a good commander, and one I noted for the future. He did not once rub it in with Candidus, and even the displaced officer congratulated his replacement on the success. Father was full of positivity once more, and reappointed Candidus, leaving both men in command of separate forces.

It is, incidentally, the aftermath of that event which in some ways has defined my life, for I am far from ignorant of the name the people give me. Caligula had his little boots, and so I have my own nickname.

It was as I was standing in the aching cold, watching the clear-up of the pass, that Anullinus joined me, and my attention was drawn to his apparel. Very sensibly, given the conditions, the general was wearing one of those hooded cloaks I had seen and so admired on the magician in Silicia. I had pointed at it.

'What is that cloak?'

'This?' Anullinus pointed at the item. 'Something I picked up in Gaul. They call it the *caracallus*. Some consider it boorishly northern, but I find it eminently practical on campaign.'

The caracallus. I nodded my approval.

Anullinus paid attention, though. Just over a month later, a cara-callus, tailored perfectly to fit me, was delivered to my tent, with a note proclaiming it an early birthday present from a friend. It was, perhaps, the most thoughtful gift I ever received.

We marched on, then, across the Taurus and down into Cilicia, bearing down on Niger's stronghold. Reports came that the enemy was gathering a huge force of new untrained conscripts in a desperate bid to hold us off at the last. Had we taken the pass by force, I have no doubt that we would have fallen afterwards to that massive army.

We met them finally at a place called Issus, the fourth day after the kalends of November. As we approached the enemy, I queried the name with Probus, one of the officers. Though much of my schooling had been astoundingly dull, I had listened, rapt, to the tales of Alexander, King of Macedon, and his conquests in the East. He had been only thirty-three years old when he died, but in his short reign he had created an empire the size Rome could now claim, defeating the Persians who had held off the Greeks for centuries. He was, even then, something of a hero of mine. And I knew the name Issus. It was there, five centuries ago, that Alexander had crushed the Persian forces of Darius. I knew every moment of that battle, for I had continued to study it even when my tutor believed I had moved on to other subjects.

'Is this the same Issus of Alexander?'

Probus threw a look of raised eyebrows my way. I was, after all, a boy of eight. 'Why yes, young man, I believe it is.'

And then I began to pay attention. I could see the terrain as our men flooded across it opposite those of Niger, and in the eye of my mind, I could see the forces of Macedonia and Persia facing off across it. And, oddly, the battle between Niger and my father was something of an echo of the world-changing battle of Alexander and Darius. I watched from the side-lines with the senior officers as the two armies clashed, the fighting brutal and non-stop. It went on through the afternoon and even as the watery winter sun slid towards the horizon, but from mid-afternoon onwards, nobody was in any doubt as to the outcome.

What was left of Niger's army broke in the failing light. It is no exaggeration to say that the death toll that day was so high that the rivers flowing down to the shoreline were red, and that a bloom of pink water was seen half a mile out from the coast, such was the quantity of men's blood poured into the sea.

Just like Darius centuries ago, Pescennius Niger himself survived the slaughter. He found the fastest horse among his cavalry and raced for Antioch, his last great bid for imperium having failed.

Candidus, then, appealed to my father. I think he needed to save face after his earlier failure, and he saw now an opportunity to rebuild his reputation. Father consulted his augurs, and agreed. Though the army would camp the night and follow the fleeing rebels in the morning, all the way to Antioch, Candidus would take what was left of his Illyrian cavalry and chase down the fleeing enemy commander.

Probus had begun issuing orders to the officers to round up the enemy survivors and have them swear a new oath to Father, but Anullinus stopped him, and it was then I learned another lesson I would eventually have call to employ. Niger's armies had fought us to the very end, even when they knew they were beaten. Such men could never be trusted as allies. The only answer was death. Every last man on that field who still breathed had to breathe his last that day. Only then was Father's throne secure.

'*I've found another head.*'

'*This one's still got the eyes in… and a silver ring.*'

The greatest battle of the war was over.

We learned what happened a few days later, upon our arrival at the enemy's stronghold. Niger had fled to Antioch, just ahead of the pursuing cavalry, but there he had realised he had insufficient forces to hold the place against us, so he had gathered a few things in a desperate hurry and then raced away east, with the intention of seeking refuge in the Parthian empire, and perhaps persuading them to help renew his imperial ambitions.

He got as far as the first major bridge over the Orontes, where Candidus and the cavalry caught up with him and his small bodyguard. There, Pescennius Niger finally met his end. When we arrived at Antioch, Candidus handed his head over to Father, who took it with an implacable expression, and then pronounced the war over.

The aftermath was somewhat predictable. Though there was still much to do, Father had to deal with the results of his campaign. Over in Britain, Clodius Albinus was yet to make a move, content as he was with being Father's heir, though even he must have known that was a temporary sinecure. And the great promontory city of Byzantium remained, holding out in Niger's name even though he was gone, but a sizeable army held the place under siege and it would fall eventually. There were no immediate threats to my father's authority, and so we dallied in the East for a time.

Proclamations were made and letters sent out. Those Roman nobles who had thrown their support behind Niger fled as best they could, but they were all found eventually, and each suffered, at least on some level. Niger's family, Father did not revenge himself upon, though he did send them into exile where they could pose no further threat. Men were exiled or executed across the empire, with one notable exception. Sometimes it is worthy of an emperor to show clemency even in times of betrayal. Julius Caesar knew that. Father rarely displayed clemency, in truth. He was a hard man. But sometimes, even his gruff shell could be cracked. Such was the case of Cassius Clemens, one of Niger's supporters.

The inner strength of the man was clear from the fact that, though Father's men tried to drag the prisoner before us for his trial, they more or less had to run to catch up as the man marched confidently into our presence. He bowed his head, a gesture of respect, no more.

'What have you to say for yourself?' Father asked, as we all became aware of the executioner's sword being sharpened in the corner with grating strokes that chilled to the bone.

Clemens remained straight and proud, looking my father in the eye.

'I was acquainted with neither you nor Niger, but, finding myself in the midst of his partisans, I was constrained to look to the moment, not with the purpose of fighting you, but of deposing the pathetic Didius Julianus. I therefore did nothing wrong, either in this respect, since I strove in the beginning for the same ends as you, or in another, by refusing to desert a man to whom I had pledged allegiance. An oathbreaker is worse by far than a direct enemy, of course. You would not have approved if any of these men who are sitting with you in judgment betrayed you and deserted to him. Do not, then, condemn us for not doing the very same to Niger. This is the time to show the people of Rome what sort of emperor you are, Lucius Septimius Severus.'

Father was so taken aback by the frankness and the marshalled logical argument that he burst out laughing and announced the trial at an end and the man free to go. Anullinus was of a different opinion, still convinced that no man of Niger's could ever be trusted again. He would prove to be correct. Another lesson learned. Thus was the last of Niger's men dealt with. It was not just the lot of unfortunate men to fall to Father's wrath, though. Whole cities had declared for Niger, and they became his immediate targets. Neapolis in Palestine was stripped of its rights, as were half a dozen other cities. His full wrath, though, he saved for the two great strongholds of Niger, Antioch and Byzantium. The latter would have to be taken before it could be made to pay, but Antioch was now ours, and we entered the city to find a frightened and desperate populace.

We stayed in Antioch for half a month, while its defences were dismantled as part of its punishment. I listened to Father in the city's forum, reading out what seemed a never-ending list of restrictions, deprivations and other penalties. The city that had been Niger's heart-land was to be made an example of.

At first, I agreed with him. Based upon the lessons of Anullinus, I could see that an example needed to be made in order to deter a repeat of such events. But this was not the same. These were not defiant warriors on a battlefield, but citizens and families in their own metropolis. As the days rolled on as the punishments were enacted, and as I reached the grand old age of nine, I became aware of the results of Father's decision, and why the same fate should not befall civilians as warriors. With Father almost constantly busy, Mother back in Rome with my brother, and no one else really around to look after me, I took to wandering, with an appropriate entourage of slaves and guards of course, for neither my father nor I were fools.

Even long before Father had claimed the purple, we had been an important family. I had grown up in rich Roman townhouses, or Governor's palaces, or sprawling rural villas. In truth, I don't think I had ever really met the ordinary people of the empire, other than as our slaves or servants or soldiers. That month, I experienced the real civil world for the first time. I explored what was left of Antioch, and gradually came to understand an uncomfortable truth.

These Syrians may speak Greek primarily, and even weird local dialects. They may look different to the average Italian. They had supported an enemy of my father's and were suffering for it. But the odd thing was that I realised, as we uncovered more of Antioch, that no matter how many small differences there might be, still the people of Antioch were Roman. We were punishing Romans for supporting a Roman. That, in itself, I found worrying. But as I came to understand the geography of the land, things became even more uncomfortable. To the south lay Arabia, a land of deserts, nomads and rebels. To the east was ever-troublesome Parthia, an enemy of Rome as long as anyone could remember. To the north-east the kingdom of Armenia, nominally a client state, but with a history of swapping to partisan Parthia if the occasion demanded. Quite simply, the East was an outpost of Rome in a world of dangers on all sides. I pictured then what would go through every mind in the East when the emperor began to chastise his own people for supporting other Romans. After all, there was another great empire, just across the Euphrates River, who might be more forgiving.

The trouble I felt only increased as I found impoverished people in Antioch brought down so low that they were hunting and cooking the city's rats, and roasting their own pets to survive.

Again, I do not shy from blood, and cruelty has its place, where it has a purpose, but *wasteful* cruelty, and violence for amusement do not sit well with me. I began quickly to form the opinion that my father was wrong. And the more I thought about it, the more I realised he was often wrong. Oh, he was a powerful man, a lion on the battlefield, and no idiot. But he had a tendency to make poor judgments, I felt. I thought back to that poor half-Jewish friend of mine, thrashed within an inch of his life, yet my father shrugged it off. Anullinus counselled patience in the mountains, his plans borne out, yet Father had let Candidus lead an attack regardless, which had cost us dearly. And now he was standing on the neck of the city that might well hold the key to the defence of the East. He should be attempting to secure their *loyalty*, not their obedience.

I was resolved. Refusing to turn a blind eye to the devolved state of the great city around me, I had our slaves throw money to every citizen we saw in trouble. Not a fortune, but enough to pull themselves out of danger. No, I reminded myself, not citizens. That was yet another right Father had stripped from them. The day I sat on the throne, I decided, all men and women of the empire would be citizens, for what right had a fat, overpaid merchant in Ostia to be a citizen if a firefighter or a soldier or a fisherman in Antioch could not. Only if everyone had the same rights could everyone hope to share in the future of Rome.

I was absolutely full of ideas and plans by the time I reached the palace. I marched into the large hall where Father was busy in conversation with half a dozen senior officers and a few togate officials.

Anullinus was the first to notice me, turning and gracing me with a mischievous grin.

'Well, if it isn't Caracalla,' he laughed, gesturing to my new hooded cloak that I had worn almost constantly during the chilly spring mornings. I might have taken offence. Probably should. The name has stuck for decades now, and it was all his doing. But Anullinus was a genuinely good man. I liked him, and had learned a lot from him. I returned his smile.

Father looked up, frowning. 'Caracalla?'

'The cloak,' explained Anullinus.

'Ah, yes. Very clever.' Then he turned to me. 'What is it?'

'Father, I think you need to reverse your edicts on Antioch.'

The other voices in the room fell silent, and my father rose to his full height, folding his arms. 'You do, do you?'

'I do.'

'Then pray tell, son of mine, where this little pearl of wisdom was born in the mind of a nine-year-old with experience of neither war nor politics?'

I was ready for it, though. On the way back I had asked a number of questions of my nomenclator, a slave with a truly astounding mind and memory. He had furnished me with every detail I needed.

'Will you seriously listen, Father? Hear me out?'

He looked to Anullinus and Candidus, and shrugged. 'I am never a man to ignore pertinent advice, boy. Speak up.'

'Antioch sided with their governor. Remember what Cassius Clemens said. Would you expect a Roman to break faith with a master? The senate in Rome had ratified Didius Julianus as emperor, and only turned on him because your legions were at their door. Yet did you strip the senate of their rights? You overdo the punishment. The *army* had to be destroyed, yes, but not the *province*. Antioch has suffered enough.'

Candidus took a step forward, raising a hand. 'You overstep, lad.' Even Anullinus looked doubtful.

But Father had an odd look on his face and waved the generals down. 'Let him speak.'

I straightened. 'You are surrounded by enemies here, Father. Parthia could turn on us at any time. Armenia is only loyal as long as we are the preferable master. Arabia is a seething land of raiders. Osroene and Adiabene are nominally under Roman control but as soon as Niger fell they sent overtures to Parthia. There are enemies here every direction we face, yet what are we doing? Crushing the spirits and demolishing the walls of one of the few great cities of the East that could stand against them. I think anger at Niger has focused your revenge on men who could be your own, and not on the men who surround them.'

It was more or less a speech I had been rehearsing all through the streets of Antioch on my way. When I finished, there was silence in the room. Anullinus was frowning, but nodding his agreement. Even Candidus looked half-convinced. Father took a deep breath and sat back in his chair.

'Sometimes, my friends, it takes the insight of uncorrupted youth to plough through the chaff and see the world for what it is. I have half a mind to cut Albinus off now and make the lad Caesar, and I would, had we the chance to deal with the man yet. But other matters await.' He smiled and pointed at me. 'Very well. I will have an announcement drafted rescinding most of my edicts. Not all, but I do take your point. Rewards too, perhaps, where they are due. But it will be other men who enact it all.'

It was my turn to frown. 'Father?'

'You are correct. The true enemies here are Parthia, Osroene and Adiabene. We need to head west and deal with Albinus, but we must bring the East to heel before we do so. Sharpen your blades and your wits my boy. The army marches east.'

IV

A Lesson Learned

When we moved from Antioch, it was, for me, with a surge of excitement. I had witnessed the site of Alexander's defeat of Darius at Issus, and we were to move further now into the territory of that great conqueror. I hoped to see everything. I hoped even to see Persepolis, the great capital of Alexander, and Babylon, where he died. Perhaps even Aegyptus, where his tomb is to be found.

Father, of course, was more focused on chastising the eastern peoples for their support of Niger. First came Osroene, which had thrown out Roman administrators and all but declared independence, fortifying their borders and seizing forts Rome had built to secure their territory. The king of Osroene had been a vassal of Rome for a century, but had now begun to look elsewhere. The Parthians, wisely, failed to come to his aid, and so Father's army marched into Osroene with little resistance and set up camp at Nisibis. There, a new fortress was constructed and a garrison put in place under Anullinus while the army was divided between Lateranus, Candidus, and Laetus, who between them set about bringing the land back entirely under control.

Again, they met with little armed resistance, though they did lose many troops through thirst, which became our greatest enemy in the East, for it is a hot, dry land. My excitement peaked in our time at Nisibis, for I learned that nearby lay another of Alexander's great battlefields, Gaugamela, where he had put an end to Darius' power for good. I managed to persuade Father to take me there, and we spent two days exploring the site of the most important victory of the greatest general in history.

After that, things began to pall a little. The summer was too hot there, and the land too barren. And while I had managed to explore Gaugamela, it had become apparent that this was the furthest we would travel on Alexander's trail. Both Babylon and Persepolis were far inside the Parthian empire, and we simply had neither the time nor the manpower to take on Rome's greatest adversary simply so that I could sightsee. Another campaign was conducted out of Nisibis, this time with Laetus, Anullinus, and Probus, sent against Adiabene, which had followed suit with Osroene, and now paid for their lack of foresight.

Apart from my pursuit of, and increasing fascination with, Alexander the Great, I think the East was a learning time for me. I watched campaigns of recovery and consolidation at work from the command level, and watched half a dozen different generals leading with different styles.

We returned west in the autumn. Father had declared the East settled, and that he had made a bulwark of Syria. Even at nine, I was less convinced of such achievements. I had formed the opinion, partially based on those of several generals, that the East was impossible to settle as long as Parthia remained to trouble us, for that land has been an enemy of the West for a thousand years, barring the brief time it lay beneath the boot of Alexander. Nevertheless, as we returned to Rome there were calls for a *triumph* for Father. We had probably taken enough heads in the war to warrant one, but with most of them being Roman, it would be unseemly, and so Father declined that honour, though he did take on the title, Adiabenicus.

I returned a suntanned and trim nine-year-old, almost a different boy to the one who had left on the campaign. Mother gushed to see me, enfolding me in her arms. I was startled to see Geta, for he had been a toddler when I left, and now was a hearty six-year-old. If I had hoped we would meet once more as brothers, with heartfelt reunion, I was mistaken. I had thought that such time without being subject to the influence of Plautianus might have softened him, changed him, allowed him to meet me on better terms. I was wrong. While Mother rushed to embrace me, Geta stood a little apart, arms folded, watching me with slitted eyes, as though I were some opponent being sized up. I greeted him somewhat distantly, and my chilly words were returned in like manner. Mother looked from one of us to the other for a moment, her expression saddened, but our reuinion took over once more and we embraced again.

That first night back together I realised one thing of import, though. Geta might still be little more than a Plautianus in training, but without his master, at six years old, he was powerless to oppose me.

Things were not to stay so comfortable, though. We had removed Niger and settled the East, but there remained another, wilier, opponent in Britannia. Now Father began to look west, even as we spent a sojourn in Rome. News that, with a war only just won, another was in the offing, did not sit well with many in Rome. Indeed, when extra taxes were instituted to raise new manpower for the fresh campaign, it triggered one particularly extraordinary event.

On the last racing day of the season, between the final two races, someone in the Circus began to stamp their feet and shout. Initially we, in the imperial box, couldn't make out what he was saying, but as more and more people joined in and it became a thunder of boots and a rhythmic chant, it was impossible to mishear.

'No more wars.'

I could see Father glowering, tempted to set the guard on the miscreants, but it was Mother who saved all their lives that day.

'Husband, you cannot win people over, nor can you tax them, after you have taken their heads. Magnanimity and subtlety, Lucius. Magnanimity and subtlety.'

And so that was what we did. We spent months calming things in Rome, making the populace happy. But Father was far from stupid, and he knew what the people wanted. He could not initiate a new campaign to remove a man who was a legitimate Caesar and make the people pay for it. But if that Caesar went to war, then the people would clamour for Father to face him as the wronged party.

It was a stroke of genius. All he had to do was provoke Albinus into making the first move and looking bad to the people of Rome. As such, he waited until I turned ten and as part of a planned great celebration in the city, he named me Caesar, his heir. The crowd applauded and cheered. It was natural. I was his son, and almost ready to take the toga of manhood. What could be more appropriate than making me his heir, second only to the emperor?

What the crowd failed to notice on the whole was that in making me Caesar, Father had effectively stripped the title, and all hope of power or succession, from Albinus.

It was not enough. It was *almost* enough, for we heard many tales of how Albinus was fortifying his territory and raising new forces. He was ready to oppose us, but not quite angry enough to do it. That winter, Father sent a steady stream of assassins after Albinus, some with knives under the guise of messengers, some with poison into his kitchens. He must have made life both perilous and extremely uncomfortable for Albinus. Finally, one of Father's more audacious attacks did the trick, and Albinus moved, bringing his forces across the water to Gaul, an overt military move, and one Father could counter legitimately with the support of the senate and the people.

As the court bustled around preparing to depart on another campaign, I encountered my own somewhat defining moment. I was being arrayed by slaves in official regalia. In fact, I had argued against it, and got my own way to some extent. Just as Father tended to do, I had opted for a military tunic, despite my age, and must have looked a little like a diminutive soldier. Atop this they had draped a very imperial cloak of purple and gold, a diadem on my brow, a belt of gold.

On the other side of the room, Geta was being prepared. He would not be coming with us to Gaul, but would be part of the procession with Mother until we left the city, a show for the crowds. He was being dressed in expensive, but very ordinary clothes. As we both turned so that slaves could tuck and primp, we came face-to-face, and Geta fixed me with a bitter look.

'When will *I* be made Caesar?'

The question threw me for a moment. It had never occurred to me that he might expect such a thing. The answer was clear, though, and I probably could have found a more careful way to break the news.

'Never.'

'Why not?' His face folded into a frown. 'I am his son, too.'

'An emperor needs an heir, but only one. I am the older brother, and the natural choice. In time, I will take a wife and have a son. Then, when I am one day emperor, my son will be Caesar. Until then, it will be me.'

'Unless you die.'

Over the years I have replayed that moment again and again in my mind's eye, trying to determine whether it was an intentional threat or mere chance. It did not sound threatening at the time, only irritated, but looking back, I cannot be so sure.

'I am going on campaign with Father, but I will not be standing in a shieldwall and being attacked. I will be in the command tent with the officers. There is no real danger.'

We left the city with much pomp and grandeur. Of course, Father had been preparing for the war that was to come all this time, just quietly and in small moves. A man by the name of Numerianus had been dispatched to southern Gaul even before Albinus moved, with a chest of gold and a remit to build a force of his own.

Numerianus' mercenary army raged through the provinces far ahead of us, cutting through Albinus' advanced cavalry like a scythe through wheat. They then secured the passes of the Alpes and guarded them until we approached. It was winter when we left Italia through those icy northern peaks. Father made a point of travelling as Caesar of old, alongside his men, sharing their hardships, enduring the weather and the conditions, eating as they did, and dressing like a soldier, as always. It made him ever more popular with the army. Similarly, I adopted the military tunic, breeches and boots, and continued to wear the hooded tunic Anullinus had given me in Asia, though now it was a little tight, for I was growing all the time. The nickname, Caracalla, had stuck for good, and I heard myself referred to as such during the journey by men from the lowest born to the highest. I could perhaps have taken offence. I would certainly have done so had I been the emperor Gaius, nicknamed Little Boots, but there was nothing really embarrassing about this appellation, and I had already been renamed once by my father anyway. Indeed, such was my adherence to the garment that when Saturnalia came and we celebrated as much as we could, travelling across Raetia with the army, Father's gift to me was a new caracallus, sized better for my larger frame. We were, after all, now in the land where they were invented, and acquiring one was not difficult.

Januarius saw us coming down out of the high places and to the green valleys of Gaul. Oddly, we were approaching Lugdunum, the city in which I had been born, while Father had been the governor there. I wondered whether, if things passed the right way, I might perhaps have my eleventh birthday in my home city. There was something about the synchronicity of that which appealed to me.

As the month rolled on and we moved into Februarius, our advance units began to come into conflict with those of Albinus, who had marched south from the Gaulish coast to meet the threat. The war had begun.

The first major clash came soon after, on the ides of Februarius. The army had been split into three on our approach, and one prong, led by the general Lupus, blundered straight into the main force of Albinus. Horribly outnumbered, the battle's conclusion was rather foregone, and he was lucky to escape with a reasonable number of troops.

Aware now of the location of Albinus and his force, our army combined once more and pressed on, very close to Lugdunum. We met on the plains outside the city, and as the armies rushed to meet one another, I took a good position on a ridge with the staff officers, watching. I had seen enough battles now in our time out east to, even at ten, have a good grasp of the strategies and tactics employed. And I knew from the first moment this was going to be a hard fight. For one thing, while we had the empire to call upon and a sizeable force, Albinus knew he had nothing to lose, and had been spending every coin he had raising forces for half a year. The armies were more or less equal. Moreover, Albinus was reputedly a notable military mind himself, and could call on a number of bright generals. The terrain gave no advantage to either side. In short, there was no clear victor from the beginning. Who would walk away with the throne would be decided in the thick of it.

The centre lines committed immediately, and our right not long after, though the left wing remained apart, each side heavily populated with missile troops and light infantry. I watched for most of the morning and afternoon as the tide of war ebbed and flowed, bodies piling up, turf disappearing into a quagmire of mud and blood. Even with the relative separation of our position on the hill, we were close enough to be able to identify occasional individual acts of heroism or horror, or of both more often than not. And we were certainly close enough for the noise and the smell to be our constant companions.

It was a titanic struggle, and little seemed to change over the hours I watched. Then, in the late afternoon, something happened. On our right wing there were cries of triumph and calls from instruments, a shrill din of centurions' whistles, and the army there surged forward. Albinus' left had broken and fled back into their camp. I cheered from my lofty perch as I watched our men pursuing them, until Anullinus stepped close and ushered me into silence.

'But we're winning,' I said, confused.

'No,' he said. 'The wing should not pursue like that. When the enemy break, they should turn and put pressure on the centre. Instead, the fools are chasing them back to the camp.'

And he was right. As I watched, our men followed those of Albinus back to their camp and broke into another small conflict there, while the main battle went on, still roughly evenly matched, without either force on the one wing to create an advantage.

Then, perhaps half an hour later, came a second change. On the other flank, the lines of men had spent hours now with shields up, taking a battering almost a hundred paces apart, as both sides' archer units threw clouds of arrows at one another until late in the day, the swarms of missiles thinned out more and more until they stopped completely, presumably out of ammunition. For a time, the two forces eyed one another warily, past the piles of the dead which had formed on the front line, riddled with arrows.

Then, with no warning, the enemy suddenly pulled back. Their withdrawal was a weirdly choreographed move, as they filtered back in lines, and then re-formed a little further away.

'What are they up to?' Lupus murmured to the other generals on the hill.

Then, the enemy suddenly let loose a volley of javelins. It was a weird and futile gesture, for they were definitely out of effective range. Following on their strange withdrawal, the whole thing was as baffling to the senior officers as it was to me, and it led to a heated debate.

'They are inviting us in,' Anullinus said. 'And anywhere the enemy invites you is a place you most definitely don't want to go.'

'But what is there to lose?' Lupus argued. 'The ground that's opened up is where they were. The other flank broke but the fools charged away before we could press the advantage there. We can't let this chance slip through our fingers. If we move in, we can drive them back, while we turn and press on the centre, too. Where is Laetus with the reserves?'

Another general snorted. 'Laetus is nowhere to be seen. You know what a weasel he is. He'll probably be waiting to see who gets the advantage. I wouldn't be at all surprised to find him changing sides.'

Now, Father, who had been standing to one side, half-listening as he watched, held up a hand. 'Let the *auxilia* and light cavalry advance the flank, but they need support. This could be a trick. I will bring the

Praetorians down to help, and someone send a message to Laetus and tell him to commit his men to the left wing now.'

Sometimes I agreed with my father, and sometimes I did not, but on the battlefield, the man might as well have been Mars himself, and it was hard not to feel a thrill as he climbed onto his horse with the vim of a man half his age, ripped his sword free and bellowed for the musicians to muster the Praetorian Guard.

It *was* a mistake, though. It *was* a trap. We'd not known what Albinus' men had been up to during those hours immobile, while the archers let fly volley after volley. Now we found out.

Auxiliary infantry were the first to charge the flank, light and fast. They wore chain shirts and carried light, oval shields and a short spear that doubled as a javelin. They ran without bellowing war cries, silent, preserving their breath. Then they reached the former position of the enemy, and we understood both what they had been doing, and that odd dance of withdrawal they'd done.

They had been digging trenches behind their shield walls, unseen by us, and covering them over with sticks and mud and ravaged turf, so that they were almost impossible to spot. Then, when they'd pulled back, they'd been careful to do so in columns so as not to disturb the traps. Our men ran straight into the trenches, and the result was utter carnage. The front line disappeared into the pits, breaking legs and arms, ribs and necks, and the second line followed them in, unable to stop by the time they knew what was happening. On the periphery, horses were breaking legs, throwing their riders, disappearing to a fractured death. It was already a disaster in the making, but it only got worse.

Aware of the looming havoc, men were hauling themselves up now and trying not to advance into the seemingly endless array of pits and trenches, but there was no relief to be had. Such was the momentum of the push that even as they stopped, the ranks behind pushed them into the obstacles, and more and more ranks fell foul. Indeed, I think that the horror of the leg-breakers only ended when they were sufficiently full of corpses that men could now walk over them.

And, of course, that was not all that awaited them, for the enemy still had javelins. As the ranks of our men struggled to cross a field carpeted with our corpses, they were now in javelin range, and deadly iron began to fall among them relentlessly.

Father was heroic, but he was foolish. Even though he saw what was happening, he raced on. We should have pulled back and reconsolidated our force, even if we lost the flank. As Anullinus had told me a few years earlier in the Taurus mountains, sometimes it is more important to recognise when *not* to fight. Father raced in with the Praetorians in an attempt to hold the crumbling flank that was now in serious danger. Laetus and his men were nowhere to be seen. To this day I harbour the suspicion that the general on that hill had been right, and that the commander of the reserves had been waiting to see which side it was more prudent to support. We'll never know the truth.

I watched it with horror. I watched the Praetorians commit to a fight they had at best a slim chance of winning. I watched Father at the head of them, in the thick of the battle, where even a general has no place, let alone the emperor of Rome. I saw him succumb to some blow, his horse disappearing. A cry of dismay rippled through the army, for the emperor had fallen.

Then he was there again, horse gone, on foot. He had his sword in hand, and it was bloodied. With his free hand, he ripped away the rich cloak he wore, which was hampering his movement, and let it fall to the mud. I lost track of him, then, as he waved his sword and exhorted his men to seize the flank, for he was now dressed in a soldier's clothes, on foot amid a sea of soldiers on foot. But his presence, both in terms of physical position and his impressive aura, was sufficient to put new heart into the men. They had been on the very edge of breaking, but now, suddenly, they were filled with the spirit of Mars and rushed into the fray, bellowing. What had almost been a disaster, almost cost me both a father and an empire, suddenly became a heroic victory. The enemy faltered. The javelins stopped. They were a drawn breath from routing.

Then Laetus appeared with his cavalry, heavily armoured *cataphracts* and *clibanarii*, like the Parthians. They charged the enemy flank, which broke in an instant. It was an impressive about-face, for certain. Now, we had the left flank, and some enterprising general had sent riders to admonish the overeager pursuers who had cost us the right flank, for they reappeared now, having ravaged the enemy camp. We had both flanks. And once you have both flanks, all you have to do is squeeze, and the centre bursts like a pressed pimple. I watched in awe as Albinus' army shattered and ran.

The battle was over.

We had won.

Some enemy units surrendered, though they faced the same fate as those who sought to flee, simply put to death by our soldiers on the orders of Anullinus. Never leave a proven enemy strength to rise once more. A lesson learned in the East, repeated in the West. What was swiftly made plain was that Albinus was not among the fallen, nor the captured. An officer of his guard was taken and questioned. Albinus had fled to the city of Lugdunum the moment he knew the battle was lost.

My hopes of a birthday in the city of my birth were dashed that night.

Lugdunum held out against us in the name of Albinus, which was stupidly heroic, and utterly pointless, since we still had an army, and they had but a paltry garrison. The siege lasted less than half an hour before some panicked resident opened a gate to us.

Father was Olympian in his rage at the city which had been his devoted land at the year of my birth, yet which had held out against him for a man who was not even one of theirs. His response was predictable. The army surged through Lugdunum on a tidal wave of theft, murder and sexual assault, and once they had found, taken, or used whatever was of value or interest, they torched the entire place.

They did find Albinus, though, and he was brought before Father in chains, his chin high, defiant, eyes flinty. They were still flinty, the chin still high, when with four blows of a spatha, one of the Praetorians struck his head from his body. This, Father sent to Rome, to make it very clear who was now in sole control of the empire, and as a warning to any senators who had favoured Albinus, of whom there had been a few. He rode his horse back and forth over the naked, headless corpse of his enemy for a while, and then the mess, along with Clodius Albinus' wife and children, who had watched the entire grisly performance with hands bound, was cast into the river.

Thus ended the last real opposition to the Severan dynasty in Rome.

We did not tarry in Lugdunum which, in retrospect, might have been a good thing. The place where I was born was, of course, also the place where the woman who brought me into the world passed from it. Memories would inevitably surface within Father, for though he clearly loved Julia Domna, he had once loved another.

In actual fact, in the end I had my birthday in a place that seems to have played something of a central role in my life, the island of Britannia. We arrived there in mid-Martius, for it had been Albinus' province, and would need a new governor. That honour was granted to Virius Lupus, the man who had first fought Albinus on the approach to Lugdunum. He was neither the brightest, nor the most inventive man I had ever met, but what he was, beyond doubt, was loyal, and so he was worth a hundred clever generals right then.

In Albinus' absence, the man who had been senior in Britannia was the procurator, a strange, rodent-like man with thinning hair and a twitch that made me nervous to watch. Like most procurators, he was a bright but single-minded man, and again, he could be counted among the loyal. If there is one constant in provincial government it is that governors and procurators will hate one another, since the former needs to spend money like water in the role, while it is the latter's duty to look after the money. That he would hate Albinus, who had emptied the coffers in a bid for the throne, seemed undoubtable.

By happy circumstance for the man, his son, a young man on his first step to adulthood, serving as a tribune in the legions, had been assigned to the Twentieth in Britannia. On the night of my birthday, three days after the kalends of Aprilis, I was sitting in the governor's house in Londinium, eating pastries and drinking wine, and one of my companions was Alfenus, that very tribune, here to visit his father. As my father went on to deal with some spot of business, and the others drifted away, I found myself in conversation with Alfenus.

He had initially been very stiff and deferential, but I had put him at his ease and told him to talk to me straight, and with the addition of plenty of wine, he'd soon relaxed.

'Your father had only to set foot on the island and the forces remaining here have professed their loyalty. He'll have to remove the officers that followed Albinus to Gaul, of course, but the men need to be left in garrison unharmed. How was it out east?'

'Hot. And dry,' I replied, wondering whether such a reliance was wise, going as it did against Anullinus' rules of war.

'It's not like that here. Most of the time it's soggy and cold. It feels wrong to not use your title. You will have to get used to it, Caesar.'

I nodded, but brushed it aside. I was eleven now, only two years from the toga of manhood. I'd been, for my birthday, named Caesar

Imperator Destinatus, officially denoting that I was destined for the throne. But I'd also seen blood and mud and shit and piss from Antioch to Britannia, I'd travelled with the army, crapped in their latrines, and endured campaigns. I was no golden prince who was going to sit above the men who were responsible for us having an empire. That, of course, was directly from the words of my father all those years ago in Sicilia. Every man is of value, no matter how low, because the empire works from the bottom up.

'I look forward to exploring what I can of the island while we're here,' I said. 'But in honesty, I prefer the East, even with the dust and the heat and the thirst. It's the land of Alexander, and I long to see his Persian palaces and his tomb.'

Alfenus snorted. 'You'll find no such legends here. Gods, but they didn't even write things down until we got here. I've been campaigning up in the North, near the Caledonii, beyond the walls. The place is barren, cold, and full of men whose idea of civilisation is being able to pull your heart out through your anus.'

I laughed at that, and he grinned.

'They're having trouble up there with both the Caledonii and the Maetae. It's been going on for years, but it's getting worse. I'll wager your father will have to send someone back here soon to do an Agricola on them and flatten the whole damned lot.'

'You don't like it here,' I chuckled.

'What's to like? Even their legends are horrible. No Leda and the swan or Paris and Helen or even Horatius at the bridge. I've talked to the wise men of the Maetae. Their legends are all about blood, drowning, murder and torture. They eat the bits of animals my family would throw away. Their language sounds like a man trying to gargle round a frog. And don't get me started on the stuff they drink.'

I laughed again. I laughed a lot that night with my new friend who, though a serving tribune, was only six years older than me. And, oddly, I learned a lot about Britannia that night, knowledge that I couldn't even have guessed at the time how useful it might be. I learned in detail of the system of walls that Hadrian and Antoninus had built across the North, and the advantages and failings of each. I learned of tribes and of gods and of the culture of the cold north. I enjoyed my time there.

We tarried two months.

Then Father was becoming twitchy again. The Parthians had been causing trouble in the East, and he was now considering it time to march east and finish what we started. And that prospect excited me.

Once again, I was to travel to the land of Alexander.

V

The Jewel of Parthia

Parthia, Winter AD 197

'There it is, Domine,' Plautianus called, pointing ahead.

Parthia.

The time had come. The better part of a year of campaigning in the region had finally brought us against the greatest empire of the East.

We'd set sail from Brundisium in the summer, messages sent ahead for months preparing the military, gathering forces in Syria. Unusually, we sailed straight there, without breaking the journey, for Father had had a goat opened on the altar of Neptune, and all signs for the journey were good. The majority of the army awaited us in Syria, but one particular unit we carried with us. The Praetorians, these days made up largely of former Pannonian veterans, had acquitted themselves well against Albinus, and were no longer to be a palace guard in Rome, but to be a core part of any campaigning army. Command of them had been given to Plautianus, who had accepted it with aplomb and grace. The appointment had not pleased me, but the man was ever a player of the game, and to everyone else he seemed to be a perfectly pleasant, loyal and capable man. Had I voiced my true opinion to Father, I would be flying in the face of all evidence.

Another new addition to our retinue was my brother. I was eleven years old, Caesar, and now the veteran of two great military campaigns. My presence might not actually have been valuable, but it certainly would not be an impediment. Geta was eight. I did not see what use he could be, though I was forced to admit I had been that age when Father first had me stomping around war zones. And while I was clearly being groomed for rule, that would not happen for him, so perhaps he was being trained for a more military role. I contented myself with the fact that, though he was with us, he was little more than an observer. Besides, his presence meant that Mother was with us, too, though once things were made ready in Syria, Mother would stay there with the majority of the court that had accompanied us on the voyage, while Father was insistent that Geta accompany us on the actual campaign. From the first days of the campaign, it became clear that Geta and his mentor had become closer during their time in Rome, while we had been in Britannia. Plautianus still had his hooks into my brother, as was evidenced by the guarded looks Geta levelled at me from time to time, though I began to see the campaign as a possibility to finally loosen those bonds, with Plautianus so busy in military command.

The situation in the East added weight to my opinion that Father's earlier campaign had done little to settle the region. The king of Armenia had all but severed ties with Rome, which was still officially his master, in favour of the Parthians, who had taken advantage of the chaos of the civil war and the withdrawal of manpower to deal with Albinus, to expand their territory and seize a number of great Mesopotamian cities along the border, claiming to be liberating them from Roman aggression.

Of course, the gathering storm of steel and the arrival of the emperor in Syria changed things again. The king of Armenia sent gifts, money and oaths of loyalty, flipping neatly back to Rome's side without an overt admission that he had ever been anything but faithful. Similarly, the Osroene king sent hostages and a force of archers to support the army. Of course, his land was currently in great danger, for the Parthians had almost reached and taken Nisibis, but for the fact that in the summer Father had sent a force there under Laetus, who was desperate to rebuild his reputation after his near failure at Lugdunum. Laetus had, in fact, done a sterling job in defending the outpost and it was to him we owed the fact that the entire region had not been overrun before we arrived.

Content that Armenia was under control and that Osroene was loyal, Father led the army to Nisibis. The King of Hatra, a Parthian vassal, had been the one responsible for the recent expansion. Though upon our arrival in Syria the Parthian forces had withdrawn to safe territory, Hatra, and old Adiabene that once more had paid homage to Parthia, needed to be dealt with.

The army crossed the great rivers, the Tigris and Euphrates, and moved into Mesopotamian territory. As we marched into danger, a new trouble for me arose in camp. Geta did not know any of the generals, other than Plautianus, whose duties kept him occupied, and Father was too busy to spend much time with him. Consequently, my brother was at something of a loose end, unable to tie himself to Plautianus as he'd expected. In the end, Father offloaded him on to me, which played into my plan to change things. 'Find your brother,' he said to Geta. 'You will learn from him.'

This was the first opportunity since before Father's rise to power for the two of us to reconcile. To heal the rift that Plautianus had so cleverly opened between us. Pushed together, with Geta removed from the man's ophidian influence, the path was open. Indeed, Geta approached our enforced companionship in a business-like manner, far from that of friends, but at least with no open sign of enmity.

'Why are they called kings here if they serve the Parthian King?' he asked on one occasion, determined to learn what he could, just as Father had commanded.

'The Parthian ruler is the Shahanshah, the King of Kings. Each of the regions that makes up his empire has a king. That way, if they conquer another land, it keeps its king, but he now serves Parthia. That's why places like Armenia and Adiabene often switch back and forth, because we also recognise vassal kings.'

A nod. He went away, deep in thought, with a notable absence of snide remarks or narrow-eyed glances. The first stone of a bridge had been laid. I hoped he would be back soon.

The following day, he pulled his horse in next to mine, with some difficulty, for he was no great rider yet. 'What's beyond Parthia?' he asked, conversationally.

I found myself smiling. In Geta's presence, a new thing. 'A people called the Kushans, and the Indians, and eventually Seres, where the silk comes from. Why?'

'Because Parthia always comes west. Why don't they attack the East?'

I, oddly, had no answer to that. I still don't. I looked ahead, to where Father rode, with his generals. Plautianus, all military might now, riding alongside his emperor, glanced back at us, and I shivered at the look he gave me.

By the fourth or fifth day of questions, things felt better between us than they had for years. We had a long way to go before there was any kind of real sibling affection, but the bridge over that gulf was well underway, and the enmity I had always felt seemed to have faded. I had hopes. They would be dashed.

The next morning, Geta did not appear. Instead, Anullinus met me at my tent with a task. Father had decided that I needed more involvement in the campaign, and so I was to join the scouting units, alongside an appropriate company of Praetorians, of course. An emperor's son is not a thing to risk easily. I left the main column with a mix of excitement and regret. The task was something new and interesting, but it would take me away from my brother and the relationship we were working to build.

It was not until I returned to the column that night that I realised what was truly going on. Plautianus had seen the change in us and, determined to drive us ever further apart, had persuaded Father to give me a job that would keep me away. In my absence, the man had clearly contrived to sink new barbed hooks into Geta, for the look he threw me that evening was one of spite, and he turned his back on me.

I resigned myself to the fact that my attempt to bridge the gulf had failed, and now I found that I was kept busy with military training, while Plautianus had managed to persuade Father that Geta should accompany him in a similar vein. Every day that followed drew us further apart.

We marched through Adiabene, and their untrustworthy king was made to regret his guile when we flattened many of his cities and garrisons. Perhaps he had been expecting the Parthian King of Kings to send help. He didn't. Adiabene was crushed beneath our heels, and we moved on into Hatra, where a similar story played out, once again without Parthian interference, until we reached the capital. Their king sealed himself up there with a solid force and refused to accept that we were in control of his land.

I watched the siege of Hatra, a high-walled fastness, with fascination. I had seen three campaigns now, but this was my first true siege. Camps were set, lines drawn, every engine available to the army brought to bear. We held our place there for twenty days, and I had my eyes opened to the brutality of a siege. The Hatrenians fought bravely, pouring down a steady stream of stones and arrows. They were inventive. They had made clay pots and filled them with horrible stinging insects from the region, and then sent them down among our besieging army, where they shattered and dispersed their contents in huge clouds to sting and bite and poison our men. The hospital area of the main camp grew at an alarming rate, new ward tents added daily, mostly to deal with illness, for in addition to the insects, the very air here in autumn seemed to carry sickness and poison.

Other pots rained down from the city, too, carrying burning bitumen, which ignited our siege engines so that rarely was a night in camp not lit by a burning onager. Our situation was further aggravated by the fact that every other foraging party we sent out fell foul of nomadic raiders from Arabia. The East was truly a boiling pot of curses for us.

We abandoned the siege on the twentieth day. There was a sense of defeat among the men, though really it was unwarranted. Yes, we had failed to take Hatra itself, but that was only one of many objectives, and we had laid such waste to the rest of this land that it was doubtful their king would cause trouble for many a year.

Some of the officers, including Anullinus, advocated a return to our own lands on the western shores of the great river, where we could spend the winter licking our wounds, heal the sick and regroup for another campaign the next year. I could see the sense in that, even though a withdrawal was rather galling.

Father was of a different mind, though, and once he got an idea lodged in his head, he was unlikely to be persuaded otherwise. He saw any return to the empire as an admission of failure that would gnaw away at the hearts of our men. No, he decided. We needed to not run away. We needed to change things. We needed a victory.

Ships were swiftly constructed, and others brought from all over Hatra and Adiabene, and the army embarked and began to travel down-river, towards the heart of Parthian power. In truth, though we had been hit hard at Hatra and lost a lot of men, we still had a very sizeable army, and once we were moving again, away from that cursed place, the instances of illness began to decline. As autumn slid fully into winter, we truly entered the Parthian world. There is wisdom in Rome's tradition of campaigning in the summer months and retiring to garrison for the winter, but that wisdom is overturned in the eastern deserts. There, a winter campaign is the only sensible option, and as the heat faded and the rivers flowed, so thirst, heatstroke and illness all began to fade. We returned to strength.

The Parthian King, Vologases, had withdrawn to his capital with most of his forces back in their own garrison, believing that we campaigned, as usual, with a view to chastising and retrieving those border kingdoms in the North, which would undoubtedly later change sides again. He cannot have believed we were coming for him, else he would have been more prepared.

We were approaching Saturnalia when we put ashore on the river's eastern bank, where scouts confirmed we were in the Parthian heartland, just half a day from the capital. Such had been Vologases' unpreparedness for such a campaign that we had all but reached his doorstep without resistance, for the great river flows past the city and the royal palace.

Of course, now that we were so close, word would have reached him, and he would be doing what he could to stop us, but there was not a vast amount he could do. As the army mustered on the land and began the drive towards Ctesiphon, we heard more and more reports coming in from the scouts we'd sent ahead. The Parthian king was now aware of us, and, unable to gather sufficient force to put in the field at such short notice, and not wishing to find himself trapped, he had gathered his fastest horses and his kin and guards and had raced away east and south, ever further from Roman lands.

Initially this drew more groans from the men, until the reality of the situation filtered through from the generals. We would not be able to make Vologases kneel before Father, but where we had ravaged Hatra and then been halted by its capital, here we had no such trouble. With the king and his best men gone, only garrisons stood between us and the jewel of Parthia.

That was confirmed as we reached the city. Ctesiphon is a vast place, not as big as Rome, of course, but easily the largest city I had seen in the East, with high walls and round towers, surmounted by very decorative battlements and coated with brightly coloured tiles. The city had outgrown the ramparts and clustered near the wharves along the riverbank, but we could see the high and delicate walls of the palace within, and we could see that the defences would be horribly inadequate given the size of our army. The number of men on the walls was far from enough to hold them, and even my inexperienced eye could tell that. Still, given their position and the solidly closed gates, it was clear that they intended to try.

Saturnalia and New Year came and went in the preparations for Ctesiphon. This was to be no easy task, thanks to Father's plans. Likely the army could have surged over the place and obliterated it swiftly, but that was not what the emperor wanted. Ctesiphon was to be a statement. It was to be Father's warning to Vologases to never again seize land on the Roman border. A statement. And a punishment.

Thus we did not want to completely destroy Ctesiphon, or to burn the city to the ground. We wanted it intact, and that meant cracking it neatly like an egg, in order to consume the contents, not stamping on it with a boot.

It took twenty-four days. Siege lines were laid, camps set up, new artillery and engines constructed to replace those lost at Hatra. Picket units were sent up to a hundred miles deeper into Parthian territory, just in case the King of Kings suddenly found a massive army and came back to face us. He didn't. Our scouts also located the city of Babylon just a day's ride to the south, and that was marked for similar treatment.

Twenty-four days. The first eighteen were spent preparing, building, planning, letting the enemy feel nervous. For the last six days, though, the siege proper raged. Ammunition was thrown with wild abandon at the walls and the defenders. This was a whole different affair to Hatra, though. Here, they were undermanned and unprepared for a siege, and the results were horrifying. By the sixth day, the walls were almost empty of men, those who remained now cowering where our weapons couldn't find them. The gates caved in late that afternoon, as the sun set. Yet the signal was not given to move. Storming the city at night could lead to mistakes, failures and indiscipline. Father wanted this done right, and so while the people of Ctesiphon trembled and awaited their fate, our army remained blockading them in, immobile.

In the morning, Father gave a speech to the army, which was relayed by every standard bearer and musician present, so every man knew precisely what was being asked of him. And very likely the speech was heard inside the walls by those who would be waiting for disaster.

'Ctesiphon is yours,' Father said to the men. 'Not mine. Not Rome's. And certainly not Vologases'. Ctesiphon is to be our answer to Parthian aggression on the border. I want the place to be a vision of Tartarus to their King of Kings when he returns. No burnings. No demolition. I want the shell of this place to stand like a mausoleum, untouched. But anything that moves within is to be either enslaved or killed. If it's a comely woman or a strong-backed man, they get roped up for the markets in Rome. Anyone else, man, woman, child, donkey, dog or chicken, is killed. I want a carpet of blood waiting for the man when he returns to his palace. And I don't care if you have to fuck your way through the women in the process. Do as you will. Anything more valuable than a brick is yours. Loot. Steal. Take. Anything you can carry back to Rome, do so. Anything that is too big or immobile, break it. Only the king's palace itself is out of bounds. The rest of the city is yours. I want Vologases to come back to a tomb full of blood and misery.'

There was a hungry cheer from the men. Rape and murder always gets their blood up after a siege, and usually a commander has to rein them in. Not this time. They were being actively encouraged. The King of Kings was going to pay dearly for what he'd done over the past few years. This was not just Anullinus' principle of keeping a beaten enemy down. This was a step beyond. Another lesson learned.

'Why are they not allowed in the palace?' Geta asked of the gathering.

I knew the answer to that. As Caesar, I was party to all briefings and staff meetings, and I'd heard the other command. The one that had been given to Plautianus.

The palace was for the Praetorians. They were to do much the same as the rest of the army, but any servant or relative of the king was to be crucified within the palace itself and left for him to find. And they were to use the king's own bedchamber as a latrine. The statement made in the city was to be doubly clear in the palace.

Ctesiphon suffered for three nights, and it suffered more than any besieged city in living memory. And once it was done, and nothing remained alive in the city but the birds feeding on the dead, and nothing more valuable than a dinner plate remained, we left. But that was not quite the end of it. Across the river lay the city of Seleucia. Unlike the royal capital, Seleucia was not garrisoned against us, and almost its entire population had fled on our approach. Father is nothing if not thorough, though. Seleucia was laid waste. Our pickets were then withdrawn from the East, and fully half the army embarked on the fleet we'd brought with us, along with the spoils of war, including piles of treasure and a hundred thousand slaves, who were marched along the riverbank alongside, under guard. They would travel slowly. The faster units remained here, the cavalry and light infantry, and the Praetorians.

And while half the army began the slow job of escorting our prizes back north towards Roman lands, we set about finishing the job. The army split up and moved about. Every village was flattened and burned, every well supped from and then poisoned, every cow or sheep butchered for meat for the men, every man, woman or child sent to meet their Parthian gods.

Then came, for me, the crowning moment of that winter.

Babylon was not what it had once been. As we approached the place, it became clear that its days as a powerful city were long gone. I know now that its power and most of its populace had been transferred to Seleucia and thence to Ctesiphon, and there was even no sign of the famous Hanging Gardens. But it mattered not to me. I was here on a pilgrimage of sorts, although made possible by the fact that we were here with the army in order to leave it an unusable ruin. We entered through the northern gate, and soldiers rushed this way and that through the streets, seeking anything to steal, murder or fornicate with. The Praetorians moved out a block or two ahead of us and surrounding us, for even in the wake of such victory, all it would take was one disgruntled local with a bow, and Rome could be looking for a new emperor.

Father sat astride his horse with me on one side and Plautianus on the other. Geta was riding close behind us, with more officers and guards, as we made our way along the main thoroughfare towards the great, ornate ancient building ahead.

'Father?'

He turned to me. 'Yes?'

'When we take the palace, don't let the soldiers wreck it.'

He frowned. 'Why?'

'In there is Alexander's deathbed. Where he spent his last hours. I don't care what happens to the Parthians and their king, but it would be wrong to desecrate the Macedonian's memory.'

He considered this for a moment, weighing it all up, then finally nodded. 'They shall have the palace, but not that room.'

I let it go at that. I could not really ask for more. We entered the palace, and as the Praetorians checked it room by room before we entered, dragging out anyone they found, I followed them, with Father, Geta and Plautianus in my wake, others following on. I could feel the excitement, the very magic of discovery in the air, making the hair on my neck stand up. I had felt a little like this at Issus, and more so at Gaugamela. What the feeling would be like in Persepolis I do not know, but here in Babylon, in the building where the great man died, I felt a connection that I had never felt before. It was almost as though the shade of Alexander walked with me through those rooms.

What had begun as a childhood interest and then became a fascination at those battlefields in the North, transformed in Babylon into something that was almost an obsession. I was moving fast, excited, my breath coming in small gasps as we moved through the rooms. We finally found the more residential part of the palace. The place was not royal now, for the Shahanshah lived at Ctesiphon, but the palace was used by a satrap, one of his governors, who had presumably fled long before we arrived. The furnishings and décor were rich, if not regal, and it was still a sumptuous place.

I turned a corner and walked through a door, and I felt it. I felt *him*. Alexander's very presence was in the room with us.

'This is it,' I said.

'Are you sure, son?' Father mused. 'We have seen a dozen rooms like this. It does not stand out.'

'I think it smells common,' Geta complained. 'And of fish.'

'That's just you,' I snapped, irritated by his comments. Ignoring the hard glare Father cast my way, I looked around the room. There was a bed atop a three-step dais, a small tiled pool, a podium, perhaps for dancers or musicians. I closed my eyes. I could see it then. I could see back through five centuries of change. I could see the great man lying on his bed, dying, his generals clustered around him, the men who would go on to tear apart his legacy.

I realised then, that there was some destiny at work here. We were in some way an echo of the great man and his father. Phillip had come into a world where the Greek peoples had become jaded and corrupt, their lands in decay. He had conquered them, facing off against great men, and even as an outsider from northern Macedonia, he had breathed new life into the Greek world, turning it into something new, something better. And then, when he was busy waging war, he made his sixteen-year-old son Alexander his heir and allowed him to act as a regent in his absence. What was that, if not a Caesar?

We had done the same. Father was Phillip. He had found the corrupt world of Commodian Rome, and even as an outsider from Africa, he had conquered his own empire, facing powerful opponents, to found it anew, fresh and reborn. And I was his Alexander, now coming of age, his heir and his regent. What world would I conquer, I wondered?

Geta was muttering again, and I turned, narrow-eyed, to meet a baleful glare.

Alexander *hadn't* had a brother to fill the air with complaints, to show no appreciation of important things, to argue that he should have a share of the power. Then, beside him, I saw Plautianus, the serpent of a man, looking around. And back through the door were Laetus and Anullinus, involved in some minor argument.

I closed my eyes again, and there he was, Alexander, dying in his bed, surrounded by the generals who would carve his empire up when he passed, and ruin everything.

Four generals. Ptolemy, Seleucus, Antigonus and Cassander.

Anullinus, Plautianus, Laetus and Geta.

The parallels were enough to raise concern in me.

'Alexander means a lot to you,' Father noted.

I nodded. 'In thirteen years he turned a country into an empire the size of Rome. It took the Roman people three centuries to do as much. He was the greatest general the world has ever known. And a great ruler, too. Only he could settle Persia, the age-old enemy of his people, and manage to make them loyal. My tutor used to tell me as much.'

Father fixed me with a look, one eyebrow arched. 'Julius Caesar was obsessed with Alexander, you know? Used to rage because he would never be able to match Alexander's achievements. Your tutor presumably told you what happened to Caesar?'

Another nod. I didn't like where this was going.

'Stabbed twenty-three times,' added my father, answering his own question. 'Even by friends. All because of his hubris. Remember always, Marcus, that no man is ever truly safe, from men or nature or gods. No emperor is indestructible.'

I nodded yet again. 'But regardless, Alexander is a figure to strive to be, Father, is he not? Was Trajan not a little of an Alexander, and he is still worshipped now?'

'A little hero-worship is healthy, yes. But don't let the obsession claim you. Obsessions are dangerous.'

With that he turned and gestured to Plautianus. 'I have something to arrange. Letters to send. Make sure this room is under guard and not touched during the chaos. In fact, have the door bricked up now, as it is. Let's make sure it stays undisturbed, for the boy.'

Sometimes I wonder if that door is still sealed. Whether no one has ever been in there since us.

When we left Babylon, I felt something of a wrench. Not only was it Alexander's last home, it was also where the partition was decided, where his generals split up his empire. Perhaps there was a lesson or an omen in that, too.

We left Parthia in the wake of the other half of the army, following the rather clear trail they had left along the line of the River Tigris. We caught up with them around Hatra, where there was a week's pause while the army ravaged the land once again just as a rude gesture to that frightened king behind his high walls.

All along that journey, I kept looking back. The idea that we had been in Alexander's lost empire with an army, but we were leaving, and letting the Parthians, a people who had no appreciation of him, the descendants of those very Persians he had conquered, overrun it once more, irked me. Even at eleven, I had resolved that one day I would reconquer Alexander's realm and add it to the empire.

We arrived at Nisibis to a rousing cheer from both the populace and the garrison there. Messages of congratulations over the successful campaign had been sent by the kings of Osroene and Armenia, and there was a general sense of achievement and victory. We were returning to Rome, and there would undoubtedly be a triumph, and this time Father would accept it. This time we had been victorious over a true enemy of Rome, not other Romans, and I felt certain that I would get to ride in the chariot with Father, despite the fact that I'd actually had no active part in the war. Again, it faintly irked me that Geta would likely triumph with us, despite a lack of involvement in the campaign.

When we finally reached the coast at Tarsus, I frowned as I watched Plautianus, Mother, Geta, Anullinus and others board a ship separate from ours, while we, the upper echelons of the imperial court, and just a single squad of Praetorians, boarded a fast, sleek liburnian. My uncertainty only grew as we set out that morning and immediately charted a different course from most of the returning Romans. As we made, what looked to me, due south, I finally questioned Father.

66

'Are we not going to Rome?'

Father gave me an odd smile. 'In a while. There is something I have a mind to do first.'

VI

The Golden Crown

Alexandria, AD 198

Instead of returning to Rome, we had taken ship with just a small entourage and made for Aegyptus. I had no idea why we were going, but the excitement was filling me. If I were truly following the trail of the great Macedonian conqueror, I had left his deathbed and was now approaching the land in which he was buried.

I was taken aback, initially, for I'd felt sure we were bound for Alexandria, which is the great city of that ancient land, and the heart of Roman control. Instead, as Februarius rolled into Martius, we made a great journey up the River Nile. I had no idea why we were detouring on such an oddly-timed sightseeing tour, but I learned over the first few days to simply sit back and enjoy the journey.

We stopped at all the great ancient temples in that land, and while I explored with a small guard, Father consulted the priests and magicians, acquiring a number of texts of secret lore, millennia old. We reached the edge of the Roman world there, where the Nile tumbles over cataract after cataract. We were warned not to travel further, which I think irritated Father, as he wanted to be the first emperor to cross that border. It was said that the land of Kush beyond the cataracts was suffering some dreadful plague. And so we turned around and travelled back down the Nile in late Martius.

I both laud and curse our journey on the Nile.

Father never did anything unplanned, and there were reasons for all of this, beyond his fascination with the arcane, which Aegyptus fed with gusto. He timed everything for the one day. I had been so wrapped up in what we were doing that the date completely escaped me. It was the morning of the third day after the kalends of Aprilis when we made the last push across the delta and into Alexandria. I was marvelling at the city, the great Pharos lighthouse that is famous across the empire, the port where Caesar burned the ships, the library, or at least what was left of it, and the great palace where Antonius and Cleopatra had breathed their last after the defeat at Actium. Alexandria truly was a city of marvels, steeped in history. I was agog when we docked, and staring in awe as we shuffled through the city towards the palace. I hardly noticed the fact that the populace were standing back, cheering as they lined the streets, their emperor in their presence, for my gaze was on everything else around me.

We entered the great hall at the entrance of the palace, and again my gaze was drawn to the massive colonnades, the shafts shaped like lotus flowers, the ceilings and walls painted and carved, a bright image of a spread-winged vulture above the door. It was only when we stopped unexpectedly and there was an odd silence that I drew my gaze back to the present, and realised that I was standing with just Father in the centre of a room full of men in broad-striped togas, officer's uniforms and rich Aegyptian dress.

Father was looking at me.

Oddly, I noticed then that there was something wrong with him. He looked thinner than usual, and his face had an oddly blotchy look to it. Still, he seemed happy, for he broke into a wide smile. I only realised what this was all about when he spoke, addressing the gathering of luminaries.

'Let it be known that on this day, as my son Marcus Aurelius Antoninus, turns twelve years old, I hereby bestow upon him the toga of manhood. Let the things of childhood be put aside.'

I blinked. It was my birthday, and that fact had completely escaped me. A slave was suddenly behind me, and I almost struggled, surprised, as he unfastened the bronze bulla on the thong around my neck and took it away, signalling an end to my childhood. Another two slaves arrived with my first toga, which they carefully draped around me, symbolising my entry into the world of men.

'I am not thirteen,' I whispered as Father came close. Thirteen was the usual year for such a thing.

'You have been past ready for years, Marcus,' Father replied. 'The time is right.'

And then he turned to the crowd, indicating his grown-up son. They cheered, but he was not done yet. He made lowering motions with his hands until there was silence once more. 'Marcus has not only grown into a man these past years, but he has grown into a wise and strong one. He has travelled from the cold hills of Britannia to the parched deserts of Parthia and overseen campaigns against enemies both internal and external. He has learned from the best. That is why, with this toga virilis, I also bestow upon him the title "Augustus". From this day, my son rules Rome at my side, as my partner in all things. Look now upon your emperors.'

As I stared at him in shock, the room erupted again into loud cheering. I had gone from being a boy and an heir, to being a man and an emperor in the space of twenty heartbeats. I had nothing to say. I was struck dumb. Once the cheering had ended, a procession of illustrious figures came to me one after the other to offer their support and their praise and congratulations.

We would stay a month, Father told me, between the visits, as the room buzzed with excited conversation. He had a number of plans. Plautianus could keep Rome under control in our absence, and Mother was there as the very voice of the emperor if Plautianus needed anyone. Unusually for a Roman family, Father acknowledged Mother's intelligence and wisdom and allowed her an unprecedented level of interference in matters when required. I hoped she would be enough to control Plautianus as he controlled Rome. Geta would learn of my elevation before our return. I could only imagine what would be going through his mind then. I should admit here and now to feeling more than a little smug that I had risen so far so fast while he was still a boy and without a title, given his insistence that he should share my role.

Father had another surprise for me yet, though. Once the celebration was over, we had a brief meal while we talked of small matters, and then, as he rose and stretched, a Praetorian centurion entered the room and bowed. 'All is ready, imperator.'

Father nodded to him. 'Thank you.' Then turned to me. 'Come. I have a birthday gift for you.'

Now I was intrigued once more, and the interest only grew as I was led to a carriage that awaited us outside. Father's lictors stood in their lines in front of the vehicle, and it was followed by a second small wagon that overflowed with soldiers, more Praetorians in lines behind and alongside.

'Where are we going?'

'It's a surprise.'

I climbed in, along with Father, who I noted with a tinge of worry, seemed to suffer a moment's trouble doing so until the centurion helped him up. He settled into the seat and we began to move, the glories of Alexandria sliding past the carriage windows as it bounced on inadequate suspension across the city. I fixed Father with a concerned look.

'Are you all right?'

He waved my worries away. 'I'm fine. It's the heat, or something I ate. Nothing to worry about.'

But I did. I had a suspicion that I dared not voice. It took most of that journey for me to stop watching him with worry. I was fascinated, though, as we passed through the city's eastern gates. We had left Alexandria, heading in the direction of Nicopolis and the delta. Whence were we bound?

The answer came as we moved past a series of impressive tombs and mausolea, older than Rome's control here, from the days of the Pharaohs. Then, finally, an impressive temple came into view as we rolled to a halt in front of it. A temple in the midst of a cemetery?

I knew what it was the moment we alighted. It could only be one thing. I felt my skin prickle. My breath came in short gasps, purely with the excitement. The temple of Alexander. Emperors and generals, senators and governors had come to this place to worship and pay respects to the great Macedonian. And it was not just a temple. This was his tomb, as well.

What a birthday gift.

Father had warned me against obsessing over Alexander, and yet here he was, feeding my obsession. There was a great deal of activity behind me, and I turned to see the soldiers unloading a crate from the other wagon. They manhandled this to the temple, and waited there.

'Come,' Father said, and climbed the stairs to the open doorway.

I did so, and we entered the temple with a sense of awe. Along with Father, I approached the altar. One of the accompanying soldiers passed us a bottle of very expensive wine, incense we had brought from Antioch, and a bag of gold coins. We made our devotions, lit the incense, poured libations, and mouthed our silent prayers. I do not know what Father asked of or promised to the great conqueror.

I asked for nothing. I had everything I could want, or so I thought. In retrospect, I might have asked for Plautianus to have an unpleasant accident, but in the end, I asked the great man's spirit for nothing, but I promised him one thing. I promised that while I sat on the throne I would bring his empire into the control of Rome, a legacy worthy of both him and me.

Devotions complete, we made to descend the stair into the tomb itself. While we had prayed, the soldiers had opened their crate and removed something a few feet across and wrapped in copious layers of cloth. This they carried behind us on the stair.

The staircase was decorated in the ancient Aegyptian manner, though with the clear influence of Macedonia and Greece. Below, the steps emerged into a huge room. The temple's attendants had descended ahead of us and lit the lamps in their niches, and so the place was brightly illuminated for us. The room was a mock courtyard, a colonnade around the edge, the ceiling painted to look like a night sky, scattered with gleaming stars. All around the walls behind the columns, I could see scenes of the great man's life, the battles of Grannicus, Issus and Gaugamela. The Gordian knot. The subjugation of Persia. A visit to the Ammonium oracle at the Siwa Oasis. Father paused then, indulging me, as I hurried around the colonnade, drinking in those fabulous paintings, reliving the history of the Macedonian anew.

When I had had my fill, finally, we approached the doorway onwards. This led into a smaller room, which held yet another doorway ahead. This room was a treasury. The room contained sufficient riches to build an empire, and it was for this reason that the temple and tomb had well-built and well-equipped guardians at all times, and only important luminaries were granted admittance to the tomb.

I marvelled. I reached out, hardly daring to do so, and touched the ivory hilt of the great man's sword, the weapon that had cut the Gordian knot and forged an empire from Greece to India. I learned then what the soldiers had brought with them. At Father's command, they unwrapped their bundle, to reveal a cuirass.

I drew in a sharp breath as I realised what it was. My eyes slid to the sword hanging on the wall. There was a space there beside it. I stared in awe at the cuirass, formed in the manner of the ancient Greeks, shunning metal. A suit of body armour made of folded and hardened layers of linen, light and flexible, yet very protective, with *pteruges* at sleeve and hem, shoulder plates doubling the density there, and an image of a gorgon picked out in bright colour on the chest of the white cuirass.

The armour of Alexander the Great.

'Where was this?' I murmured, still in awe as the soldiers returned the cuirass to its rightful place amid the great man's panoply.

Father gave me a smile. 'Caligula took it from the tomb and wore it on his triumph across the bay. I felt it was time it was returned to its owner.'

I nodded my agreement. I was almost stunned into silence and immobility by it all. Once that was done, and a few small gifts were added by Father, enhancing the collection, placed there reverently by Praetorians, we moved through into the last room.

As long as I live, that scene will probably be the one I remember best.

The room was not overly richly decorated, merely painted such that the walls and ceiling looked like open sand giving way to a canopy of night-time sky and stars. The only content of the room was an oversized couch of gold, after the manner of the ancient Aegyptians, and on that couch lay a golden coffin.

Alexander had been buried as a pharaoh, mummified and placed within that golden coffin, but, like those pharaohs who had gone before him, the coffin was formed in the likeness of the great man. The golden crown that had been brought here by Augustus lay atop the coffin. I don't know how long I spent looking at that face, but it was long enough that the Praetorians were getting bored and twitchy, shuffling their feet. Finally, Father cleared his throat meaningfully.

I straightened and turned.

'Thank you.'

Father smiled, and we left the tomb then, climbing back to the world of men. I was the last to leave, looking behind me as I went, my gaze lingering on that gold casket and the body of the greatest general in history.

I wasn't quite the last to leave, for a temple attendant doused all the lamps behind us and then followed up. At the top of the stairs as we emerged, there was a great deal of activity, and I frowned as I stepped back out into the main temple. As soon as we were all out of the tomb, Praetorians closed the heavy doors to the stairs, then locked the three locks and handed the keys to Father. This done, they then fed a huge heavy chain through the door handles and locked that too, passing this key also to Father. I turned at heavy grating sounds and saw more Praetorians heaving great stone slabs through the temple door.

'Father?'

He gave me another smile. 'That was your birthday gift. You will be the last man ever to look upon Alexander. Caligula robbed his tomb, and I have put that right. But now it will be sealed. Let the man rest in peace, undisturbed and at no risk from robbers.'

I nodded slowly. In a way it was awful, to seal it forever. But he was also right. It was too important to let such risks stand. And there was an indescribable thrill in knowing I would be the last man ever to visit Alexander's tomb.

The rest of the day passed in a sort of strange, blissful ennui. Father tried to interest me in affairs of state over wine in the palace, but my mind was still wrapped up in Alexander. I could think of little else. The next day, I begged leave of Father to visit the Siwa oasis, but he declined. It would take half a month just to get there and back, and it was dangerous, across hundreds of miles of open desert. We needed to be in Alexandria, and then, soon, back in Rome. I was to be presented to the people as Augustus and emperor. Such things could only wait so long. I knew that he was right, largely because it must have been burning him not to be able to make the journey himself. Siwa is the home of one of the greatest oracles in the world, and Father was ever an adherent of such things.

'Besides,' Father added, 'your brother will be waiting, expectant.'

I frowned. 'Expectant for what?'

'I shall make him Caesar. As you are now emperor with me, it is only right that your brother take a place as heir in the dynasty.'

I bit my tongue. I wanted to point out that even as his co-emperor I was still his heir. He didn't need another, and especially not one likely to be directed by Plautianus. And as sure as anything, the day Father passed away, Geta would not be my heir, for by then I would have a wife, and sons. But I did not want to anger Father, or distress him, so I held my tongue. After all, Geta's title would be little more than a sinecure to keep him content, while we ruled Rome.

Over the next few days I explored Alexandria, and I had the best armourer in the city found. I commissioned from him a new cuirass for myself. I had grown again in the months since Hatra, and I would need a new cloak too, but for the cuirass I needed something special. I wanted something in gleaming bronze, which was clearly the armour of a Roman emperor, but I wanted it to include as far as possible all the motifs of Alexander's cuirass. I would have the tied-on shoulder plates, and the gorgon, and my pteruges would not be of leather, but of hardened white linen. I would be an emperor of Rome, but I would also be a new Alexander.

As I enjoyed our time in Alexandria, though, I saw two things that began to dismay me, and both involved Father. Firstly, his health declined. I had noticed him stumbling a little, and he continued to lose weight. Then he went through a phase of night-time fevers and sickness, and the blotchiness had grown into a sort of bumpy rash in places. With the illness, he also became irritable. In fact, quick-tempered, I would say. And that led to the second problem.

Alexandria has the largest population of Jews in the empire these days, and from time to time they suffer under heavy-handed governors. They put in an appeal while we were there. They sent rich and powerful men from their community asking Father to rescind certain edicts and to ease their burden. They had very much chosen the wrong time, for Father was exceedingly tetchy.

They asked for reasonable things.

Father responded with one reasonable request: that they do honour to the Imperial cult. An obeisance at the temple of Augustus and Rome in the city as a sign of their loyalty. I knew how that was going to end. I'd had a Jewish friend once upon a time, after all, and their people interested me. I listened as they explained how they could not do so. In their cult they have ten unbreakable rules handed to them on tablets by their god, and one is that they bow to no other deity.

That problem, of course, has ever been at the heart of their troubles with Rome. They cannot accept Rome's gods or its divine emperors, and consequently no emperor can ever trust their loyalty.

The result was predictable. Father dismissed both the envoys and their requests. When they returned to their enclave there was trouble, almost rioting. Soldiers were called in, and legionaries killed. Father exploded and ordered a series of executions. I endured that time with a stony silence. I was Caesar and must concur with Father in such matters, but in the privacy of my heart there was a rather untraditional sympathy for the Jew, born of my earliest friendship. The whole thing rather palled our time in the city, sadly.

But my concern for the Jews became a peripheral thing when placed beside my concern for Father. I made some enquiries of the priests and physicians who were attending him, and none of them seemed to understand. Then I took my suspicions instead to the navy. I spoke to the commander of the small fleet that had conveyed us up the Nile when we first arrived in Aegyptus, and those suspicions were quickly confirmed. Within hours of our arrival at Alexandria, members of the crews had come down with the same symptoms as Father.

They had somehow managed to contract the plague that ravaged Kush beyond the southern border, perhaps from the very scouts who had warned us of it. The disease had then passed through the crew on the return journey, the effects showing up as we returned to Alexandria. Father must have caught it at some point on the voyage, for he was not far behind the sailors in displaying his symptoms. I asked the man how they were treating the sailors. He gave me a bleak look and a shrug.

'This disease is well known from the South, Domine. There is no cure. Anyone who shows symptoms is given over to the priests. They lock them up alone in rooms for twelve days, delivering food through a hatch with no direct contact, and if they are still alive after twelve days they usually survive.'

I shuddered. What kind of world was this we were in? When I had been a boy in Rome or Sicilia or Pannonia, any illness would prompt a huge series of potential treatments and cures from the physicians. To blindly assert that nothing could be done and just watch them either live or die seemed backwards, almost barbarian.

Father, then, would simply either recover, or succumb to the disease, and there was nothing I could do about it. That night, as I lay and worried about him, I finally fell asleep, and dreamed more than ever before. I recognise that the quantity and quality of my dreams may have been a result of the large quantities of Aegyptian date wine I had consumed as I fretted. I dreamed of many things, but one in particular stayed with me as I woke in a sweat early the next morning.

In no less than three of the fevered dreams of that night I had seen a bull. I had imagined that I was with Julius Caesar and his soldiers as he visited the shrine of Alexander, and wept that he would never be the conqueror the Macedonian had been. Caesar's legionaries had borne his Taurus bull emblem on their shields. I had dreamed of the land of Crete, where athletes leap over bulls, grasping their horns. And I had dreamed of the sacrifice of the bull at the festival of Venus Caelestis in Leptis Magna. Just the sheer overwhelming presence of taurine imagery told me that these were no mere wine dreams.

When I awoke, I dressed hurriedly and sought out the senior priest who had been attending Father.

'Aegyptians worship many animal-headed gods. I've seen their statues. Which is a bull-headed god?'

The man frowned. 'We have no bull-headed god, Domine.'

I felt deflated. I had been so sure.

'Unless…' the man added with a thoughtful look.

'Yes?'

'Do you know of Serapis, Domine?'

I shook my head. 'Tell me.'

'Serapis is a lord of healing and wisdom.'

I felt a shiver. Of course he was.

'He is both man and bull. He is a great lord of the delta, and particularly of Alexandria.'

Of *course* he was.

'It is said that the first temple of Serapis in the city, even in all the black land, was laid down by Ptolemy. He brought the great statue here from Sinope, as he was instructed in a dream.'

I shivered with a frisson of divine energy. *Ptolemy.* Alexander's general and right-hand man. Of course.

'Where is this temple?'

'It is in the city, Domine. Easy to find. Shall I show you?'

I nodded and told him to meet me at the palace gates in an hour. I was still sweaty and raddled from my interrupted night, and this was no state in which to present myself before a god. I had slaves fetch my best military tunic and fresh clothing, and paid a quick visit to the baths, making sure I was appropriately clean and neat, and then gathered my lictors, who Father had assigned me on my birthday, and met the priest at the gate, where he had a small gathering of attendants and three Praetorians. Carriages were brought. I would happily have walked, but the priest was old, and I humoured him and used his vehicles. It took perhaps half an hour, arriving at the very south-western edge of the city.

I knew I was doing the right thing the moment I set eyes upon the Serapeion of Alexandria. It was easily the largest and most impressive temple in the city. Indeed, I was so sure of myself and of my purpose now that I all but leapt up the staircase, taking them two at a time, my lictors struggling to keep up, the priest ambling at the back as fast as he could climb.

One hundred steps of white marble led to a magnificent gateway in the middle of a portico. I hurried through, excitement and urgency driving me. The temple itself was immense, and stood at the centre of a huge precinct, surrounded by that portico. There were doors into rooms built all around the edge, and fountains and pools positioned around the wide paved space. The nature of the god could hardly be mistaken, for much of the precinct was occupied by sick plaintiffs, suffering from any number of complaints, all here to seek the god's grace and heal themselves. A cynical man might suggest that cramming so many diseases together was more likely to spread the illnesses than to cure them, but perhaps that would not be correct. This was Serapis' home temple, after all.

'What are they?' I demanded of an attendant, pointing at the many doors.

'Libraries, my lord, some of what remains of the Great Library. Dedicated to the healing magicks and arts. All the knowledge of medicine and the workings of Divine healing are gathered here.'

I took a shallow breath, not wanting to draw in too much of the surrounding illness. I turned to the lictors with me. 'Gather any man you can find to help. Have those libraries searched for anything that might help with the Kushite plague.'

That was it. All my attendants and even the priest who'd led me here were set to searching for a cure. They might find something useful, probably not. But that did not concern me. They were doing something to help. And I, too, was going to do what I could.

I entered the temple itself. The three Praetorians tried to accompany me, but I told them to help search the libraries. I went in alone. After so many days in the city, my identity could not have escaped anyone, and the moment I entered, attendants and priests ushered everyone else out, barring the most senior priest, until I was alone. He asked, very politely, how he could help me. I told him I needed no help, and he left with the others. I was alone in the temple with the god. His statue was immense, seven or eight times my height, his arms reaching out, his brightly-painted marble form both majestic and realistic, resembling, appropriately, Aesculapius. Before him stood the various altars and offering tables. I had brought nothing. There was nothing in Alexandria that I could offer the god that was worthy of the boon I sought. But I had my own idea.

As the door shut with a clunk, leaving me alone in the echoing divine presence, I bowed my head to the god and then raised it again.

'I ask a boon, Divine Serapis.'

And I knew now, here, that this was my new god. My new deity. My personal devotion. Caesar had his Venus and Domitian his Minerva. Serapis was my heavenly presence.

'My father, the emperor of Rome, who will one day sit with you among the gods, is plagued with the illness from Kush. He fades before my eyes. But I hear that some survive this disease. I ask you to watch over him. To use your powers to shelter him from death and to see him returned to health. I know this is no small request, and so I bring no mere incense, or wine, or gold. Instead I make you a promise. I offer you the greatest payment I can think of.'

I folded down to my knees, something I do not do lightly.

'I vow to you a new temple. As this great Serapeion rises on the hill above the city of Alexander and Ptolemy, so shall a new temple to your glory and worship rise on the hill above Rome, the centre and the heart of the world. The Serapeion of Rome will be greater even than this. The greatest temple I can decree. This I vow to you in the hope that you will save my father.'

And with that I used some of the wine left by the priests to pour a libation to seal my offering.

I left, taking only my lictors with me, leaving the rest to search the libraries. Indeed, within the hour, I had a veritable army of people examining the libraries. They never found anything. I'd not really expected them to. I watched, tense, hopeful, for the next few days. From what I had learned of the course of this disease, confirmed by the cases among the sailors, the next few days were critical. If he was to die, it would be imminently.

His fever broke on the third day. I hurried to his rooms in the morning, as I had every day, a gaggle of priests and physicians in my wake, more hanging around outside the doors of his apartment. I knocked and was admitted. The previous evening, I'd thought his end nigh, for he could hardly speak, curled and twitching with pain, sweating into his sheets, those sores erupting on his face and arms.

I entered that morning to find him sitting up in the bed.

He fixed his gaze on me.

'I find that I am hungry, son.'

And that was it. Relief flooded through me. Over the next few days he was attended regularly, but his recovery was swift. Best of all, I understood that in most cases the skin deformation that covered the victims would end with scabs falling away and leaving scars that would last for all the victim's life. If ever there were confirmation that Serapis had heard my plea, it might be found in the fact that hardly any mark touched my father from his disease, and as the end of the month approached, there was no real visible sign that he had ever been ill.

Of course, it was the invisible signs I should have looked for, but I was just so grateful that he had recovered. Now he was well, and we were to return to Rome, two *augusti* together.

For now, I was an emperor of Rome.

Part Two – Divided

'Miseram pacem vel bello bene mutari'

Even war is a good exchange for a miserable peace

—Cornelius Tacitus

VII

The Chariot of his Fame

Rome, Summer AD 198

'How is your father?'

I tried to turn, but the slaves who were adjusting my garb would have been thrown from their task if I did, so I limited it to my head, which just drew a gasp of despair from the man attempting to comb my unruly hair into an imperial coiffure. To the side stood Marcus Opellius Macrinus, currently praetor of the treasury, one of Father's favoured lawyers, and one of the few men with enough balls to speak to me directly without fawning all over me. I liked him, partially because I knew that whatever he said to me, he meant.

'He's all right. There are after-effects of the illness. He gets out of breath quickly, and his feet hurt him, he says, but he is walking and talking and his mind is still sharp. I do think it was the work of the gods that he made me Augustus and co-emperor just in time to be of use to him when he feels less strong.'

'And is your brother the work of the gods also?'

Geta. Caesar. Heir to the throne after me. I needed a wife. An heir. Someone to put in the line between us. Geta, prodigy of the hateful Plautianus.

'He is most definitely the work of the gods. Good taste prevents me from saying which ones, though.'

That made Macrinus laugh out loud, a hearty, booming sound. He had a huge laugh. A huge voice. In fact, he was a huge man, another African, but this one from Berber lineage, darker-skinned and with a penchant for piercings and tattoos.

'So you are involved in your father's triumph? You ride in the chariot?'

'Yes. With Geta, too.'

'And you're now pontifex maximus?'

Rome's high priest, a ceremonial title really with very few duties, overseeing the various cults and priesthoods. I nodded. 'I am.'

'So what happens at the sacrifices at the end of the triumph? Do you have to jump out of the chariot, change hats and then race your father to the altar in order to officiate?' He grinned, white teeth in swarthy face. 'If you have to help with the sacrifice, do you have to keep jumping backwards and forwards between the priests and your family and swapping hats?'

Now I chuckled at the image that created. 'Stop riding me, Marcus. You know I've just delegated the role for the day.'

His grin remained. 'I shall be watching the procession ahead most carefully. Every pace you take weighs in coin, you know? I have people desperate to account for every denarius. I considered not marching in line myself. I could save the treasury the price of a hundred and twelve loaves of bread if I stay home.'

Moments later my head steward announced that I was ready. I looked at myself in the huge bronze mirror. The slaves had gone to work on me. I have a serious face, given to a natural frown, and even at twelve, lines had begun to form on my brow from that expression. The makeup they had applied had almost removed my habitual look, replacing it with a bright and sunny countenance. Even laughing with Macrinus, I didn't feel *that* bright and sunny. Combine that with the *toga picta* of imperial purple shot through with designs of gold thread, and the gilded laurels set and pinned to my hair, and I looked more like I ought to be lying on a couch in a languid position and propositioning sailors, than celebrating a military victory.

'Start again,' I grunted at the slaves. 'Wash this shit off my face and just cover up any pimples.'

I could feel the disapproving gaze of the master of *cosmetae* as his staff hurried to clean my face. It would be hard without disturbing the rest of my attire, but they would try their hardest. Geta might let them primp him. He was still too young to know better, but I doubted Father had let them turn *him* into a painted trollop.

It took another half hour to get me to a state that I was happy with, but which the attendants did not feel was too understated. Then, finally, I joined the others, and Macrinus, with a last jolly farewell went about his own preparations. Father, predictably, looked more or less the same as me, serious and not over-made-up, more military than glorious. Geta, surprisingly, had opted for the same. It frankly pissed me off that he was here and wearing the toga picta of a triumphant general. Admittedly, I'd not given a single order or commanded a single man during the whole Parthian campaign, but I had been with them, at the front, into the sacked cities, in the command briefings. I'd even accompanied the scouts. Geta had mostly sat back in a chair in his tent and played with himself, unless he was following Plautianus around or asking questions. I might be able to argue a right to be part of the triumph. Geta was only there for the dynastic look of things.

Indeed, I had felt a surge of hope the day before when Anullinus had pressed Father on the matter. I wasn't supposed to be listening in. I just happened to be nearby.

'He's just a boy, Lucius, and one with no involvement in the campaign. Having him in the chariot degrades the achievements of you and Marcus.'

'I have noted of late something of a rift growing between the boys. I need to nip that in the bud. I will not have my family torn apart by arguing brothers. If Geta had been there and Marcus not, I would still have had Marcus in the chariot. We are a dynasty, now. Like the Julii or the Flavii. And I need all of Rome to see us united. A dynasty that cannot work together cannot survive for long. I will close the rift between the boys.'

I heard a grunt from Anullinus, indicating that he was less than convinced, and then a less welcome voice.

'Indeed, Lucius,' Plautianus murmured, a serpent hissing in Father's ear. 'I would say that perhaps at the moment Marcus has pre-eminence and Geta rather walks in his shadow. I know this is natural for older and younger brothers, but if you are trying to sell them to the people as sharing in a dynasty, then perhaps you could further advance Geta, to bring him closer to a level?'

Bastard.

Fortunately, Father stepped on that one. 'For now things are best the way they are, though I want the boys more like brothers than opponents.'

That seemed unlikely, at least as long as Plautianus was around.

We travelled the city in that great triumph in the chariot behind Father, and because he was required to face front and look glorious for the crowds, he would have missed entirely how little success he was having healing our rift, for we did not even glance at one another that entire journey. It was a slow and laborious business, for the pace was set by a thousand of the slaves we had brought back from Parthia. That, of course, was but a fraction of the huge number we had taken, but a thousand is enough to herd around the streets, believe me. Behind the slaves came the spoils of war and the trophies of captured arms. I had wondered how we were going to achieve such a thing, given that our spoils had all been looted by the men for their own enrichment on Father's orders, and little really came back for the empire as a whole. It should not have surprised me that the Villa Publica in the Campus Martius houses, among other things, a huge collection of fake spoils of war that can be trotted out at a day's notice, and fill the wagons for a triumph without any messing about. Triumphs were rare enough that few people were ever likely to notice a repeat appearance.

Following them came all the senators and magistrates, including Macrinus, then our lictors, all in their military red, lines of hard men. Then came us. A trio of imperial glory, one oblivious, the other two clearly ignoring one another. Behind us came the officers on their steeds and then the best veteran cohorts of the army.

I am, as I've mentioned, not a man easily given to smiles, but as we sacrificed on the Capitol, Macrinus' image of me leaping back and forth and repeatedly changing hats would not leave my head, and at one point Father fixed me with a pointed look and hissed that I needed to display more decorum.

I was, in the end, rather relieved when it was all over.

I spent a month enacting tedious edicts issued by Father, all of which seemed designed purely to benefit the senate and to mollify them. Then I had a visit from Father, and I noted, with some pleasure, Macrinus in his wake. The man was grinning, something that usually intimated he had thought of a private joke he was in too good a company to voice.

'Father,' I began, trying to head off the coming encounter, because I'd been trying for three days to bring a matter to his attention.

'What?' he muttered as the rest of the entourage came to a halt. He had that look I recognised as trying to hold onto his point while he listened to another.

'Your building programme.'

'What of it?' It was one of the major talking points at the time. Father had decided that one of the main signs of legitimacy for an emperor was to build a new forum, a new palace, new entertainment venues. He'd planned a huge bathhouse, but that would have to wait, for he would first have a great triumphal arch for his Parthian campaign, other monuments in the forum, a newly commissioned grand marble plan of the city, a whole new palace on the Palatine with a baths and a grand *nymphaeum* that would separate it from the start of the Via Appia, and a complete rearrangement of the imperial guard barracks across the city.

'I want a temple,' I said.

Father waved a dismissive hand. 'Rome has a temple to every god. I have had to push every last decision for building past accountants who frowned at me once for every denarius I cost them. I've even had to delay some projects. Whatever it is, write me a note and I'll add it to the list. This is different, I have good news for you.'

'Oh?' I was interested, but I had also had my plan halted by treasury officials. 'Still, this is important.'

He paused, his frown deepening. 'What?'

'I vowed a temple to Serapis. In Alexandria. In return for your continued survival.'

Father gave me a thankful, warm look. 'I do appreciate that, Marcus, but there are half a dozen dilapidated temples in the city we can rededicate for a remarkably small cost.' He was starting to shuffle from foot to foot. Standing still hurt his feet these days, since the illness.

'You don't understand, Father. I vowed the greatest temple in Rome. Your health was worth it.'

He gave me a look again, but I had him. It had all been for him, after all.

'All right. Start looking at sites for it. I will make some room in the budget somehow. I am founding three new legions, and quartering one of them at Albanus near Rome. Perhaps I can slip some money towards it from the military budget.'

I grinned. Creative accounting. Excellent.

'And now,' Father announced, 'meet your new brethren.'

It was my turn to frown then as I scanned the ranks of men behind Father. Mostly young to middle-aged men of senatorial rank. Eleven of them. I would be a twelfth.

'The Arval Brethren?'

Father smiled and nodded. I felt a thrill. A man can be elected to a number of priestly roles without any real competence or piety or plan, right down to the high priesthood I had only just given up. But the Arval Brethren was different. Twelve priests in a cult so close that even emperors not initiated had no real idea what they did. Twelve priests who were chosen for life. Father had longed to be chosen, yet it never happened. Apparently, for me, it had.

Macrinus.

My new friend was one of them, and it seemed likely he had pulled the strings to get me recommended.

'Thank you,' I said simply.

'Not my doing,' Father replied. 'But congratulations, my boy. You have risen high in Rome. Tonight we will celebrate.'

Four hours later we did just that, though it was not a high point in my life. Macrinus had already taken me out to taverns frequented by soldiers and got me drunk on some truly horrible drinks, long before I ambled into the palace where Father had a night of wine and entertainment arranged.

There was something of a blind spot with Father. He might be perceptive and bright, but not where Geta and I were concerned. He simply failed to note anything wrong between us more than mere brotherly quarrels, and believed the rifts he could see to be small things easily healed. He also failed to notice how drunk I was when I turned up that evening. I managed to mutter and mumble my way through a few brief encounters with Mother and Father, and was standing on a balcony overlooking the Circus on my own, trying to sober up a little, when my brother found me.

'Why you?' he said waspishly, by way of greeting.

I was now thirteen. He: ten. I was a man with the toga of manhood, an emperor... and an arval brother. He was Caesar, an heir, but still a boy.

Plautianus stepped onto the balcony behind Geta, then, and put his hands on the boy's shoulders in an almost fatherly fashion. Geta clearly thought he was due more than he received, urged on by Father's old friend, while Plautianus had hitched the chariot of his fame and career to the Geta horse, hoping, I suspected, to use him to tie himself into the imperial family. Gods, but I hated Plautianus, and all that did was start to make me start to hate Geta, who was becoming a young facsimile of the man.

'Three names were put forward for the Arval Brethren,' Plautianus said. 'One can be discarded when compared to the sons of an emperor. But I have seen the result of the votes. Geta won. Yet it is you who have been chosen and not your brother. Why?'

I regarded him with a hard, dark look, the one that remains on all my statues. You'll have seen it.

'I have no idea. It is the decision of the brethren. Geta was unlucky.'

'In that he didn't have a Berber friend to talk them round?'

My expression hardened, if that were possible. 'Remember to whom you speak, Plautianus. You are a friend of my father, but, like him, I am emperor of Rome. I suggest you find somewhere quiet to think on your ambitions and their cost.'

Plautianus had the good sense to bow his head, say nothing more, and withdraw, leaving me alone with my brother. I tried to dig down through all the layers of shit that lay between us. I took a few steps forward. It says something about our relationship that he flinched and stepped back, but I pressed on and took his shoulders in my hands, fixing him in my gaze, brother to brother.

'It does not have to be like this,' I said. We had almost built a bridge, once. Almost closed that rift. Could it still be done?

'What?'

'Always a competition. Anger at what the other has. We are brothers. All I wanted when you were born was a brother I could share with, explore with, get into trouble with. There is still a chance for us to work together. I know you think Plautianus is your friend, but what he is doing is setting us against one another, and all so that he can come out on top. Surely you can see that?'

The look he shot back at me was the nail on the crucifix. He couldn't. He couldn't, or wouldn't, see what Plautianus was doing.

'Everything is taken by you,' he said, and there was acid in his tone. 'I get nothing but your leftovers. I expect that one day, if you die, I'll be one of the Arval Brethren, but not before. Because you got there first. Caesar. I only got that because you didn't need it any more. I was only taken on campaign because you were now one of the officers. I'm your shadow. I'm the forgotten one. And that's not fair. At least she's *my* mother.'

I rounded on him then. 'This was *never* about our mothers. I don't even remember the woman who birthed me. Mother brought us both up as her own. I've never thought of her as anything but my mother, and you as anything but my brother.'

I stormed away from the balcony after that. I have no idea what Geta did, though he undoubtedly ran into the arms of either Mother or Plautianus.

The days passed in the ennui of government: a seemingly endless roll of documents to be signed and sealed, announcements and speeches to be given, senators to be wined and dined and appointments granted in return for gold in the imperial coffers. I was approaching my fourteenth birthday when I encountered Plautianus in a good mood in the palace corridors. I didn't like that. Plautianus in a happy mood was as worrying as Geta in a happy mood. Neither was something to smile about.

'Ah, Marcus,' he said in an expansive voice as he bumped into me and hugged me as though we'd always been the closest of friends. 'Have you heard the good news?'

Whatever it was, I doubted I'd consider it good.

'No.'

'Veturius is retiring as prefect. Your father has named me the sole prefect of the Praetorian Guard. It is a rare honour not to share the role.'

Wonderful. A unit with a confirmed history of supporting usurpers under a single commander, and an oily, ambitious one, at that.

'You must be very pleased.'

'I am. And I have a notion of how to repay him.'

I didn't like the sound of that at all. 'Oh?' Guarded. Vague.

'You know I have a daughter. Sweet little thing, Plautilla.'

I had no idea. He could have fucked a frog and had tadpoles for all I knew or cared. 'Oh?'

'She's only a couple of years from marriageable age.'

His leering look told me everything. I marshalled the only argument very quickly. 'Geta is too young. He'll barely have taken the toga of manhood himself before she's of age.'

'That's why I was thinking of you.'

A hundred responses whipped through my head in less than a heartbeat, and had I had a sword at my waist, it'd have been a thousand. I forced my face into a teeth-clenched humourless smile. 'How generous of you.'

'Your father and I... we are both of Leptis. We are outsiders in this great city, and no matter how powerful we become, there are those who will always think of us as second class. It would do us all well to tie our families together.'

He grinned and walked off.

'Yes,' I thought. 'My family rule an empire that, barring the conquests of Alexander, controls the civilised world. Your family are provincial hopefuls. I wonder who would get what out of *that* deal.'

Within a matter of days I had made my counter-decision and brought it to Father's attention. Emperors of old, who were more concerned with purple robes than with the order of rule, had met with their *consilia* in rooms of state, while flautists warbled and Aethiopians danced, oiled Grecians wrestled and slaves ran in and out with sweet-meats. They would wear their best togas or silk tunics.

Not so my father. His meetings of state were in a simple room off the old *stadium* garden of Domitian, where the new palace was being constructed. It was a utilitarian room, graced with simple, effective furnishings, and with small plates of basic foods and an average wine. I was co-emperor with my father, Lucius Verus to his Marcus Aurelius, and I walked into the room and took the seat beside Father. His was a throne in all but name, and mine was just only a little less. Others entered one by one, and when we had *quorum*, I cleared my throat.

'Now we are all here, I have a proposal.'

Father chewed his cheek. 'Plautianus is not present.'

'It cannot be helped if he is late.'

Father shot a look at me. He knew I'd done something. In fact, I'd engineered a little display among the more purse-loyal guards to keep their prefect busy. He'd be along before the meeting was over, but he'd be too late. 'Go on.'

'Do you remember Quintus Aemilius Saturninus?'

He nodded. 'A good man.'

'One of the best among the *equites*. He was Prefect of Aegyptus during our visit, and did everything he could for you, and maintained control of the Jewish quarter during the troubles.'

That you caused…

'Yes, yes. I know the man.'

'He is back in Rome and looking for position. I have spoken to him, and he would have me bend your ear with a view to sharing the prefectship of the Guard.'

I held my expression to my usual fierce intensity, fought the triumphant grin.

'I vouchsafed the prefectship solely to Plautianus. It does not need a shared command.'

'Just as the consulship was designed for two men, so that neither ever held the reins of state alone, so also the prefectship of the Guard, Father. Two prefects means that neither can ever move to usurp without being countered.'

He digested this, and I watched him mull it over, his ties to an old friend and the promises given, placed against the danger of a one-man army. In the end, he nodded.

The days continued to pass in relative peace after that, albeit with a cold glare reserved for me by Plautianus every time we were in the same room. Indeed, a year passed with little to note its disappearance other than my father displaying a tendency to lameness in the feet and Geta taking a step further towards adulthood.

It was during the summer, when I was involved in the Arval Brethren's duties that this all came to a head. We'd done the day of festivities in the city, surrounded by whooping citizens, drunk and enjoying the atmosphere. Tomorrow we'd do the same, and the people of Rome would flock to the temple for the donatives of baked goods, the wine flowing freely. For the night in between, though, we celebrated the harvest with the goddess, or at least with a dozen of the best whores the city could provide, down in the sacred glade off the Via Appia. We would celebrate fertility in our own way, twenty-four bodies writhing in the undergrowth. It was my first time. Or at least, my first time not with one of the palace slaves who'd been instructed to 'make me a man'. It was my first time with a woman who wanted to be with me, even if it was just for the money.

It was one of the more irritating moments of my life, when things were just getting interesting, because it was at that moment that Macrinus appeared over a shrub with an armful of wine. As I thrust and grunted, then barked in surprise, he grinned. 'You not done yet? Mine was with child half an hour ago, I reckon.'

I finished. Actually, I finished rather accidentally, thanks to the interruption. Once the girl was gone and I'd pulled a tunic on, Macrinus rounded the shrub and planted his ample backside on the seat beside me, facing the shrine.

'You're going to have to do something about Plautianus, you know?'

'Oh?'

I mean, I agreed. I'd thought much the same. But I had no idea anyone else had been keeping track.

'You know he's acquiring power, land and money at a rate not seen since the days of Sejanus?'

I shrugged, my expression darkening. I had heard rumours. Plautianus had been getting his enemies killed and taking their estates, using his Praetorian and palace connections. In truth that was nothing new. 'He kills his enemies. I detest the man, but I can't fault him on that. I'd have done exactly the same in his position.'

'No,' Macrinus replied. 'I know of at least three men who would happily rip his head off and shit down his neck-hole that he hasn't done anything about. He's not killing his *enemies*. He's killing anyone who stands between him and power. I'm quite surprised my name hasn't come to his attention yet, being close to you, Domine.'

'So?'

'Have you heard about Quintus Aemilius Saturninus?'

I shook my head, concerned now.

'Appointed co-prefect so recently,' he said, 'sharing power over the Guard with Plautianus. No longer.'

I felt the earth shift under my feet. 'Yes?'

'Poor bastard. He was found last night. He'd been set upon by a gang. Nowhere on his body escaped the beatings. A physician consulted and noted that a human has 206 bones and that less than a third of that number had survived unbroken on Aemilianus. He was a shadow of a man.'

I shook my head sadly. He'd been a good man, not to mention my appointee to the post, which irritated me.

'That's not the half of it, though,' Macrinus muttered.

'Oh?'

'A reliable witness claims that the men were off-duty soldiers. That they were wearing military tunics and boots. White tunics...'

White tunics?

Praetorians?

'Are you telling me that Plautianus has had the shamelessness to murder his co-prefect almost straightaway?'

'I don't think he liked the idea of sharing power. Of course there's no evidence. Even the witness could only testify to the *likelihood* of who they were, and he wouldn't stand a chance of recognising the individuals out of the thousands of serving Praetorians. Unless you torture every last Guardsman, the matter will simply blow over.'

I found myself fuming over that. I could see no way to bring the matter out in the open, and accusing Plautianus of murder without any evidence would just be an embarrassment. I did not enjoy the rest of the festival that night, nor indeed the next day back in the city. I really wanted to make Father aware of the situation, but I couldn't see an easy way to do so. Outside the family, Plautianus was his closest friend, and the man he most trusted. I had no evidence. I knew the man was a snake, but I could hardly prove it.

The solution hit me when I was going through my correspondence a few days later. There was only one man Father would listen to regarding the matter. He wasn't in the city at the moment, for he was currently governing Crete and Cyrenaica, but perhaps I could persuade him to intervene. I settled straight away into writing a carefully worded note to my uncle, Father's brother, then rushed the missive off with the imperial couriers.

Then I waited. Nine days, the couriers had told me. A nine-day journey from Rome to the provincial capital at Gortina. I waited the nine days, checking on weather reports. All was calm and good. The letter should have been with my uncle at that point. Then I waited ten more days – the return journey and a day for uncle to compose a reply. Nothing came. I continued to wait, becoming more and more impatient and frustrated. Every day as I waited I became aware of reports of important and rich men falling to Plautianus, who was becoming worryingly rich on their stolen estates. It took a little over a month in the end for the reply to reach me.

I opened it with trembling hands, hope filling me.

Nothing.

My uncle never mentioned the case itself, though he alluded to it somewhat obliquely, clearly covering his back in case the letter fell into the wrong hands. The message to me was clear. Without any evidence, my uncle was not going to step in between Father and his best friend. The brothers had always been close and trusted one another implicitly, but something like this could drive a wedge between them, and he was not willing to risk such a thing.

Plautianus was now openly playing the villain, yet Father saw nothing amiss, and the man, while being rather blatant, was also clever enough to leave no evidence of wrongdoing, and to have a perfectly reasonable excuse for everything he did. Moreover, he had my brother in his camp these days, and Geta would simply gainsay me.

I would find a way to bring Plautianus down. I vowed it.

Unfortunately, my scheme would have to wait. Word had reached the capital of incursions by the nomads in the deserts south of Leptis Magna, and Father had taken offence, it being his homeland.

We were to prepare for war, and Africa awaited.

VIII

In Cold Blood

Garamantia, Africa, December AD 202

I fought two wars that next year or so. The first I fought with Father,
for the empire. The second I fought against Geta, for my future. I didn't
know about the second conflict for a while, though, as we concentrated
on the southern borders of the empire.

Our force was nothing like the one we had fielded against Parthia,
and I learned that first few months a valuable lesson in tailoring any
army to the campaign that required it. Parthia was an organised and
civilised empire like our own, with its own armies and fortresses and
generals and plans. As such, we could field an army composed principally of heavy infantry and skirmishing cavalry like those of old, for
we knew our enemy and knew that most of the action would be either
sieges or fought out in the open.

The campaign against the Garamantes was different. I had read my
Strabo, and my Pliny, and so I knew as much about them as was possible
for a Roman who'd never encountered them. They had evolved from
the Berber tribes of the desert periphery, those same peoples from
whom Macrinus' line had sprung, but they had begun to move in
the direction of civilisation. They had formed from tribal groups into
towns, had begun at least rudimentary farming activity, as well as
mining and salt refining. These they traded with Rome across the
border. They had even begun a kingdom with a noble hierarchy. One
might say they were a civilisation in the making, part-formed. But what
they did not have was a true army. While they had moved in the direction of modernity in many respects, their military activity remained
solidly in the area of raiding and skirmishing warbands, mounted on
horses and camels, relying on their secret ways to travel from water

source to water source in the forbidding sands. No standard Roman army was going to bring them to battle. Thus we employed mostly like-for-like. We had two legions with us, just in case, the Third Augusta from Lambaesis and Father's new Second Parthica taken with us from Italia. But they were just our core and reserve. They were outnumbered eight-to-one by units drawn from everywhere that bred men hard for desert life. We had Mauri cavalry from the far west of the African continent, we had Berbers from across Africa and Cyrenaica, we had Aegyptian units both foot and mounted, we had slingers from Crete and Hispania, archers from Africa and Syria, and even Arabian horse. The army conversed with the weirdest polyglot of Latin, Greek, Berber, Aegyptian, Arabian and Aramaic.

But they were equal to the task. I could see from the moment we landed at Leptis Magna that the army assembled beyond the walls was made for this land. We tarried in Leptis for a number of days, and I started to think that perhaps Father was enjoying being back in his homeland too much to press on. The truth became apparent soon enough as four triremes put into the port one afternoon. They were bringing the aforementioned Cretan archers to join the army, and with them came the governor of the province that had been suffering the raids. My uncle.

He and Father embraced at the dockside, kissed cheeks and grinned. They were so similar that for a moment I lost track of which was which, but then my uncle spotted me standing nearby and hurried over, flinging his arms around me.

'Marcus, my boy, but you are a reflection of your father. The cut of a military tunic suits you. But what is this? You wear a warm cloak? Is our African sun not to your liking? It seems to have formed worry lines on your forehead.'

He was ribbing me, and I knew it. I had been wearing a military tunic long before the last time I'd seen him, and all the world knew of my adherence to that cloak, for the nickname that clung to me had already become better known than my actual name. I fixed him with a fierce look.

'You have become fat. Too much time in a governor's curule chair, I suppose. Is that why Father summoned you to war? Do we need to find you a fat horse?'

His look wavered between offended and amused, and I was relieved when it settled on the latter. 'You have a sharp tongue, nephew. I have a mind to employ it against the enemy, since my bulk prevents me from getting too close. I think you would do well in the front line.'

That made me laugh, and we embraced again.

The evening was one of reunions and humour, but it ended early with the call of a horn. We were marching to war, and no one wanted a thick head in the morning. Before we took to our beds, though, once Father had shared a last joke with his brother, I caught up with my uncle on the way to his accommodation. Catching the look in my eye, he dismissed his attendants and waited, while I sent my lictors to find somewhere to wait. Moments later we were alone.

'I need to talk to you about Plautianus.'

His expression darkened. 'I doubt there is anything you can say that you've not already said, far too blatantly, in a letter that could have been intercepted by anyone. In case I wasn't clear enough in my reply, I think the man is a complete toad, but I will not move on him without evidence.'

'How can there be evidence if no one investigates him?' I countered in exasperation.

'I did not say I was not investigating. Dear nephew, the moment you revealed your suspicions, I activated a score of spies throughout the palace and the Guard. If he takes a shit in a suspicious way I'll know about it in a few days.'

I cracked a smile. 'Thank you.'

'No. Thank you. I don't like the idea of men playing my brother, and it sounds suspiciously like that is what Plautianus is doing.'

I felt better as I went to bed that night. I had a true ally at last.

The next morning we moved out. As I watched the army ahead of us, ploughing out into the great southern unknown, a notion occurred to me and I found Father and waited for an opportunity to speak to him.

'Give me command of a unit, Father,' I said.

He frowned. 'You are emperor, Marcus, like me. You have command of all the units, and all the commanders.'

'But I rode in the Parthian triumph and I'd done nothing. You have led men in battle. I haven't. Father, I'm sixteen. At my age Alexander went to war with the Thracians, savaging them in the name of his father. Rome will not respect me without some evidence of war skills.'

'You overestimate such things. The best wars are ones that are won without a fight. I have fought in my life when I had to, and only led men when I did not put my future in danger.'

'I will not throw my life into the jaws of the lion, Father. Just give me a unit.'

He huffed and puffed out his cheeks for a moment. 'Fine. A reserve unit. The Berber chieftains from south of Leptis regard me as a close friend, and sent a number of their units as my personal guards. I give you one. Five hundred mounted Berbers. Try not to get them, or yourself, killed.'

I grinned. In truth, I was a tiny bit disappointed. I had pictured myself leading armoured heavy infantry like some great hero, or at least Roman cavalry. Not swarthy nomads with spears and dun tunics on ragged desert steeds. Moreover, when I was presented to them as their new commander, they made obeisance and said all the right things, but I could see in their eyes that they resented being put in the charge of an adolescent with no battle experience. I was determined to change that.

I took my cue from Father's own history with his army. I rode with them, and I ate with them. I slept among their number and prayed with them, to my own gods and to their strange ones. Still, I could not inveigle myself into their trust.

Our first encounter with the Garamantes came entirely by chance. We were yet fifty miles from any supposed presence of their peoples, and the army had stopped during the worst heat in the middle of the day, putting up shades and drinking precious water. I was on the left wing of the army and gave my Berber riders orders to set up in the shade of an overhang. To my astonishment, they completely ignored the order and set up some distance further on. When I demanded of the senior officer why they had done this, he replied that they had set up within walking distance of water. Shade they could make with blankets. Water was more important. In truth, it probably pissed me off more that they were right, and that I'd overlooked that, than their insolence did. But I was damned if I was going to accept insubordination. I reached out and gave the officer a ringing slap on the cheek with the back of my hand. I was young, but he was a short man, and so I had height on him, and I was no reedy youth now. I was probably over-hasty, for one of my rings left a cut across his cheek. His hand sprang to the dagger holstered across his belly and it left the scabbard by an inch. I glared at him.

'I am emperor of Rome, and my command was wilfully disobeyed. Some emperors would have had your unit decimated or cashiered for such behaviour, and you know that. If that blade leaves that sheath I will see you crucified on the sands for your presumption.'

His glare matched mine, but I was not going to back down. 'My command was wrong, but you could have come to me and made a suggestion. That would have been the correct thing to do. The chain of command respected. You also know this. Now learn that I am not to be trifled with. If you do not need the shade, then you do not need rest. Your riders will do a three-mile probe to the south-east, and I will come with you to be sure that *this* command is obeyed.'

He backed down. I was relieved. I didn't want to fight the man. He spoke to the others in their own tongue, and the wave of resentment that hit me was palpable. We moved out the moment they had repacked their things. We rode for some time into the desert, all but one man I had sent to my father to explain where we had gone. I let them move into their own formations, because arguing with them further would hardly help. We rounded a huge rock formation, and there, suddenly, were the Garamantes.

I stared in shock. There had to be four or five thousand of them. Not enough to win a pitched battle with our army, but they had somehow come within little more than a mile of our forces without being noticed. Were they the only ones, or part of a larger trap? Our men were fell out, lying under shades and drinking water. The massacre that they could potentially start would carve a huge hole in Rome's forces.

I turned to the officer, who knew what these men were capable of, and whose eyes were also wide.

'Take half the men. Ride for my father with warning. We will delay them, and buy you time.'

'Domine, it should be you who...'

'*Ride*, you bastard.'

With half a dozen commands in his native tongue, the man led more than two hundred riders away. I looked at the rest. 'No one sells their life cheap. We fight them and we hold them, and the moment they have us we fall back, and we do it again. We do it all the way back to the army to give them time. Understand?'

They did. They gave a roar.

No one argued with me now. The whole army was in danger, including many of their countrymen, and I had offered my life to help. The Garamantes gave a horrible ululating cry and ploughed towards us. It was at that moment that I realised how wrong I'd been. I'd wanted shiny legionaries and written off these grubby men in tunics. But the Garamantes came, not dissimilar to my own men, and my riders reacted. First they formed and threw their light spears, which peppered the attacking line and disintegrated it. While the Garamantes were recovering from the missiles, I led them forth, ripping swords from scabbards, and we hit them like a spiked hammer, like Charon at the end of a gladiator match, crushing heads with his massive mallet to be sure no one was faking.

I fought for the first time in my life. I actually fought, and I killed. In fairness, I have to say that I did not enjoy it at all. I was sick and frightened. And since that very day I have followed the advice of Anullinus and my father and only started a fight I knew was already in the bag. That day I took a flesh wound to my left thigh and another to my left bicep, but I killed three men in cold blood. By the time we broke off and rode away, I was coated with blood, mine and that of others. My riders were whooping with the heady feel of victory. Because we had not just delayed them, we had stopped them. So savage had our attack been that they made no attempt to chase us down.

We rode back to the army laughing, and when I met my father, he already had them marshalled and moving, ready for trouble. We found three such smaller armies that day, but because we had sprung their trap early, we dealt with all three separately and it was us, not them, who had the initiative.

That night, when camp was set, I was called over by my men, and initiated into something. I still couldn't say what it was, but they painted my face and tattooed my hand, and we drank something that tasted like Charon's piss while we cheered gods I'd never heard of. My men had accepted me, and that marked the start of a lifelong companionship I have had with the Berber cavalry.

The campaign was a tough one in the following days, largely because of the difficulty in bringing the Garamantes to battle. The bands of warriors tended to lurk in their hidden places and then emerge unexpectedly, hit us hard and swiftly, and then melt away into the deserts and rocks before we could do little more than take the stragglers. We managed pursuit and some damage thanks to the general makeup of our forces, who were at least at home in such conditions, but even with an army tailored to dealing with such a campaign, we learned a new hard truth in those days. The denizens of the African deserts hide their paths and their water sources and stores, and they are impossible to locate without local knowledge. They could simply disappear and we could only chase them down as far as our own supplies could follow. Thus we did a little damage to them and covered a great deal of territory, but they managed to carve chunks from our army throughout that time. Things were starting to look sour when we hit upon the solution.

We came upon one of their towns. A cluster of brown stone buildings hugging a rocky promontory, narrow curved streets, coloured canvases stretched wide, casting the alleys into shadow, ingenious water systems bringing liquid life from the rocks nearby to allow the town to survive. The place was surrounded with mudbrick walls. We began to lay siege to it, but it was clearly going to be a difficult proposition. We hadn't brought siege weapons with us, for they would have made our journey in the deserts impossible, and there were simply no trees around to create machines from. Additionally, any siege had to be brief, for they had a good supply of food and water, while we were living on fumes at that point. We tried a full assault, but their arrows and javelins made short work of any infantry attack, so we settled in.

The breakthrough came from the Berbers in our army. They located the town's water supply for us. Nearby rose a large rocky plateau, and water was to be found deep underground beneath it. The Garamantes had sunk a shaft down to the water and then cut a channel that flowed underground all the way to the town, with access shafts periodically along the route. Father seized the opportunity. We set out the engineers from the two legions, and in two days they used one of the access shafts to block the flow to the town and divert it into a new shaft that brought it out where we instead could access it. The town fell mere days after that, as thirst settled in. Now that we knew how to deal with their towns, we left this one little more than a rubble field full of corpses and looked for another.

The water systems were all similar, and each time the Berbers managed to locate the shafts so that we could cut off the towns and bring them to their knees. We left three towns as bodies and rubble before the Garamantes decided we had to be stopped and came to find us. Then, we were able to deal with them on our terms, and the whole campaign changed.

The battle was fierce, but very much a foregone conclusion. We laid waste to them, and somewhere in the deserts south of Cyrenaica there is an expanse of sand that is little more than skeletons protruding from the ground. We set up camp that night with a sense of closure and victory. We had the location of their capital now, where the king reigned, and we had obliterated the bulk of his forces.

I was laughing with the officer of my Berber cavalry, who had once again acquitted themselves well that day, earning badges of distinction from Father, when a Praetorian interrupted us and announced my uncle. Tactfully, the officer backed out of my tent and went to celebrate with the rest of his men, and I grinned as my uncle entered. My grin slid away in moments as I caught his expression.

'What is it?' I asked as he walked across and took a seat opposite me, reaching out and pouring wine for us both, without even adding water, I noted.

'I have had news from Rome.'

I waited. We'd had tidings here and there throughout the campaign, for our supply lines led all the way back to Leptis Magna, and couriers could move fast along it. But this was clearly more than just news of events in the city. My uncle cleared his throat.

'I suspect that Plautianus has his hooks into your brother.'

'This I already knew.'

He shook his head. 'But he has become brazen. He has somehow gained control of the treasury officials and issued new coins. They show your brother on one face, and on the other depict him seated on a throne with an orb, laurels and sceptres. The legend is *Securitas Imperium*.'

The security of the empire.

Geta.

The arrogant bastard.

'Father will tear him apart for that.'

He shook his head. 'No, he won't.'

'What?'

'Plautianus is promoting your father's son, the dynasty, the safety of the empire. Why would your father argue with that? Nothing there is overtly beneficial to Plautianus. He's brazen, and he's definitely becoming worryingly powerful, but he's clever enough that he leaves no trail of treachery. There's still nothing for which I would take the matter to Lucius. But the moment we return to Rome, we need to start looking at how to stop the man. And I will increase my eyes and ears on him while we are here.'

The news rather soured our victory that day.

The next morning we moved on, leaving that boneyard behind. It took five more days ever deeper south into the desert to find Garama. Like other Garamantian towns, this one was walled and impressive, built close to a source of water. Unlike the other ones, this one was not going to let its water be cut off so easily. What remained of the forces that their king, Igider, could call upon had been pulled back to this place, though undoubtedly many hundreds of raiding tribes remained in the deeper desert fastnesses. They had used what time they had to fortify, and the line of their water supply was now guarded with small brick forts, heavily manned.

The terrain up on those plateaux was not conducive to a lot of our military. The legions would certainly struggle, and any standard cavalry unit would have trouble, and so the job fell, of course, to the irregular desert units, and my Berbers were among the force dispatched. We were given one of the central targets, and we approached that fort carefully, for it was filled with archers and men with supplies of spears and rocks. We dismounted some distance from the ramparts, for this was not a job for horses, and began to approach carefully. The land of gold, brown and black was dotted with rocks and ridges, ravines and dips, and my men had been born and bred in lands such as this. They moved forward like lizards, darting from cover to cover across bright hot patches of sunshine. Rocks and arrows and javelins arced out, but with little effect, for by the time my swift men were in the open long enough to be seen, they were back in cover and twenty paces closer to the wall. There was no order to the advance, no commands given, no signals. They did not move as a unit, and yet every heartbeat brought them as a group closer and closer to the enemy. I had lost four men on the approach. Four out of more than four hundred. They were that fast. That good.

To be honest, I was hardly involved. I went with them, for not to do so would have destroyed all my credibility among them, but I knew I had neither their speed nor their stealth, and they knew it too, so I came along towards the rear, out of the worst of the danger, and following paths already well-worn by my men.

We hit the fort suddenly. They had seen our approach, but the last sixty paces were taken at a run, swarming from all sides. We took a few more casualties then, but still surprisingly few for the circumstances. The Berbers are a strange people. Their warriors look wizened and wiry, dark and weak. They are anything but. They were fast and strong and brave and shrewd. They poured across the sands and swarmed up the walls of that mudbrick fort like the lizards they had so emulated on their approach. I was close to the action as I raced in their wake, watching them flow like a tide across the ramparts and slaughter the defenders, men of the deserts, just like them.

I was careful. I managed to get to a lightly wounded enemy and deliver the killing blow, bloodying my sword so that the riders could see that I was with them, killing like a warrior, without actually putting myself in any danger.

The fort fell swiftly, and the others along the line followed suit. The next few days as we settled in around Garama were taken up by engineering works and enemy sorties. As our legionaries toiled to cut the water supply from the capital and divert it for our own use, King Igider knew his time was up, and so sent what forces he could to stop the works. It was a hopeless cause, of course. It was the heavy legions that defended their own, and could fight on their own terms, and every sortie was smashed and driven off with little real danger.

Without water, they fought for nine days, which shows how hardy they were. They killed a number of our men, both legionary and auxiliary, but all this was, really, was the death throes of a kingdom. On the ninth day, their king sought a meeting with the emperors. Father and I sat on thrones beneath a canopy, with the court and senior officers gathered around in the shade. We sat drinking cold watered-wine, surrounded by tables of fruit and drinks. Igider was made to stand in the burning sunshine, hungry and thirsty, with his own courtiers and chief warriors.

He offered terms. He offered eternal loyalty to Rome, a promise of peace, tribute in terms of every commodity they traded, and a number of hostages equal to the number of men we had lost. For most campaigns, those terms were excellent. Many an emperor would have made such a request expecting it to be turned down. This was different. Father had a personal interest in this. This was the militant tribes on the border of the empire ravaging his homeland. That, he would not stand for. He had a counteroffer:

Obliteration.

Just as Anullinus had always advised, the enemy were neutralised completely. The king and his party were killed where they stood. Garama was taken by the end of the day and every living thing within put to the sword. The buildings were demolished, the walls torn down. Our brutal campaign against the Garamantes had reached a horrifying conclusion. We had demolished most of their towns, their army, their capital and their king. Garamantia was no more. A lesson I had learned in the East and then in Lugdunum was brought to bear once more with brutal efficiency.

We celebrated beside the carcass of a kingdom. More so because without realising it we had passed into the new year, and Father had an announcement. He had selected the consuls for the year, which the senate would ratify in due course. He had already sent the orders back to Rome. The consuls were to be my uncle, returning victorious from his stint in Cyrenaica... and Plautianus.

I wasn't sure what to think about that. A glance at my uncle confirmed that he was equally uncertain. He hated the man almost as much as I did, and the idea of serving in Rome's chief magistracy alongside him would be galling. Yet it might also provide unprecedented opportunities to prove the man's criminal activities. Uncle was to return to Rome and take up his position with immediate effect. He would take with him the Second Parthica to reinforce his authority, for they were based just a few miles from Rome.

When I asked Father what we had planned, he gave a languid stretch. He stood, stumbled a little with his aching feet, and straightened. 'We are in the land of your forefathers, Marcus. While we are here, I will show you whence your blood sprang. And I shall make Leptis magnificent. I shall have the place a new Rome, with a grand forum and more. An arch, celebrating the new security of Africa. The city shall be unparalleled outside Rome itself.'

Moreover, while we tarried, he would see to the defence of the provinces, for never had Rome been in a better position to solidify the southern border. That led to a planning meeting one night in the city. A dozen officers and politicians had notions of how best to reinforce the Limes Africae that Hadrian had begun a century earlier. They all had conflicting notions, and each had holes in it. I listened to them all, and as each idea was put forward, I pointed out those holes.

'The problem with a turf rampart is that it cannot be raised in a desert,' I said.

'A ditch is an easy thing to dig in mud, but in the rock of the African wasteland?'

'A palisade will simply become a catch for drifting sands until it is buried.'

'Hadrian's defences are already half submerged in the desert.'

Finally, Father turned to me. 'You seem to find fault with all of this, Marcus. What would *you* do?'

'I would take my lead from Agricola and his systems, or Domitian's border on the Rhenus. No solid barrier can be constructed and maintained without eventually succumbing to the desert. Forts should be placed at regular distances, or as regular as possible while placing them on good routes for supplies and back to cities and oases. Larger forts should be positioned at any point where desert raiders are known to work. The forts should be manned by peoples who are familiar with the deserts, for only they are suited to working in these conditions. Then, once that system is in effect, each commander can take control of his own stretch of border and construct extra fortlets or towers as he sees fit to keep the border secure. It needs to be a fluid system, allowing for change and working *with* the desert, not in defiance of it.'

I had learned much in my time in Britannia talking to that young tribune, and now I could see how such systems could be applied. Father nodded slowly. So did a number of others. I was given the overall control of the border, while Father began his building projects in the city. For two months I worked on the plans, with the various officers and local leaders, and by the time we were ready to set off back to Rome in the spring, the southern border was as carefully planned as it had ever been.

But that time was also one of worry, for word continued to come in, not to my uncle any more, but *from* him to me. Plautianus had come up against Mother. She had taken offence at him at last, and the two were at loggerheads.

My return to Rome was clearly overdue.

IX

A Piece in a Game

Rome, Aprilis 9th AD 203

The following month was chaotic. We arrived back in Rome in early Martius, and had less than a month until Father planned to celebrate the *decennalia* of his rule with a grand festival in the city. As such, he immediately launched into the planning of the same with his consilia, while I was left with the minutiae of rule. I would turn seventeen before the festival, and now my beard was beginning to fill out, making me look more and more like Father, and giving me more of a grown-up appearance, which sat well with the fact that I was Rome's de facto ruler for a month.

We had returned to find Plautianus in an unprecedented position of power. Mother had attempted to curtail the growth of his power, seeing the threat he presented to her husband, but even Mother, who has the strength and wisdom of Minerva, could only do so much without the emperor there to support her. And so Plautianus had begun a counter-offensive. Where Mother used her friendships and relationships with the more powerful families of Rome to intervene in Plautianus' activity, he began to undermine her, to produce witnesses to supposed depravities and other unacceptable behaviour for a woman in her position. Noble-women tortured for affidavits, unreliable lawyers, fictional scenes. He was low.

However, my uncle was already onto the man. He had spies in the man's household, and now, as Plautianus sought once again to expand his power, so did my uncle expand his observations. The Urban Prefect, Fabius Cilo, a man more loyal to Father could never be found, was solidly positioned in Plautianus' camp. Best of all, through a little networking, my friend Macrinus had found himself one of Plautianus' direct clients. The man was building a faction in Rome. Just as the Circus has racing factions, so now did the court have political ones. I stood on one side, with my uncle and a number of men I trusted implicitly. Plautianus formed the other, his group centring their support around my brother. And their faction was full of eminent men, too. Cilo and Papinian, Coeranus and Caecilius Agricola, Castor and even my old tutor Euodus. Notably, among their number could be found Cassius Clemens, once Niger's man, who had talked his way out of a death sentence in Syria. His reappearance here only strengthened my belief in Anullinus' old maxim that a sensible man never left enemies alive to rise again.

I went against Uncle's advice in my first days back. Seeing this clique forming, or in fact almost fully-formed already, and knowing that Plautianus was playing Geta like a piece in a game, I had to do something. Geta might well think he was on top with a powerful network, but he was just the figurehead for the real power. I had to warn him. I cornered him alone in a room of the palace.

'Cut your ties with Plautianus,' I said, flatly.

He turned, frowning. 'What?'

'The man is a serpent. He is trying to control Rome. Eventually, I have no doubt, he will try and succeed Father in our place. He seeks power and he's using you. I think he saw from the start that he would never be able to use me, but you were younger, more susceptible. He is not your friend.'

His eyes narrowed. The answer was spat at me. 'You just cannot stand the notion that I might be in the succession, now, can you? When I was just a toddler, and no threat, you were fine, but now that I'm Caesar and there are men in Rome who see that I have every bit as much right as you to the throne, you're getting panicky.'

'Don't be stupid. Don't be blind. Can't you see what he's doing? Gods, Brother, but he's even trying to bring Mother down, because *she* can see it.'

He took a step closer, eyes blazing, straightening up to me. When had he got tall enough to do that? 'You stain Mother's soul by even speaking of her. And she's *my* mother, not *yours*.'

I was getting angry. Little good would come of that, but I couldn't stop myself. 'She is my mother. Always has been. She was my mother before you were even born, you little rat. Plautianus keeps producing witnesses to her debauchery. How can you stand the man?'

He snarled. 'Plautianus assures me that these accusations are all false. It's not him who is producing them, *Brother*, but clients of his. He is *defending* her against them.'

'Oh, wake up. She's powerless now. He's declawed her. She can't move against him any more, because she's only a few steps away from being taken through the courts for things he's invented.'

'You're just jealous,' he rumbled, turning and walking away.

'And you're being fucking stupid,' I replied, running after him, to leap in front of him. He tried to step round me, but I got in the way. 'When Plautianus falls, and he will fall, our dynasty will be in danger if we're divided. You have to *listen* to me.'

'If I had a dagger I'd gut you now,' Geta hissed.

I was so surprised that I blinked, silent. Then the anger hit me. I punched him. I punched him so hard that he was damned lucky I didn't break his jaw. The glare he gave me as he stalked away, clutching his face, could have cut through steel.

I tried in half a dozen ways to bring the matter to Father's attention, and even to Mother's, but there was little I could do. Father was busy and waspish, and when I intimated that his sons might be less than devoted brothers, he just waved his hand and told me that there could be no division in the emperor's house and to 'sort it out'. Mother was more approachable until I dropped the name of Plautianus into the mix, at which point she withdrew, suggesting that she dare not even speak his name now, for the things he claimed to be able to prove would tear us apart. Indeed, she seemed to have withdrawn entirely to a world of stoicism, her salon filled with eastern philosophers daily. I finished up with my uncle once again, who told me that things would be different when Plautianus fell. Then, Geta could be made to see.

And so I did what I could. I continued to provide passive opposition to the man in the court, while administering to the empire as Father finished his lavish preparations, often in collusion with that very serpent. Then, on my birthday, I received the most unwelcome gift of my life. I was engaged in a discussion over additional finances being freed to strengthen the Raetian border, for I hardly felt like celebrating that year, and my parents were clearly too busy to care anyway. I was in my military-style tunic and boots in one of the palace libraries, poring over a map with two generals, three bean-counters and a clerk, when the door clunked open and Father strode in, business-like and forthright.

'Felicitations, son,' he began. 'Happy birthday. And what a gift I have for you.'

I frowned. That didn't sound likely. He'd been too busy with his decennalia to spare me more than a few moments for days, and hadn't even bothered to wish me a happy birthday until long after noon that day. I had a sinking feeling, and with good reason.

'Oh?'

'I have a match for you.'

My eyes narrowed. Marriage had been floating around at the back of my mind now for the past year, I admit, and all the more so since my last encounter with Geta. I needed a wife, and with her I needed a son. Then there would be no reason for Geta to be involved in the succession, and he could be safely shuffled out of the way, while I secured the future of Father's dynasty. But I hadn't expected anything sprung upon me. I'd assumed that once this chaos was out of the way and we were safely settled back into life in the palace I would be able to look at prospective brides and work through a system of selection in consultation with Father. Having my part in the decision-making taken from me was only the start of the trouble, though.

'Who?'

'Plautilla.'

I felt sick. The world spun around me. The ground had been ripped from beneath my feet.

'No.'

His eyes bored into me. He was taken aback by my reaction. 'Explain.'

'I will not be married into that man's family. He is a snake. He conspires against me. Against Mother. Against you. He builds webs. Yes, he's not a snake, he's a spider. He builds webs of control. He's already got Geta and a score of Rome's most influential in his web. And now he tempts me into it with a daughter? No, Father. He doesn't want a match for us. He wants more influence.'

'He is my friend,' Father reminded me with a very ominous tone. His fists were clenching.

'Marry her to Geta.'

'Your brother is too young. He'd have her I'm sure, but he's only just taken the toga virilis. He's barely out of childhood. Plautilla is of good marriageable age, should be fertile, for her mother produced seven living children, she's pretty enough, she's allied to our house, she's of good African blood, like us, and she comes with a sizeable dowry.'

Yes, I thought, bitterly. A dowry paid for by all the innocent men of Rome Plautianus had killed and dispossessed.

'Plautianus thinks that the decennalia is a good time to tie our families, to strengthen the African connection in Rome, to celebrate the continuation of the dynasty, and he's right. It should be now.'

'I will not marry that woman. I will not have him as a father-in-law.'

Father's gaze took on a coldness I had never seen turned on me before.

'You are Augustus and emperor of Rome, Marcus, but only on my say. I am senior emperor and your father. You will respect my wishes in this, for if you do not, then you cannot be relied upon in the office. You will marry Plautilla and smile as though it is the happiest day of your life, or I will strip you of every honour and title I have given you. I have another son who might perhaps be more grateful.'

The chasm below threatened to swallow me. Plautianus for a father-in-law, or to lose the succession to Geta. A blade to my front and a blade to my back. And whatever path I chose, Plautianus would get more hooks into our family and into the governance of Rome. I was cornered. Trapped.

'What will it be?'

I straightened. I had to force myself to unclench my teeth. 'You are right, Father. The dynasty must come first. When will it happen?'

The tension in him eased, and a smile returned, though it was a little guarded. 'It will be quick. We are short on time. The announcement will be given at the decennalia, in five days. The marriage shall follow swiftly.'

Gods, but even condemned men languishing in the carcer are given longer than that. I nodded my understanding. I may have smiled. I remember trying, though it probably came out looking more constipated than joyful.

I dismissed my planning meeting once Father had gone. I did not feel like work that day, and decided that I might stop having birthdays altogether if this was the sort of thing that was to happen. I simmered in anger and irritation the rest of that day, and then once more began to concentrate on work, ignoring entirely the fate that now hung over me like a bunting-festooned sword of Damocles.

The sixth day before the kalends of Aprilis came around all too soon.

The populace were ecstatic. The celebration began with a show of imperial largesse that would have bought over even the most reticent of publics. Every soldier in the city, and every civilian who was entitled to the grain dole, was given ten gold *aurei*, one for each year of the emperor's reign. A fortune. I could only imagine how the praetors were sweating, thinking of the imperial coffers. I heard from them later that he spent two hundred millions *sesterces* on that day, on gifts alone.

The first day of the festival would be largely filled with games and performances, and then finish with a banquet on such a scale as had not been seen since the hedonistic days of Nero. I might actually have enjoyed it all, were it not for the part I had to play in it. The impending nuptials between myself and that harpy were to be part of the celebration. I was to accompany the bastard and his stinking offspring from their house on the Little Aventine, via the forum, and up to the palace. Then we would join Father's main procession and travel once again through the city by a winding route to please the people, to the Flavian amphitheatre, where the games would begin.

I met the wedding party at the gates of his house with my retinue. I had my lictors ready, bundles of sticks in hand, for any trouble, and an entourage of senators, freedmen, soldiers, servants and slaves. I was on horseback, but had been told by Father in no uncertain terms that from their house I was to ride in the litter with Plautilla. It churned my stomach even anticipating it.

The litter was brought round, an open thing so that we could be seen by the crowds lining the street. Plautianus himself, and all his clique of villains and sycophants, would follow on either on horseback or on foot, with only my lictors and guards ahead. I settled into the vehicle which was then lifted by sixteen Arabian slaves and carried steadily through the streets.

I will admit that I had already formed an opinion of Plautilla long before I met her, based entirely upon her father. I was wrong. I had assumed her to be wily, grasping, dangerous and devious. She was none of those things. What she was, instead, was utterly vacant. In my seventeen years in the world I had met men and women from all walks of life, but I had never met anyone even remotely as empty-headed as Plautilla. She was pretty in a sort of plain, vacant way, and had been carefully made more so by her cosmetae. She fixed me with a smile.

'You must be Marcus.'

What a stupid thing to say in the circumstances. I toyed with a sarcastic reply, but settled for a noncommittal grunt. Behind us, and in front of her father and the others, came the dowry, and I have to admit to being impressed there, at least. Fifty patrician women could have been dowried with what Plautianus gave my father. Of course, it had all been stolen from patrician families over the past few years, and he was only giving Father money he'd extorted from loyal Romans, but still, it made the people marvel. When Plautilla noted me looking at it, she smiled even wider.

'Think how many shopping trips we can have. I can have a *stola* made of gold.'

I rolled my eyes. 'You'd have to have it hinged so you could piss comfortably.'

I thought it would insult her. Offend her. Instead she gave a girlish giggle. I sighed. It was going to be a long morning. Indeed, I had to listen to her stream of drivel for an hour, all the way to the palace. She never stopped talking, and it was all formed of the fluff from between her ears, with no sense and no substance. I knew two things about her by the time we got to the palace, and, in fairness, she was such a pointless girl, I don't think there was really anything else to know. Firstly, she seemed to have missed out on being born with a brain. Secondly, she was captivated by wealth. She wanted it, and then she wanted to spend it. Already by the end of our first journey she had planned how to spend every last sestertius of the dowry following us, all on fripperies, rubbish and jewellery. I know I'm somewhat labouring over this point, but I simply cannot describe in adequate words how much I detested the girl. Had Father not dangled disinheritance before me as a threat, I might well have leapt from the litter and run. I was tempted, even then.

We joined the imperial party at the palace. The dowry was escorted inside to rapturous applause from the people. While we waited, the others joined us, and I could not miss the snide grin on my brother's face, nor the knowing look he shared with Plautianus. We then set off in a grand procession once more, passing through every sizeable street so that the people of Rome could marvel over their emperor and his family. Two hours we travelled, with that endless shrill, wet, empty-headed monologue of shopping and clothes going on in my left ear. I have never been so grateful to finish a journey, and I have trudged through barren deserts in my time.

If I had hoped for relief, though, I was to be sadly mistaken. I was seated at Father's right hand in the amphitheatre, with Geta at the far side, and then Mother, but Plautilla was placed on my other side, where she took up her brainless monologue with barely a drawn breath. By the third hour, at least I was learning how to tune her voice out of the sound around me.

One thing I noted as I looked around, trying hard not to listen, was the empty seat. It took a while, checking on the gathered family members, luminaries and courtiers, to work out who it was who was not here, and when I did, it came with a lurch. My uncle was absent.

Ignoring the steady stream of drivel, I turned to Father.

'Where is Uncle?'

'He felt unwell. Decided to spend a few days down in Baiae, taking the waters. Shame he'll miss it, but better he gets well, eh?'

A new suspicion began to form then. Three people stood staunchly against Plautianus. Mother, he had silenced with the threat of public and very shameful revelations which, even though they were clearly false, could not easily be proven so, and would ruin her public image. *I* had been silenced by hanging the millstone of Plautilla around my neck and by his closeness with my father, which would not allow for accusations. The least active of us was my uncle, the one who was being most careful, yet Plautianus must have known how he felt. That now, of all times, my usually robust uncle might fall foul of some illness I found highly implausible.

The opening ceremonies of the games almost passed me by as I tried to ignore the stream of consciousness droning in my ear, while wondering how Plautianus might have managed to feed something to my uncle. And the more I thought about it, the more I worried. It had to be poison. The timing was too suspicious to be pure accident. And if it was poison, was it just something low-grade, keeping him out of the way, or was it something lethal that was only beginning to take effect? I found it hard to believe that even Plautianus would be so brazen as to murder my uncle, but the nagging feeling would not go away, and it soured most of the decennalia for me.

I tried to distract myself by focusing on the entertainment.

In the middle of the arena was an impressive construction. It was shaped like a boat, with opening doors in both bow and stern. I wondered what Father had planned, and the crowd waited with eager anticipation. Then, the true entertainment began.

The boat began to disgorge animals. Sometimes one door would open, and hunters would spear them from the deck of the boat. Sometimes both doors would open, and two species who were either deadly enemies, or were hunter and prey, would be released to kill one another in a display of natural savagery for the entertainment of the people. It was bloody, and it was fascinating. Some of the animals I had never seen before, and a few I had never even heard of.

At one point, just as the elephant was being removed from the sand by a hundred slaves with ropes, a creature was released that was utterly vicious in appearance, like a dog or wolf, but with characteristics of a lion, too. A big thing, and there were five of them. Ten men were sent out to hunt them, and as we watched the contest, which was uneven and weighted towards the success of the animals, I turned to Father.

'What is that?'

'No idea,' he replied with a shrug. 'The arena entertainment was planned by Plautianus.'

Urgh.

The snake leaned forward, having heard.

'It is a crocotta, from India. They are very rare, and I believe this is the first time they have ever been seen in Rome. A spectacle, is it not?'

I grunted a reply, but he was not to be put off. 'One hundred animals today, and then one hundred more on each day of the festival. Seven hundred in total. But the animals are only a prelude.'

'Oh?' Father asked in interest.

'When the combatants come on, I have arranged something really special. Gladiatrices.'

Even I was impressed. Gladiators were not a cheap commodity, and in the numbers required to fight at a festival of this magnitude, they would break many a treasury. But gladiatrices, women fighters, were far rarer, and so fetched an even higher price, especially if they were talented or pretty, or both.

We watched the animal hunts and pitched natural battles for another hour. In fact, over the seven days of the festival I doubt there is an animal in the world that we did not see hunting or hunted on the sand of the arena. Bears, lionesses, panthers, ostriches, asses, bison and more.

The people were truly excited now, and as the break came about while the boat was dismantled and removed, the last carcasses shifted and the sand raked clear of blood, the populace of Rome seethed around the cavea finding purveyors of snack foods and small wine jugs, and then settling back into their seats only as the editor rose to announce the next round of games. He gushed over my father's achievements and imperial bearing for a while, called for another ten years of rule uninterrupted, and, rather cheekily I thought, for an end to costly wars, and then announced a very special event. Forty gladiatrices were to grace the sands, depicting the Amazons under Queen Penthesilea, coming to the aid of the Trojans. They would fight forty gladiators depicting Achilles and his Myrmidons.

We knew how the fight would go, of course, for it was an epic retelling of the tales of Troy. Penthesilea and her women warriors must die, for Troy fell and Achilles won that fight, but she would die gloriously and heroically, and the people would cheer her even in death for Troy was the progenitor of Rome, of course, and the Greeks won the war only by treachery.

Plautianus was announced as the man behind today's entertainment, and I saw the bastard rise and bow to accept the adulation of the audience. But he'd made a mistake that day.

The two sides burst from the gates onto the sand opposite one another, to a fanfare of musicians that was almost lost anyway beneath the roar of the crowd. Even Plautilla had stopped yapping now, entranced. I watched as the two armies approached one another across the sands. It was Macrinus, seated just off to my left beyond my soon-to-be-wife, who spotted the problem.

'They're not gladiatrices,' he snorted.

I frowned. 'Oh?'

'Look at them. No muscle. No meat on their bones. They're stringy. And they move like they're terrified.'

It was true. As I watched I could see that they displayed none of the usual traits of gladiators. A suspicion forming, I looked around. Plautianus looked worried, and well he might. I realised instantly what he'd done, as did most of the others around me. It would have been near impossible to find forty gladiatrices, and so either Plautianus, or whichever *factor* he had left in charge, had simply bought forty female slaves and armed them. Anyone who has watched a fight in the arena can tell you that sparring to entertain a crowd is a skilled business, and takes years of training and a certain mental strength. Simply arming a slave does not produce the same effect.

We watched the battle. We had all read the Aethiopis of Arctinus in our childhood. We knew how it went. The battle was hard fought, for Penthesilea was all but a match even for mighty Achilles. But then he manages to kill her in her moment of greatest glory, the Amazons are overwhelmed, and as they fall the Greeks mourn the passing of such a great enemy.

That was not what happened. Plautianus or his people had armed weak women slaves, but had pitted them against veteran myrmidon gladiators. The result was carnage that lasted about fifty heartbeats. To give the gladiators their due, they knew how poor it all was, and tried very hard to look like they were struggling, but the poor women had no idea. They should not all have died. They should have taken a few small cuts and fallen in a grand pretence. Instead they fell in droves, cut down because they had no idea what they were doing.

The first day of Father's decennalia ended on something of a sour note. There was no cheering as that supposedly epic clash ended half an hour before the planned time. Fully half the spectators left then, not bothering to watch the rest of the fights. While I stayed and would have liked Father's celebration to have been more successful, I have to admit to a small smug part of me that almost cheered every time I heard Plautianus' name spoken of disparagingly in the following days, which was often, among both high-born and low.

The banquet that finished the day was not as successful as had been hoped, either. I have no idea whose idea it was, but the repast that was offered to the great and the good of Rome was not the usual fare. Someone had formed the notion that it would be a great way to celebrate my father's first ten years with a banquet that was a blend of good quality Roman food, and African delicacies, celebrating my family's origin. What they hadn't realised was that the people of Leptis Magna, and Africa in general, eat very much the same things as we do in Rome. Whoever had had the brilliant idea had latched onto the diets of the Berber tribes as being authentically African, and so some of the foods we were served were all but still kicking and some were truly eye-watering. Some even *involved* eyes. It was not an easy success as meals go. Everyone ate less than usual, tried some unusual dishes, and plastered fake smiles across their faces as they tried hard to swallow things they would normally discard. Everyone except Macrinus, of course, who celebrated his Berber heritage, and tucked in with gusto.

By the ides of Aprilis, while the festival was still in full swing, a law banning women from fighting in the arena was passed, with no public outcry. The festival came to an end, and despite early teething troubles, it was generally considered a rousing success. Father's reputation only grew with it, certainly. I had little time to consider it all, myself, for I was married the day after the festival ended, the empty vessel that was Plautilla still yapping away most of the way through the ceremony. We consummated our marriage that night, for to not do so would have been unthinkable. It was one of the emptiest experiences of my life. I prayed she would prove to be with child as soon as possible so that I would not be required to repeat the process too often.

That week I increased my nightly visits to the more attractive slaves of the Palatine. Better a slave than an idiot, after all. And then Father encouraged us to take a trip. To get out of Rome for the summer, as was traditional, and to get to know one another somewhere more conducive. I was all for it.

That was why, only nine days after our wedding, Plautilla found her bags packed and a carriage awaiting to whisk us off to the resort town of Baiae down the coast near Neapolis. Our entourage was ready, but I had more reason for my trip than to explore the emptiness of my wife's head.

My uncle had still not returned to Rome.

X

The Playground of Emperors

Baiae, Maius AD 203

I walked into the atrium of the villa with a sense of dread over what I might find. I pictured my uncle bleeding out his last, perhaps prophetically, for Father always put a lot of store in dreams and images as portents. In actual fact, what I found was my uncle sitting in one of the side rooms with a slave massaging his back.

'Marcus? This is a surprise.'

I regarded him carefully. I still expected some sign of dreadful poisoning. 'I… I'm married. Father wanted me to take her away from Rome for the summer.'

He nodded, though his expression had darkened. 'He sent word once the proposal was dealt with. I cannot say I agree with his decision, though it's his decision to make, and any objection I raised would have been too late anyway. Is she everything you'd dreamed of?'

'In the more panic-inducing night sweats, yes. She's greedy, spendthrift, empty-headed and irritating.'

'A vast improvement on her father then.'

I had to give him that point. She was a dreadful woman to know, let alone be shackled to, but at least she was relatively harmless. 'I'd been told you were ill.'

'I was. Really quite ill, in fact. I've been here for some time, and the ministrations of the excellent physicians, combined with the healing waters and simple pleasurable relaxation seem to have done the trick. Your timing is superb, in fact. Last week I feared I might die, I was still so ill. Then I turned a corner, and now I feel much, much better.'

'Do you know what it was?'

'Something I ate. And clearly something natural. I have an excellent food taster, trained in the same place as Halotus, Nero's taster. They produce the very best. Since the phenomenal rise of Plautianus I thought it wise to employ additional security, including a taster. Phaeon has eaten everything I have for more than a year now, and he is hale and hearty, which begs only the conclusion that I had a natural reaction to something that was no more poisonous than a turnip.'

I sighed with relief. 'I had feared the worst. Especially given the timing, with the bastard now managing to worm his way into the imperial family. But I had been dubious whether even he would be brazen enough to make an attempt on your life.'

'Oh, I don't put it past him at all. He has your father fooled into thinking he's a boon, sent by the gods. Your father will hear no ill of the man. I will stay a few more days and then return to Rome. Now that I'm feeling better, I think it's important that I get back into that maelstrom and watch for any slip-up the man might make. If we are both in Baiae, no one is watching him.'

I nodded my agreement. 'But I would rather it was I who went back. Here, I am trapped in a hedonist's paradise with that horrible woman.'

'Your father expects you to summer somewhere away, and he's right. That's normal. If you go home, Plautianus will think it odd. Let's play everything as though there was nothing wrong, and keep him content that he is in no danger.'

'What am I supposed to do at the seaside with a moron for a whole summer?'

My uncle gave a hearty laugh. 'You are in Baiae, Marcus, the playground of emperors. You are seventeen and this place has been entertaining the rich and powerful for hundreds of years. If there is a pleasure to be found in the world, you'll find it in Baiae. What was it Horace said? "No bay in the world outshines delightful Baiae." Ignore your empty-headed harpy and enjoy the delights while you can.'

He frowned. 'Although, perhaps do not ignore her completely.'

'Why?'

'She is the daughter of Plautianus. Stupid and irritating she may be, but she has been in her father's house for more than a decade. She might know things, even by accident. And if she is the idiot you say she is, she might be enticed to let them slip.'

I conceded that point, too. I made my excuses to Plautilla over the next few days. She seemed quite happy, knowing that I was spending time with my uncle, and as long as the supply of coins never ran out, she was quite content on her own. I watched Uncle carefully over those few days, and my uneasiness returned. He claimed to be feeling fine now, but he was still spending a lot longer in the latrine than any man had a right to, and his mood was erratic. I might say he had become quick to anger and easily given to melancholy, but in fairness that is not a bad description of *me* either, and there was nothing wrong with me. I put it aside, and we worked through everything we could think of on Plautianus, to little avail.

He returned to Rome a few days later full of purpose. I would follow on in the autumn, but would spend the summer trying to relax, looking like the perfectly content young newly-married emperor, and carefully asking pertinent questions of Plautilla.

By the end of Julius I came to the conclusion that the girl had spent an entire life more or less oblivious to everything that went on around her, unless it involved makeup, clothes or a purse full of coins. I truly do not think she was dissembling. I don't think she was capable of such a thing, or even of spelling it. I began by asking carefully framed questions that were a little oblique to my actual goal, so as not to spook her. I wanted to know what information Plautianus had on Mother, and where he kept such information. He would have to have a solid copy for evidence, and that would have to be stored somewhere. I fussed around with some documents I'd brought with us, noting that I didn't know where would be safe to keep them in the villa we occupied. I lightly dropped into the conversation my query.

'I can't find anywhere that looks safe. Where does your father keep *his* records?'

'Oh, in a cupboard, I think.'

That was what I was up against. Having delivered that fascinating little nugget of non-information, she started to rattle on about some necklace she'd seen in a jeweller's in town.

'A cupboard doesn't sound very secure,' I prodded.

'I don't know. Maybe he locks it or something. Do you think I'd look good in pale yellow?'

You'd look good in a cinerary urn, I mouthed silently to her back.

My lines of questioning went on a lot like that. Gradually, as it became clear that subtlety was something as alien to Plautilla as poverty, I began to become more and more direct with my questions. It reached an apex by the kalends of September, when I almost lost my temper.

'Has your father ever told you he would like to be emperor?'

She blinked. 'Oh, wouldn't that be lovely. Then you'd *both* be emperors. I'd be married to an emperor and have one for a father. Do you think we could arrange it?'

I gave up. It was like interrogating a brick, only a particularly thick brick.

I spent less time with her after that, and a lot more time whoring my way through the ladies of Baiae. One night, when I returned, a little drunk and smelling of perfumed women, Plautilla met me in the atrium. She looked unhappy. I swayed a little.

'I'm not pregnant.'

'No.' Shame, really. Making an heir to get in the way of Geta's plans was about all she was good for, after all. 'That's probably because we only slept together that once, after the wedding.'

'Yes. I don't like this. Even my slaves are asking why we do not share the bed more often.'

More often than never?

I sighed. 'I'm a busy man.'

'It's almost as if you don't like me.'

Oh gods, but the woman was thick.

'Listen...'

'I sometimes wonder whether you have another woman.'

I snapped. I had honestly tried to hold it in, but I'd had months of this drivel, cohabiting with a spendthrift brainless dolt who probably reported everything I did to her father, or at least would do when next she saw him. I was having to send back to Rome for a new chest of gold every nine days to keep her shopping habit fed, I had learned nothing of any use, and had endured just too much. And she was now accusing me of things that I was blatantly doing right in front of her. I was unkind. I didn't care.

'Gods, but you're stupid, Plautilla.'

'What?'

'I roll home, pissed as a deckhand after a storm, smelling of the bedrooms of four of the best whores in town, one of whom taught me something truly wicked she learned in Syria, and you only have a suspicion I'm seeing other women? Of *course* I'm seeing other women.'

She went pale, but paused for only an extended moment before she began to nod slowly. 'I understand. Some men are charged more than others. Some take lovers, but as long as they always come home to their wife, it is accepted. I thought we would be different, but I can manage this.'

'You stupid woman,' I snarled. 'All you are is a hole in my purse through which gold leaks like the waterfalls of Tibur. You have so much space between your ears they could store grain in your head. Your only saving grace is that you're not your father, and yet you come with the added peril of him anyway.'

'Marcus?' she said. I honestly think she was shocked and confused. An imbecile could have seen what was wrong between us in a couple of months. She had spent half a year with me in ignorance.

'I need an empress, Plautilla. I need a mother to the children we will have, a consort to the ruler of the world, who understands finance and politics and war. My Mother can teach things to generals, she can out-argue philosophers, can advise Father on treasury matters. *She* is an empress.'

'She's not your mother.'

I know I'd passed the line of acceptable and polite already, but that was the final straw.

'I cannot divorce you. My father thinks our match and the connection of our families is important. I can't divorce you. As long as *my* father thinks that *your* father is a loyal friend, I'm stuck with you. But, my little dove, Father is almost sixty years old, and I am his heir. The day that I take on the purple alone, your father is going to meet the edge of a blade, and you? I know you are no traitor, but I simply cannot stand the sight of you, and your father *is*. You, I think, will enjoy a nice frugal exile on a rock somewhere.'

I turned my back on her and walked away. I was a little drunk, as I said, but my words were not just wine-fuelled anger. This had been building for months. My only regret, both then and now, is that I could not hold my tongue longer, because what I really did not need was Plautianus realising I was so set against him.

There was nothing I could do. I spent that night whoring and drinking again, until I could hardly see. When I rolled home at around dawn it was to discover that Plautilla had left with most of the entourage, returning to Rome.

I tarried in Baiae for five days. It took most of that to sober up. Perhaps the gods were unhappy with my actions, for during that brief time, the mountain Vesuvius exploded as it had on the day it buried Pompeii, though in a smaller manner. Fires blazed on the mountain for two days, and the earth shook and rumbled repeatedly. I heard voices in the forum predicting doom for the empire. I felt certain there was a doom in the offing, but I thought it might be a little more centralised than that. After those five days, when the mountain had settled, I gathered my people and we set off north once again, heading for Rome.

We reached the capital just after the kalends of October. I went first to my apartments in the palace, and changed. I needed to bathe and clean myself down. I was surprised as I entered to find Plautilla awaiting me. She would have known I was coming, of course. When there is an *adventus* of any nobleman entering the city, the population is aware before they reach the fifth mile marker. When it is an emperor, their progress in their journey is noted and anticipated by all. But after we had parted so, why was she there at all?

'Hello.'

She bowed her head demurely. 'Husband.'

'Why are you here?'

'I am your wife.'

'I thought I'd made my position clear.'

She fixed me with a hard look. 'So did my father. My duty is to stay here with you and be a good wife, and as good an empress as I can be, though clearly I'll never be good enough for you. Father has commanded me to fulfil the role for which I was born.'

I nodded. I hated her, but less than her father, and while I would never be a husband to her, that did tug at my sympathy a little. She was a piece in the game of men, with no strength or power, just value. I straightened. 'There is plenty of space in the imperial apartments. You find your rooms, I will have mine. We will smile for the public on state occasions. That is all that is required. I will see to it that you have a small stipend to keep yourself supplied and entertained, though nothing on the level you enjoyed in Baiae, for even Crassus spent less than that. But I will not countenance being spied on for your father. Are we clear?'

'We are.'

And that was the end of that. I attended the baths and changed my attire, then went to find my father, only to discover that he was out somewhere with Plautianus. Not wanting to spend time in the palace, in case I bumped into my wife, I moved on to the next visit in my plan. My uncle.

He lived in a spacious villa on the less-fashionable Viminal Hill, and I approached with my lictors, guards, slaves and freedmen in the usual procession, admitted by my uncle's staff into the grounds, where we approached the main door. There I left most of my entourage, just freedmen and slaves now, which I continued to shed as we passed through the sprawling structure until I reached his door alone. I knocked and a voice bade me enter.

As the door creaked closed behind me, my heart fluttered at what I saw.

My uncle lay on a couch beside a table, and he looked as close to death as I've seen a man while he still breathed. The voice that had admitted me was that of one of his slaves, who stood beside the couch.

'What's happened?' I asked, scurrying across the room to them. The aroma of vomit and diarrhoea clung to that side of the room, and clearly emanated from my uncle. He turned a look on me and I felt panic and grief at that gaze, for he looked agonised, lines of pain drawn across his face over months of this. My uncle made a series of motions with his hands, the slave watching intently, and then the tall easterner standing by the couch cleared his throat.

'The master wishes you to know that the illness that drew him to Baiae came back in force upon his return to Rome. He finds it painful to speak, but I have been his silent communications in the court for some years when he wishes to pass information in secret, and so now I am his voice while he does not speak.'

I shivered. Too much pain to talk?

'If Baiae helped, why not return? Why stay here?'

Another flutter of hands, and the man who was now my uncle's voice translated. 'This time the illness came on strong and fast. It has robbed the master of much of his strength, and he does not feel up to any journey longer than that to the latrine.'

'I... am dying.'

127

His voice was little more than a scratching sound, like the *scrit, scrit scrit* of a pen on a wooden tablet. I felt tears well up, partly at the sound, partly at the sentiment. Still, even as he spoke, his fingers danced their language.

'The master has felt it important to continue the task of investigating his enemy even from his sickbed.'

That was why he'd not left? He'd suffered as he continued to work on Plautianus?

He lapsed back then, convulsing, and at a call, three more slaves and a physician hurried in bowing their heads in respect as they veered around me to go help my uncle. I waited for a moment, and then gestured to the physician. 'Tell me everything.'

He ministered to my uncle, and then, when his patient had sagged back, breathing heavily, the physician approached me. 'Domine, your uncle weakens slowly. I have prescribed a number of treatments, but all they have done is calm the symptoms a little. I have nothing now that is not palliative.'

'But what has caused it?'

The man tapped his lower lip. 'I cannot say for certain, for by the time I was called in, the damage had already been done. If I were to make an educated guess, however, Domine, I would suggest that your uncle had somehow ingested a lethal dosage of a plant-based toxin, and my money would be on hellebore. This cannot easily be done by accident, of course,' he added, darkly.

Hellebore. Poison.

'But he employed a taster.'

'Yes, Domine. It is a puzzle.'

'Tend to him as you can.'

I was wrapped in a shroud of worry and fear, but underneath it lay a solid layer of hatred, because I knew full well what serpent was behind all of this, for all the apparent lack of evidence. I spent the day, and several that followed, investigating with the help of my uncle's staff, especially his food taster, Phaeon, who was part of the puzzle. I still had not been to see my father since my return, though I noted neither had he come to Uncle's villa. Periodically I checked in on both the physician, who seemed quite capable even though there was little he could do, and his patient. It took us days to piece it together, and it was only when we recreated a meal consumed of an evening in the household that it dawned on us what was happening. Everything I ate, the taster ate, and I realised that I was at risk, for this was how my uncle had fallen, yet I had to know. It was as I was about to take a mouthful that the taster blinked in realisation.

'The condiments, Domine.'

'What?'

'I taste the food as it leaves the cooks. Your uncle added condiments afterwards. It has to have come from them.'

It took little in the way of investigation to find the culprit. The jar of silphium smelled wrong. The physician took it to examine and confirmed after a few hours the presence of lethal quantities of hellebore in the mix, the sharp taste of the deadly plant masked by the sharp taste of the condiment. The problem was that there was now no way to identify how the poison had been introduced. It had been here for over half a year, long before our sojourn in Baiae, since before the decennalia and the marriage. Silphium is used in small enough quantities that one introduction of the poison would probably last for a year of meals. The physician also confirmed that it was a subtle measurement, low enough to hide the presence within the condiment, and not enough to kill outright, but enough that with regular ingestion the effects would be critical and gradually weaken and cripple the victim.

Another investigation turned up a kitchen slave who had apparently run away in the Februarius of that year, had been run down by the slave-hunters near Albanum, and had died before he could be brought in. It seemed almost certain that this slave had introduced the poison, but had died before any information could be drawn from him. I knew, I absolutely knew, that somehow Plautianus had induced the slave to add the poison to my uncle's kitchen, but there was simply no way to prove it.

It was now late October. I had been back in Rome for only half a month, but already I noted a decline in my uncle's condition even in that time. I was determined to bring the bastard responsible to justice. I had devoted all my time back in the city to my uncle, but now I made my way to the palace and found my father, who was leaning on the balustrade and looking down upon the Circus Maximus. Plautianus, of course, stood nearby, and so did my brother. Father turned.

'You seem to have been avoiding me since your return.' His voice was hard, his manner unhappy. 'Could that be because you insulted the wife I urged you to take, and defamed my oldest friend?'

I fixed my gaze upon him, challenging, unwavering. 'Your oldest friend lies dying in his bed on the Viminalis. And it is the doing of the very man you defend, though I lack the proof to have his head stricken from his body.' At this, my gaze lifted to Plautianus, who returned it with a glare laden with hatred. I could similarly feel Geta's gimlet eyes boring into me, where he stood beside his treacherous sponsor.

Father's manner changed in an instant. 'Dying?'

'He has not drawn the matter to your attention, because he still seeks the proof to bring down his murderer, and he thinks that every day he buys will allow this bastard another chance to slip up and reveal his true nature, and I have followed his lead all this time, hoping for the same. But I do not think he has long left now, and Plautianus is too clever to let you see what he really is. I think the time has come. You need to visit your brother while you still can.'

All thoughts of anger at me had fled Father with the revelation. He strode from the balcony, summoning his lictors, and I followed. So did Plautianus and my brother. For once, I was grateful. Perhaps in my uncle's presence, Father could be made to see them for what they were. I caught up with the old man as he strode through the palace. I could see him wincing with each pace. His feet hurt him every day, now, and he was wheezing with deep breaths. He was not well himself, though his was the lingering effects of the Aegyptian malady, causing him troubles, as he was truly no longer a young man.

'Why have you not visited him in his illness, Father?'

'I had affairs of state to occupy me, Marcus. You were away with your wife, after all, and so I had everything to do. Plautianus and your brother helped me, but they lack the authority you command in the empire. I have been meaning to visit him for some time, but it never seemed to happen. He never asked me to come.'

I nodded. 'He would not. He keeps to himself and hopes to unravel Plautianus' schemes.' I cared not that the man was in earshot following us. Let him know I was on to him now.

We picked up Father's entourage through the palace and took a carriage from the gate to save his feet. Geta joined us in the vehicle but for some reason Plautianus did not. It was too much to hope that he was not coming, of course, but he was probably finalising some nefarious scheme even as we travelled. We climbed the Viminalis and reached my uncle's villa, were admitted, and made our way to the room where he now habitually lay in pain. As we entered, Plautianus had rejoined us. I flinched as we crossed the threshold into the room, for that odour of vomit and diarrhoea was stronger now, and the others were similarly assailed by it.

'Gods,' Father gasped as he gagged on the smell.

My uncle looked up. His face was waxy and grey. He looked like the freshly dead already. Father took a few steps towards him. We remained close to the door, all three of us, though I made sure I was a few steps from Plautianus and Geta. I noted in a moment of worry that the ophidian bastard was wearing his sword. We were outside the *pomerium* at the villa, but only just, and while it was legal to bear a weapon of war in public here, it had not been throughout our journey. Still, he was prefect of the Praetorians, and they had dispensation. I could not help but register, though, that he was the only one in the room who was armed. If there was trouble, how many could he kill before my uncle's guards reached him to put him down? My hand went to my belt, where my eating knife hung in its sheath. If trouble began, I would cut his throat with that, I decided.

The slave who was my uncle's voice had no need to speak. The dying man's hands writhed, fingers forming signals, and my eyes widened as my father nodded, and answered with similar gestures. I realised then that this must have been happening for years. When they were younger men in the dangerous court of Commodus, they had been able to communicate unheard by others. And now they were doing it again. I had no idea what they were saying, but it was important, clearly. The effort was exhausting my uncle, and finally, he twisted a shape and then sagged back, wracked with shivers, breathing heavily.

Father turned, and he was angry. His gaze was cold as it fell upon Plautianus.

'I have defended you, old friend, against the accusations of even my own son. We have known one another since we climbed trees together and played soldier with sticks and stones in the gardens in Leptis. I have trusted you, relied upon you. You helped secure my throne. I have been blind to you, though. Blind to what you have been doing. I should have known, for I dreamed that Albinus had returned to challenge me, and so clearly *something* was wrong.'

I felt a thrill of victory. Whatever my uncle had said, it had carried enough weight, claimed enough evidence, to persuade my father at last.

'I am still your man, Lucius,' Plautianus replied. 'I have never stood against you, never plotted against you, never sought your throne.'

I was sure that was a lie, but I could not prove it. Father shook his head. 'No. I believe that. I believe that you are still my man. But what you have done is detrimental to the empire. No man should be allowed to get away with the things you have done. And I still would not believe it of you, but my brother has gathered evidence. You may not seek to bring me down or to challenge me, but I believe you see a future in which your family occupies the throne. That will not happen. I have a son, and any child your daughter gives him will be ours, not yours.'

Plautianus was managing a wonderful expression of wounded innocence. Really, the man should have been on the stage. Father straightened. 'I shall make sure that your excessive powers are curtailed. You will bring down no more noble houses of Rome to fill your coffers. You are the prefect of the Praetorian Guard. I expect you to act like it, for the preservation of the imperial safety and the honour of the state. And you will be held in check. Another prefect will be assigned and we shall have a return to dual-command, and this time your co-prefect will not mysteriously die within days of appointment. Do you understand?'

Plautianus nodded. 'I have only ever sought to serve. Anything I have done, I have done to strengthen our position, to tighten the bonds of our families, and to remove potential mutual enemies, even if I have become wealthy in the process. I will ever continue to do so, but if you feel it necessary to place restrictions upon me, I accept that gladly, in order to enjoy your ongoing faith, Lucius.'

It was masterful. Wounded innocence. An admission of his guilt that had somehow turned it into something heroic and honourable. If I'd thought the bastard was going to fall that day, I was wrong, but at least Father had had the veil of deceit lifted, and would watch Plautianus for trouble. As Father returned to his brother, crossing to join him, Plautianus turned to me, and I knew from the look he cast my way that the blame for all of this he placed on my shoulders. Uncle would not be around for long, and Plautianus had set his target on me now. He would be seeking my downfall, and I had to be careful. I would also need to act. And soon. Geta was throwing me evil looks, too, as if I'd expected anything else.

My uncle died within the month. A great statue was raised in the forum in his memory. Marcus Flavius Drusianus was appointed as co-prefect of the Praetorians, the first check on Plautianus' power. The man settled into the role of the perfect, loyal servant.

That, I was sure, would not last long.

XI

Practice Races

Rome, Junius AD 205

The year after my uncle's death was one of portents and signs, and of great change and even greater surprises. The first of those was to come one morning not long after his funeral, when I bumped into Plautilla in the imperial apartments. We had very carefully arranged our schedules so that the chances of us meeting were minimal, barring state occasions when we would be required to attend together. It was a tried and tested system. We were trapped in marriage. She hated the sight of me now, and I had always hated the sight of her. And yet that morning we almost bowled each other over in a corridor. She looked shocked, shaken, which in turn shook me, because I'd never considered her bright enough to experience shock.

'What is it?'

She fixed me with a look of blind panic.

'I...'

'What?' I demanded.

'I am with child.'

I gaped, open-mouthed. I must have dropped to the floor, for slaves came running to help me up. It seemed that the one time we had joined, after the wedding, had been enough after all, and she was dull-witted enough to miss all the signs until it was unmistakable. For some time I bounced around Rome as though a weight had been lifted, almost happy. I was going to have a child. Geta was going to be out of the succession. Moreover, if we had a son, I could get rid of Plautilla to some distant place and stop worrying about her.

I should perhaps have paid more attention to my brother in those months. With Plautianus shackled, devoid of most of his former power, my brother had lost his most powerful supporter, and with the announcement of our child on the way, his succession was now moot. He was slowly losing everything, and I should have seen that such a thing would lead to repercussions.

—

On the day of the birth I remember pacing, drinking unwatered wine. I remember Father offering me platitudes that he probably thought were sage advice and Mother offering me pearls of wisdom that she probably considered mere platitudes. I remember the obstetrix's assistants hurrying into the room just as I had reached the pinnacle of tension. She was beaming. I felt a swell of exaltation.

Then it collapsed.

'You have a daughter, Domine.'

Fucking wonderful. I roared my frustration and thumped an angry fist into the wall. A daughter! All that time, the tension, the wait, only to be landed with a tiny, needy version of Plautilla. A son would have been an heir, would have made her very existence worthwhile, but a daughter was of no dynastic value to me. I ranted on that very subject as I punched the wall again and again, but Mother pulled me away before I broke my knuckles, rather darkly and pointedly reminding me that not all women were worthless. I went into the room to find Plautilla clutching the mewling child with a look of love and relief. I told her flatly that the girl had to stay in her side of the palace, and walked out.

I never saw her again. The child had weak lungs and lasted just a month.

Geta wore a disgustingly smug look around the palace that month. His place in the succession was reinstated, and he knew that if Plautilla and I rarely crossed paths, there was little chance of a second child to spoil his plans. I had never wanted to punch my brother in the face more than I did at that time.

It led to a rather frank discussion with my father that almost caused a rift between us. There had been a number of worrying events in Rome: a sea creature of monstrous type and proportions had entered the harbour of Augustus at Ostia and attacked an imperial trireme; an image of Father was shredded by bears in the amphitheatre; and, foremost, a comet was seen in the skies over Rome, its trail pointing from Father's new palace to the mausoleum of the Augustan emperors. It lingered for days, suggesting the demise of the Severan line. Father's favoured interpreters foretold a series of disasters awaiting us all.

'You will take your wife back into your rooms.'

'I will not.'

'You will, and you will fuck her and bring us another child.'

'I would rather fuck a hog, Father.'

He rose then, pushing himself upright from his chair, eyes blazing. 'You will do as your father... as your *emperor*, commands, boy. Take her back.'

If anything, his anger simply brought forth my own, two lions staring at each other over a carcass. 'No.'

A finger was levelled at me, shaken. 'You will take back your wife and sire an heir, or I will look elsewhere for my own.'

My lip curled. Geta? Probably. And another time, that threat might have been enough to cow me, but my blood was up, and I was ready for a fight. 'Then do it. Cast me, tried and tested and strong, aside, and raise my weak, snide, sneaky brother in my place. What value a dynasty then?'

I had respected the strong father of my childhood, and in many ways I still did, but I was Caesar now, and I had to stand my ground.

'You *defy* me, boy?' he hissed.

'I will not *demean* myself further with that creature,' I snapped back.

I have to admit to being surprised when he took a step forward and delivered me a stinging slap to the cheek. I was even more surprised when I returned the gesture. I had grown strong, and this was no boyhood blow. I hit him hard, and he staggered back, almost falling into his chair.

'You made me Caesar,' I snarled. 'Have the courtesy to treat me like one, not like a wayward child to be knocked into line. Or if you truly want to put me aside for a weakling, then do it. But I will have no more of that woman.'

For a moment, he stood there, fist clenching and unclenching. I think he was trying to decide whether to punch me. For certain I would have punched back. In the end, he levelled that finger again. 'You will do as you are instructed, or you will be stripped of your power. Your name will be torn from history, like the monster Caligula. I will *not* be defied by my own son.'

But perhaps there was a touch of fear in him, for instead of facing me down, he turned and marched away, angrily, leaving me seething in the room, my tongue heavy with retorts unsaid.

It was Mother's voice of reason that settled it all. She persuaded him that losing me was too much to bear, and me that I needed to come to some arrangement with him. I met him in one of the libraries and agreed to try once more, and if Plautilla failed to produce an heir from that one meeting, I would be allowed to divorce her and find a more fitting consort. That night I read every medical text in the library when he left and applied every suggestion for contraception. Then I went to her and we both spent a night we hated.

Nothing came of it, of course, but Father would have us see out a year to be sure.

-

The new year came around, and in a bid to heal the divide in his family, Father made Geta and I consuls together. It failed, of course. In an effort not to spend time with anyone, for everyone was now annoying me, I spent more and more hours at the Circus, where I found solace from my family, and developed something of a rapport with the Blues faction. As the winter wore on into spring, I became more and more tied to them, becoming their de facto figurehead in Rome.

For those who do not know the races, I will tell you that the chariot teams are split into four factions. The Blues and the Greens, each of whom can field more than a dozen chariots with renowned riders, and each of whom has a school and stable complex half the size of my father's palace, are the city's two main contenders. Every season it is hotly debated which of them will finish on top. The Reds and Whites are younger factions, and less successful, though they take home a reasonable share of the prizes each season. But the true contest is always between the Blues and Greens.

It so happened that in the spring of that year, a name arose on the African chariot circuits. Euprepes had become the most famous racer south of the sea and, having won every great prize from Mauritania to Aegyptus, he was keen to come to Rome and test his mettle against the best the empire had to offer. I was thrilled. The idea that a rider from my family's homeland had achieved such fame and wanted to come to Rome was simply wonderful. I arranged everything. I secured an enormous sum, largely from my personal funds – and it was enough to almost empty my coffers that year – just to entice the man to join the Blues. I received an agreement by letter, and it was all arranged: we would have the great Euprepes.

He arrived in Rome on the kalends of Maius and immediately went to the camp of the Greens.

We were baffled, stunned, and very, very angry.

It emerged that, at the very last moment, the Blues had been outbid by the Greens, their offer reaching the famous charioteer halfway across the sea, a courier racing by fast ship to intercept his. How they could have known our bid was beyond us; it was not public knowledge, and it really was a truly huge sum.

It was only on the first day of practice races that the full reasoning came clear. With no crowd – because the day was for team practice only – two of the blue chariots and two of the green entered the Circus Maximus. I went with Celer, the Blues' most successful rider, for I was learning the ropes from him then, and had even ridden a few circuits myself. Then the Greens came in, and one of them, of course, was the infamous Euprepes. Beside him, chatting like an old friend and dressed like a champion rider himself, came my brother.

The stinking little shit had even invaded the place I went to get away from them all. He'd never shown even a modicum of interest in the races until he saw in them a way to get at me.

It all fell into place. Only someone with access to the palace records and accounts could know how much I had set aside for the man and then top it. Geta was the one who had swept Euprepes out from under me. I vowed revenge in that moment, not just on my brother for his underhanded wiles, but also on the fickle rider who had shunned me for a few more coins.

The revelations led to a costly and destructive day.

The practice races were supposed to be just that; they were not proper races, which are dangerous. The unenlightened will tell you that the matches in the arena are the bloodiest spectacle of Rome. They are fools. More charioteers die each year than gladiators. A race in which even half the chariots cross the finish line is considered an impressive one. Pits are dug and mounds raised to bury broken horses every month, and riders are remembered on funerary steles more often than any other sportsman.

This was supposed to be a practice day.

The Reds and the Whites had joined us while I was glowering at my brother. They quickly took in the atmosphere and decided they could do without the day of training, beating a hasty retreat. I was angry. *Really* angry.

'Celer.'

'Domine?'

'I know you've not much to go on. You saw him ride in. What do you think?'

Celer snorted. 'He's a provincial hopeful, Domine. I've seen his sort off more than once.'

'Good. Take him out in the first race. I want him smeared across the Circus walls, ground into the sand. I want it to be impossible to tell in the wreckage where the man meat ends and the horse meat starts. Do I make myself clear?'

He gave me a grin. 'It shall be so, Domine.'

I retreated to the stands. I was sitting close to the track, below the imperial *pulvinar*, and Geta was seated on the far side, opposite me. The two *quadriga* lined up. This was no real race, and the carceres remained dark. The contestants were lined up on a groove cut across the sand. A Circus slave dropped the linen marker, and they were off.

The two chariots began to move, picking up pace and then hurtling along the side of the Circus, racing for the turn at the end. I watched with tense anticipation. They cornered well, both of them, and had I been of sound mind, I might have labelled them of roughly equal skill. But I was angry and with deadly intent. I prayed and wished for destruction for the African traitor as he cornered, but the two chariots were fine and raced along the far side in front of my brother with hardly a hair to separate them.

I lost them for a while there, on the far side of the *spina*, my view impeded by all the decorations along it, until they cornered again at the start. They were keeping pace, far enough apart to avoid disaster, and Celer was now on the outside. I watched as he tried to manoeuvre Euprepes into a place where disaster would befall him, but the African was surprisingly wily. They reached the end once more almost neck-and-neck. There was a moment then where they came hair-raisingly close together, and I thought it was all going to happen, then they separated, chariot wheels slamming back to the gritty surface and slicing away as they turned, heading once more down the far straight.

All I could see were the flashes of both chariots between the columns, the decorations, statues and bronze dolphins as they raced in a blur of colour. Then something happened. One moment two chariots were racing, the next, Euprepes of the Greens was emerging into the turn alone. My eyes tracked back along the spina and found a shape that might have been Celer's chariot and horses. There had been a disaster. Euprepes slowed and brought his vehicle to a halt near the carceres, for there was no need to continue the race now. The victor was clear.

My eyes raked the spina, picking out any detail. Then they rose to my brother opposite. He wore the oiliest grin, and not for the first time that year I had the urge to smash his teeth down his throat. He was playing with something, twirling it in his hands. He had the *fasces* from one of his lictors, and was sliding the rods from it one at a time and twirling them in a somehow meaningful way. I was sure in an instant that somehow the bastard had thrown a rod and caught Celer, or his chariot or horses, mid-straight, and caused the accident. I was furious. Livid. Had we been closer I might well have killed him on the spot.

As it was, I was actually more concerned with the welfare of Celer than punishing my brother. He was the Blues' best hope for the overall laurel that year, and I was tied closely now to the Blues, with friends in the camp.

I was out on the sands swiftly, hurrying across the hoofprints and wheel-ruts. I threw a look at Euprepes where he sat, impassive, that would have nailed most men to a wall, and then rounded the spina. The blue chariot was a mess. The vehicle was gone, and only one of the four-horse team had escaped unscathed.

Celer himself had somehow survived the disaster. He was on his hands and knees, throwing up into the sand as Circus slaves ran around him trying to help. He was battered and bloody, but he lived, and it looked as though somehow, miraculously, he had even avoided breaking a bone. Then he looked up, and his gaze went straight to Geta, confirming for me precisely what I had suspected. I intercepted the Circus medical staff, who were hurrying to help, and wagged a finger at the head physician.

'Anything he needs, he gets. I don't care how much it costs. Send to the palace if you need to. Make sure he's well, and with the will of the gods can race at the next meeting.'

The man looked dubious as to that last, but bowed his head in understanding and they ran on to help Celer. I had something else in mind. I stormed towards the stands where my brother still sat, trying to balance a fasces rod on his index finger.

I'm not sure what I intended. I had no weapon, but my hand habitually went to my sharp eating knife at times like this, and I might well have cut his throat had I been able to reach. Fortunately for him, access from the sands into the seating is rare and restricted for obvious reasons, and so I came to a halt before him, almost vibrating with anger, but unable to get to him. I have said before that I have no trouble with either violence or cruelty when they are directed appropriately. I hate them being wasted. They were not wasted that morning. I would have impaled him or hung him on a cross that morning, and I would have held a banquet to celebrate doing it. The anger I had long held against Geta had hardened, becoming loathing.

'You seem vexed, brother,' he said, hitching that infuriating smile up.

'Don't play innocent, Geta. I am well aware of what you've done, right from subverting Euprepes to the Greens to almost crippling our driver. Celer knows, too.'

'Too bad there are no independent witnesses,' Geta sneered.

'I suspect a spare rod might be found in the wreckage.'

'Several,' Geta replied, standing and hurling his handful of sticks across the sand into the pile of broken timbers and flesh.

'If you weren't hiding behind the barrier, I would beat you to a pulp, you little rat.'

'That would hardly be a fair fight, though, would it?' Geta barked. 'I'm sixteen, you're nineteen. You've had a military career, I've been kept in study. And since you seem to set such store in fairness, it would be hypocritical of you to beat me senseless, would it not? I wonder what Mother and Father would think?'

'You can't hide behind your new green friends,' I spat. 'They don't have Plautianus' power. Shit, even Plautianus doesn't have Plautianus' power now.'

'How about a race?' he said, gimlet eyes gleaming.

'What?'

'And I shall offer you important stakes. If you win, I'll step away from the races and leave you to it. If I win, you walk away from your Blues.'

Overconfidence can be a killer, hubris more so. I accepted in an instant, for in my immediate reasoning, I could only assume that Geta would lose. He was younger, thinner and weaker than me. He could not have had the practice I'd had with the horses and chariots. I had every advantage.

The wager was set.

I hurried back to find the staff who'd accompanied Celer to the Circus. Every chariot has its support staff, numbering quite a few very skilled and devoted people, for even the slaves of the racing factions are loyal and true to their colour. Thus, two score people had come with us from the faction's headquarters, and we'd brought a spare vehicle and beasts, too.

I had trained a number of times, and I knew what I was doing, but a rider bonds with his team, and the vehicle I habitually used was back in the stables.

'Domine, you're not used to this team or this vehicle,' said the head *equisio*.

'I'll make it work.'

'Can you not delay until we bring your chariot?'

'No. I will use this. It ends now. I want that *Caesar* out of the Circus for good.'

'All right, Domine. Three things to remember, then. Your left trace horse is Tipo, and he's got a tendency to pull hard. You have to counter his instincts and keep him in line, or he'll try and take your team off left or right more than you intend.'

'Why race him then?'

'Because he's fast and strong, and Celer is used to him and knows what to do. This chariot is slightly heavier than the one you use, so bear that in mind. It will make momentum more of an advantage or disadvantage, especially coming into the turns. Just try to adjust in your head in advance. And thirdly, you don't have your own kit. That means you're either going to have to borrow kit which might not fit well, or go without, and you know how dangerous that can be.'

I brushed it aside. 'I can wear the leathers. The helmet I can live without. Let's face it, if I come off head-first, that's not going to save me.'

In no time I was striding out from the carceres in my military tunic with the purple band to remind people of my status, clad in the banded leather of a rider, my hook-knife at my belt ready to cut me free if I found myself in trouble. I wore only a bandana to keep the sweat from my eyes and leather bracers to prevent chafing at the wrists. I had good solid boots, and crossed to the chariot, climbing up onto the platform with a confidence I should have watched. Even as I brought the vehicle out into line ready for the off, I could feel everything I'd been told. The weight was new, and Tipo was trying to pull me further than I wanted. I countered it easily but would have to remember that in the press of the race.

It should have been a warning when Geta rolled out. He was dressed like a true charioteer, and rode with an ease that suggested he was well used to that chariot. He had, of course, planned somehow to get me into a race that day, and had given himself every advantage he could. He'd brought his own gear and team and vehicle, while I was riding with strangers.

We lined up. Euprepes had the rag to drop, and now stood on the stands nearby, waiting while the last of the mess caused by Celer's crash was removed from the sand, and the blood was raked in. I looked up, watching the flights of birds and the weather. I set only limited store by the omens of nature and the gods, but my father lived by them, and it sort of rubbed off on me at times. There we were, two brothers just ten paces apart, waiting for a competition that would leave one of us free to enjoy the Circus without the other.

Euprepes gave us a warning, and then dropped the rag.

We set off. I was swiftly surprised by how competent Geta was. He'd been practicing more than I had expected, and had a reasonable mastery of his team and vehicle as he shot away across the sand. I, on the other hand, was struggling to pick up speed, thanks to the vehicle's weight. I am prone to fits of temper which sometimes override sense. I can be impetuous. I was so on this occasion, blithely assuming I would win without any difficulty and thereby overlooking my disadvantages. The chariot groaned and lurched to speed. When it did so, it picked up more pace than I was used to, and though Geta had gained an early lead thanks to the start, it was clear that my top speed was faster than his. I pelted away along the straight.

That was the point I reined in my own exhilaration and anger. I'd sleepwalked into agreeing to this with such a heavy vehicle. I'd also been told about the horses, and I wouldn't be surprised again. I judged the turn coming up fast, the empty stands ahead the only watchers. I had to steer to the left but the horse, Tipo, was going to try to oversteer, so I had to make sure I kept control. There would be an advantage, I thought, to the vehicle's weight in the turn. Too sharp a corner could result in one wheel lifting free of the track, which would be an incredibly dangerous moment. This chariot, though, was heavy enough that that was less likely.

I hit the turn hard, slowing only at the last moment, and leaned into it. I could feel it, then. Tipo was heaving me to the left, trying to come closer to the spina than he should. I nudged him with the reins, pulling him back a little, exerting my control over him, and, thank all the gods, he responded well. We spun around the end of the spina at speed but with both wheels on the ground, and I felt a wave of joy and hope. Geta had the lead, but I would catch him soon. Now that I was up to speed it would be an easy enough thing, and I had the hang of the turns already.

My joy evaporated as I finished the turn and came into the straight. In a heart-stopping moment, all hope exploded, for there, right in my path, was Geta's chariot. He'd had enough of a lead that he should be halfway along that straight, but he wasn't. He was only just around the turn, and right in my way. He'd begun to turn the chariot as he slowed, by the looks of it, so that he presented me with a three-quarter angle. I couldn't understand what he was doing. Was he insane? I had but a moment to decide what to do. I could pull left, but the space between him and the spina was minimal, and there was a strong chance I would collide with one or the other. I could race straight into him, in which case we might well all become grave fodder. Or I could try to execute a sharp turn in the opposite direction of the one I'd just come out of, which was extremely difficult. It was realistically the only option, though I have to admit to a temptation just to hit the bastard and see what happened. Still, sense won out.

What happened remains something of a blur even now. I would be willing to swear, with my hand on the altar of Apollo, that I saw

Geta cutting himself free of the reins and leaping from the chariot in the other direction, running for the relative safety of the spina. I could never prove it, of course, and there were no other witnesses, but I'm sure that is what I saw, and it all adds up to a deliberate attempt by my brother to ruin me. I don't know whether he truly intended injury or whether he was just trying to knock me from the race so that he could win.

I hauled right on the reins, and the team turned. In the panic of that moment, I suspect I forgot to counter the urge of Tipo to oversteer, though, as I say, it's all something of a blur. The chariot turned sharply. Too sharply. I know I ripped the knife free of my belt to cut myself clear of the reins as he had done, but I was too late. I sawed into the leather, but the chariot tipped and rolled before I managed to cut through. The rest is chaos in my memory. I remember agony, flying grit and sand, blood, the screaming of horses, the splintering of wood, distant shouts of alarm, and then silence and blackness.

The next thing I knew I was coming around from unconsciousness. I was still lying on the sand, with the Circus slaves and physicians and attendants all around me. They had white faces as they murmured among themselves and cast anxious glances down at me. My eyes hurt. They had sand in them, as did my nose and mouth. I coughed it out, and that also hurt. Everything hurt, though gradually things were resolving so that I had more of an idea what was happening. I tried to lift my head, and that now hurt more. Still, I could see the pile of timbers and broken spokes that was all that was left of the chariot. I could see two dead horses, including Tipo, and two living, wandering out across the sands, ignored in the chaos.

Then I saw my leg. It lay at a funny angle. I frowned and moved it.
I passed out again.

When I next came around, almost all my pain was in that leg, which was now facing the right way, strapped and splinted. It had been broken, and quite badly. I felt a shock of fear, then. I had spent long enough with the army to know that a broken limb would sometimes heal well, but could often cause life-long problems. At least with my elevated status, they would not simply lop it off to save time as many army medics would.

I hissed and grimaced as they lifted the stretcher, and a flood of anger and hate washed over me as we passed Geta. He had a strange look, which I realised was a smug smile covered by a fake shell of concern for the benefit of the witnesses.

'I trust you will live up to our agreement and stay away,' he said.

Had I the strength I'd have sat up and throttled him then. 'Neither of us finished, you little rodent. This is not over.'

Not by a long way.

XII

These Nine I Cast

Rome, Februarius 22nd AD 206

It took me six months to recover from our race. The court politics played out in the visitors I received. Mother visited me daily, and she always brought treats and something to build my spirits. My aunt, visiting from Syria, called in regularly, trying to keep my humour up. The luminaries of the Blues from the Circus came once after every training day, when they were released from work for relaxation. My father visited when he could, which was not as often as either he or I would have liked, but with me laid up with a leg in the air, his workload had doubled, and he had to attend to the business of empire as well as looking after his son.

Geta came once. It was almost a month after the 'accident,' and he came to gloat over the edge the Greens had gained with Celer out of commission, and to demand once more that I step away from the races altogether as per our wager. I refused flatly, and that was that – the last time he came.

I spent my time in convalescence planning. As long as Plautianus remained, I could never truly free myself from his daughter, I could never free my father from his companionship, and I could never remove the possibility that he might suddenly do something unexpected in support of Geta. He had been declawed, but he remained nonetheless, oozing his way around court and raising threats to stability. One day I would free myself of all threats but for now Plautianus was the first.

I got to know the Praetorians. The units the Guard place on patrol around the palace vary, rotating through the members of the Guard, but certain units with certain officers have routines, and over the months I selected the most likely bunch. Each cohort has ten centurions, and so, whatever cohort had the palace detail, there were 800 men on duty looking after the Palatine, the various other imperial residences in Rome, our extensive country estates, and covering protection duty for any member of the imperial family not currently in residence.

I needed a way to work out who was loyal to me and who was not, and that took some thought. In the end I settled upon Euodus. I knew that my old tutor favoured Geta. He had been staunchly in my brother's camp the whole time, and so he was my catalyst. I would wait until one of the centurions from my chosen cohort was commanding on the Palatine, and I would make sure to summon Euodus while he was present. When the old man arrived, usually flustered and nervous, I would make some unreasonable demand of my brother, claiming it to be a response, and use Euodus as a messenger. For instance, when Saturninus, the centurion of the First Century was on duty in my apartments, I arranged just such an exchange.

'What is it, Domine?' the gangly old man asked nervously, panting from the exertion of running to my side.

'My brother continues to demand that I relinquish my position with the Blues and sign a document confirming that I will no longer attend the Circus.'

'I am aware, Domine.'

'But I am feeling whimsical, Euodus. Please take this to my brother, since he will not admit me.' I held out a sealed document.

'Might I ask what it is, Domine?'

'It is an execution warrant for the Green who won today's race trophy. He is accused of race-fixing and of cheating.'

The old man's face creased into a frown. 'But the races are still running. The winner has yet to be determined. I do not understand, for you do not even know who it will be, Domine?'

I grinned, nastily. 'And it will infuriate Geta. Do it, old man.'

And I sent him on his way. As he left, I watched the centurion on guard very carefully. In the days of Commodus, the Praetorians were political animals bred in the world of emperors and as at home with the machinations of court as they were in their camp. Since my father had dismissed them all and replaced them with grizzled veterans from the Danubius, that had all changed. They were not subtle these days. They were soldiers, given to saying what they thought. That first day, when I tried it with Saturninus, I felt sure I'd found my solution. As Euodus shuffled away, I paid attention to the centurion. The tutor squirmed past him, giving him the wide berth that academics generally adopt with soldiers, and as he vanished, Saturninus grinned. I managed to catch his eye and rolled my own.

'What do you think his answer will be?'

'He'll tear it up, Domine. But only after he's turned purple and exploded.'

'That's what I thought. It gets boring lying here day after day, Centurion. Taunting and irritating my brother is my only entertainment.'

'Then might I suggest something, Domine?'

'You might,' I answered, intrigued.

'I happen to know which girl he particularly favours at the moment in the palace. If she were to be removed from availability, I suspect it will rile him more than anything.'

Time for my serious test.

'Your prefects would not be happy if you helped me against my brother. Plautianus is my brother's man, after all.'

'And Drusianus is yours, Domine.'

That was that. Plautianus might be Geta's, or more realistically the other way round, but it appeared that Drusianus could be trusted, and now so could Saturninus. I should probably have spent more time making sure of them, but I tend towards a precipitative nature, and sometimes leap into decisions. On this occasion, it came out well. Over the following days I got to know Saturninus, who visited me even when not on duty. I spoke to the prefect Drusianus. Between their recommendations, and using the ploy of annoying Euodus to test the reactions of centurions, I began to build a list of men I trusted and men I did not. I tried to keep it all within the one cohort, because the wider one spreads a plot, the more likely it is to be uncovered.

Over a month and more, I settled upon three centurions from the First Cohort. All three had become my confidantes, and all three I decided I could trust. The other seven in the cohort were either clearly in favour of my brother or were of the most dubious and easily bought loyalty. Such men I could do without. I had three good soldiers and seven expendable, all of powerful centurion rank in the Guard. And I had Drusianus, who had taken such a dislike to his co-prefect that he had naturally become my man.

I let them distance themselves from me, for if we were to conspire then it would be better if we were not noted together too often. Then, one night, while I was closing in on full recovery, I summoned all four of them in secret to a private meeting. We met in a largely unused part of Tiberius' old palace, my trustworthy slaves and freedmen making sure we were not disturbed.

'The time has come,' I announced.

The four men looked at one another and at me. They were unsure, yet curious. As they sat in the indicated seats, four burly slaves brought in an altar dedicated to Apollo that I'd commandeered from elsewhere in the palace. It was placed in the centre of the room, and the slaves then left, making sure the door was sealed.

'We are alone,' I confirmed. 'And even wagging ears cannot hear us. I hope I have not been misled that you are all men loyal to both my father and me?'

The rousing chorus of agreement was heartening. I nodded. 'Before we proceed, I would like every man to place a hand on the altar and swear to Apollo that they are brothers in this, that treachery will be visited with Divine vengeance, that they will remain loyal to my father and me to death and beyond. Will you do this?'

There was a nerve-racking moment as the four men looked at one another again. To edge them into it, I placed my own hand upon the altar, leaning from my seat and moving my leg a little stiffly. I thought for a moment that my faith had been misplaced. Then Drusianus placed his hand beside mine. Then Saturninus, and then the other two centurions. They each gave their oath, and I had them, for no man would risk angering Apollo after taking a vow on his altar.

'It begins like this.'

–

It took only a month for the plan to take effect. Drusianus had several very violent and noisy arguments with Plautianus in front of plenty of witnesses. In the end, he proclaimed that he could no longer hold his position in the Guard when his co-prefect so clearly undermined him at every opportunity. He walked away from his post, without actually resigning his commission. Plautianus seemed to treat this as a victory, and took full control of the Guard once more. My favoured centurions in the First Cohort managed to inveigle their way into his good books and were seen to be Plautianus' men. In fact, seven of them already were, so it would not have been a difficult ruse to create for the others.

I became nervous as the appointed time approached. We had settled on the Parentalia festival in Februarius to make our move. It seemed likely that the focus on family at that time would nudge my father's opinions in the right direction. The festival arrived. Nine days of festivities, ending with Feralia and a ritual meal which was for the family alone. As such, we had a rare moment of solitude, for meals and occasions on the Palatine were almost always busy state occasions. On that day, in the grand *triclinium* on the Palatine, there was Father and Mother, Geta and me. Even the attending slaves delivered the meal and wine and then left us alone.

'I see you are almost back to normal,' Father said with satisfaction. 'I presume there will be no more ridiculous stunts in the future. I have only two sons. I do not wish to waste even one.' It was a joke, but a dark one.

I limped a little still, but I had now foregone my walking stick and was back to more or less my old self. Not quite. I was wiser. Wilier. Cleverer. Nastier.

We settled into the meal, and I wondered when it would happen. Indeed, I probably shot my gaze at the door a hundred times that night without meaning to, expecting it to burst open. I seriously worried that something had gone amiss as we finished the last of the meal and settled to drinking wine, Mother looking at Father with a supportive expression, knowing that he missed his brother at such times, Geta and I studiously ignoring one another. Father finally stood, reached down, and picked up the black beans set aside on the table for the ritual. With eyes closed, he cast them as hard as he could. Two went through a window and the rest bounced from the wall.

'These nine I cast. With these beans, I redeem me and mine,' he said in sonorous tones, and then repeated the mantra eight more times, slowly turning to face in all directions as he did so, finishing facing the way he had begun. His eyes snapped open and he cleared his throat. 'Ghosts of my fathers, go forth.'

As if that had been some specified code word, the door to the room burst open. Two of Father's lictors stumbled in backwards, trying to hold someone back. Father's hand shot to his belt, gripping the dagger he habitually kept there, just as mine reached for my eating knife. I had expected a messenger. Something noble, stoic, acceptable. Not a fracas.

Indeed, as I watched, it became clear that there were four sides in this struggle in the doorway. Father's lictors and a few members of the Praetorians who had been on guard were working together, struggling against an armed party. Another small unit of Praetorians, including the three centurions for whom I'd been waiting, were busy drawing blood with other Praetorians. It was chaos. Praetorians fighting Praetorians while other Praetorians tried to stop them both, all while the lictors tried to keep them away from the emperor.

Oddly, it was my father's sheer presence that drew a halt to it. As one soldier collapsed to the floor, gurgling and with blood gushing from his groin, Father shouted.

'What is the *meaning* of this?'

The struggling ended. The guardsmen on duty and the lictors took advantage of the moment's pause to back into the room and create a defensive line between this commotion and the emperor.

'I bear grave news of treason and plots, Domine,' Saturninus said, and as he did so another of the Praetorians leaped at him and threatened to start the whole fracas over. The man was pushed down, where lictors dragged him back upright, one of the rods from their bundles held across his throat, prepared to crush his windpipe if he tried anything.

'Speak, centurion,' Father said.

Saturninus stepped forward. 'A plot is afoot to remove you from the purple, Domine, both you and your fellow Augustus.'

'Go on.'

The man with the rod beneath his chin, who I now recognised despite the lack of an identifying crest as one of the centurions I had confirmed as an enemy, struggled, which only strengthened Saturninus' case.

'Hold that one,' Father commanded, then to Saturninus: 'Tell me.'

'Your enemies plan to turn your own guard against you, Domine. The officer class of the First Cohort has been bought entire by Plautianus.'

'Not this again,' snapped my father. 'We have had this out. He is my friend.'

'No, Domine, he is not. He sinks his hooks into your line. He has the Caesar already in his grasp, but he cannot gain the favour of your heir, and he cannot supplant you without ending the line.' He saw my father drawing up to deny it again, and hurried on to get his words out, treason in the open. 'Look to the ousted prefect, Domine. Drusianus is gone. I know that you appointed him to limit the traitor's power, and already the man is gone, and Plautianus has sole control of the Guard once more. Domine, this is no rumour or hearsay, for I myself have been made party to it all.'

Now, Father was interested. His mouth closed. He frowned.

'I was drawn into the conspiracy,' the soldier went on, 'along with all the centurions of the First Cohort. He thought to buy us with gold and promises, as though we were the corrupt Praetorians of old. But we are not, Domine. We are of the powerful Danubius legions, loyal to our emperor and steadfast in resolve. We were bribed, but we were also threatened. Death stalks me now for betraying the prefect's trust, and will do so for my colleagues. Three of us remain loyal to you, Domine, but seven even now whet their blades to carry out the traitor's orders.'

Father shook his head. 'I cannot believe it of Plautianus. No. He has been dangerous and powerful, and even corrupt, but he has always been loyal.'

The centurion stepped out forward once more. The lictors and guards moved to intercept him, but the centurion removed his blades and cast them to the floor. Disarmed, he reached into his belt and held up a scroll case bearing the seal of the Praetorians.

'Let him approach,' Father said, and then stepped backwards and sat down. Too long on his feet hurt him these days.

Saturninus did so, keeping safely and appropriately distant from the imperial person, but proffering the scroll. I watched with interest. I had told them that their word would not be enough. Father was blind to the danger of his old friend, and would need proof of some sort. Drusianus and Saturninus had conferred and told me that they could provide something. How they might find proof of treachery when the whole thing was a lie manufactured by us, I could not fathom, but it appeared now that they had.

'A Praetorian seal is proof of nothing,' Father noted as he slid the document from the case and unfurled it. But as his gaze slid down the page, I could see the certainty drain from him. 'How did you come by this?'

Saturninus bowed low. 'I say again, Domine, the traitor sought to secure my hand in the deed. You will find such a letter with all the centurions of the First Cohort.' In support of his words, the two other centurions I trusted in that gathering fished out just such a scroll case.

My father's expression hardened. 'This is still hard to credit.'

'Yet you recognise the handwriting, Domine?'

A long silence. Tension. An empire, a *world*, in the balance.

'I do.'

I was stunned. Somehow, against all probability, they had managed to secure proof of treason apparently written in Plautianus' own hand. Of course, that wasn't the case. It couldn't be. But it was convincing enough to sway even Father. All I could think was that they had spent painstaking hours with purloined documents from Plautianus' office, copying out the words they needed to create a damning document. Sealing it with the prefect's seal was easy enough, for they would have access to Drusianus' ring. It was so neat and clever it could have been written by a Greek playwright.

He spent a long time looking at that document. Finally he looked up again, and his gaze fell upon the soldier with the rod beneath his chin. He flicked a finger to the man holding him. 'Kill him.'

It took little more than a squeeze to crush the man's throat, and the centurion collapsed to the marble tiles wheezing and screaming hoarse screams, scrabbling at his flattened windpipe, desperate for air. He wheezed and gasped, and thrashed and shook for some time until he fell still. Father's expression remained dark. 'Cast the body into the Tiber.' Then he looked to his lictors. 'Find a courier. Have a message sent to Plautianus. Tell him his presence is required urgently in the palace. Tell him a plot has been unearthed.'

As Praetorians took the broken body away, and one of the lictors hurried off to have the message sent, the rest of the soldiers and lictors formed up in the room. Eight more bodies in the corridor marked others who had fought to help Saturninus see the emperor, or to stop him, and they too were removed. Slaves appeared from somewhere and cleaned the floor carefully before retreating. Father motioned for Saturninus to retrieve his weapons, which he did.

We remained there for some time. Mother's expression was a complex one. I could read in her face a careful sombreness and disbelief, affected for the sake of her husband, but beneath that a deep and heartfelt satisfaction that her enemy may finally be brought down. It felt extremely odd, for no one spoke in that dreadful quiet.

Then we heard the small party arrive outside. We heard a smaller number admitted. We heard the footsteps thin again until finally a single pair of military boots approached.

Plautianus rounded the corner and approached the doorway at speed. Then he saw the Praetorians and the lictors. He turned, seemingly suddenly aware that he had lost his entourage en route. Instead of his loyal men, all that followed up behind now were the emperor's own guards, those he trusted implicitly. Plautianus came to a halt in the entrance to the room, eyes screwed tight in suspicion.

'Domine, you called for me?'

'Why, Gaius?'

The prefect's frown deepened.

'Why *what*, Lucius?'

'I am your emperor, Gaius. You will address me appropriately.'

That put the prefect more on his guard than ever. His hand went to his belt, dancing across the pommel of his sword, a dangerous move in the circumstances.

'Why what, Domine?'

'Why would you kill us?'

'Kill you, Domine? I have no idea what you are talking about.'

Father threw the letter at the man, who caught it and gave it a quick read. 'Preposterous.'

'It is your writing. I have known you a long time, Gaius.'

'It is an excellent forgery, I'll grant you, but a forgery it remains.'

'I wish I could believe that.'

A new voice chimed in then, and I felt a twitch in my cheek at the sound. 'Plautianus is ever loyal, Father,' Geta proclaimed. 'But like all steadfast men he makes canny enemies.'

'Says the one man who would walk clear of the murders,' I snapped. 'The one man Plautianus already controls and who could be made to sign over the whole empire to an ambitious prefect. You are blinded, brother, blinded by your alliance with this criminal.'

'Oh, fuck off Antoninus,' my brother spat, earning a sharp look from my father.

'Quiet, the pair of you,' he barked. Then to Plautianus: 'Defend yourself.'

155

'How? And against what? I do not know of what I am accused or who by. I see only this flimsy evidence. Have the accusers stagger under the burden of proof, Domine, rather than demand I prove my innocence.'

I flinched. This was a dangerous moment. I could see Father wavering.

Before I realised what I was doing, I had taken a step towards Plautianus. As he opened his mouth to speak again, I punched him in the jaw. The attack was so unexpected by everyone in the room, myself included, that he did nothing to defend himself, and the blow was a powerful one, sending him staggering back.

'You can prevent me killing people and taking their coin,' he spat at me, 'but no amount of blaming me for your impotence and your unmanliness will cover your shame, boy. A *eunuch* could have given my daughter children by now.'

I roared and leapt for him again, my rage getting the better of me. Of all people it was Father's strong hands that grasped my shoulders and held me back, though once again his gaze was hard and flinty as it fell upon his old friend. Plautianus had made a mistake in reacting as he did. Father did not take insults to his line well. Again, silence fell. I knew this had to be the time. If it didn't end now, the bastard would slither out of trouble again and we'd never get another chance. My brother was watching his main supporter teeter on the precipice; he would do whatever he could to prevent the fall. My eyes fell on Saturninus. He had his blades out, and his gaze was on me, seeking only an order, permission.

'Saturninus!' I barked sharply.

That was all he needed. He leapt and lunged. The blade sank into Plautianus' neck, but the centurion did not stop there, bearing the prefect back and down to the floor, where his knife skittered free. I did not understand why, but as the pair writhed on the floor for a while, blood everywhere, finally Saturninus rose, and I noted that Plautianus' sword was half-drawn, his hand wrapped around the hilt. The attack had been so sudden it seemed unlikely the prefect had begun to draw his blade even with his neck slashed through. So either Saturninus had set that up to look suspicious, or...

'What was that, centurion?' snapped Father.

'He was drawing his blade, Domine,' Saturninus said, head bowed.

'It's true, Father,' I added, quickly, confidently. 'That's why I shouted the warning.'

The centurion took it up once more. 'His plot was undone, Domine. He had no choice. But it is the duty of the Guard to protect the emperor. It was *my* duty.'

Father looked into the man's eyes for some time until his gaze slid down to the bloody heap that had been his oldest friend. When he looked back up, he nodded slowly. 'There is much to do,' he said.

–

Over the year that followed the death of Plautianus, the repercussions were severe. Plautianus' entire family, right down to distant cousins, was driven into exile, their property taken by the imperial treasury, their names struck from all rolls. Blessedly, that included Plautilla, and the last time I ever saw my awful wife was as she was escorted from her apartments by Praetorians, a gaze of utter hatred levelled at me. The manufactured conspiracy was investigated and unpicked through interrogation and torture, though its lead commissioner was Drusianus, the very man who had helped create it with me. Through the careful manoeuvring of clever men, and tortured confessions – for in truth a man being tortured can usually be made to admit to anything – the truth of our accusations was confirmed.

Cilo and Macrinus, as men put into Plautianus' circle by us purely to help bring him down, were saved and honoured, the former retaining his position as Urban Prefect, the latter now appointed Procurator rei Privatae. Coeranus was sentenced to a life in exile, and he was one of the lucky ones. Two dozen of Plautianus' close confidantes fell badly in the following days, and so unpleasant was their demise that Caecilius Agricola did not wait for them to come for him. One night he dismissed his family and staff, drank more unwatered wine than any man should, then smashed his cup and opened his veins with the shards. Cassius Clemens failed to talk his way to freedom a second time, and his demise was brutal and protracted.

I hoped that now, with Plautianus gone, and with him the influence he'd exerted over Geta, perhaps the gulf between us could at last be crossed, our relationship brought back from the very brink. I would give him but a short time to grieve over his wicked mentor, and then attempt once more to build that bridge.

Father's proscriptions cut through the self-important meat of Rome like a cleaver through a leg of lamb. Men fell everywhere. It was a good time to be away from Rome, which was fortunate, for that was what Father had in mind. One night, as news was brought of the latest bloodbath in the villas of the wealthy, Father rose from his chair and placed his palms upon the table.

'My sons are still distant.'

Mother nodded, her expression sad. 'It has been thus for some time, Lucius. Plautianus had thought to play father to our youngest, and I fear the longer such foul influences play upon them, the harder it will be for them ever to come to terms.'

'It is the fault of the snake pit that is Rome, Julia,' he said. 'Rome corrupts, you know? You came west with me when the world of Commodus was already falling apart, but I remember him as a young prince. He was a good man once, a bright one, who could have made Rome golden. He was a prince with promise until he spent time in the world of Roman politics. Men like Cleander, of whom even Plautianus was only a pale reflection, twisted a good emperor and turned him into what you remember. I will not have that of our boys.'

'What will you do?'

He slapped his palms on the table hard enough to rouse both my brother and I so that we looked around at him. 'We leave Rome,' Father announced.

'Where to?' Mother enquired.

'To Tibur for the season, my love. Hadrian's villa. You will love it. It is grander than any palace, five times the size of the Palatine, and with every amenity you could want. It is away from the blood and the ordure of Rome, yet close enough, just half a day's ride, that I can continue to run things from there, especially with the help of my sons, who, with luck, will find in our solitude a connection they have sadly lost. And when the summer comes, we will go to Campania like any sensible Roman, and enjoy the coast.'

'That sounds delightful,' she replied. 'Just what we all need.'

And so it was done. We were to disappear from the intrigues of Rome and enjoy the rural life until Geta and I had healed our rift and the Severan family was whole once more.

Part Three – Conquest

'Qui desiderat pacem, praeparet bellum'
Let him who desires peace, prepare for war

—Publius Flavius Vegetius Renatus

XIII

A Whirlwind Visit

Tibur, AD 207

Father thought that Tibur and Baiae might offer a chance to bind his family back together. I initially thought as much, too, but the problem seemed a high mountain to climb. Geta had taken the fall of Plautianus very hard, and saw me, quite rightly as it happened, as the reason for the man's death. He blamed me, and though I could see a wavering in his attitude now, cracks in the façade of his anger, he could not yet bring himself to speak to me. It would take time yet, and, wary of ruining any chance, I backed off and left him, hoping he would slowly heal. It was short-sighted, for all it did was give him time to stew, and the ongoing distance between us preyed on our parents' minds.

I forget how many times over that year Father brought his sons together, sat us down, and tried to solve the problem. Sometimes he would be patient, cajole, explain, wheedle, attempt to use both family ties and simple logic. And sometimes he would make harsh demands when the mood was upon him, angrily attempt to force us together. Perhaps he would have succeeded, had my brother and I not both carried the Severan quickness in our blood. Each and every one of his attempts to heal our rift would provoke Geta into making some barbed comment about my part in it all, and he would then press me until I snapped and spat back curses at him. Each time, even going in with the best intentions, I came out angry and having only helped to widen the rift.

Mother had a more positive approach. One day when Father was out hunting, she called us to her study, dismissed the philosophers with whom she'd been consulting, and sat with us, watching us carefully in silence for a time.

'I love you both, you know that?'

Without even a glance at one another, we both nodded at her.

'And it tortures me to watch this happen. But I also realise that if there is ever to be a healing of this rift, it will be of your own making and not forced by your father. One day, perhaps, you will realise that there are enough dangers out there facing you both without adding those from within. But for now, I cannot bear to watch you tear each other apart like this. I shall persuade your father to leave you alone. To return to Rome, and to grant you each roles that will keep you apart. Perhaps with an enforced distance between you, the fires will cool, and you will start to realise that you could be the greatest of allies, rather than enemies.'

And that was that. Mother was always shrewder and more insightful than Father, and she was absolutely right. Father was at times rather heavy-handed, and had a tendency to make rash decisions, a tendency which has come down through the blood to his children. Perhaps if he'd not attempted to bring us together, he'd not have driven us quite so far apart.

She persuaded him just as she planned, and by Martius we were in Rome again. Despite Mother's advice, however, Father insisted that we celebrate my decennalia. It had been ten years now since I had been raised to the purple, and I was twenty-one years of age. Three days after the kalends of Aprilis the city exploded with festivities, from bouts in the arena to fake ship combats, to plays, to street markets and processions... to races in the Circus. I felt rather smug returning to the Circus Maximus and taking a ceremonial lap around the spina in a gilded chariot while Geta, who'd repeatedly demanded that I relinquish all rights to the place, watched with our parents. That probably did little to help our relationship heal, but I could hardly help it.

In fact, all the festivities really did was drive home a blade of bitterness and jealousy into my brother's heart. I was being displayed as the golden emperor who reigned alongside our father, who had achievements and was beloved of the people, who was his heir and who would take up the mantle when he was gone. Not only was Geta not so honoured, he never would be, for he would never be Augustus alongside us. The decennalia was to him confirmation of his removal from the succession. Of his failure. Just as at Tibur, Father's decision had done little to help bring his sons together.

Apparently deciding that we needed to be further separated, I was called to Father's study in the palace on the very day the festivities ended.

'I have had communiques from the governors of Raetia, Noricum and Pannonia over the past few months requesting extra funds and manpower,' he announced. 'It seems the tribes beyond the river are beginning to rise once more. It has been decades since their defeat under Marcus Aurelius, and paying them off ended with his successor, of course. Now they move once more.'

I nodded. 'The Danubius border was going to come under pressure again eventually. Is it serious?'

'No, I don't believe so. There is no desperation in the requests. For now it is just a rise in activity, with a few raids carried out across the river against small settlements and farms. But the problem is that I have a number of similar requests to deal with. Optatus, Sabinus and Secundus beg for funds and troops all along the Danubius, but I have calls for men and gold also from Maximus and Procilianus in the Syrias, and from Alfenius in Britannia. I have only so many resources to send, and too many places to send them. I am inclined to send those resources to Syria. Britannia has three legions to guard a relatively short frontier, and for all the history of the Danubius, that border is home to one of the strongest concentrations of legions and auxiliary forces in the empire. They should be able to maintain the border with the men they have. Parthia, however, will have had its sights set on us since the day you and I stood in the wreckage of Ctesiphon. Give me your thoughts, Marcus.'

A consultation between emperors. My advice was sought, and not, I know, as a sinecure. I had proved myself in my time, particularly in Africa against the Garamantes. I looked at the map on the wall.

'I agree. Syria is the priority. We must deter Parthia from deciding to annex parts of the East. A new concentration of troops would do that. Britannia has a wall that should be able to hold it safe with the appropriate manpower. Many years ago, when we were there, I learned much from a tribune on the island. The wall is only eighty miles long, with a garrison of more than twenty thousand men and two legions within easy marching distance, a third in reserve. If Alfenius worries over a border of eighty miles with such resources, then he is misusing them and should be replaced.'

I leaned back and folded my arms. 'The Danubius is, indeed, where the problem lies, but I do not believe it is a problem with manpower or funding.'

'Oh?'

'Like the *fossatum* in Africa, which we found in disarray and overrun by both sands and bandits, most of our borders have not been carefully managed since the days of Hadrian and his successor, almost a century ago. Times have changed, and the frontiers have fallen into decay. Domitian, Trajan, Hadrian and Antoninus all fortified the Danubius and the Rhenus, but no one since. I think the problem lies with the organisation and the defences of the frontier, not with the army that mans it.'

He nodded slowly. 'You may be right. What would you do about it all?'

'I would tell Alfenius to put his own house in order, send support to the East, and assign administrators with a good eye for defence to reorganise the border from Raetia to Pannonia, possibly even all the way to Dacia along the rivers.'

He laughed. 'When did you become such an emperor, Marcus?'

'The day you raised me to it.'

He huffed, took a swig of a drink from the wooden cup on the table and leaned back in his chair. 'You dealt with the African border after we crushed the Garamantes. That was five years ago, and we have heard of no trouble since then. Your plans clearly worked. Will you do the same on the Danubius?'

I looked across at the map. 'An imperial visit is always an uplifting thing for the army and the people. If there have been raids, a personal appearance would certainly do no harm in rebuilding confidence.'

'It is agreed, then. I will have men and gold sent to Syria. Alfenius can deal with his own affairs, and you will ride for the Danubius. Take a cohort of the Guard with you. The First seem to favour you, take them. And soon. In the coming days, if you can.'

And that is how by late spring I had left Rome and travelled north. I reasoned that, since there had been no requests from the Germanies, the border was still solid and secure all along the Rhenus. The problem area seemed to lie along that great west–east stretch of the border from Mogontiacum in Upper Germania to Aquincum, where the Danubius turns south. This, then, was where I would concentrate, though I would try and include Moesia and Dacia in my plans, taking a new strengthened border all the way to the Euxine Sea.

I arrived in Mogontiacum at the end of Aprilis and met with the governor. As I suspected, Optatus was simply mismanaging what he had to hand and failing to identify the issues. The area of the upper Rhenus and upper Danubius had always been the weak point of the northern border. Domitian had recognised this and had pushed the border forward to a better defensive line and reinforced it with a chain of forts and fortlets. Hadrian had decided that this was not sufficient, and had added a wooden palisade running the entire length, sealing off the region between the two rivers. His successor had added a ditch and, for the more easterly section, a stone wall. Clearly, this was still not enough.

I spent nine days touring the region and reorganising the system, a whirlwind visit. In even that short time I moved garrisons to dangerous spots that had been overlooked, reinstated a few of the smaller fortlets that had been abandoned in more recent decades, and set things up so that the troops assigned to the frontier had a much better coverage of the area. I listened to tales of the more recent raids and troubles and found where the palisade had been torn down and warbands had taken cattle and slaves from Roman lands. I identified the difficulties in controlling such places, and so we planned leg-breaker ditches, *lilia* pits and the like, to strengthen those areas. In the days since Hadrian and Antoninus, the forests had crept closer once more, and so I ordered half a mile of land outside the frontier cleared, providing a much better field of view, and added to the height of the towers, giving them a better range for archers and spearmen. They were all small tweaks, largely repairing half a century of neglect, but I was confident that they would do the job, and Optatus was satisfied with the results. He was a civil administrator at heart, and a good one, but with little in the way of tactical nous, and he appreciated my help.

I moved east, then, in mid-Maius. The Raetian limes from there to Castra Vetoniana, a region of perhaps a hundred miles, was similar in nature, and the problems were attended in much the same manner. In a matter of days I had dealt with what I saw as the real trouble spot, where the border had always been the weakest. From there, the Danubius became wider and much more difficult to cross. The problems would be different all the way down to Aquincum. What I found there, once again, was half a century of decay and misuse. Units occupying forts too small for them or too large, having been moved around; units split between forts and out of communications reach with each other. Forts positioned in places that would have made excellent forward positions for invasions, as was likely the original intention, but which were in woefully inadequate positions for good defence.

One such was Lauriacum. The fort there had been constructed for a massive garrison, but was occupied by five hundred worried-looking spearmen. It lay on low, marshy ground not far from the great river, and had unimpressive walls. With a little investigation, I found a far better site two small tributaries to the west, three or four miles away. It was on higher ground with a better field of view, controlled all those tributaries, and was closer to the main military road that ran from west to east. This was one of the regions that had suffered badly from recent raids, which meant that the Marcomanni on the far bank were not averse to putting men in boats. A new, large and heavily manned fortress lying close to the various rivers, with better communications and supplies, would be able to react to troubles faster and more efficiently. I had the Second Italica Legion transferred in from a site where they were of little immediate use, and the unit of spearmen reassigned elsewhere. Such was my reorganisation of that border. New heavy fortresses with solid manpower were planned, covering the danger spots, drawing units away from less important places, and all, again, in a matter of days, where the governors had taken months to do nothing.

As the kalends of Junius approached I moved on and settled into the Pannonian Limes. I had little worry for Carnuntum at its heart – that great city and fortress had ever been the centre of Rome's military and administration in the region, and little change was needed, for it would take a truly brave enemy to attempt to cross the river there.

I was in Brigetio in early Junius, settling into the largest garrison on that stretch of border. I spent my time in an office with maps of the region to either side and before me various military and architectural treatises that I used as my basis for defensive systems. I was attended by officers from the region, including the four Pannonia legates, but also the commanders of both the Fifth Macedonica and Seventh Claudia, come from Dacia and Moesia to attend on a reorganisation that might affect their own provinces.

We were held up in Brigetio by a series of summer storms, though I enjoyed my first few days there. The fortress was the home of the First Adiutrix Legion, one of those which had proclaimed my father emperor back at the fall of Pertinax, and remaining our most loyal of all military units. Indeed, some third of the Praetorian cohort that had accompanied me from Rome had been promoted from this legion fourteen years ago, and many of them renewed old friendships. Our relaxation was not to last for long, though.

As the winds howled and the summer rain beat down, with Vulcan's hammer smashing at his anvil echoing across the sky, trouble found us. A unit of cavalry lancers, the Ala I Ulpia Contariorum, was based at Arrabona, twenty-five miles west along the river, one of the sites I planned to look into when the weather broke. I was too late. That stormy morning, five of its riders limped into Brigetio, injured and exhausted. One fell from his horse, dead in the saddle, even as I emerged from the headquarters building, wrapped as ever in my caracallus against the rain.

Officers were rushing from every direction to converge on the stricken horsemen, while outside the walls, a crowd had begun to gather despite the weather, seeing the men ride past.

'What tidings?' demanded a senior tribune, reaching the men first.

'The Quadi, sir,' the rider answered, breathless. 'They came in the storm.'

My heart lurched. The smallest unit in the area would be five hundred men, and I believed this *ala* to be of a thousand riders. If a few injured survivors had come here with news, how many of the Quadi were there? The tribune pre-empted my question as I joined the growing officer corps around the battered arrivals.

'How many?'

'Four thousand, sir. Maybe five. Our scouts from the fort had word of the crossing and the commander sent three *turmae* out to send them packing, for we presumed it to be just another raid. The turmae were overrun and killed. Two more sent to check on them were battered and harried all the way back to Arrabona. We'd lost a hundred and fifty men before the Quadi reached the fort and laid siege to it.'

'How did you get out?' I asked.

'We are the survivors of the second scout group, Domine,' he answered bowing, eyes lowered as he realised to whom he was speaking.

'We watched the Quadi reach Arrabona and then rode here with the news, via the forts of Ad Statuas and Ad Mures.'

I turned to the gathering of generals and officers. 'Why would the Quadi risk a large incursion? 5000 is not enough for an invasion, but far more than any small raid requires.'

Attius, the legate of the First, shrugged. 'Driven by a poor harvest, I would say, Domine. The weather has been too wet this summer for the farmers of the region, and the Quadi do not have the grain reserves to fall back on like the empire. Arrabona has well-stocked granaries, but is one of the weaker military targets in the area.'

I nodded. 'And since the breakdown of relations with Rome they can hardly ask for help. Raids are almost to be expected, but incursions on this scale cannot be tolerated. We need to remind them of our strength and deter them from such moves. Attius, can your First take on four or five thousand Quadi?'

The man simply nodded, but beside him, Piso, visiting from Dacia, gave a vicious smile. 'I brought half a cohort of the Fifth Macedonica with me too, Domine, and you have a cohort of Praetorians. I suspect they'd love to wet their blades with Quadi blood.'

I nodded. Over six thousand veteran legionaries and Praetorians should be able to break four or five thousand tribesmen. The signals were given, horns sounded, and the legions mustered on the parade ground outside Brigetio, each man huddled beneath his cloak against the warm rain that hammered down relentlessly.

In half an hour we were on the move, a strange force, centred on the First but bulked out with parts of a dozen different local or visiting units – every man who could be spared. We armed light, leaving behind all non-essential equipment. Arrabona was some twenty miles from Brigetio, and with a forced march we could reach the place in four hours, so there would be no need for camp supplies. We marched at speed.

To everyone's great relief the storm broke in the early afternoon as we approached the forts of Ad Mures and Ad Statuas, two forts close together, guarding a dangerous crossing point, too strong a position for the Quadi to consider. We picked up the garrisons there, a small *vexillation* of the First and a mixed Thracian cavalry and infantry unit, and paused just long enough for the men to eat, before moving off once more. Though the rain had stopped, it had battered down now for so many days that the ground squelched beneath us and the gravel roads were little more than rivers of grey water. We gratefully removed our cloaks, for though we had needed them against the rain, it was high summer, and the temperatures were far from chilly.

Just an hour from Arrabona we found the survivors of the Ulpia Contariorum. Three hundred lancers, half of them wounded, all exhausted and on tired horses, their position half marching camp, half hospital ward, *capsarii* at work on the many injuries. They had fought to defend Arrabona as long as they could, but their commander had ordered a break-out when it became clear they were doomed, and they had simply barged their way through the Quadi to freedom, losing men in droves on the way. I did not castigate them. They had suffered losses of seven men in ten and had fought for a whole day. No one could ask more of a unit.

We pressed on, hungry now for vengeance for what the Quadi had done. Starving they might be, but there could be no accepting such an attack. It was a warm, sunny, damp mid-afternoon when the scouts returned and informed us that they had sighted the enemy. Orders were given and we moved into battle formations as we approached, creating a wide front, with the First at the centre, supported by the Praetorians on the left and the cohort of the Fifth on the right, the riders and auxilia at the flanks. Arrabona lay abandoned, but intact. The Quadi were not here for conquest or revenge, but for theft and pillage.

They had already raided the granaries, but were now in the process of taking their ill-gotten winnings back to their own lands. A flotilla of boats of native style, alongside a few small stolen Roman ships, were tied up at the bank while the tribesmen loaded the stolen grain aboard. The bulk of the Quadi remained on this bank, guarding the grain that was yet to be loaded, and the officers looked to me. I gave the order.

As the army swept forth, I found myself regretful. I had not been expecting war or campaigning, and I had no real place leading men here. I discovered in that moment that I missed commanding my Berber riders, and it was heartening when the tribune in command of the Praetorian cohort bowed and sought my orders. I rode over to meet him, and as the army began to surge forward, I joined that tribune in command of the Praetorians.

It was not a strategic conflict. There was no time really for tactics or plans. The enemy were stealing grain and we had caught them just in time. The Roman force, which outnumbered them by almost three men to two, charged, bellowing cries to Mars, Minerva, Bellona, Jupiter, Mithras and half a dozen local gods. The Quadi went into something of a panic. They had learned we were approaching only moments earlier, as the legion hoved into distant view, and their leaders did what they could. The tribes turned and surged forward to meet us, or at least two thirds of them did, while the rest continued to work, getting the grain boats safely into the water and out of our reach.

The fight was short and brutal. Historians will always tell you of flanking manoeuvres and heroic generals plugging gaps in the lines, horsemen breaking shieldwalls and so on, and on occasion these things do happen. The vast majority of battles, though, simply involve two great forces smashing into one another, howling, stabbing, slashing and battering until one loses either heart or too many men, and breaks. It is a simple question of numbers and endurance, and often tactics do not even come to bear. Such was the fight at Arrabona. I was almost involved. I came so close to the action I thought I would be able to blood my sword, and such is my nature that I do like to bloody it once I've drawn it. But the Praetorians' and their tribune's very reason for existence was to make sure the imperial family was safe from danger, and every time I almost reached the fray, there were suddenly Praetorians between me and the Quadi. Still, it can have escaped the attention of few that I was in the thick of it and trying to do my part.

The Quadi broke first, after a little more than half an hour of combat. Though they were desperate, and trapped on our side of the river, they were exhausted. They had been on this grand raid for over a day without sleep and had spent much of it fighting or moving grain, while we were well-rested and had covered the distance in five hours. Moreover, they were poorly armed and hungry, while we were Rome's best veteran soldiers, heavily armed and well fed. It really was a foregone conclusion.

The Quadi fled back to the river, where their colleagues were still loading boats. Dozens of vessels were already out in the water, ferrying their prize back towards tribal lands, and already almost half the grain stores had gone, the rest standing in piles of sodden sacks on the near shore. The officers looked to me for instructions. I glanced at the panicked Quadi on the shore. They could probably be made to surrender. Be enslaved. But I was angry. How dare they think to steal the grain needed by our own hungry people? Marcus Aurelius had been right to attempt their conquest and overthrow. I looked to the men.

'No quarter.'

And that was that. I watched, impassive, as the Quadi were cut down to a man, every last figure butchered – Anullinus' old maxim in play. When the only surviving tribesmen were the ones out in the water on boats, we surveyed the situation. I gestured to the sacks of grain stacked waiting to be ferried, and turned to the others. 'The grain is wet. Can it be saved?'

One of the men called over his quartermaster and asked of him, then approached me with the answer. 'It may be salvageable, Domine, but likely no more than half of it. They have had it all out in the rain far too long for comfort.'

I nodded slowly. 'Save what can be saved. Have it returned to the granaries to dry out, and we'll see what we can do.'

'What about them, Domine?' Piso asked, and I followed his finger out across the water.

'If we cannot have the grain, then neither can they.'

I watched as the legions began to ferry the grain back to the fort of Arrabona and the safety of its granaries, and as the artillerists hurried up to the fort walls to man the weapons there. The Quadi had left the artillery alone. They were no engineers, after all. In moments, the legions were cranking back torsion weapons and loosing fist-sized stones or foot-long bolts out across the water from the heights of the fort defences. The Quadi had presumed themselves safe out on the river. They were wrong. I watched as boat after boat took a rock or a bolt to the hull and began to wallow, gradually disappearing below the surface as their crews shouted and wailed desperately. We did not get them all, of course, but we sank enough to make our point. The Quadi had thought to cross in the cover of the storms and steal a season's worth of grain from a weakly guarded store. They had learned a hard lesson, for they had managed to return with just a handful of grain sacks that were probably already too sodden to save and would start to germinate before they could be used, and had lost thousands of their warriors in the process. One thing that everyone seemed confident of was that such a move would not be repeated in a hurry.

I stayed at Arrabona for four days as things were settled, the dead buried and the sacks checked. It seemed that more than half the grain could be saved, which was a relief for all. The ala based here were given a donative of imperial coin and I vowed to grant honours to them for their service. But they were also badly diminished, and I pledged to ship them out until they could be restored to strength. The First Adiutrix put in a temporary garrison, and I gave orders for all the forts from here to Brigetio to be enlarged and strengthened with good stone walls and towers.

The brief campaign over with resounding success, I returned to Brigetio and continued my work there. By the end of the summer, a statue had been raised in my honour at Arrabona, paid for and dedicated by Piso, the legate of the Fifth, and Egnatius Victor, the Pannonian governor. I was immensely pleased, of course, though deep in my soul I was a little embarrassed that my entire part in the battle had been trying to get to the fight and being held back by my over-protective Praetorians. Still, as autumn came around, everything was in place, and the Quadi had sent gifts and tributes across the river in the hope that I could be mollified and would not send a force there in retribution. The border was settled, and I was satisfied that my changes here, along with those all the way to Germania, would prevent future troubles. I spent the autumn and the early winter continuing on down the Danubius, heading towards the Euxine Sea and speaking to officers and governors, tweaking the defences and fortifications as I went. I spent two months in Dacia, where the borders shifted from time to time, and incursions were not uncommon. Piso and I reorganised the defences there, and I devoted more imperial funds to the task than I really should have. I spent time throwing spectacles for the people in the towns there, granting honours to the military garrisons and generally being a golden imperial presence, and the people reacted well. By the time Saturnalia approached, the whole province of Dacia had given a special place in their hearts to myself and to Father.

It was three days before Saturnalia when a message arrived for me via dispatch rider. My father needed me back in Rome. The situation in Britannia had apparently deteriorated seriously and needed our urgent attention. It seemed I was to go directly from one war to another. Despite the urgency of the message, I allowed myself Saturnalia, for the people of Albanum had devoted considerable attention and funding to special celebrations for the presence of their emperor. Soon, though, the festival was past, a new year beckoned, and so did Britannia. I was sad to leave, but my work was done here, and new ground awaited.

XIV

For Britannia

Britannia, AD 208

I had enjoyed my time on the Danubius. Even with the summer storms, the times of deprivation, the work and the battle against the barbarians from across the river, I had enjoyed it all.

Before I left Dacia, other messages had started arriving for the governor and higher military officers there, and I had some idea of the scale of what Father was planning from the fact that he had called upon the Danubian fleet, based in Dacia and Moesia, to send a number of vessels to join the force he was assembling. If he was bringing ships from the Euxine Sea, where else was the army being drawn from? It was useful, though, for the fleet was able to convey me and my entourage, and even the Praetorian cohort, back to Rome in the process. We sailed then from Tomis in the worst season for sailing, and took almost a month to reach our destination.

I returned to Rome via Ostia Portus with the usual adventus. I was met at the fifth mile marker by senators, priests, dancers, musicians, acrobats, fire-eaters and a gushing public, and from there was escorted into the city like a hero of old. As we approached the forum on the way to the Palatine, I was greeted by a sight that immediately set my teeth on edge. Statues to the two consuls for the year had been set up near the curia, and they were very clearly Geta and me. I'd not been told I would be consul again.

'You took your time,' Father grunted at me by way of greeting as I walked into his office.

'It is winter,' I replied in a similar tone. He looked up at me from a map, and gave me a curt nod. 'I needed you back. Britannia requires our attentions. There have been troubles in the North, spurred by the tribes beyond the walls. Alfenus Senecio, it seems, was not magnifying the danger there a year ago. He has fought a battle in the North and claims a victory over one of those tribes, but he seems to believe that has just driven more tribes into revolt.'

I shrugged. 'Tribes who revolt need to be either punished or bought off. Britannia is so distant, so small, so unimportant in the grand scheme, I would have given Alfenus a chest or two of gold and told him to buy peace with them. He has the most impressive wall in the empire and a massive concentration of manpower. He should at least be able to keep the peace.'

Father shook his head. 'I am of a mind to finish Agricola's job. I will see the north of the island subdued and added to the province. Once the system of bringing them into the empire is underway the military can be thinned out and men spared for use elsewhere. I am not gathering a punitive army, but an invasion force. We go to add Caledonia to the empire, Marcus.'

I pictured what that tribune from long ago had told me of the north of Britannia. Hilly, wet, cold, primitive, few resources worth mentioning. It did not sound to me worth the effort. At least Dacia had gold. And since the day we'd stood in Ctesiphon, I'd had plans brewing in the East.

'If we simply bought them off and settled things for now, we would have the forces available to go east, Father.'

'No,' he said, his tone flat, final. 'Our work in Parthia has given them something to think about, and now that we have bolstered our frontier there, the old enemy has withdrawn from any danger zone. There is no pressure in the East, and we have received overtures. The Parthians need time to recover, and we have already bought generations of peace there. Now we will complete the North.'

I pictured those dusty, sandy palaces of wonders out in ancient Persia longingly. Alexander's domain. I had vowed already to add those lands to the empire. Now, here, we had the chance, and instead Father intended to use them to add a soggy swamp on the fringes of the known world to the imperial bosom. A hole to the whole, you might say.

'Alexander's empire, Father. We could extend the borders all the way to India with one campaign. We could secure the silk road from their grasp, secure the spice and incense routes through Arabia, and permanently remove a thorn from Rome's side. Imagine what we could do...'

'No, Marcus. The decision has been made. We are for Britannia.'

There would be no further argument, and the strategy was then laid before me. I do have to admit to being impressed at Father's plans. I might not agree with the need for this campaign, but he was determined to do it right. Agricola had conquered the North a century and a half earlier with three legions and auxilia numbering about the same. We would have a force three times that size. Agricola had been the first man to recognise the value of the navy on the island, and had utilised the local fleet to good effect. We would have a massive fleet drawn from all around the empire. And where Agricola's conquest had been fleeting, thanks to disasters drawing the manpower away before consolidation could begin, Father was determined that this time we would stay. He made a good case for it, and by the time we left Rome, I was almost in agreement. *Almost.*

There was one niggling problem. Father's health had declined a little further in my absence that year. His feet were now hurting him so much that he rarely walked more than a mile, and was much more reliant upon horses and litters. His breathing was shallow, to my mind, though the *medicus* I consulted surreptitiously assured me that there was nothing wrong with him. Certainly, with the exception of walking too little, he acted as if there was nothing wrong. Agricola had been at the peak of his life in Britannia, while Father seemed to be fading. Would he be up to the task, I wondered?

The army had, of course, been moving since late in the previous year. It was late Martius before we embarked at Ostia with half of Rome's toga-wearing fools and half the empire's administration in our retinue. All but one cohort of Praetorians was with us, as well as sundry units drawn from the local provinces. We used the Misenum Fleet to take us to Britannia, and there found the massed forces that had been marching north and west for months assembling in a huge temporary camp at Gesoriacum on the coast of Gaul and being ferried across on a daily rota by the Germanic and Britannic Fleets.

Geta was to be assigned a command in the campaign, and I realised that for the first time in countless years, I was in a strong position to bridge the chasm between us. It had been a while now since Plautianus had gone, plenty of time for my brother to recover. Father would be concentrating on the campaign and not on misguided attempts to help that only hindered. Geta was being given a strong position with a chance of glory for the first time, and had no cause to feel overshadowed by me. It was an opportunity.

I used my time aboard the ships for Britannia, and in our overnight stops, carefully. I tried to speak to Geta directly, alone, more than once, and was greeted only with cold distance. The fire of anger seemed to have gone from the looks he threw my way these days, but what I saw in them was little better. Shiftiness. Duplicity. It reminded me so much of Plautianus that it made me shiver. I had thought that with the man gone, his influence would fade, but I now began to worry that the effect of that relationship had been permanent enough even to outlast death.

As such, I tried to find oblique ways to bring us together. On the voyage north, I repeatedly engineered evenings with the commanders and generals of the army, pondering tactical and strategic issues of the coming campaign, and trying to draw my brother into the discussions, to open up a dialogue with which I could work. Sadly, it seems I had inherited from Father not only my anger, but also his tendency to attempt reconciliations that only ended up having the opposite effect. In trying to draw Geta into military discussions, I only ended up highlighting how little he knew, his ignorance of all things military. By the time we were approaching Britannia, we were no closer to reconciliation, and instead, the officer class were beginning to worry about the young Caesar taking a command role among them.

My plans had backfired on a monumental scale. Father, persuaded by the voices of all around him that Geta was not made for a military campaign, decided on a new course for us. As we rode north across the verdant landscape of Britannia, making for the trouble zone and the old walls there, the campaign was rearranged. Father would take overall command, of course, as was expected, and I would be his second in command, naturally. But there the military leadership ended. Geta was out of the staff. Instead, he was to be given control of the civil sphere in Britannia. It seemed that Alfenus Senecio had not survived his campaign the previous year unscathed. Some illness he had contracted was weakening him, and so Geta was assigned as *iuridicus*, a viceroy to deal with the governance of the island, while we continued to press the war in the North.

Things are done a certain way in Rome: the war season starts with the Tubilustrium festival in late Martius, and ends with Armilustrium in mid-October, when the war trumpets are put away for the winter. It was already into Junius when we arrived on the island, and it would take months to have the army moved north and made ready for campaign, given the sheer scale of the force Father had put together. By the time we were ready to move, winter would loom, and we were given to understand that winter north of the wall was not something to be treasured. So we arrived in the northern city of Eboracum, where we would set up court for the duration of the campaign. From here Alfenus and my brother would administer island and empire, while Father would oversee the grand plan, and I would deal with the on-the-ground minutiae of command.

It suited me. While Father spent most of his time sitting down in the governor's palace in Eboracum, or lounging in the baths, soaking his sore feet, and Geta pored over lists and accounts, I was given free rein by Father to deal with all things military in preparation for the next year. I took to the task with gusto. First was the matter of defence.

Sounds idiotic, I know. We were readying an invasion, yet I looked to defence? But there is a good reason. Any people, when faced with such an event, might just take any opportunity to break their enemy. We would spend the winter in garrison, organising, and so the Caledonii and the Maetae, and the other tribes in the region might take the chance of hitting garrisons here and there, weakening us before we began. As such, I would look to the old defences in the region and make them stronger, just as I had done in both Africa and along the Danubius.

Over a few months of late autumn, I took a hand-picked force to explore the region in which we would be campaigning and the various defensive systems that kept the enemy away. My force constituted Praetorians, Batavian horsemen, members of the Sixth Legion from Eboracum, and, to my great delight, Berber cavalry, who had been brought all the way from the sands of Africa for the campaign. We explored the length of the wall built by Hadrian, which was south of the real danger zone. As such, I reorganised the forces there and had changes made and repairs begun, removing the line's status as a border and utilizing it instead as a massive reserve garrison and storage depot. At the extreme eastern end lay a fort on a hill by the river, where the garrison was struggling under the weight of grain that was being shipped in to support the army. I had the garrison reduced, but the fort expanded and reorganised to contain masses of granaries, turning it into the army's grain store for the campaign. Moving north, we found the abandoned wall of Antoninus, half as long, but with a stronger concentration of forts. This I rejuvenated, returning the forts to active status, moving forward garrisons to it from the southern wall, and expanding the military systems between the two walls. This would be the frontier from which we would launch our great campaign. From here, I explored further that autumn, moving into lands that had seen no Roman boot since Agricola.

From that wall, a road led to an abandoned fort of immense proportions and impressive defences. This I had garrisoned, and sent messages to move strong forces into the area. It would make an excellent headquarters for a northerly push. From the fort, a ridge followed a line to the north and east, all the way to the sea, and along it from beginning to end were the long-broken remnants of forts, fortlets and signal towers unused in more than a century. At the time I had not the manpower with me to re-form this line, but it would be one of my first goals when we advanced.

While we stayed in that impressive fort of Alauna, we had two surprise visits. The first, not long after our arrival, had come from the north, from those brooding purple hills that marked the start of Britannia's trouble. The Caledonii, it seems, are not a tribe, but a collection of tribes gathered under one flag, in the manner, I suppose, of the provinces of the empire. They are individual and all very different, but they exist as one, and when threatened they fight as one. When not threatened, of course, they fight each other.

The leaders of the Caledonii were distinguishable principally in three ways. First, they wore more bronze and gold than their fellows. Secondly, their guards and lackeys hung around them. Thirdly, they seemed to have acquired good Roman cloaks, belts, rings and brooches. In some ways they seemed too hard to be trying to be Roman. They came in a haughty manner, riding light chariots pulled by small ponies. Initially, my men were not keen on letting them into the fort, but in the end they did so at my command, leaving the bulk of their retinue outside, only an honour guard to accompany them.

Their haughty manner disappeared when they spoke. It seemed of the four leaders who had come, two could speak a reasonable level of

Latin. The other two either couldn't, or, more likely, refused to. Thus they had a man speak for them as a translator. Their words came across immediately as rather obsequious. They represented the Caledonian confederacy. They regretted such troubles as had been caused over the past few years and blamed dangerous sects within their own people, telling us that the problem was being brought under control. They would take oaths that no future raids or troubles would come across into Roman lands, and would provide us with tribute... if we agreed to stay behind the 'old stone wall'.

I would have liked to have given them the answer I knew they would get from Father – a sword in the gut – but while I had the authority to do so, we were still in our stage of preparation, and I was hoping for a peaceful winter while we organised. As such, I told them that I would need to pass this to the emperor, my father, and until he made a decision we would occupy such positions as we currently did, but would move no further. They were temporarily satisfied with this, and offered their hope that we could come to an arrangement. Then they left, and we continued the preparations for conquest.

A matter of days later we received a deputation from the other confederacy of tribes, the Maetae. This group occupies the lower lands, between the Caledonii and the wall of Antoninus. They had more to lose than the Caledonii, of course, for they were a closer target, living just north of the old walls. Here I truly learned to employ something I had begun to understand in the presence of Plautianus. That man could silver-talk a Vestal virgin into a threesome, and there was no trusting anything he said, but I had discovered from the very beginning that he was unable to force the lie into his eyes, and there, if you watched carefully, the truth always lurked. That was something I found also with the Maetae. They offered a heartfelt alliance. They told us how they had always suffered border raids from the Caledonian tribes, while they were a lowland people with more in common with the tribes that now paid at least lip service to Rome. They told us they welcomed Rome's presence, and would even supply us with food and scouts to help us move north and east against the Caledonii. They were so damn convincing that half the officers with me were ready to shake their hands.

I saw their eyes.

They were much cleverer than the Caledonii. They saw that we had come in response to the raids of the past few years and neatly laid the blame with the more northerly confederation of tribes, with whom they'd clearly had feuds since days immemorial. They offered to support us as we crushed their enemies for them. Of course, they could not know that conquest was now our goal. It had been a century since any Roman presence had been felt north of the wall. They assumed we were there purely to chastise and then withdraw. The Maetae were using us against their opposition. Well, two could play at that game. I gave warning looks to my officers and then fixed a trusting and innocent expression, not an easy thing to do with my face, I can assure you, and came to an agreement with the Maetae. We would leave them alone while we moved against the Caledonii, and they would give us aid. I was very careful with my wording, for I do not like to break my word. I never once promised that we would not move against them. Just not yet.

And so, the north of Britannia was prepared for the coming war. Half the enemy thought we could be persuaded to leave them alone, and the other half thought they were using us and would then be left in peace. And all that time, what was actually happening was that some way south, where they could not look, so many thousand iron-clad soldiers were gathering and training, equipping and preparing, that they could stand side-by-side and their weight might sink the island.

As winter set in, I left things to be settled there and moved back south to the old wall. My plans were already being put into effect. Forts were being redesigned, monumental double-arched gates turned into single ones with blocking stones, barracks and workshops replaced with granaries, roads driven into forests, fortlets and signal stations reinstated connecting the far north with our campaign bases.

And then back to Eboracum.

I had been away for months only, and the difference in that place was immediately visible upon my return. The fortress on one side of the river was filled to the brim, and other units had set up semi-permanent camps around it wherever they could. On the near side of the river, where the civil town sat behind heavy walls, the place seemed to have been cleaned, partially rebuilt, cleared of mess and vagrants, lined with imperial guards, and the governor's palace had been massively extended and enriched, with a new bath house and a barracks attached, its own perimeter wall patrolled by Praetorians. Father had made this place fit for the court, for wherever an emperor travels, he is always the centre of government and so, in effect, Eboracum was now Rome. A massive bridge of heavy stone was almost complete, replacing a century-old wooden one. The whole fabric of Eboracum was becoming an imperial centre.

Other changes had begun, too. From what I was told upon my arrival, the civil administration of both Britannia and the empire as a whole was largely being run from a series of offices filled by Geta and his cronies, including the lacklustre governor of Britain whose mismanagement was largely responsible for our being here in the first place. It appeared, beyond expectations, that my brother was showing some talent in the job.

While I had been laying the groundwork for Father's planned invasion of the North, Father had been soaking his feet in healing waters and enjoying the delights of Eboracum, and had, more or less, promoted Geta to run the empire.

Satisfied that all was running smoothly, and before I had a chance to find Geta and interrupt his work, I went to see Mother. She was not in the palace, and I found her, of all places, on the almost complete new bridge. Small skiffs shot back and forth across the river carrying the daily traffic, for the bridge was closed to the general public until complete. For now, legionary engineers from the Sixth were busy working on it, Praetorians having sealed off both ends, and Mother stood at the centre of the length with Papinian, the Praetorian prefect, the two of them talking in low tones while they watched the sluggish grey waters pass beneath.

'Marcus,' she said, turning and noticing my approach, 'I did not know you were back.'

She hurried over from the parapet and threw her arms about me. I let it happen, enfolding her in my own embrace and patting her lovingly on the back in the process.

'I've been here but an hour. Things have changed. Geta is running the empire?'

She nodded, turned back and gestured to Papinian, who bowed and walked away, far out of earshot like the protective Praetorians, leaving us more or less alone.

'Things have been organised the way they must. Your father is not well.'

'He's not been well for a year or more. It was still a risk putting my brother in such a prominent role. Lucky that he seems to have some talent.' But I could see the concern writ upon her features and I felt a nagging worry scythe into me too, then. 'How ill *is* he?'

'His feet are unbearable. He manages a few steps at a time, walks perhaps three times daily. His gut hurts him and he is tired all the time. Worse, because he is in pain all the time, he sleeps little, and the exhaustion has made him vague and forgetful, not to mention cranky. That, Marcus, is why Geta is running the administration. Your brother is Caesar. His word is now that of the emperor. Next spring your father will go with you to the North, perhaps in a litter, perhaps on a horse...' I realised there were tears in her eyes, and that I really wasn't expecting. 'And I do not think he will come back,' she finished with a shudder.

'He cannot be that ill.'

'He hides much. He was ever a man of action and of strength. He will not wish to fade and rot in bed. He will want to go out on campaign, like a general of old. The real control of the campaign is going to come down to you. Even if he is in his best days, you will still be stronger, brighter and healthier than him.'

She took a step away from me.

'And that is when your brother will be elevated.'

I blinked. 'What?'

'In the new year. You will rule alongside your Father and help guide and command the campaign in the North. But your brother will be made Augustus, a co-emperor alongside you both, for he now rules Rome in many ways. And when your father's health...' she faltered then, tears brimming once more. 'If your father does not come back, there will still be two emperors.'

I fought the many emotions crowding my head, then. For years, I had hated my brother, had been almost at war with him. I had been adamant that he would never find a place in the succession, for I was the older brother, bred for rule, and I would have a son to follow me as Caesar. Yet since the fall of Plautianus, the possibility of a reconciliation had been dangling tantalisingly before me. Geta's elevation might just possibly be that one thing needed to bring us back together, since we would effectively be equals...

…but what if it didn't? What if Geta clung to the ghost of Plautianus and continued to hold me to account? What if he could not accept a reconciliation, and instead took his raising as an opportunity to oust and replace me? It was a thorny problem. To do nothing and smile was to risk everything for which I hoped. But to make a move would very likely end any possibility of ending our feud.

I made feeble excuses to Mother and left her to it. I was faced with an impossible choice. The only thing I could do was to speak to Geta, to gauge where we stood, to weigh up the options with more information to hand. But the last time I'd seen him was when we landed in Britannia, and my attempts at including him had effectively stripped him of military command. I remembered the bitter looks he'd thrown at me then. Would a season of scribbling in ledgers while I rode with the army have lessened his irritation? I doubted it.

Unable to decide upon the best way to go, in the end I made a foolish decision that was neither option. I went to get drunk. I found a *caupona* near the end of the bridge, where the Praetorians following me protectively emptied the place of its customers so I could drink in safety, and I did just that. I drank what passed for wine, both watered and unwatered. I drank their beer, which tasted like wine that has already been drunk once. I even tasted some dreadful spirit they make out of rotten fruit, which left me feeling slightly sick and with a sore throat.

I drank far too much.

And a man in that state should never be allowed to make important decisions. I rose, suddenly, lurching a little, swayed, and then marched towards the door, set upon a path of confronting my brother. If he could be made to see reason, perhaps all would be wonderful. If not… my fingers toyed with the hilt of my eating knife.

As I reached the doorway, figures moved to block my exit. Papinian, with half a century of Guardsmen. He shook his head.

'Go home and cool off, my emperor,' he said.

'Get out of my way.'

'No. I have the orders from your mother to keep the two of you apart. You know me, Marcus Aurelius Antoninus. You know I am no mad killer, no power-seeker. You know me for a man of law and reason, of philosophy and truth. Listen to me now, I cannot let you hunt your brother. Go to the fortress, find the baths, find a group of soldiers and play some dice, find a whore and play some bed games. And then, when your blood has cooled in the morning, I will arrange a meeting with your father.'

For a moment, I frowned, wondering why he thought I intended to 'hunt' Geta, before I realised I was still gripping my eating knife, and my face was probably creased into anger. It is my natural look, after all. I was impotent. Only me against Papinian and half a century of Praetorians. There was nothing I could do. In the end, I did exactly what he said, on all three counts. But all that night I was plagued by an image of my brother in the robes of an emperor, at my shoulder, where my son should be.

In the morning I went back to the palace to meet with my father.

My blood had cooled, as Papinian said it would.

It had cooled to ice. Reconciliation or no reconciliation, I would share my throne with no man after Father.

XV

Caledonian Strongholds

Caledonia, AD 209

I never had the chance to confront Geta following that binge, which may or may not have been a good thing. From my meeting with Father onwards, I was kept busy with the military sphere, then sent north once more. Where our scouts and native geographers told us there were swamps, and by the gods there were some swamps up here, we spent the winter having legionaries construct raised walkways through them for ease of movement. Where there were thick forests, the legions cut thoroughfares through the middle. We built harbours, forts, ditches, ramparts. The winter was busy, and all the work was mine to command, for Father's increasing disability kept him in the palace in Eboracum. All this work kept me safely away from Geta, of course, who was just as fully occupied with trying to bring the unruly province back to full working order, locked away in rooms with men with bald heads and pointy beards who complained about money all the time.

So it was that I only actually saw my brother three times through the whole winter, and never when we were alone. Never personally enough to discuss my problem.

Martius came, the trumpets were given their ritual preparation, and the army prepared to move. In an impressive moment of unity; the entire family came together to try and persuade my father against taking an active part in the campaign. He could hardly walk now, and used a stick when he had to, preferring to ride or, even better, sit in a comfortable litter. His digestion caused him endless trouble, and he was becoming weak, which was strange and disconcerting to see in my ever-robust father. Mother, I, and even Geta, tried to argue that he stay in Eboracum. I'd been well-trained for what we must do, after all, and had spent the winter preparing. But he was insistent. He had begun this campaign and, though he was quite aware that it would probably be his last, he was determined to be part of it, to add Britannicus to the epithets of his name.

We moved north with the spring, watching the world change around us. I began to see a certain strange, rugged beauty to this hard land, where before I had always seen it as wanting. With the disappearance of the snows, the mists and the grey, it became a world of bleak hilltop wonders, secretive valleys and, towards the east, rich, green farmland. I could finally see why someone might want to own the place. The grain from the east would be good, and if those hills held any sort of ore deposits, the place could perhaps be made to pay for the cost of its conquest.

Our first contact was, once again, with the Maetae. True to their word, they supplied us with native scouts who knew the terrain and their neighbouring tribes, including slaves and hostages taken from the Caledonii many years ago in local wars. They supplied us with extra goods, and aided our transport north.

The Caledonii awaited.

Of course, they knew now that there would be war. We would be no surprise, for their overtures in the autumn had gone unanswered. I hoped that the delay had cost them important time to gather forces and organise. I had read my Tacitus time and again over the winter, familiarising myself with the campaigns of Agricola here over a century ago, for, alone of all Romans, he led a successful war up here, while all others had failed and withdrawn.

Agricola had concentrated on marching up the East, along that flat land, supported by the navy on the coast. Despite a few troubles, he took control of all the lowlands with seeming ease. His problem was that the Caledonii would not meet him in battle willingly. They attacked in the night, or came by surprise and massacred garrisons. It was only by starving them over several years, by blocking them off from their farmland, that he forced them to meet him on his preferred terrain, where he overwhelmed and destroyed them. It seemed to me that this was the solution, then. Fighting on their terms would never work, if we campaigned in a traditional manner. We had to emulate that great general and bring them to fight on ours. We would reoccupy all the system that he created, and attempt to repeat his success.

All my plans unravelled the day before we moved out from Alauna. As evening set in and the army made camp, utilising the ramparted enclosures that had been here for a hundred years already, I spoke to the gathered generals and my father. I tapped the great map on the wall.

'Here, and here, and here, here and here are fort positions that were designed specifically to seal off the easy approaches into the Caledonian highlands. It is my intention to ignore the more recent forts in the low areas and concentrate on blockading the tribes. I understand that their hills and valleys are not even particularly good for grazing, and the tribes rely heavily upon grain from the East and upon low grazing lands out this way. The longer we can cut them off, the more hungry and desperate they will become. Like Agricola before us, we can force them to come out from their hills in force, and destroy them on our terms. Once we've broken their main army we can afford to begin the process of moving into their territory and securing it, but until then we run the risk of being destroyed in detail like Varus' legions in Germania.'

The various nods told me eloquently that the officers saw the sense in my plan.

'No.'

I turned with a frown. Father was drumming his fingers on the chair arm.

'No?'

'No. It took Agricola four years from this very position to bring them to battle. Had Domitian not withdrawn the troops, it would almost certainly have taken another four to mop up the endless pockets of resistance that arise after such a victory, and place forts for control. I cannot tarry here so long. Two years. I give this campaign two years. We have a force much grander than that of Agricola. We have an extra century of knowledge and experience. We have the Maetae as allies. We have advantages he did not. I vowed to the senate when they balked at the cost of this enterprise that the campaign would be swift and decisive and that Britannia could be settled and profitable within a few short years. I cannot afford to drag this out.'

Now the generals were nodding in agreement with my father, fickle bunch that they were.

I was ready to argue my point, for I knew damn well I was right, and so did every military mind in that room, but I also knew the look on Father's face, and knew that there was no debate to be had. His mind was made up. I waited, sullen and frowning, as he laid out a different plan that involved, to my mind, a near-suicidal decision to extend the army up the East as far as Agricola had ever reached, to the great glen that cuts the highlands in half, and then move into their territory from several positions by early-to-mid-summer. His plan split our large army up into small forces, and then marched them directly into the enemy's open arms, fighting on their terms. I was aghast. I waited until the generals were dismissed, and then sent away everyone, from Praetorian to body slave, until I was alone with my father.

'Stupid,' I said.

'What?' He was angry with me, but I could see that he no longer had the vim and energy he'd once had to scold me. He looked more exhausted than furious.

'You know my plan is the right one. You were always the strategist. You were the one who taught me even as a boy that the best war of all is the one you don't have to fight. And now, while I offer you a route that could bring us victory with just one fight on our own terms, you intend to throw away thousands of lives in a campaign that offers at best a dubious chance of success.'

'Careful, boy.'

'No. You made me co-emperor for a reason. I wear the purple, and though I love you dearly, I will not sacrifice my position and the safety of the empire on the altar of family.'

'You go too far.'

I sighed.

'I will do as you say, Father,' I announced, rather surprising myself in the circumstances. 'It does not do for an emperor to be openly defied by his peer, and so I will commit to this costly campaign for the public eye. But in return, you promise me this: when the season is over, and we have gained nothing, which I fear will be the outcome, you let me command the next season.'

His eyes narrowed. I was playing a dangerous game, and I knew it, but I was being forced into it.

'Agreed,' he said, finally. 'I will lead this season, and you will lead the next. There shall not be a third, though. Mark my words.'

I nodded, angry but silent. That threw out my plan to emulate Agricola and slowly starve them into a suicidal battle. We would attack them, instead.

We marched north. We occupied all the forts from Agricola's day, dredging the naval basin he had created for the access of our fleet. We took effective control of all the flat arable land in the east, and moved into the highlands repeatedly and in various places, wherever the scouts advised us of Caledonian strongholds. It is not generally appropriate for an emperor to place himself in danger, in the actual thick of a battle, and so I spent most of my time in the rear echelons in command positions. Despite that, though, there are precedents. Domitian rode with his army against the Chattii, after all. Thus, despite the strictures of wearing the purple, I managed to involve myself in one of the pushes. We had an army of immense size, and I had to give it to my father that his tactics, while costly, were actually effective. Each of the vexillations of the army that moved into those forbidding hills was the size of a reasonable invasion force on its own.

The point at which the highlands come nearest to the coast is close to one of our naval bases, Portus Lapidaria, where the hills begin to rise mere miles from the water's edge. There is an old camp there, from the first campaigns in the region, a sprawling mass of odd shape that covers a whole hillside. From there, I led a force of half a legion, three thousand auxiliary infantry, a unit of Hamian archers and, best of all, a mixed force of cavalry, of both Berber and Germanic origin, the former light and fast, the latter armoured and brutal. From the camp we moved west in the height of the summer heat.

We followed a river that quickly shrank as it rose from a lazy flow to a cold, fast and babbling brook, which led us into thickly forested hills. It was not good terrain for us, though thankfully our native scouts could direct us to clear ways and open paths that wound through the territory. We caught the scent of our prey half a dozen times over the first two days of our advance. We found settlements that had been abandoned recently enough that they had not yet begun to show signs of decay, but never did we find the enemy. It did occur to me that there was every possibility that we were being led into a trap, a fly to the Caledonian spider, but we could not abandon our advance. It would be unthinkable for a general to march back out without drawing blood, marking himself a failure. For an emperor to break off the pursuit would look like fear. I braced myself for the worst and we moved on. We were managing little more than a crawl in terms of marching speed, due to the dreadful terrain and the need to be aware of potential danger at all times.

Three days in, we reached a large river flowing through these hills and down towards the east. A mile upstream we found a fordable point, and we found our first trouble. I was careful, of course. First I sent over scouts, and then the Berbers to create a patrolled perimeter. Then over went a cohort of the legion to create a solid force. I would not be caught moving into the unknown. There I learned a valuable lesson about how wily these northerners are, and how naïve we were. I was thinking myself safe, having created a heavy bridgehead across the river, and was crossing the bulk of my force. All was fine.

Then the Caledonii hit us... from behind. I had been so careful looking ahead that I'd lost my cavalry rear guard without even realising it, for the tribe had been moving with the stealth of a shadow through their secret ways behind and alongside us, following us for miles. With three quarters of my force on the far bank, they came suddenly from trees and undergrowth in a great howling, furious mass. It was truly a sight to behold, for they had moved right up to us, hidden at all times, and now they emerged *en masse*. One moment we were alone and safe, the next we were besieged by howling Caledonii, and with hardly a breath in between.

I would like to say I fought valiantly. In actual fact, the single century of Praetorians who accompanied me as my personal guard did everything they could to keep me from danger. I was driven by them through the bulk of our forces to the river, and, while our army fought a valiant defence against the tribe, I was escorted across the water to the safety of my legionaries. There I watched and marvelled. The Caledonii were carving huge chunks out of my force, who were trying to fight their defence while also crossing the river to safety. It was all but a massacre. Finally, my officers managed to turn the tide, stopping the advance and bringing extra forces back to the beleaguered bank to turn and push back against the tribe. We suddenly started to gain an edge. Where we had been wheat to the Caledonian scythe, now we were advancing.

And in that moment, they were gone.

At the first hint that they were in danger, they melted away into the landscape as fast as they'd appeared. It was breath-taking. I sent scouts to locate them, but there was no sign. They had gone, and I had learned a hard lesson. I tried to decide whether to turn now and follow them, or to press on into native lands. My generals were largely for the former, wanting revenge for that attack, and I have to admit that I was now hungry for their blood. I try not to get annoyed for no reason, and I do not like wasteful bloodshed, but this was starting to drive me to it. The native scouts explained to me that I would not find the tribes, though. They would have split up and gone many ways. We would not find them in force unless they wanted us to. Ahead, though, some twenty miles further into Caledonian lands, there was a fortress that was still being constructed. It was planned as a meeting point for the tribes in their endless wars against their neighbours, but it would surely be manned now, with Rome at their threshold. I agreed. Better to seek somewhere they would want to defend than to try and chase ghosts across this dreadful landscape.

A day further took us at best ten miles, and into new perils. We were feeling relieved for a while to be moving in easy open ground, heading north-west along the grassy bottom of a shallow valley. The logs came without warning. Hundreds of tree trunks, recently felled and stripped of branches, suddenly rolled from the edges of the woodland above us on either side of the valley. The assault covered a distance of hundreds of paces, relentless and unavoidable, from both sides. A tree trunk does not sound tremendously destructive, but I tell you now, you have to see such a thing to believe it. Dozens, scores, even hundreds of my men were broken and crushed by the rolling, bouncing timbers, each as heavy as ten oxen. By the time the assault was over, all in the space of fifty heartbeats, I had lost a tenth of my infantry to the trees. Bodies lay crushed and mangled, the living envying the dead as they lay with legs at impossible angles, white bone jutting from bloodied flesh. My men were released with a roar, and raced up the hillsides for revenge.

They found no one.

The Caledonii who had done this deed had already gone, melting away once more without sight or sound. They had killed hundreds of my best men, and we had not even scratched them in return.

That night my fury peaked. I raged in my tent, vowing that their people would pay for this, throwing cups and glasses, bellowing incoherently at my officers. I vowed first that I would conquer this land, but by the end of my ranting, as I collapsed, exhausted, into my cot, I had changed my mind. I had decided that this land was undesirable after all, and that the only answer was genocide. Not just Anullinus' execution of surviving warriors in order to prevent a second rising, but more what

Father had done to the Garamantes. Obliteration. The complete and deliberate depopulation of the whole of Caledonia.

Consequently, late next afternoon when we reached the hillfort for which we'd aimed, I gave my men a specific command. No living thing was to survive that afternoon. Even the cats and dogs were to be killed and burned. Anyone taken alive was to be crucified on the prominent ramparts of the fort as a warning to the others, an omen of what awaited every Caledonian that fell into our hands.

I have been accused of being cruel, but I have said before that my cruelty was never wasted, never unprovoked, and on this occasion, I revelled in it. I sent my men against that hill, which was almost complete, the ramparts solid, though with areas not quite finished. The heavy infantry marched up the hill, supported by the auxilia, heading directly for battle with the natives who swarmed about the long, barrow-shaped hill, preparing to defend it. My light and heavy horse I sent around the footings of the slope, partially to guard against anything unexpected, partially to spear any Caledonian who made to flee the hill. I kept with me a century of Praetorians, a century of legionaries, and all the archers. I also kept two dozen riders who covered the area around me for over a mile, making sure there would be no repeat of that first massacre, natives swarming over my command position while the bulk of my force was elsewhere.

I'd planned it well, for the enemy sprung a trap, two extra forces pouring from the forests to either side, trying to outflank my infantry, to fall upon their rear, but instead they met my Batavian and Berber cavalry. I've no great taste for the taking of scalps or heads in general – it seems unnecessary and a little messy – but that day I encouraged it. As it happens, despite being from opposite ends of the empire, the Germanic Batavians from their forests by the river, and the Berbers from their desert sands, both like to take a head from a body in battle. By the time an hour had passed and the battle was clearly ours, the Roman cavalry sported grisly decorations, with heads and scalps hanging from hands, shoulders, spears and saddles, every horse and every rider spattered or soaked with blood, and invariably not their own.

They did just as I commanded. I had once intervened with Father's chastising of Antioch, and now I perpetrated far worse. But again, there was reason. There was a goal. We had two years to end this, and so I let the blood flow freely. I even saw one over-enthusiastic soldier attempting to crucify a chicken, laughing with his mates as he did so. Such was the fury of the natives that three quarters of them died in battle, refusing to submit, even their grey-hairs and children grabbing knives and sticks and hoes and trying to kill Romans. The quarter that were injured or captured were dealt with harshly. They were crucified as per my orders, and not one had their legs broken to speed their demise. They would suffer for two or three days, starving as their joints slowly separated and sinews snapped. And I was not risking another Caledonian force coming to save them, either. We camped there in sight of the hill for four days until the last of them perished, just to be sure no one survived. I know that other Caledonians saw them. Our scouts never found anyone, but every morning they located fresh tracks and trails around the hill that petered out into nothing before they could be followed too far. Caledonians saw their people die, but could not get close enough to help them.

Four nights we listened to the screaming and groaning from the hill, though every hour of every day it diminished as they went to meet their gods. Only when the hillside was naught but a graveyard did we leave. I led my reduced force back out to the lowlands, where our tale was told across the army, moving from camp to camp. In the months that followed, other generals in the campaign took their cue from my lead and the tactics of terror began to be felt by the locals. All summer long, they sprung traps, launched unexpected night-time assaults, surprise attacks. They poisoned water supplies we relied upon, and even blocked our path with livestock so that we had to spend time herding and butchering simply to traverse a valley, while they prepared traps for us. In short, they led us a bloody dance for several months, and our men said the campaign was the most brutal they had ever experienced, even those who had marched on Niger and Albinus, and those who had sacked Ctesiphon.

But our revenge was in scale. Never since the salting of Carthage has an enemy been so viciously scourged as happened to the Caledonii that year. Burnings, impalings, dismemberings, crucifixions, all manner of horrors were to be witnessed on every hilltop from the Wall of Antoninus to the northern sea. And it was not only the men of warrior age that suffered. Every Caledonian taken was killed. Men, women and children, babies and pets. Every last one, no matter their age, gender or profession. All were tortured to death in full view of anyone who cared to see. And the campaign ran on beyond the usual season, too. Father was not ready to return south for the winter, and neither was I or any general in the field. We had changed the whole nature of the war, and we would prosecute it to the end now. A straight invasion, as I'd noted, would never succeed, but this was something new, and something terrifying. A war of terror that might just cow the bastards after all.

Even the men were calling for more. That alone should be a surprise. They were fighting hard, and suffering. We were taking no slaves, which meant that the extra coin that came to a legionary for such things was absent that campaign. Yet none complained. The Caledonii had so ravaged our men that they cared more now for revenge than for profit. Of course, Father had increased their pay more than any other emperor already, so money was not really an issue for them.

The end came in November. Far beyond the campaigning season, through autumn and even into winter we brought death, torture and cruelty to the Caledonii, and finally, they had had enough. A deputation arrived at Alauna. The confederation had many kings, who ruled as a council. Our work that year had whittled a substantial council down to three men, all of them old, sad and broken. The three kings of the Caledonii came with an honour guard, who were removed at the gate, so that the old men walked into the fort alone, tired and beaten. They stood before Father and me, trying to maintain what little pride still remained for them, but they were not to be permitted even that. Kings they were, but Praetorian *optios* struck them behind the knee with their staffs, forcing them to the ground where they could grovel properly.

They asked what terms the emperor would offer for peace. To my relief, he gave them a hard look and replied, 'Total capitulation of all the lands and tribes between the walls and the northern coast.' He would settle for nothing less than Rome's total overlordship of the island. They agreed, broken and hollow. There was no other choice, of course.

I knew, even as I watched them, that this was only a temporary peace. Agricola had had them in this position lifetimes ago, but Rome had taken its boot off their neck, and they had slowly become defiant and belligerent once more, historical proof that Anullinus was correct. Right now they looked defeated, but I wondered how many generations it would take for them to recover. Unless Rome was willing to keep this northern land fully garrisoned forever and permanently hold them down, or we killed every living thing north of the wall for all time, there would always be another war.

I pried information from scouts that night, and my whole attitude changed then. Yes, the country was ruggedly beautiful, and there was good farmland on the east, but the highlands of the Caledonii held nothing of value. There was no ore to be had, no gold, no grazing, nothing. To conquer and hold this place would cost a fortune, and would gain Rome nothing. I resolved then to let the campaign finish and Father have his triumph, but I agreed in the end with my predecessors. The place was too troublesome and worthless to bother holding. The line of the wall had been well chosen.

The Caledonii returned to their lands and Father had installations put in place further inland than ever before, including a fort at each end of the great long lake that cut the highlands in half, imposing an unprecedented control over the Caledonii. It would never last, but in the short term it looked good.

Before winter made travel impossible, we spent some time in the North, Father and I, where he learned with fascination of these cold northern lands. We watched impossible coloured light dance across the skies, surely the work of some native god warning us to go no further. We noted how short the days had become here, and saw creatures hitherto unseen by any Roman. It was a relief after the season of war.

The relief was not to last long, though. As winter truly set in, we rode south through our conquered land, back to Eboracum, where my brother had been busy in my absence.

XVI

A Trinity

Caledonia, Winter AD 209

'What was he thinking?' I snapped angrily.

Father threw me a level, guarded look. 'The punishment of these Judean cults is nothing new or unacceptable, Marcus. Such decrees have been quite common in Africa, and I have given my blessing to them.'

'Yes, yes,' I hissed, still spitting fury. 'I understand the logic. They do not bow before the divinity of Rome, its gods and its emperors. They are a danger to the state because they bring disapproval among the gods. I know all of this. Personally, the Jews I've known have been quite acceptable and amenable, and I hear the Christians are the same. But whether they deserve to be punished or not is immaterial. This is simply not the time.'

Again, that steady look. He was holding in an anger of his own. 'I consult the omens very regularly, Marcus, you know that. The future of our dynasty and the peace of the empire itself cannot be certain while rogue elements in the state continue to defy the gods. If we want this island complete, we need the gods with us, not against us. Your brother was thinking quite levelly.'

'No, he fucking wasn't.'

His eyes hardened, but I was undeterred. 'We're gone for a little over half a year, stomping around soggy valleys in the North and fighting lunatics, and he takes it upon himself to order the execution of Christians across the settled half of the province. Just what you want when you're trying to carry out a war is for the part of the land you *do* control to move towards revolt.'

'There is no hint of revolt.'

'Not *now*, no,' I barked. 'But that's because he had the killings stopped. This priest down in Verulamium, this Alban fellow, he was immensely popular. Taking his head turned every Christian on the island against us. You realise, I assume, that there are a lot of them these days? Maybe as many as you'd find in the Mithraic caves? There are Christians in the army, too. Gods, but there are probably some in the court and the administration. It's not like they have it tattooed on their foreheads, especially when Geta is merrily having their friends burned and beheaded.'

'It has been policy for a long time. Even the blessed Trajan and Marcus Aurelius had them executed when they refused to acknowledge the gods.'

'But they did not hunt them down, and especially not in a warzone when they are busy fighting that damn war. I know you want to protect him. He's your son, and while it pains me to admit it, he seems to have a talent for bean-counting and administration. But this whole Alban affair proves that he doesn't think it through. He's an able administrator, but that does not qualify a man to rule. He's dangerous to have in full power, and you know it as much as I.'

'He remains in the role, Marcus. My decision is made. And before the consuls are chosen, he will join us as Augustus. He will rule alongside us. We will be a trinity, such as is to be found in the gods of the Capitoline.'

'If he is a god, then he is one of those we saw in Aegyptus, with the animal heads. The baboon one is my guess.'

With that, I turned and stomped from the room. I was angry. I was angry at everyone, in fact. At Father for being blind to what he was allowing and standing by his foolish decisions. At Mother for not intervening, despite the fact that she had to see what was going on. At this Alban priest for pushing things so that my brother noticed him. At Geta for being an idiot who took it upon himself to unsettle the province that we were busy trying to unite, by beheading popular Christians. He was a fool, and had spent his whole life trying to edge out of my shadow and into the succession. He should never be Augustus, yet now he would be. Officially, he would rank the same as me. My only hope now was to divorce Plautilla, off on her island somewhere, marry and have a son. But I couldn't do all that while I was in Britannia and at war. It would have to wait until we got back to Rome.

Unless it was not Father who failed to come back from Britannia...

-

The snows settled across the land and the north of Britannia looked like a crisp, white sheet. The consuls were chosen, the administration was busy trying to settle the island despite the fact that Christians were now burning temples in the night in protest at the way they were being treated, attacking priests in armed gangs and then melting away into the streets before they could be caught and identified, all in a manner reminiscent to me of Caledonian warbands. I was dealing with the usual troubles that occupy a military commander over the winter of a campaign: supply issues due to the weather holding up traffic, shipping unable to sail thanks to the winter seas, the steady increase in illness and injury over the period of hard weather, and so on.

The Maetae, of course, must have been sitting in their fortresses and watching us carefully, well aware now that they had not bought our friendship, but merely time, with their supplies and scouts. Our army now occupied installations all the way up the east to that great glen, and surrounded the highlands, blocking every approach and controlling Caledonian access to arable farms and good, low grazing land. It was clear now to everyone that we had come north of the wall to stay, not merely to punish, and the Maetae could be under no illusion that they would be part of the empire within the year. What they would do about it remained to be seen. The Caledonii, on the other hand, knew their independent world had ended, at least for now. They knew we held their lives in the palm of our hand, and they had no choice but to come to us, begging, which is precisely what they did.

Word had come to Eboracum that a deputation from all the Caledonian tribes sought an imperial audience to discuss the future of their people in relation to Roman rule of the province. When we had left them in late autumn in the North, we had imposed total control, and they had accepted that. Now that everyone's ire had cooled and they'd had a winter of hunger and deprivation, they needed more. They needed Rome's help now, to keep their babies fed and their homes warm. Without our permission there was nowhere for them to farm or raise livestock. They would slowly starve into extinction. During the campaign, that would have suited me perfectly, of course, but if Father intended to include them in the empire and to bring Rome's control to the northern shore, they would need to change. They would need to Romanise, and the first step in such a move is to come to new agreements, to secure their loyalty with gifts that will change them forever. Agricola knew this, for Tacitus said as much. The toga would become fashionable. They would adopt the lounge, the bath, the banquet, and in their ignorance, they would call civilisation that which was in truth part of their slavery.

Father agreed readily. If the Caledonii were ready to come open-armed to Rome, then the process of conquest would move on, and he was hungry to complete it speedily. The Caledonii would meet us between the walls. They were nervous of travelling south of the walls and into a world that had been Roman for so long, for it was alien to them. But between the walls, the world was still in that half-light of an imperial dawn, lacking the trappings of empire, but occupied by tribes that accepted the dominance of their southern neighbours.

We would travel to meet them. I offered to deal with it all, for Father's health continued to deteriorate, and he was barely able to shuffle across the palace now, but when it was mooted that perhaps my brother might be a better choice, for he was a civil administrator while I was seen as little more than the emperor's sword arm at the time, I hurriedly changed tack. The last thing I wanted was to give the bastard more power. I flopped back on myself, instead encouraging Father to handle the matter personally.

The compromise did not please me, particularly. All three of us would go, in a show of imperial unity, a grand display for the barbarians. We would meet the Caledonii and offer them civilisation in return for their permanent loyalty and the acceptance of the Pax Romana.

The procession that rode north that Januarius was grand indeed. All three emperors, along with the majority of the court in its finery, two cohorts of Praetorians, two cohorts of the Sixth Legion from their Eboracum base, my favoured Berber riders, and assorted hangers-on. We must have looked as though we were on our way to a fresh invasion rather than a political meeting, but there would be no doubt in the minds of the Caledonian leaders that they were now our subjects, and that was largely the point of it.

Geta rode on the far side of Father each day as we made our way north, glaring at me periodically, and we shared not a single word with one another. The placing was clearly deliberate, to keep us apart, and Geta was quartered separately of an evening too, each of our rooms being allocated with a separate cohort, such that there was no chance for us to meet at all. We crawled north, twenty miles a day, with carriages and horses and a massive entourage, and hardly ever did my brother and I meet, and never spoke, separated by our father during the day and by the Praetorians during the night. Six days we travelled, four up to Corio on the wall of Hadrian, and then a further two to the fortress of Trimontium which lay between the walls in the lands of the Selgovae.

I had a bad night at Corio. An hour after the evening meal, one of the few times Geta and I were to be found in the same room, for the three of us were the guests of the town's magistrates, I fell ill with a stomach ache. I summoned the court physician, who had accompanied with us to tend to father's ongoing illness, and had him look me over. He announced that I had eaten something that disagreed with me. He told me that while I felt dreadful, I would be fine in the morning. He gave me an emetic, which I really did not need since I was ready to puke like a fountainhead already.

In the morning, I felt dreadful, and was pale and waxy, but as the hours passed and we made our way north again, I began to recover, and by the end of that day I was almost myself again. The general consensus was that I had overdone the oysters at Corio, a rare delight hardly found in northern Britannia, shipped south from the coastal lands of the Votadini beyond the wall. It was assumed that some had gone off in transit, and I had certainly eaten my fill of them. It was a perfectly logical explanation.

But I had seen my brother's face that evening, and the look he bore I could only describe as triumphant. I cannot prove that he attempted to poison me, but I remain convinced of it to this day. I never ate in the same room as him again after that.

We reached Trimontium to find that the Caledonii had been there for some time awaiting us. They had come in a surprisingly large number, and were camped a safe distance from the fort itself. They had been disarmed, of course, especially with the emperors coming to visit. New kings had arisen among those tribes we had battered the previous year, and so a full council of the Caledonii came out to meet us. They came with an honour guard of their best warriors, but those men were unarmed and remained a few paces behind them, far enough not to pose a threat. The kings stepped out ahead as we approached.

We had formed into what must have looked like a military wedge. Father sat astride his horse at the lead, with Geta following at his right shoulder and me at his left, the closest we had been to one another for a year or more. Behind us came half a dozen generals and senior military officers, and then a gathering of courtiers in their most glorious tunics, togas being impossible to ride in. Like Father and Geta, I wore military uniform, though unlike them, I had my habitual caracallus to stave off the bitter winter winds. Behind them all came the army, though the eagle-eyed might have noted that another few squads of Praetorians had peeled off to each side and hovered at the edge of things protectively, supported by a unit of Arabian horse archers, who could have put arrows in any native that moved before they could reach us. We were bold, not stupid.

As we approached them, my gaze played across the gathering. I recognised the three elderly kings from whom we'd accepted the surrender in the North, though they had recovered some of their dignity in the intervening months. The new, younger kings bore a strange mix of haughty pride in their elevation and humble defeat in the fact that their rule was to be tempered by bowing to a Roman master.

They posed no threat. I could see in their eyes only acceptance. I could also see that this was temporary, however. I'd said that they had been defeated before and yet returned to strength after Agricola, and I knew they would do so again unless we held them down, and the small amount of pride I could see returned in the eyes of those kings confirmed that. It had taken but months. Unless we kept them in a servile state at the tip of a sword, it was only a matter of time before they recovered their independence.

I was musing on such things even as the initial greetings were made, and I blame what happened on my mind being elsewhere. As I looked at the deputation and pondered on the likelihood that this entire campaign would count for naught within a decade, my gaze fell upon one of the kings' guards, who had strayed closer than the others, keeping near his master. Somehow, despite the entire deputation having been disarmed, that warrior had managed to keep a sword at his side, and his hand was on the hilt as he took another step forward. In reality, what could he have done, alone with a sword against the might of Rome? But I'd been distracted and taken by surprise. As I saw his fingertips dance on the frosty hilt of his sword, I felt the blood rush to my head and before I realised it, I'd torn my own blade from its scabbard and brandished it, thrusting it forward towards the warrior.

Foolish.

A commotion broke out immediately. No one else had seen the armed native. All they saw was me suddenly bellow incomprehensibly, rip my sword from its sheath and apparently thrust it in the direction of my father's back, for I was at his left shoulder. Praetorians were moving immediately, senators howling in shock, and my brother capitalised on it in an instant. He must have known I had no murderous intent towards our father, yet he cried a warning to him and hauled on his reins, barging his horse between Father and I protectively.

Father turned, his eyes wide with surprise at the bared blade that wavered in my hand and the younger brother who'd pushed between us. He never said a word. His eyes demanded an answer to the unspoken question, though, and I shook my head, face solemn, answering in kind as I thrust my blade back into its sheath and tried to recover my own poise. It was difficult. The disaster had been seen by all, yet understood by none. By nightfall, the story that I had made to kill my father was all over the camp, and probably spreading out among the native tribes, too.

Father dismounted and stepped up onto the tribunal that had been prepared, and then sank into the curule chair at its centre. He managed so well to disguise the pain and discomfort he felt that the Caledonii and the gathered nobles of Rome were probably entirely unaware of just how much it troubled him. I saw his eyes, and it was impossible to keep the pain from them, tears welling up with every step.

Still, he managed to maintain his imperial dignity throughout the meeting. The Caledonii acquiesced to every imperial demand without argument, a sign of just how desperate they were, and how thoroughly we had beaten them. In return for an oath of loyalty to Rome, the senate and the emperors, they were to be granted access to their ancestral farmlands in the east, under the watchful eye of the garrisons who would remain in the region on a permanent basis. Rome would send engineers to help them make the best of their resources and in return they would send south tributes and taxes like all citizens of the empire. We would even send them grain from our new stores at Horrea Classis to alleviate the starvation they had endured following their defeat. This is the way of Rome. The hammer and anvil to crush resistance, then the offer of aid and civilisation to entice them into a new world. The Caledonii were ready to accept. Again, I was of the personal opinion that the moment we removed even an ounce of our military control, they would begin to recover and dream once more of independence. Still, for now, things looked good. All being dealt with to everyone's satisfaction, the Caledonii returned to their camp, accompanied by a few of the officers from the northern forces who would make the detailed arrangements for exchanges.

Father limped back to his horse and mounted with difficulty, and we rode back to the fort of Trimontium, where we would stay that night before returning south. The commander of the garrison had naturally given over his own 'sumptuous' quarters for our convenience during our visit and moved into one of the centurions' rooms. Father entered first, and then Praetorians escorted both my brother and myself inside and to our individual quarters. They were probably so attentive because of their ongoing orders to keep the pair of us separate, but to any observer it would look horribly like I was being arrested.

We went to our rooms and I changed into dry, warm clothes. I would have liked to use the baths, but we had a schedule in order to keep myself and Geta separate, and he was in there first. As such, I was sitting in my room, musing over the disaster of a day when there was a knock at my door. It was Papinian, the Praetorian prefect, with two of his men. He was there to escort me to Father.

I walked with them, trying not to feel nervous, though I was. Father was in poor health these days, but he had once been a lion of a man, and there was still that in him, I knew. At the door of his office, the two soldiers stepped aside, and Papinian escorted me in. Father sat behind his desk, still in the clothes he had worn on the tribunal, and Castor, his *cubicularius*, sat to one side. Papinian strode to the other, and the door was closed behind us, leaving the four of us alone in the room where I took a seat opposite Father.

At a nod from Father, Papinian produced a sword, blade bared, and placed it on the table between us, the hilt close to my hand. I shivered.

'I would like to think there was some explanation beyond the obvious,' Father said, eyes glittering. I made to interrupt, but he waved me down. 'You will have your chance to speak, Marcus, but not yet.

There is a sword here now, and only one. It is the only blade in the room. If you really have it in your heart to slay me, you will never have a better chance. You are young, strong and armed, while I am old, weak, and unarmed. Castor will do nothing, and Papinian is under orders to accept your commands, and has been since the day we arrived on this island, for you are every inch the emperor already.'

An uncomfortable silence descended on the room. The sword loomed, larger than an army in that moment, the thread upon which an entire empire hung.

'Speak,' he said.

'I was foolish.'

'You certainly were, but that is no explanation.'

'I saw one of the Caledonii armed. I'd been off in my own world and in the moment I noticed, panic, I think, took over. I saw a threat. I drew my sword. I don't know what I meant to do, but I do know it was never meant for you, Father.'

He nodded slowly. 'I have been trying to understand why you would want to kill me. You already have everything that you need to rule, and soon enough I will be among the gods and no longer sharing power with you.'

'I was foolish.'

'You are impetuous. You always have been. I was, too, in my youth, and so was your grandfather. It is in our blood. But like he and I, you must learn to rein yourself in. You must impose control over yourself. Situations like this cannot be allowed to develop. It looks appalling to the people. We are a dynasty.'

'Yes, Father.' I felt somewhat humble, a little like a child being upbraided. Possibly something like how the Caledonii had felt after the war, facing us.

'And I want a promise from you, Marcus.'

'Father?'

'You will give me your word here and now that you will accept your brother as your co-emperor and make no move against him.'

'Father, I...'

'No. It is a command. You will give me your oath and abide by it. And if you cannot do so, then you had best pick up that sword right now and strike me down. I will not have my family divided. I have tried time and again to persuade you to make peace and to reconcile. I have pleaded, I have bribed, I have pushed, and yet the two of you are as distant as ever. I will beg and push no more. I give you this now as an imperial command, and the way things are looking it may be one of the last I ever give: you will give me your oath that you and your brother will rule in harmony. I no longer care whether that harmony reaches your heart, but for the good of the empire, you will fake it like a professional actor. Do you understand?'

I nodded. What else could I do?

'And in return, because I know that every war has two sides, and you are not alone in the blame here, I will make the same demand of your brother.'

Another nod. So that was it. I would have to accept the matter, unless I wanted to stand up and usurp my own father. Deflated, I found myself giving Father my oath. I promised to treat Geta as an equal to Father and myself, and to make no move on him lest Father decide to strip me of the purple.

We rode south the next day, making for Eboracum once more. Geta continually threw me looks as we rode that made it clear how just such an oath had been torn from him that night. On our way south, we paused for a time at the great wall of Hadrian. I had made so many changes in the year we'd been on the island, and Father had spent most of his time in the city or with me in the North. He'd not seen the wall or my alterations to it. So we tarried there for eight whole days, touring its length.

It was as we were on our way back, leaving Luguvalium in the west, when we encountered a strange scene. A small group of soldiers from the Ala Augusta based in the fort there happened to be close to the road, dressed in their cavalry sports armour, all decorative and with gleaming faceplates, colourful plumes and bright spears with streamers. As we approached, the Praetorians coming closer protectively, the riders stepped their horses back and bowed their heads.

I was content, but Father motioned for us all to stop, and then turned, and levelled a finger at one of the riders.

'What is the meaning of this?' he demanded. I frowned, unaware of what he had seen. The rider, too, seemed surprised. He reached up and removed his gleaming facemask, the ebony-coloured face of perhaps an Aethiopian beneath. His gleaming white eyes were confused.

'Domine?' he asked, head bowing once more.

'*This*,' Father snapped, gesturing from shoulder to shoulder in an arc under his chin.

I realised now. The man was wearing a garland of cypress boughs. They were all in such garlands, something to do perhaps with their favoured gods or with some ritual of the cavalry, but now that I looked at it closely, it struck me how much that particular one resembled the garlands that festoon a tomb following the death of a loved one. Still, the rider apparently did not understand. He looked down at the garland and then up, frowning.

'Domine, you have conquered all. You are a god, my lord.'

I saw Father blanch, then. 'I will be a god in good time, soldier, but not yet. Not yet.'

And he kicked his horse and sped away, Praetorians hurrying to follow him. I shook my head. The rider was still baffled at what he'd done wrong. To him, the garland was part of his routine, and no imitation of funeral decorations. To him, he had offered the greatest of compliments to his emperor, and not intimated that he was dying. I would have liked to have explained it to the man, but we had to ride fast now to catch up with Father, who, ever slave to omens and superstitions, was now worried that the gods were seeking his end.

We travelled at speed to Eboracum, where he made sacrifices at the temple of Bellona.

In the days that followed, life in the city was difficult for me. Father was increasingly lame and ill, Mother constantly worried about him, and I was living with the constraint of an oath to treat my brother as an equal. I was almost glad when word came in the spring that the Maetae had risen in arms. Better to march into war than remain in that terrible position in Eboracum.

The North called once more.

XVII

A Few Taboos

Caledonia, AD 210

It is often through the slightest and most accidental of things that we become aware of what is really important. I rode out from Eboracum with our gathered force of Praetorians, vexillations of the Sixth Legion, the imperial horse guard, and sundry other units, and made for the wall of Hadrian, where we would collect a good deal of extra strength, finishing our force as we moved to the Antonine Wall.

I was in sole command, now. I had struck a deal with Father, if you remember, that he would command the first year, and I the second. I suspect he would have argued that now and taken full command anyway, but the fact was that he was unable to do so, even if he wished. Over the late winter and early spring, his health had declined once more and he was rarely to be seen on his feet at all now, or even out of his apartments in the palace. He looked sick, he winced whenever he moved, his appetite had all but vanished, and every time the court physician left his room, he shook his head sadly. Mother had the final say, of course, telling him flatly that I was going alone.

I did wonder what mischief Geta might get up to in Eboracum in my absence, having for the first time since we arrived on the island an unimpeded and constant access to Father. I stewed on that all the way north. But on the whole, my spirits were relatively high in the circumstances. Father had wanted the war finished this year, and it looked very much as though he would get his wish. The Caledonii were cowed, for now, at least, and the Maetae, while clever, were a smaller confederation and inhabited much more accessible lands than their northern neighbours. I felt sure we could deal with them much faster than the previous year. And deal with them we would.

Father had made it clear. He had given the order, to me and to every senior officer in the army. There was to be no quarter offered to this tribe who had supported us and then rebelled. Their lives and indeed their entire world was forfeit for their betrayal. Extinction was what Father sought. Every male we found was to be killed. Every last one, no matter whether he be warrior, greybeard or babe in arms. In a fit of particular fury, he even ordered that any woman found with child be killed lest their progeny be a boy. Thus would the Maetae vanish from history.

I won't bore you with much of the details of the campaign, but for me, four moments stood out that summer, and each is memorable not for what was happening with the British tribes, but for what it meant for me personally.

The first was before we even reached the warzone. We were encamped somewhere in that endless sea of bleak hills that lies between the walls, where the tribes might not like us, but they are at least peaceful and accepting of our presence. We were settled for the night in a series of camps just north of the fort at Bremenium which I had reoccupied for these campaigns. I had taken to a habit of which the Praetorian officers disapproved for the potential danger it wrought. I'd started it that previous year in the far north. Of a night, when the camp was set and the men had eaten their meals and were playing dice or writing letters or polishing armour, I would go among them. Slipping from the headquarters, I could be anonymous in my hooded caracallus, for the garment was not entirely unusual among soldiers in the north-western provinces. As such, I could move about the camp and gauge the mood of the army without the habitual guardedness a man adopted in the presence of his emperor. On the whole I had learned good things, and had found a new appreciation of my men.

On this occasion, I was among the legionaries of the Sixth when I heard the first voice of dissent. It was not that I didn't hear negativity at times, of course. It is a soldier's lot to complain about his conditions, his commanding officer, the food, the weather, late pay, wet socks and the like. But this was different. This was not one man, but a tent party of eight, and when eight men discuss some matter, it is always worth listening.

'All I'm saying is that if centurion "I'm so noble" Fuscus had just fallen in with the others, we could have been back in Eboracum with dry beds, warm women and cold beer.'

'I'm not arguing with you, Catus, but it is what it is. At least we'll get prizes for the war, while those back in garrison will get nothing.'

'You're fooling yourself, Lucius,' grumbled a third man, pausing in the rubbing of oil into a blade. 'Look at last year. A whole people crushed and nothing to show for it. No loot, no slaves. And anything better this year? No. The old lion says kill them all. There'll be no prizes this year. Just rain and blood. That's what young Antoninus wants, you know? Rain and blood. Never seen a more miserable-looking fucker.'

Someone pushed him roughly. 'You've never been close enough to the emperors to see that much, you knob.'

'He's right, though. Caracalla just wants war and blood. Nine years I've done in the Sixth. Nine years, and even with the governor's wars, we spent most of the time in garrison. Comfort and warmth. Then along comes Caracalla and we're off in the North, catching illnesses and getting killed. Mark my words, when the old man dies, we'll be moved to wherever there's a war. Here, Germania, Parthia, Marcomannia. His brother… now *there's* where we should look.'

My ear twitched at that.

'I'm not convinced that Geta's any better, though. I mean, yes, he's generous to a fault, but he's never spent an hour on a battlefield, never visited a war, never even seen a Briton. At least Caracalla's fought with his men, knows what the empire faces. What can Geta really offer us?'

'Gold, you fool,' grunted a taciturn one in the corner.

'And peace to raise kids in Eboracum,' added another.

'Stop torturing yourselves with this,' said the one called Lucius. 'It doesn't matter what we think or what we want. It's a chain of command. You know how it works. The tribune's Geta's man, so his centurions are Geta's men, so we're Geta's men. Personally, I'd like to shove a stick up the young one's arse and see his brother rule, but unless you're prepared to argue with the *centurionate*, our opinions count for shit. Soon the old man'll be gone, and we all know there won't be two emperors for long.'

This was new, and more than a little unsettling, information. I walked on, thinking hard. The Sixth were based in Eboracum, where Geta had been for over a year. He would have had plenty of opportunities to get his claws into them. And once you have the commanders of an army, you generally have the rest, according to conventional wisdom. So I couldn't rely on the Sixth, apparently. Had the rot stopped in Eboracum, or had it spread?

I walked about the camp, listening now with an ear for repeats of those sentiments. To my dismay, as we marched north, I heard similar from the mouths of plenty of men, not all of whom were of the Sixth. Auxiliary units, legions from the South or those we had brought across the water, even the small naval detachments travelling with us to deal with river transport. It seemed that Geta had been busy in my absence with more than just administration.

I had been forced to accept equality with Geta, but could I really be held to that when my brother actively worked against me?

The second night after that, as we approached the wall of Antoninus, I managed to corner Papinian as he left an inspection of his Praetorians. I steered him away from the crowds, towards the corral of the Praetorian cavalry, a small squad of his men hovering protectively but respectfully far enough away to allow us a little privacy.

'Does my brother own the army now?'

The prefect turned a frown on me as I leaned on the fence and looked out over the proud horses, grazing in the evening gloom.

'Domine?'

'Cut the Domine rubbish. We've known each other a long time. You're a close friend of my mother, my father trusts you, and we've fought battles together, you and I. It seems that Geta has bought the loyalty of the Sixth in Eboracum with gold and promises of other benefits. And I do not think it is just the Sixth. He has begun to turn the army against me. We all know that Father is in serious decline. How many of us harbour even a hope that he will leave this island? And you know there will be a scramble when he goes.'

'No,' Papinian said straight, eye-to-eye. 'No, there will not.'

It was my turn to frown. 'Oh?'

'I don't care what provisos you put in your oath to your father,' the prefect said, expression carefully neutral. 'I am not Geta's man, young Augustus, but neither am I yours. Until he joins the gods, I am your father's man, and through him, your mother's, too. It is their wish – nay, their *command* – that there be peace between you, that you rule together. As long as I draw breath, that will be my goal. I will not take arms against you, Marcus Aurelius Antoninus, but do not ask me to do as much against your brother. The Praetorians are here to protect the imperial family. *All* of them.'

And that was that. With a respectful bow, he backed away. I could not count on him. But whatever he believed, there would be a struggle, a reckoning, as was now clear. My brother had already tried to poison me once, and was now turning the army against me. Distasteful and harsh as it may sound, I was beginning to wonder seriously whether there could be only one son of Severus. If Papinian would not side with me, then he was going to be opposed at some point, for he would attempt to protect my brother from me. As I turned, something caught my eye and I glanced back. For a moment, I thought I'd seen the figure of a man among the horses, but at second glance he was gone.

–

We gathered the army at the wall and moved on in force, heading now into Maetae lands. The villages we found were deserted, their strength pulled back to defensive places, well aware of our approach and our intentions.

I was doing my rounds one night in the rugged wilds of that northern world, grateful to discover that there was more support for me, and less for Geta, among these more northerly units who had been far from his silver tongue, but who had fought the Caledonii with me. I stepped away from a unit of German horse and towards my favoured Berbers, who I felt sure I could always rely upon, when I became aware of a figure moving at a tangent to intercept me. As he neared, he inclined his head and murmured, 'Domine?'

The Praetorians shadowing me moved forward to protect me. I might be incognito, but I had eight heavily-armed guards within reach, also incognito, for I am no fool. The man approaching was insolent, clearly. He knew who I was, for he had called me lord, had he not? And yet he approached thus in a manner no common man approaches an emperor. I was tempted to let the Praetorians have him, but I was intrigued, and not just by his insolence.

The man wore the tunic of an officer in the *equites singulares*, the imperial horse guard. He was, I realised as he came closer, of immense size. A veritable giant, with a prominent brow and hands that could crush a ship. He was an impressive specimen. He would have made a phenomenal wrestler or gladiator. As a horse guard, I wondered to what fabled land they'd had to look to find a horse that could bear his weight, for most cavalry steeds would see his toes dragging along the ground even mounted. I had a moment of clarity then, and suspected that it was his ghostly shape I had seen that night in the horse corral.

Fascinated, I gestured to my Praetorians and they fell back once more, though their hands remained on their weapons and their eyes alert. I beckoned to the giant.

'You are forthright to your emperor, soldier.'

The big man's head remained bowed. 'Sometimes, one must break a few taboos to change the world, Domine.'

Change the world? Now, I was *really* intrigued.

'Go on.'

'I… I overheard your discussion with the Prefect Papinian, Domine.'

So it *was* him with the horses. 'I know. You were in the corral.'

That surprised him, and he straightened. 'No insult or offence was intended, Domine. I was caught in the imperial presence, and I did not know how to leave it without making myself known, so I remained quiet and slipped away.'

'Change the world, you said?'

He nodded and finally his head came up. He had the build and the face of a brute, but there was a fierce intelligence in those eyes that belied his form, and I adjusted my thinking quickly. 'Papinian is only one of the prefects, Domine.'

I nodded. 'Laetus. He remains in Rome.'

'Aye, Domine, but I know without doubt that he is your man, and not your brother's. You cannot rely upon Papinian, but he is not in sole command.'

I nodded my appreciation of this. 'And you? And the Singulares?'

'The Singulares adhere to your father, Domine. I cannot say how they would waver if he were to pass, but some of us are your men. Some of us have seen the blood fly and the steel gleam on the battlefield, and have seen our emperor in the thick of it, one of us. Your brother plays at rule, but it is like a child with a wooden city. Only a man who knows how the empire works can hope to rule it well.'

I smiled. The words of my father, so long ago, came floating back to me then. *The powerful always think that the empire works from the top down, but you have to have seen both ends to know the truth. The empire works from the bottom up.*

It seemed that my brother had never learned that lesson. He had bought off the officers of units, expecting that loyalty would trickle downhill, but loyalty is not water. It does not flow with the gradient. Loyalty comes in blocks and has to build upwards.

'Are there others who can be relied upon?'

The big man shrugged. 'Plenty. The procurator of the province hates your brother, for he has done nothing since his arrival but interfere in the man's business. And there are others. Not the senior officers, though. Your brother's gold has bought many a heart this past year.'

An idea was forming, and with it came a smile.

'I think that perhaps I can counter that. It is in the nature of powerful men to think they are in control. Often they are not. My new friend, I think we have work to do. What is your name?'

'Maximinus, Domine.'

'Maximinus the Thracian, I would say from the accent. We have much to discuss.'

–

We marched on into Maetae lands, but now I had a new focus. In reality I gave little care about the future of this northern swamp. The tribes were permanently restive, untrustworthy and violent, and the only way to keep them under control was to keep your foot on their neck forever, which no emperor could afford. Sooner or later the place would be abandoned again as it was after Agricola's victory. All we needed to do was teach them all a lesson and deter them from thinking about coming south and causing trouble again for at least a hundred years. That would be easy enough, especially with Father's standing order for the campaign. But my new focus was to use the campaign instead to bind the army to me, the way Geta had been trying for the past year. But I would do it differently. I would capture the hearts of the soldiers, and let the officers panic when they tried to turn them against me. The words of the soldier that first night at Bremennium gave me the idea I needed.

Against the Caledonii there had been no bonus and no loot for the army, for we had killed them all and burned what they left. This time

I was bound by the order to kill every male of the Maetae tribes, but beyond that the strategy was mine to create.

I pulled together all the scouts and I sent them out with specific remits. We were not looking for their strongholds to crush as an invader normally would. We were looking for their population centres, those hidden dells full of the ordinary tribesfolk, and we were looking for their holy places and their royal sites.

As we moved against the first of these that was located by my riders, I had all the carpenters and engineers among the force pulled out to one side. As they stood on the open grass waiting for my words, they were baffled, for there was nothing for them here but war.

'You are excused the duty of massacre today,' I said. 'Look around you, to left and right. What do you see?'

There was a long silence, and eventually a brave soldier raised his hand.

'Yes?'

'Trees, Domine?'

'Yes. Trees. I want them stripped down and turned into mobile cages. Use the spare wheels among the wagons, and any we take from the raid, and make any others you need. There are plenty of beasts of burden in their fields for us to use. The scouts tell me that this place houses maybe six hundred locals. Assuming half of those are women, I want cages for three hundred slaves.'

One of the senior officers close to my side cleared his throat. 'Domine, we have instructions…'

'To kill all the *men*,' I finished for him. 'The women will all go to the slave markets. Supplies have been low since the Parthian War, and prices are at a high now. The army has bled and suffered for two years up here and with little recompense. It is time they were paid for their work.'

There had been a few muted cheers, but now the noise exploded across the gathering, and I knew that soon my words would be on the lips of all the army.

I stood with my officers and watched our forces roll across the Maetae. This tribe was far from the largest we would find. The bulk of their warriors had taken refuge on a hillfort, sending the others to some deep, hidden valley. We had ignored the fort and its defenders and marched instead on that enclave of women and children and their farm animals.

I watched the slaughter and the rapine. It was eye-watering even from a distance. We lived up to Father's orders. Most of the males here were old men or boys, but each one met the edge of a blade. The women were rounded up and herded into fenced enclosures while the carpenters built the mobile prisons that would carry them south, taking ship at Horrea, and thence to the slave markets of the empire. At Horrea they would be sold to the ubiquitous slave traders, and the profit added to the war chest for the army.

The next day, the warriors whose families we had taken came for us, anguished and furious, leaving their hillfort. They did not last long. We left them crucified on their walled hill for all to see.

And so it went. We found the people of the tribes instead of their warriors, and we took their women for the empire. By the second month we no longer had to ship the captives south, for now it was known that we were actually taking slaves, the traders followed us on campaign and bought them fresh from the field of battle. They tried to argue us into selling them men, too, but an imperial command is an imperial command, and so the men would all die. And when the menfolk came for us, driven to suicidal fury by what we'd done, we killed them and stripped them of anything of remote value, selling it all to the traders in our wake. Any animals, supplies, or loot we found, it all went to the army.

And when the scouts located a royal stronghold, we took it by force, for there we would find gold, and silver and precious stones. Slowly, inch by inch, the Maetae ceased to exist, and everything they were and everything they had became gold in the army's coffers. By the end of the second month we had too much really to carry in official carts, and the first donative was paid to the men. The soldiers queued up for their month's wages and found it to be a little more than triple what they expected, their share in the spoils of the war. I had a feeling Father might argue with me about that, when it could have gone to the imperial treasury, but I cared not. I was looking to the future – to a future without Geta.

Every now and then the scouts would find us a religious site. Here, I made a command decision that in some ways defied my father, though I believed he would have agreed with me, for he was ever a superstitious and overly gods-fearing man.

We let the priests live. There were some in the empire who believed our failure to conquer Britannia was a result of our massacre of their druids, which had turned their gods' ire on us. I would not repeat the mistake. So the only Maetae males who escaped our war that summer were their priests. But when they were kicked from their houses, we took their gold and their bronze. Nothing from the actual shrines, mind, for stealing from a priest is just stealing from a man, while stealing from a shrine is stealing from a god. Still, it was known that the richest men of all these old tribes were always the priests, and that proved to be true as our gold stocks grew again and again. Indeed, just to be sure, I had our army put up altars to their local gods here and there, showing our respect.

All summer we moved across Maetae lands like wildfire. In our wake, we left nothing but deserted settlements, empty hillforts, burned and crucified men and the wheel ruts of slaver wagons. Perhaps much of my reputation for fierceness and cruelty comes from that summer. I was implacable. Unstoppable. I was the fury of Rome come with a sword edge to remove the Maetae from history, the way poor emperors are removed by their successors.

By autumn, there were worried comments among the senior officers. By this time, my secret eyes and ears had been at work all season and I knew who was already solidly lodged in my brother's coin purse. Not surprisingly it was these men, beginning to worry at my popularity with the army, who began to advocate a close to the campaign and a withdrawal south once more.

I refused them. My excuse was that the work was not yet done. I told them that I would not leave the North while the Maetae could raise a voice in resistance. They would be extinct before we went south. It was perfectly reasonable, and actually quite sensible, especially since the autumn was unusually mild for this far north, and Rome does not like to leave a war unfinished.

Of course, it also suited me personally, for the longer we campaigned here, the more the soldiers were mine. The more we killed and enslaved and looted, the more gold there was to distribute among the army, binding them ever tighter and making Geta and his pet officers more and more irrelevant.

And so we marched on into the late autumn and the winter. Only when the snows started to come did we relinquish our grip on the North, taking our spoils and leaving the wasteland that had been the Maetae to the crows. We'd not killed them all, of course. Once it had become clear that we were bent on total extermination and that their revolt was little more to us than the stamping feet of a petulant child, what was left of the confederation fled north into the highlands, into the blasted hills and shadowed valleys of the Caledonii, seeking aid and succour from a people who had been their enemies since the days gods walked the world.

The last of those four most memorable moments that season came as we travelled south. I was seated in the office of the commanding officer at Cilurnum on the wall of Hadrian, alone, working on a missive to send ahead by dispatch rider, informing Father that we were but days away. There came a knock at the office door. I called for entry, knowing that no one could reach that far without being known and trusted by the Praetorians on guard. I was somewhat pleased to see the massive looming shape of Maximinus Thrax in the doorway, that officer of my horse guard. He bore an expression of triumph, which pleased me, for I was sure he was my man through and through, and what pleased the Thracian giant would undoubtedly please me.

Then, as he entered, head bowed, and moved to one side, others came. This, now, was much more of a surprise. There were officers here I had sounded out over the summer and felt could be relied upon the day I turned on my brother, but there were many who had taken Geta's coin and promised their support, who I knew had given their oath against me. They continually filed in. My guards are not stupid, of course, and none of the officers were armed, and for every four that entered, one of my guards came with them, hand on hilt, protective of their master and watching the assembly. By the time the steady stream of men was finished the room was packed, just a space left around me. Twenty-one men, all of the rank of tribune or prefect or higher, each a man of import, wealth, power and influence. And each of them being watched by my armed guards.

The door closed.

'Yes?' I said.

There was an odd silence. No one seemed to want to speak, and eventually it was probably the oldest man among them who stepped out to the front. He was the camp prefect of the Sixth Legion, and a man I knew to be so far in my brother's purse, you could barely see his arse above the coins.

'Domine, the time has come for you to rule.'

I had to really fight hard not to grin. Even those who had been my staunchest opponents, it seemed, had come over to my side. Of course, it's easy to support one candidate when the men beneath you have no incentive either way, but when your soldiers have begun to forge a bond with the opponent, that loyalty becomes rather stretched. That was not the only surprise, though.

'When the time comes, this empire will have one emperor,' I said with an air of finality. 'I thank you for your loyalty, and hope I can rely upon it when the time is right.'

'The time *is* right, Domine,' Maximinus put in, stepping out front now. 'Your father was a great emperor, and brought us peace and stability in a time of chaos. But he is dying, Domine.'

'I know,' I said simply.

'You do not understand, Domine. This war is almost done, but your father will not finish it. He may never see it end. New leadership is needed now.'

My gaze hardened. 'If you are suggesting usurpation...'

'No, Domine. An emperor's life is sacrosanct. But he can no longer command the army nor the administration. It is the considered opinion of your staff that your father should be asked to step down in favour of your sole rule.'

I tried to picture Father's expression if I tried. With or without him, he intended for me to rule alongside Geta. That he might step down and put me in sole command was a farfetched dream. Father, after all, did not know that Geta had already tried at least once to remove me, and was working towards a coup. I stood, hands flat on the table before me.

'My father will rule Rome until he draws his last breath. It is the way of things. When he is gone, I alone will reign, and I will be grateful for the support of the loyal armies of Rome on that day. And believe me, I am certain that day draws nigh.'

They shuffled out, a little deflated. Where they had come up with this fanciful notion that I would push Father aside and take his place I do not know, but it was heartening in its way.

Four moments that summer, then. I had learned in camp of my brother's intent to steal the army out from under me, and it had become clear that there would be a contest between us. Then, in the North I had found new allies among the officers, and learned that all was not lost. Then I had initiated a campaign that brought gold to the purse of every soldier, ever heightening my popularity. Finally, as we bore down on Eboracum once more, it transpired that my success in winning over the army was so overwhelming that they sought to put me on the throne, alone, *now*.

Not bad for half a year's work.

And things were about to change, for in Eboracum my father had taken a turn for the worse.

XVIII

Be Harmonious, Enrich the Soldiers, and Scorn All Other Men

Eboracum, Winter AD 210

We rode back into the city that had been the de facto capital of the empire for the better part of three years tired, travel-worn and soaked to the skin with the winter weather that had been hard on us all the way south. The army had shed units all the way, dropping them back at garrisons on the two walls and at forts between and south of them, only the Praetorians and the Sixth Legion staying with me as far as Eboracum. As we lost each officer on the way back to their commands, they had, to a man, elicited promises from me that I would call on them the moment I needed them. Even having lost many of them en route, by the time we approached the palace on the civil side of the river, I still had a small cadre of men at my back who would see me take the throne sooner rather than later. In fact, the only officer in my retinue that would stand in my way should I seek to oust Father was Papinian. Thus it was that I felt enormously self-confident as I marched into the complex and sought out Father.

I was shocked when I laid eyes on him. He had gone downhill rapidly in my absence. He lay on a couch looking grey and pallid, and had he not been permanently trembling, I might have thought him gone already. I found myself casting a quick prayer and an offer of an altar to Serapis as I entered the room. Mother was there with him, of course, her face filled with concern, even fear, and a deep love. That caught in my throat, but there was the business of empire to be carried out, and no matter how much I loved her and worried for Father, it was my duty to make a report and to discuss the matter with him first – the duty of a returning general.

Other empresses would have left, or been dismissed, while the menfolk talked. Not Mother. She remained seated close to her husband as I squelched across the marble and sank into a seat with the sound of a sodden cloak being wrung out. The officers, also not dismissed, stood in a gathering behind me, near the door, and I could all but feel them willing me to demand Father step down. Looking at him, they had a point, for there seemed little about him now that could command an empire.

There was an awkward silence, broken only by the steady drip of rainwater from my seat to the floor below and Father's short, sharp breaths.

'You were successful.'

A weak and scratchy voice, far from the booming tone of my youth. Not a question, either. Father knew how successful I had been from the various reports I had sent south throughout the year. This was to be just a summary. I simply nodded.

'You did things differently,' he wheezed. 'Not the way I would.'

I shrugged. 'It was effective. The Maetae are cowed, though for how long I cannot say. None of these tribes will ever truly accept domination.'

'They should have been obliterated, not cowed. *Then* they would accept domination.' Something of the old strength had crept back into his tone. Anger was giving him presence once more.

I felt a touch of annoyance at that myself. I'd done more than anyone could have hoped to in that year in the North, but it simply wasn't feasible to annihilate the whole confederation. It sounded good in planning, looked good on reports, but the truth of that hilly, bleak world north of the walls is that some were always going to get to safety in the highlands and harbour thoughts of revenge.

'It is neither feasible nor a reasonable use of our resources to hunt down every last tribesman and put him to the sword.'

'That was the order I gave.'

'Father, the tribe is scattered and broken. They are currently no threat. The problem now is that with almost a year concentrating entirely on the Maetae in the lowlands, we have taken our eye from the Caledonii.'

'The Caledonii rise?'

I shook my head. 'We have had no reports to that effect yet, but the winter tribute they promised has not come, and I find that suspicious and worrying.'

'That could be the weather.'

'Possibly,' I admitted. 'Or possibly they watched what we did to the Maetae and decided they would rather fight to the last than submit. Sometimes you can push someone too far, and to them obliteration becomes a better option than what we offer. Father, this island is never going to be whole. And it *shouldn't* be. That's why the walls are there. Nothing north of them is worth the effort. The tribes will always rise again, and the feeble resources the land offers are not worth the cost of controlling them.'

He sagged back. 'I wanted it done in two years.'

'That was a dream,' I said, irritated again, now. 'A *fevered* dream, at that. Two years is not enough. It took Agricola twice that. And I doubt, having met these tribes and looked into their eyes, that even he and Domitian would have been able to maintain the victory. The north is uncontrollable. And worthless. At the very least, though, two years was not enough.'

'Then the war shall go on,' he snapped. 'A third year it is.' There was a hardness to his voice now, a disapproval, an echo of the man who had once been dubbed the Lion of Leptis. 'If it takes another year,' he said, 'then let it be so. I will be Britannicus before I die. This province made whole shall be my last legacy.'

He propped himself up on an elbow with considerable difficulty. 'And if you cannot do what must be done, then it will fall to an old soldier. This time I shall ride out in Martius and lead the army. And I shall have every head north of the wall bowed to Rome, or stricken from its body. The north will be part of the empire, whether it be cowed, or empty.'

I was angry now, rather than merely irritated. He was being a fool, and we all knew it. Mother opened her mouth to calm the situation and remind him of his condition, but I beat her to it. 'The only thing you'll lead in this condition is a funeral procession.'

It was a terrible thing to say, I know. But I was angry. And it was true. How he even got to and from the latrine I didn't know, but the very idea of him mounting a horse was laughable.

'You mock me, boy?'

I bridled. 'I speak plainly, Father.'

'You would prefer I place your brother in command?'

If ever there was a way to poke a bear with a sharp stick and provoke a reaction, this was it. 'Geta couldn't lead a campaign,' I snapped. 'You're blind to his faults because he's your son, but you know that *I* am the man for the army, that I am blooded and trained, with a record of success. Geta has never led an army or faced a foe. You want this over in another year? It would take him *ten*. You know that, and I know that you make the suggestion purely to rile me.'

'No,' he said, with grudging agreement. 'Not Geta. But not you, either. I shall lead the army.'

'You are being foolish.'

'I grow weary of your defiance. Get out of my sight. You are dismissed.'

I turned and marched out, still sodden and dripping, and angry as ever, concern painted on every military face as I passed. I could almost feel them willing me to turn back and demand what they saw as the only realistic solution: that he step down in favour of me. I could feel their frustration as I walked past them and left Father to his fantasies.

Outside, in the corridor, I bumped into the court physician, accompanied by a man who I suspected to be the medicus of the Sixth. They paused, heads bowing.

'Domine, how is he?'

'Stupid. Rash. Unyielding.'

The man sighed. 'As always. Domine, your exalted father is failing. My ministrations no longer work to heal, nor even to prolong. All I can do now is to keep the pain away. To make him comfortable.'

'Perhaps you should be administering something to hasten his departure,' I grunted.

He stared at me in shock. 'Domine?'

I shook my head, sagging a little. 'Nothing. If he is in pain, then perhaps it is his time. That is all.' My thoughts strayed to all those officers gathered, who'd urged me to step up and replace him. Was it such a stupid idea? There was still time to turn back and make my demand.

No. Patricide is the worst crime in the empire, punishable with the *poena cullei* – the offender tied in a sack with a snake, a dog, an ape and a cockerel, and thrown into the river to drown, if the animals did not kill him first. No, never patricide. I'd been offered the blade once and had turned it down, after all.

I gave the medicus a weak smile. 'Try to keep him comfortable. He is labouring under the impression he will lead the campaign north in just a few months.'

The man gave a dark chuckle. 'He has grand and unfeasible ideas, then, Domine.'

'I know it. Thank you, gentlemen. Do what you can.'

But as I left and went to the baths to get myself clean and warm and then find dry clothes, I was repeatedly assailed by images of Father lying there, hardly mobile, barely alive, and the notion that perhaps it was my time to rule would not abate. I had to force myself to think of something else as I reached the palace baths, shivering and cold.

My timing was poor. I slipped out of my sodden clothes in the *apodyterium* of the palace baths and left them in one of the alcoves, a Praetorian nodding his head in respect as he guarded the place, slaves rushing to take my clothes for cleaning and replace them before I needed them again. Slipping into the protective wooden shoes left for bathers, I clacked through the place, naked as a babe with a towel over my shoulder. I should have cleaned myself with oil and strigil first, of course, and *then* used the pools, but I was cold and damp, and all I wanted was warm water. I was an emperor. Let someone else worry about the cleanliness of the pool water afterwards. I walked into the steamy atmosphere of the *caldarium* and over to the pool's edge, and then slid down and into the water. It was only as the steam drifted clear that I then saw Geta across the pool.

My eyes instantly shot around the room to see if we were alone, fantasies of murder flitting into my mind. Of *course* we were not alone. He had a Praetorian standing protectively in the corner, and the one who'd nodded to me at the door had followed me in. Papinian had standing orders with all his men, and there was no way they were going to leave my brother and me alone in a room together. With good reason, too. I tell you now that had we been alone I'd have drowned the bastard there and then, and poured a celebratory drink afterwards.

'I *thought* I smelled shit,' Geta snarled. 'I should have realised you were back.'

I said nothing. I had nothing to say to him. I simply glared at him, picturing him slipping beneath the surface, eyes wide, face bloating, water rushing into his lungs. It was a comforting image. In my imagination his flailing arms and glassy eyes were the portal to my new world.

'Father is not long for this world,' he said, eyes narrow.

I just grunted. *Drowning, arms flailing...*

'He will be among the gods soon. Mother is insistent that we will share the empire, you and I.'

'Then Mother is more of a fool than I thought.'

'You will not defy her.' A statement? A question? A threat? All of those?

'No,' I answered, although I wasn't entirely sure that I meant it. Defy Mother or share the world with him?

'Neither will I.'

I looked through the steam into my brother's eyes, where the truth always lies. There, I saw something that made me uncertain that he meant it either.

'We will never share the empire,' I said.

There was a prolonged silence. We both knew what that meant. No matter what we said, as long as Mother was alive, we would have to defy her to end this feud the only way it could now end. In blood.

'I find I am not enjoying this,' I growled. 'Something in the water offends me.'

I slid from the bath and found my clogs once more, the tiled surface of the floor sizzling to the sole. It is petty, I know, but I enjoyed watching the multi-hued slick of travel grime floating out in ripples from where I had been towards my brother. Without a further backward glance I clacked out of the place.

It was clear that time apart had only widened the gulf between us. In our youth, I had hoped for a brother to share all with. In our adolescence, I had discovered that this was not to be, and that Geta and I would never agree or share siblings' love. Now, as adults, it was slowly becoming painstakingly clear that we could not coexist, and that only one of us would live to be an old man.

As I walked back through the palace, I passed the hall of emperors. A gallery that had been created for the imperial visit when we first landed on the island. I passed Julius Caesar. He was never an emperor, of course, but who could argue with his inclusion. I passed Augustus and Tiberius, and then Claudius. No Caligula. As I walked on, I realised Nero was missing, too, and then the Flavians, but without Domitian. Nerva, and all his followers until Commodus, who was similarly missing. A hall of emperors, but only the ones we were allowed to remember. None of those damned ones. No one whose name had been scratched from history, no matter the reason. Caligula, who had been a poor, battered soul, and despite all the good he'd done, was gone from history. Nero, Rome's most popular emperor, but gone because of the opinion of others. Domitian, who had strengthened the borders and rebuilt the administration and the treasury, who had saved the empire from the Chatti. Gone. Commodus, who I remembered as golden and glorious. Gone.

It struck me then, as I walked past those impassive faces, that even Geta's demise was not enough. If I simply killed him, I ran the risk of doing what he'd done to that damn Christian priest called Alban. Geta had created a martyr, and had almost started a revolution. I would not do the same with him. The day I saw the light leave Geta's eyes, I would need to add him to that list. To be truly a sole emperor, it was not enough that he died. He had to never have existed. And more so than those emperors who were missing from this corridor. Everything. Every hint he had ever walked the world had to go. Every coin. Every chiselled line, every bust, every law his name went to. He had to have gone from not just Rome, but from history.

By the time I was back in my apartments, I was decided. Geta must be the emperor who never was.

The winter rolled on, becoming steadily colder and wetter. Father continued to decline. The physicians, when pressed, gave him a few months, no more, though they couched this in the most delicate of terms. The consuls were chosen as the new year came around, and I could see Mother's hand in that too, for Pomponius Bassus had been a friend to me, and had been with us in the East. He, I was sure, would support me in any bid for sole rule. His partner in the consulship, however, was Hedius Lollianus Terentius Gentianus, a man who was known to espouse the supremacy of my brother as the legitimate child of both emperor and empress, a hopelessly self-important prick who did not like me at all. Carefully chosen consuls, then, who would keep one another in check, neither of them able to support one of us alone. Similarly, the governor and procurator of Britannia were replaced, for it had become well-known that the governor was in my brother's purse, while the procurator favoured me. Their replacements were unknowns with no prior connection to either of us, and therefore theoretically neutral.

She knew what she was doing, of course. Mother could see that Father's end was near, and she was putting in place everything she could to make sure that her two sons cooperated, by force or by law if necessary. Our power bases were chiselled away bit by bit, on Mother's instructions. The officers who were known to support me were shuffled back into garrisons, while those who Geta had bought were sent far away. By late Januarius, the only person I knew I could count on, who had any access to me or the court, was Maximinus the Thracian, that insightful giant cavalry officer in the imperial guard. Back in Rome, my Berber friend Macrinus would support me, of course, as would Laetus, the other Praetorian prefect, but neither would be able to help me here on this remote island. Similarly, I doubted there was anyone Geta could call on. And with Papinian and the Praetorians firmly obeying the order to keep us apart, our hands were more or less tied.

The kalends of Februarius rolled around, and with it came the next attempt on my life, or so I believe. I had employed a food taster of my own ever since that evening with the 'bad oysters' at Coria, for I could no longer trust palace employees. On the eve of the kalends, I settled in for the evening on my own, a list of potential senators I could lobby for support when the time came on the table beside me, irritably crossing off far more than I underlined. My taster tried the pork meatballs in olive tapenade, one of my favourite appetisers, and smiled for about ten heartbeats as I fumed over my work. Then he frowned, hiccupped twice, clutched his stomach and keeled over, his legs and arms shaking uncontrollably as frothy vomit fountained from his mouth. He was dead in another ten heartbeats. I was entirely put off my dinner, and more than a little vexed. I had the kitchen slaves tortured for information and then executed, of course, but it came as no surprise when no lead came up, and nothing pointed to the brother I knew damn well was behind it. Oysters in the North, and now meatballs back in Eboracum. He was being unimaginative.

I toyed with the idea of a return blow. I could probably get poison into his food, and if I thought it through, I could probably do it just as subtly, leaving no evidence. The problem was that I didn't want to. It was not that I didn't want rid of him, but I wanted him to watch me do it. I wanted it to be direct and personal. I am not a man for poisons and assassins. Give me a blade and a target, and that is where I will find myself content. And so I survived the poisoning attempt and let Geta go on nervously, waiting for the return blow that would never come.

The day after the kalends, Maximinus, the Thracian giant, was the victim of a knife attack in one of the alleys of Eboracum's civil settlement, while pottering along on his way home from a bar. Two locals jumped him. One managed to stick a short blade through the cavalry officer's arm, miraculously passing between the bones and severing nothing critical. By the time a few passing legionaries found the fracas and came to his aid, the big man had broken one man's head, even using the arm with a knife through it to fight with, and was smacking the other repeatedly against a house wall. He was escorted to the fortress surgeon and stitched up forthwith. He considered the wound little more than a scratch, and while it is not unknown for thugs to attack an officer on his own in the narrow streets of the city, it seemed awfully convenient to me that it happened to be the one officer in the whole of Eboracum upon whom I could entirely rely who happened to be jumped by thieves. Geta, of course, wore a mask of innocence at all times, even as he planned and plotted and made his attempts.

The third day of Februarius gave me a moment's relief, as there was no attempt on my life, and nothing happened to any of my friends. That evening, though, I learned to my disgust that the new governor and the new procurator of Britannia, who had arrived together in the south the previous month, had entered Eboracum that day, seeking an imperial audience, and were immediately whisked away, wined and dined by my brother. They were unknowns with no ties to either of us, but Geta was now urgently plying them with treats to secure their support.

On the fourth day, a slave came to find me. I was summoned urgently to the imperial apartments. There, outside Father's door, I found the court physician speaking in low tones to one of his orderlies. As I approached, he looked up and dismissed the servant, bowing his head. 'Domine, I fear the time is almost upon us. I have urged your father to rest, but he is insistent that he speak to you, and to the Augustus Geta.'

I nodded and stepped past him, opening the door. Before I could say anything, I could hear footsteps behind me, and I glanced back to see my brother approaching with a slave. I turned and walked into the room. I stopped, sharp.

I have never seen a man so close to death without a sword in his gut. I could almost hear the boatman's oar sploshing as he came to collect Father and carry him to the land of the dead. He was trembling, lying flat on his back. His hand had slipped from beneath a coverlet, and it was shaking uncontrollably. His face was almost white, like a marble statue when the paint has all but worn away. He looked small and frail, two things I had never thought to see in the Lion of Leptis.

I frowned. Beside him, on the table where one might expect a plate of nibbles, stood a funerary urn, a decorative example, but locally made, and with the lid lying to one side. I heard a throat cleared. Mother sat on a chair nearby, her expression grave, her eyes red-rimmed and cheeks puffy from crying. I gestured to the urn. A question.

'He says he does not understand how such a thing can hold him when even the world is too small for him. A clever man to the end, and a lover of a dark joke, your father.'

I looked at the urn. So small. So... final.

'How is he?' asked my brother, stepping into the room behind me.

'How do you fucking *think* he is?' I snapped without turning.

Mother made a hissing noise. 'Can you two not keep your bickering down even by your father's deathbed?'

Deathbed. Father had always been there, at the heart of everything we did. And in the more recent years, since the chasm between Geta and I had widened to the extent of threats and violence, Father had kept us from open war. He was the control, the command, the empire. And he was dying.

'Is that them?'

It was a weak voice, feeble, cracked and almost a whisper, like a spring wind through reeds. It made me shiver to hear my powerful father so diminished.

'It is,' Mother said.

'And we are alone?'

Behind me, the room's door shut with a quiet click. 'We are,' Mother confirmed.

Father turned his head, apparently with great effort. He was racked for a moment with shuddering coughs, and then fell back, breathing shallow, almost in gasps. It took some time for him to build up the strength to go on. Finally, he settled into a steady rhythm once more.

'It is the old illness, you know?'

I nodded.

'The one from Aegyptus,' he went on. I realised that he was looking at us, but could actually see nothing. He was blind, at the end. 'It never really went away,' he said, 'that illness. But your devotion to Serapis, I think, saved me. I should have died there and then in Aegyptus, as did so many others from that trip, but the gods thanked you for your devotion and granted me another thirteen years, and for that I am grateful.'

'Would that they had given more,' I said quietly.

'No. I have come far enough. I am not a young man. Just short of sixty-six years in this world, and I have come further than any man ever, from our origins in Leptis to rule of the world. I have beaten enemies both inside and outside the empire, settled the throne after a civil war, and rebuilt the treasury. The people will, I think, speak my name with kindness, and what emperor could want more?'

I remained silent. I didn't know what to say.

'Will they call me Britannicus, you think?' he asked, almost plaintive.

I nodded, though he couldn't see it. 'Even if the conquest is not complete, the tribes have paid heavily for their acts these past years. No man since Agricola has seen the North so settled. Whether we keep the North or not, we have conquered it.'

Behind me, my brother said, 'You will be Britannicus, Father. I will see to it.'

It rankled that he'd pitched in and said exactly what I was about to, but now was not the time to argue with him.

'Promise me that you will see the North finished,' Father said.

I rolled my eyes. The north could never be held. I knew that now, and I'd said as much to him. But behind me, Geta made that promise, and though I hated to do so, I echoed it, for if I did not, perhaps there would be a case for Geta gaining control of the army over me.

He fell silent again now, breathing in tiny gasps. He tried to say something, but no sound came out. After several attempts he rested once more, building up his strength. Finally, he beckoned with a crooked finger. Geta and I stepped close to his bedside, the closest we had been to one another in years. He smelled of sweat and rotten meat. I gagged and hated myself for it. Father took a deep breath.

'Be harmonious, enrich the soldiers, and scorn all other men.'

I nodded. So did my brother. Wise words on two counts, that was. The harmony part less so, though, and far less likely to happen.

We stood for a long moment, watching Father's chest rise and fall, rise and fall, rise and fall, and then it fell for the last time and he lay still. Mother let forth a cry of anguish, and Geta and I stood beside the body of our father. With unspoken accord, we both looked across at our mother, and then to one another. Father was gone. If we had been alone, we would probably already be clawing at each other's throats with intent to kill, but not with Mother here, not like this.

I straightened. The emperor was dead, and Geta and I shared the rule of the world.

For now.

Part Four – Brothers

'Quodque initium novum alio initio finito evenit'
Every new beginning is the result of another beginning's ending

—attrib. Lucius Annaeus Seneca

XIX

The North Settled

Eboracum, Februarius AD 211

The days that followed Father's passing were strange. Even as his body cooled, the tug of war began, and a strange, three-way struggle it was. Neither Geta nor I saw fit to sully Father's passing with bloodshed of our own, and so our feud settled once more into that tense, unspoken thing. Yet we both began jostling for position, knowing that the time was now near. At the same time, however, Mother began her own machinations in earnest. While both my brother and I began to secure our own position, Mother began to secure Rome against us, and such was the force of her personality and intellect, and such was the empire's respect for the newly widowed empress that everyone bowed to her will without question. While we prepared for the inevitable clash, she did everything she could to prevent it.

My officers, the ones I'd brought south who were now ready to draw blades in my name, even against my brother, were all sent away by her, but in my father's name and ratified by Papinian. She was not stupid, though, for dismissing or transferring such men could trigger insurrection. Instead, each was lauded for his part in our victories and given promotion to either higher military rank elsewhere or to public office back in Rome. Within a day my military power base in the city had vanished. I was not alone, though. While I'd been fighting in the North, Geta had similarly continued to build a strong support among the remaining military and civil spheres in Eboracum. These, Mother now had removed in subtle ways. The Praetorians had their standing instructions confirmed: in the name and memory of the emperor, they were to continue to uphold his wish that his sons be kept from conflict with one another. They were no longer our bodyguards, but part peace-keeping force and part jailors.

That day saw more upheaval in the state and in the court than any since the passing of Commodus, though few outside our *familia* would recognise it for what it was. At the end Father had accepted that he'd failed to bring us together and had instead wrung from us an oath of peace. Mother and Papinian would use that and the memory of a beloved emperor to keep us from conflict as long as they could. Even she must have known the time would come, though.

And while we all went about such business, administrators and freedmen prepared Father. Clearly, he would have to be cremated here, and then transported back to Rome for a state funeral. His body was arrayed in his best military garb the next day, just before the various officers departed for their new posts, and carried out to the forum of Eboracum, where a great pyre had been stacked up by the men of the Sixth. Praetorians stood around the periphery and behind them the people of the province watched, their faces bleak. The members of the court, the senior officers and the top men of Britannia attended in the square with the emperor's family. The priest murmured through his officiation, animals were sacrificed, and all those deemed worthy were allowed to approach the pyre and place their gifts and offerings upon it around their emperor. Then, on that chilly, grey Februarius morning, Geta and I took brands from the coal-filled braziers at the edge of the forum and approached the pyre. I wonder how many of the watchers noted that we never shared a glance throughout the ceremony, and that even in honouring our father we did so by approaching the pyre and firing it from opposite sides, out of view of each other as we both spoke promises that no one else could hear, and ones that, frankly, would have made Father extremely angry had he been able to listen.

We stood there for hours as Father was rendered down to ash, whereupon his remains were gathered up by the priests and their attendants and taken away to be placed in an urn for transport to Rome. The ceremony concluded with little more than a sigh and a silent departure of the crowds. There was no need for an announcement of succession, of course, for I had ruled as emperor alongside Father for years, and Geta had been our colleague officially for a year or so. As far as the uninformed public was aware, the succession would proceed smoothly and they still had two emperors.

We couldn't take the remains back to Rome, though. Not yet. We had started something in Britannia, and it remained unfinished. The Caledonii still had not lived up to their promises and sent their tribute, and that left a question hanging over the North. We had come to Britannia in response to their raids, and although I had no intention of solidifying our conquest, for Father was gone, and with him the impossible dream of making this province whole, we could not leave until we were sure those raids had stopped for good. Moreover, I had my own plans that relied upon another sojourn in the North. Mother had managed to dismiss my military support in Eboracum, but all across the warzone there were other officers in garrisons who were ready to support my bid for sole power. Mother had only delayed the inevitable.

'I will see the North settled before we leave,' I announced that evening as Father's consilia met for an initial session with my brother and me. 'I will not drag things out. The north will never be tamed, and a withdrawal to the walls is inevitable. But those who live beyond it need to know that doing so is our choice, not theirs. They need to stay cowed for generations. It will take two months, in my opinion, to put them down. They are fewer in number now, and we know their strong places. I will pull from them promises of peace.'

There was a general nod to this. Everyone was aware how costly this war was becoming, and no one wanted to see it drag over another year. Even my brother agreed, though I imagine that was because he saw getting me out of the way for two months as an opportunity to gain further power and influence.

Of all the people there – Mother was not, of course, for it was not her place – Papinian was the only one who had an idea of what was going on in our heads. He'd been charged with keeping us from one another's throats for long enough now that he knew us, and it was he who spoke up, the lone voice of dissent in the room.

'This is a task for your generals, Domine. Your place now is in Rome. Both of you.'

An attempt to halt our work. I felt the irritation building. 'Your opinion is noted and duly ignored,' I said in a flat tone. 'I shall not wait for *tubilustrium*. I will travel north in two days, and take the bulk of the military with me. We will crush the Caledonii and their Maetae refugee allies so thoroughly that they cannot raise a warband for a hundred years.

By late spring I intend to be in Rome, but until then I will finish things in the North.'

And gather my officers to my cause once more.

Geta was nodding his agreement. With me out of the way, and almost certainly Papinian and his Praetorians as part of the force too, he would be much freer to gather his own support.

The prefect was shaking his head. 'That is not possible.'

I blinked. I was actually surprised. I know that Papinian was a friend of my mother's and had been set to keeping us apart by Father, but to deny an emperor in his council was something that could easily see a man killed. It was very brave, and very foolish. I could feel the anger rising, and was seeking to contain it. It would not look good if I exploded in a rage now and ranted and threatened bloodshed. But I would not be gainsaid by this man.

'You forget your place,' I hissed.

He turned a look on me, and when he spoke it was in what he probably thought was a conciliatory tone. 'My place is between you and your brother, Domine. Your father and mother both made that clear to me.'

'My Father rests in an urn, now, Prefect. Do not think to impose commands upon your emperor. Such things can have nasty results.'

He shook his head. 'I was stomping around battlefields with your father when you were too young to shit without help, Marcus Aurelius Antoninus. I know what needs to be done. There is no value to seeking glory here. Your father is Britannicus now. Look elsewhere.'

I stared, livid. No one spoke to an emperor thus. I was struggling not to step across and slap him.

'Mark those names, Prefect. Marcus Aurelius Antoninus. The names of an emperor.'

'Yet I remember you as Lucius Septimius Bassianus, child of a Syrian house.'

That was it. I'd had it with him. I was a few short breaths from demanding his head, and again had to force myself to maintain my calm. When I spoke, it was through clenched teeth.

'You are dismissed, Papinian.'

He straightened. 'Then I shall return to my quarters and make ready for the campaign,' he said stiffly.

'You do not understand,' I said. 'You are dismissed from the *prefecture*. You are no longer commander of the Praetorian Guard. Gather your things and return to Rome, and when I am less angry with you, I may consider finding you a position that suits your talents but does not stand you in my way.'

His face set in a stony look, and he turned to Geta, probably expecting my brother to gainsay me, for it would be a natural assumption that we would disagree. We always did. We would argue about the colour of the sky, even. But not on this. On this we were in unusual accord, for we both saw the coming conflict and neither of us wanted Papinian getting in the way.

'You are dismissed,' my brother said.

Papinian looked from one of us to the other, and then turned, taking a deep breath, and marched away. I wrapped things up then with the consilia. Little more needed to be said, and Geta had nothing particularly to add. Most of all, I was angry. Papinian had provoked me, and I knew I was close to snapping. It is dangerous to deal with the business of state in such a mood, and so it could only be a good thing that within a few moments we were departing and I was stomping through the halls of the palace looking for something innocuous on which to take out my frustration.

Sometimes a man becomes a victim simply by being in the wrong place at the wrong time.

I was halfway back to my apartments when I bumped into the Thracian giant Maximinus, who had been looking for me, his arm still bound in wrappings from his injury. It was not common for the imperial cavalry guard to have free access within the palace, but I had granted as much for this man, for he was now my only certain ally in the city.

'Domine.' He greeted me with bowed head, face solemn.

'What is it?' I snapped. I was in a foul mood.

'Domine, there are rumours beginning to spread. Bad ones.'

I frowned. 'What sort of bad rumours?'

'A tale that just before your father died, you ordered the physicians to do away with him. Some even say that this is what actually happened and is the cause of the emperor's demise.'

I stared at him. Such rumours could do appalling damage. They had to be stopped. I thought back. That day I'd been angry after a fight with Father, I had made some stupid comment in the corridor to the medical staff who attended upon him. I'd been alone. I'd left the officers in the room and I doubt any of them could have overheard the exchange. That made it damn clear that these dangerous rumours had spilled from the lips of those very healers. There had been the court physician, Galen, and the medicus from the Sixth whose name I did not know. Two men. Both of them in senior positions of trust, who should know better. I fumed. The problem with rumour is that once it starts it is near impossible to stop. Geta would undoubtedly promulgate it and use that rumour to his advantage, blackening my name.

Another setback, and all because of the flapping mouths of two stupid men.

I clenched and unclenched, clenched and unclenched my fists angrily.

'Follow me.'

Moments later I was at one of the many guard rooms around the palace used by the Praetorians. As I barged through the doorway, face more thunderous than usual, the soldiers shot to their feet, knocking chairs over and spilling drinks in their surprise. They lowered their eyes in respect as I came to a halt, trembling.

'I have orders for you... nine men,' I said, eyes counting heads. 'Find the medicus of the Sixth Legion in the fortress across the river, and Galen, the court physician. Do not speak to anyone else, and do not accept any other tasks until this is complete. Find those two men and take them by force down to the waterline below the new bridge. I want each of them beheaded and their bodies cast into the river. Have the heads spiked and displayed on the bridge parapet. Have the phrase 'rumour monger' written on both foreheads for all to see. Do you understand?'

No one looked up. In fact, with their eyes still lowered, yet wide with shock, they looked at one another. No one spoke.

'Do you *understand*?' I bellowed.

They did. A chorus of agreement.

It was a little hasty, I admit. And in the long run it hardly stopped ill rumour, but simply added the murder of respected physicians to my list of crimes. Yet one, if not both, of them was guilty, and I was angry. I doubt anyone would spread rumour again without more care.

I marched off and left the soldiers to their work.

Three days I tarried in the city. My orders were carried out, and as the cohorts of the Sixth marched across that new bridge in Eboracum, setting off for our last campaign in Britannia, they tramped between the grey, staring heads of two respected physicians bearing their warning against the spreading of rumour. All I could do was hope that while I was away, Geta did not manage to take advantage of the absence of Papinian to gain too much control. On the bright side, I had plenty of support in the North, and I was taking the bulk of the Praetorians and the Sixth with me, so there was little he could do to gain a hold among the military.

It was upon reaching the wall that I discovered my mistake. I had underestimated Mother, which was foolish, for I'd always known how clever she was. I had reasoned that she knew only the avid support on the faces of those who'd accompanied me back to Eboracum, but it seemed that she had been far shrewder than that. Even as we'd stood around that pyre in Eboracum and watched the Lion of Leptis rendered down to ash, letters had raced north from the city, penned by the empress and countersigned and sealed by Papinian while still the Praetorian prefect, transferring and promoting almost all those men I'd painstakingly worked to bring on side during my campaign in the North. How she had identified them so fast I do not know, but as I came to forts expecting to find men who were ready to butcher Geta to put me on the throne, I would find instead only complete unknowns in command.

The glorious, clever woman had pulled the rug from under my feet. I was still powerless, or as powerless as an emperor could be, at least. My only hope was that she had been as thorough with my brother. I had hoped that with the end of the war in the North I would have sufficient power and control to seize the empire whole and tear it from my brother's hands. Now, it seemed, he and I were once more evenly matched. Moreover, Mother and Papinian had carefully selected as replacements men who could be relied upon to support both her sons with equal vigour and obey the imperial command, the only exception being when those commands were turned upon a brother. Mother was determined to keep her sons both alive and well, even if we would never see eye-to-eye.

As we moved north the same story played out at almost every fort. Here and there I found a supporter she'd missed, but on the whole my power base had vanished. We moved into Maetae lands and as we did so I tried everything I could think of to bring the army in the North back to my side. I was confounded at every move. The officers had been put in place with imperial edicts, and each had been carefully worded so that it would now take the order of both ruling emperors to dismiss or transfer that officer. Geta would have to agree to it too, to remove them. Gods, but Mother was clever. And that meant I was stuck with officers who would never favour one of us over the other, and who I could not get rid of.

As for the army, while I was still popular with them, they could see little gain now in supporting me over my brother, and the promise of loot and slaves was a paltry one, for in the past two years we had stripped the Maetae and the Caledonii of everything of value. There was little anyone was going to take away from this season's fighting but blood and hardship.

We travelled the territory of the Maetae and found just a wasteland. Our campaign the previous year had utterly brutalised the tribes of that confederation and had left them with barely enough men and women to survive, let alone populate a landscape. I have read that after Caesar's seven years of war with the Gauls, there had been so many deaths and so much destruction that it took five generations for the land to recover. In truth, even now, Gaul is still a shadow of what it should have been. Such is what we had done to the Maetae in one year.

We found small villages here and there, and whenever we did, we killed and enslaved, looted and burned, but it was like a nailed boot grinding an ant into the ground – hardly glorious or lucrative. We moved north again and within half a month of leaving Eboracum we were into the highlands where we had campaigned that first year, when we had learned how dangerous the Caledonii could be and had only cowed them with the utmost brutality. Here, there were more signs of life. We had destroyed many of the Caledonii, but they were still strong enough to form small warbands, and that was all they needed for their subtle and horrible mode of warfare. Our men began to suffer those attacks we had met the first time we'd come here, but there was a difference now. Back then, they had fought with the ferocity of an invaded people and with the belief that they could achieve victory. Now they fought with that glum pessimism of a people who know that they are already defeated and are merely clinging to a ghost of what they were.

Our reprisals, on the other hand, were more horrific than ever. There was nothing worth taking from these people anyway now, and the troops would not be bought off with what we could find, so we butchered, burned and crucified our way across the North. For the first time in the history of Rome, we went north of that great glen that crosses the highlands, and even built a small temporary fort just to the north from which we hunted down the last of their warriors. It was not a campaign to be proud of, and I would not demand a triumph, despite the fact that the body count probably warranted it.

By Aprilis we were standing knee-deep in damp bracken on some gods-forsaken soggy hilltop in that northern land, confirming with the scouts that there was nothing left to destroy within twenty miles in any direction.

We had burned and executed everything we found for the better part of two months, and for the last six days we had found nothing. It seemed we had emptied the North of life. Of course, we all knew that was not true and that the survivors were in hiding. Such is that land of blasted moors and deep valleys that a tribe could disappear within them and never be found. That was one of the reasons the place could never be held for Rome.

We needed to finish this now, and so I had to meet with the most important survivors. I sent out messengers. I would have bedecked them as traditional Roman envoys of peace, with white flags and olive branches, but no olive tree would grow in this cold, damp climate, and so I had to rely upon white rags alone.

The locals must have understood the symbol, for after two days of sending out scouts, a deputation finally arrived at the gates of our main camp, near the sea at the great glen's eastern end. They were far from impressive, and the warriors of the guard looked either too old to fight or too young, all weary and defeated. The leader was in no way a king like those we had met in previous years, but he seemed to carry authority, and when he was introduced, it was as a man who spoke for both the Caledonii and the Maetae.

'We have nothing left to give,' the man said in a broken tone and with no preamble. His gaze was lowered, though more through exhaustion than respect, I believed. 'No tribute to send. We starve and have nothing. Rome has taken or burned everything from the wall to the end of the world.'

I simply nodded. 'I no longer seek tribute. But you will be pleased to note that unlike my father, who sits now among the gods, I have no interest in maintaining control of your horrible land. Why you would want it, and how you survive in it, is beyond me. I am here simply to tell you two things. Firstly, that Rome is withdrawing from your lands to the southern wall, though we shall maintain a few small northern outposts to watch over the situation in the North. We shall trouble your people no longer.'

At this he finally looked up, though a Praetorian centurion stepped closer and used his vine stick to push the man's head forward, gaze respectfully down once more.

'The second thing is that you should take this as neither our failure nor your victory. It is simply our wish to abandon this hole to its fate and concentrate on lands that are worth our effort. Our soldiers will ever look to the north on this island, and there will be no repeat of the decade of raids and belligerence that brought us here three years ago. Should any warband come within arrow reach of the wall, we will return in force, and the next time not even a tree or fern will survive in this land. Do you understand me?'

There was no dissembling among them. No confusion. No discussion. Each of them, from prince to pauper, nodded and murmured their understanding. We had an agreement. It had taken two and a half years of war, and I had abandoned Father's dream of a united island, but we had avenged ourselves for the troubles that had brought us here, and I had secured two things. We would have a good, solid northern border and could concentrate on the profitability of the province, and it would be many generations before the tribes of the North felt even remotely confident in approaching the wall.

The war was over, the tribes cowed.

–

We travelled south once more, not with a sense of glorious victory, but at least with the feeling of a solid success. As we moved back towards Eboracum and civilisation, I carefully assessed every installation we had manned over the three years. Anything north of the Tavus river had its ramparts slighted and any structure torn down. Our bridges were demolished as we pulled back. The great ditches of Alauna were left intact, for the place would be the natural position for a forward post should we ever need to return. South of that we left a few temporary garrisons at the wall of Antoninus, each of which would remain until we were certain that the northern tribes would live up to their promise of peace.

The northernmost remaining fort would be Trimontium, and after that, just the outlying forts and the main solid border of the wall of Hadrian, which would from this day form the northern edge of the empire. This time I did not bring south with me a cadre of officers eager for me to seize sole power. This time, I returned tired, cold and ready to leave the province.

As I walked once more into the great procurator's palace in Eboracum, I was greeted as a conquering hero, and directed to the *aula regia*, where I found Mother in Father's throne-like seat. She looked extremely regal. I had always known that she had more of a hand in the ruling of the empire than any empress before her, but I had never seen her display her unprecedented power so blatantly.

As I entered the room, I was announced with all of my titles, and my full name, to which I had appended Severus since Father's passing. Similarly Mother was announced, and I almost chuckled as I met Julia Augusta, Mother of the emperors, Mother of the camps, Pia Felix, Mother Vesta, Empress of Rome.

At a gesture from her the various lackeys, slaves and soldiers departed the room, the door closing and leaving the two of us alone.

'Impressive,' I said. 'It would appear that Father lives on, just in a dress now.'

She gave me an odd smile. 'Expediency. You and your brother drive me to great lengths to maintain the empire. Until the bad blood between you can be settled and the empire protected from your arguments, I must maintain sufficient authority and respect to keep the two of you in order.'

My eyes narrowed. This was an echo of Papinian's assertion that he, a mere soldier, would tell an emperor what to do. She could see into my head, though. She knew what I was thinking.

'You are emperor of Rome, Marcus, and I will do nothing to diminish that. But I raised you and made you what you are, along with your father. I am your mother, and all of Rome knows me and knows my strength. You will not set yourself against me, and I tell you this now.'

I paused for only a moment before bowing my head. 'Of course.'

'Good. I have had the same from your brother. The empire is at peace. It is the most stable and peaceful it has been since the days of your namesake. Our family is popular, and we have won great wars in the East, the South and now the North. There is no corner of the empire where we are not respected and admired. This is the legacy of your father. A strong military, a strong empire, and peace and prosperity after decades of disaster. I will not allow the struggle between my sons to ruin that legacy. Do you hear me?'

Again, I paused. 'I do.'

But I also knew that this could not last. The loss of Father was still a raw wound for both family and empire, but sooner or later it would be scabbed over and become a scar, and then we would come into our own. For now, though, Mother was right. We needed peace, at least until we were in Rome and the empire accepting of the new regime.

'Good.'

As if somehow ears had been on our conversation, the great hall's door opened once more, and in walked my brother. He looked surprised to see me, but managed to contain all but a little flicker of irritation as he came to a halt just out of reach of me, facing Mother. The timing was too convenient to be accident. Somehow Mother had arranged it.

'I have had this from both of you, now you will both listen and take in that to which you have agreed. I know, sadly, that you will never be friends. That you will never be in concord. But sometimes what we want as people must take second place to what *Rome* wants, and what Rome wants is harmony and strength of rule. You have both agreed to submit to my will in this. What you think in the privacy of your head and what you do in your private lives now does not concern me. But as far as the people of Rome are concerned, from the most powerful senator to the poorest beggar, you are brothers and emperors of Rome, with no division.'

We shared a look. We had agreed, but we both knew that this agreement would not last.

'We will do what we must,' she went on, 'to keep you two from one another's throats, and somewhere along the line an agreement will be found that will allow you both to function without bloodshed. For now you will wear the mask of fraternity all the way from Eboracum and into Rome. Now go and prepare. We depart in two days.'

And yet, as we nodded and turned, leaving, neither Geta nor I could bring ourselves to look at each other. Our war had not ended, but merely been paused.

XX

The Menagerie

Rome, Maius AD 211

I had given my word. So had Geta. Our peace, such as it was, lasted hours. By the time we were ready to move, taking Father's ashes back to Rome, I was already speaking to the various senior officers appointed by Mother and Papinian, and working on them, persuading them of my right to sole rule, that I was Father's true heir. They were all polite and obedient, and yet none of them were entirely willing to discard Geta, such was the hold that Mother, and the ghost of Father, had over them.

Word of our journey went ahead, of course, and so we were greeted every afternoon, as we reached the next stage of the trek, by the toga-clad *ordo* of each town. Gifts were thrown to us, garlands in evidence, rose petals, entertainments and so on. An imperial visit to a town is a huge thing, even if the emperor is merely passing through, and I think we were all sick of the glorification and the enforced jollity and splendour even by the time we reached the southern shore of Britannia. I am not at all sure what the provincials must have thought of us, with Mother travelling in state as though she were every bit the emperor, and her two sons moving entirely separately, each with his own column and entourage, not even looking at one another. We must have been a strange imperial visit. And then, of course, there was Father's urn, transported in its own carriage, which drew reverence and awe from each and every soul as we passed.

It was a slow journey, too, which did little to ease the tension between us. Any state journey that involves the entire court is always a slow thing, but when combined with a grand funeral procession back to the capital, it was extremely tedious, and the month came to a close before we had even left Britannia.

We crossed the channel in the late winter, which is a troublesome time in that wild stretch of water, yet we managed to do so without incident, and landed in Gaul in Martius. Our arrival in Gesoriacum was a grand affair, for we were welcomed as conquering heroes, the general word being that we had successfully suppressed the north of Britannia, and no hint that we had not added it to the province as had been Father's wish.

We tried in public to maintain Mother's fiction that we were in concord, but in effect it proved impossible. We made a cursory attempt to keep our bickering in the private sphere, but it simply did not happen. We both spent every spare moment attempting to bring important men over to our side, blackening one another's name. We were each accompanied by lictors and Praetorians, which is a good thing, for had either of us shown any vulnerability on that journey, I am sure we would have exploited it with a naked blade, no matter what promises we had both given Mother. It came to a head the day we reached Durocortorum.

As we crossed the lush fields making for the city, the distant hills little more than a purple ribbon on the horizon, there came a shout of furious panic from my brother's carriage where it rattled along on the far side of the road, ten feet from me on my horse. The entire column came to an immediate halt as Geta leapt from the vehicle. I was garbed as a soldier as usual, with my caracallus wrapped around me, riding a cavalry mount, while my brother wore a civilian tunic and travelled in a carriage. This, I'd hoped, had said much to the military minds among us.

Geta leapt to the road and jumped up and down, bellowing and brushing at his torso as though to rid himself of something. I watched, entertained by the display, until finally he stopped this show and stood, trembling, his eyes rising slowly to me, narrowing as they did so.

'You.'

'Me,' I answered, with a sneering smile that I simply couldn't keep in.

'You failed.'

'I did?'

'You think to do away with me before we reach Rome? Well, you failed, brother of mine.'

I shrugged. 'I would love nothing more, but my sword remains sheathed, as I promised Mother.'

The reason for the halt became clear as I looked over his shoulder. One of his Praetorians had leapt from the carriage, holding a snake perhaps two feet long and patterned brown and black, gripping it just below its spade-like head. The soldier held it at arm's length, regarding it with a worried look until one of his companions grabbed it and pulled it out of his hands, breaking the thing below the head and casting the writhing, broken shape away into the grass.

'Asp viper, Domine,' the soldier said. 'Very dangerous.'

Geta's eyes glittered. 'Nice try,' he snarled at me.

'What is this?' said a new voice.

We turned to see that Mother's carriage had now pulled up close by and she was leaning out of the window, pulling aside the curtain.

'Paccia's son tried to kill yours,' Geta said angrily. 'Poisonous snake, just like him.'

I bristled. The reminder that I was not Julia's natural son was deliberate provocation, and I struggled to maintain my temper.

'Marcus?' she said, turning a meaningful look on me.

'Nothing to do with me. Gaul has snakes, and not just ones like him.'

'A likely story,' Geta hissed.

'When the time comes, I will see you to the next world on the tip of a blade, sweet brother, not through something like this.'

'Might I remind you of your promises?' Mother snapped. 'If you cannot be trusted to maintain civility even on the road, then it is time you were separated.' She called over Valerius Patruinus, the current Praetorian prefect, and a man loyal specifically to her above all. The arrangements were made before we reached the city. We were to make camp outside Durocortorum, Geta to the north, I to the south, while Mother would provide the grand imperial visit for the city. The next morning we moved on according to her new plan. The imperial procession split into three distinct columns. Mother, with an appropriate imperial entourage and military escort, set off on a direct route, following the great road south-east to Lugdunum and then down the Rhodanus, taking ship at Massilia and hugging the Italian coast back to Rome. Geta was set a path that carried him to the south-west, far from the rest of us, around the Arvernian hills and thence to the port of Narbo, taking ship there. My route was to take me further east, to Argentorate and then over the Raetian passes and down into Italia. It was cleverly done, for not only did it put a whole province between Geta and I, and negate any possibility of the two of us meeting until Rome, but it would also take both of us a lot longer to travel than Mother, who would arrive in Rome considerably ahead of us, allowing her to put plans in place before our arrival. I won my own little victory as we separated, for it was not until we were well on our way that Geta would have realised I had taken Father's urn with me. That must have infuriated him.

Just how expertly Mother planned the journey was made clear when I finally sighted Rome in Maius and learned there that my brother had just put in at Ostia Portus. Our routes had been so expertly worked out, and the officers commanding the columns given such explicit instructions that, even having travelled hundreds of miles apart, we had reached Rome within a day of each other.

I will admit to a little smugness that of the two of us it was I who entered Rome first. Geta would still be making his way upriver as I entered the northern edge of the city. My adventus was, of course, anticipated, but then so was that of my brother. The senate, careful to not to show favour to either of us, divided and attended two separate approaches, half at the north to meet my procession, half at the riverside dock to meet that of Geta. Likewise, the people of the city were divided between the two sites, and so my adventus was only half that one might expect of a returning emperor, though at least I was the first to arrive. The people of Rome chanted as I traversed the streets, calling me Britannicus for our victory, though that appellation belonged in truth to Father. Laurels were cast before me, and the arcades of the city were lined with souvenir stalls.

In fact, our arrivals were so closely timed that my brother's ship put in at the Navalia even as I reached the Palatine through cheering, crowd-lined streets. He was but half an hour behind me.

I arrived at the magnificent façade of the imperial palace on the hill to find Sempronius Rufus, Mother's cubicularius, waiting for me at the palace door. Our arrival had been anticipated, and Mother, ever intent on the safety of both her sons while maintaining a public appearance of unity, had organised everything. I was escorted very politely and deferentially to the wing of the palace that Father had constructed a few years earlier. This, apparently, was to be my personal living quarters, while the old Flavian palace on the far side of the Stadium Garden was to be Geta's. We would live separate private lives, yet both palaces had access into the main rooms of state where we could greet the city's luminaries together in a show of familial concord. It was a master stroke, fitting of our mother's shrewdness and wisdom. The only problem was that, though we had both taken the oath to her that we would work to maintain this façade, and not knife one another in the palace corridors, the longer we existed in close proximity the more strained we would become, and the more likely it was that the oaths would be broken.

I settled into the palace that afternoon, using the baths and cleaning myself up after the long journey. We would have only that one day before our ability to put on a show of brotherly conduct would be tested, for now that we had returned his ashes it was time for Father's state funeral. The people had waited three months, after all. Still, as Geta returned and was escorted to his half of the palace, it became apparent that even an afternoon was too much. Though we lived in separate palaces, there were far too many places where the complexes bled into one another, with open connecting passages, various doors, and that great long open garden between us. We'd been home for less than three hours when we bumped into one another in the open space that connected to both palaces and where the menagerie was housed.

'Fuck,' I said, laying eyes on him as we both stepped into the mani-cured lawns and hedges. 'Will you piss off and leave me in peace?'

'Find your own garden, arsehole,' he snapped. My Praetorians gathered close, as did his, and for a moment we must have resembled two small armies, waiting for the call across the battlefield. I was damned if I was going to let the runt have the win here.

'This is the only garden in Father's palace. The old Flavian palace has access to the *main* gardens. Go stink up the air there.'

'That's public space. Mother is insistent that I don't use it. This is the only private garden. You don't even like gardens. Just blood and shit. *That's* your world.'

'If you don't fuck off,' I hissed angrily, 'I may have to break my word to Mother and put a knife in your ribs.'

At that his Praetorians put their hands to their sword hilts, which led mine to do the same. For a long moment we glared at one another, a single insult away from open violence. The tension was broken by a gentle, almost musical voice calling out from the walkway around the top of the garden.

Quintus Marcius Dioga was one of Mother's favourite courtiers, an equestrian and long-time adherent of the family, another son of Leptis Magna. He was one of the few men in a position of power in the city who commanded respect from all, even the senators, and his voice carried a strangely sing-song tone that at once soothed and yet held a core of steely command.

'Domini, it is the empress' wish that the garden be a mutual meeting-place, part of both palaces, and a location where the emperors can meet in neutral territory and discuss issues.'

We shared a look, Geta and I, and in that look we both knew how little chance there was of that happening. 'I shall not tread the same lawns as that animal,' Geta snarled.

'Likewise,' I snapped, and the pair of us turned and walked away, slamming the doors and shunning the garden from that moment. Indeed, by the time Somnus claimed us that night, finally home and wrapped in our sheets in separate palaces, we had sealed every connecting door and passage, having them all blocked and bricked up. And even then, we each set men on guard at any point of ingress, for we were under no illusion that if there was the merest chance of an assassin slipping in, then it was likely to happen.

By the time we rose in the morning, we had also managed to secure completely separate staffs, with separate kitchens and storerooms. There would be no poisonings, for there would be no access there. We even had our separate baths.

Mother had made the funeral arrangements many days before we returned, and we spent a few hours preparing ourselves. For once, Geta shunned his usual purple tunic, and I my military garb, and both of us wore the black of mourning. Appropriately attired, with our faces painted by a cosmeta in pale white lead and with our eyes and turned-down mouths picked out in black, we joined Mother in the rooms of state, for she now quartered herself in the old Tiberian palace in order to show favour to neither of us.

Father's urn was placed in position at the centre of the great triclinium, the state dining-room, on a table draped with black silk. The black tables and tiers of black seats were already in position. Neither of us would speak as we met, for to do so would only begin an argument, but Geta and I exchanged looks instead of blows until Mother silenced us both with her own. We travelled then in state from the palace, surrounded by men and women in mourning, even the Praetorians eschewing their traditional white for appropriate black. The city was eerily silent as we led the procession, Father's urn carried by a veritable giant of a man, held high for all to see. As we passed, the silence was broken by the weird surge of moaning and wailing of the people of Rome for their deceased lord. It came in waves as we passed, ebbing and flowing. From the Palatine we took a snaking route in order to display the urn to as many as possible, finally arriving an hour later at the Capitol. As Father's urn was lowered into place, I realised that the man now carrying it might be a giant, but he was a different giant to the one we had set off with. It made sense. No man could have carried it aloft for an hour, and yet I had not noticed any change, so smooth and subtle had it been.

On the Capitol, Geta and I both attended upon the priests with their togas over their heads in the traditional manner. We watched and recited appropriate lines as the priests of the Capitoline triad sent up their prayers on behalf of the city and the empire that the great gods of Rome receive the emperor into their number. Firstly, the priest of Juno, then of Minerva, and finally of great Jupiter, all begged that Father be accepted into Olympus. A hog was sacrificed at the close of the rites.

The ceremonies over, our entourage threw coins into the crowd, each freshly minted with images of our deified father, and we took a more direct route back to the Palatine. There we returned the urn to its place and unwrapped the wax mask of Father's face that had been fashioned very carefully and resembled him in heart-breaking detail. The mask was applied to the reclining figure at the head table of the room, which had been placed in position in our absence. The figure was attired in Father's usual military manner, and the resulting manikin was unpleasantly realistic.

Once Geta, Mother and I had settled ourselves into position, the doors were opened. Senators and men of note and power, all in funereal black, filed into the room and took their assigned places to the left of the emperor, while their wives and the powerful matrons of Rome fell into place on his right. According to tradition, none of the women had adorned themselves with jewellery, and all wore staid black.

A day-long meal was then undertaken in silence, all in the presence of the emperor in his urn and the facsimile of him on his couch. The open end of the room was taken up during the feast by a succession of choirs from all the provinces of the empire singing paeans to the emperor's spirit. Periodically, through the meal, a man dressed as a medicus would enter, the room pausing as he approached the wax effigy and announced in grave tones the emperor's rapidly failing health. Each time the ritual was completed, the emperor's condition worse with each iteration, the choir would wail until the medicus left the room.

Finally, as night fell, the feast ended, the singing stopped, and all filed out from the palace once more. Again, now, the city's streets were filled with people, and again that wave of sobbing and moaning crested and dipped as we passed. Now, though, the procession was different. First it was led by Father's lictors, then a squad of Praetorians, and then the men and women of Rome's highest circles. Then came Father's urn, once more held aloft for all to see, and then Mother, Geta and I. But now there was another sight for the people of Rome, for the entire couch with its reclining effigy of Father was borne aloft with us, carried through Rome.

We reached the appointed place on the Campus Martius, close to the river, and there, at the centre of the wide, open space, stood the wooden house, formed from kindling and dry, seasoned timber. We could smell the unguents, perfumes, incense and dried fruit that adorned the edifice from even a street away, such was its heady odour. Hangings of black and gold were draped all across the wooden house, bearing the signs and names of many gods. As we fell into place in the wide square, the public gathered at the periphery, held back by Praetorians, the couch and its effigy were carried into the building and settled into place, the soul of the emperor no longer tied to his earthly remains, but now housed within the effigy. The bearers returned and closed the timber doors, allowing more drapes to unfurl and cover them.

As braziers were set up around the square, the imperial horse guard arrived and pranced in perfect precision around the building, doing honour to their departed emperor in a manner so old even Romulus must have learned it from someone. As they filed out, and I wondered behind which gleaming cavalry mask my friend Maximinus Thrax had lurked, in came the charioteers, carrying out their own homage. I had managed to pass the day with barely a thought for my benighted brother, but watching the champion charioteers of the four factions riding around that structure, I was dragged all the way back to that day in the Circus when Geta had first tried to kill me, for his favourite, Euprepes, was still there leading the Greens, while the blue champion was a lesser man since our champion had been mangled that day.

My lip was twitching in anger as they departed, and I had to force upon myself appropriate serenity as the rites were carried out. Finally, in almost an echo of Father's cremation in Britannia, Geta and I stepped out and grasped a brand from the braziers, approaching the structure from two sides. We torched the building and stepped back, watching it roar into golden life. The smell was incredibly intense even in the wide open, for the burning incense, oils and so on created an odour that filled half the city for the next hour.

We stepped back to the edge, beside Mother and the urn that contained Father's earthly remains, and there we all watched with bated breath, tense.

An emperor can be remembered in three manners. On occasion they will be neither honoured nor hated, as with the ancient Tiberius. If they have brought upon themselves a bad name, they can be disposed of with ignominy and have their name damned, to such an extent that their images and names are scratched out and they are removed from history. But a beloved emperor will undergo rites as we had observed that day and night, and with the appropriate sacrifices and the goodwill of the gods, he will be accepted among their number. It was not a given thing, of course, that the Olympians would wish it so, and we waited with a great deal of tension.

The relief we all felt as we saw the eagle was palpable. In the darkness, it seemed to have emerged from the burning roof of that funereal building, and with a single cry, soared up into the night sky and away into the darkness. Father's spirit had risen to join the gods. A great cheer arose from all around, and I had a tear in my eye, I must admit. Beside me, Mother was sobbing with sorrow and relief at once.

A prosaic friend once told me that the ritual is a sham and that the priests of Jupiter have a captive eagle ready for any such event, carefully working its release into the ritual. To that friend I snorted and told him that he could believe such things and dishonour the gods if he so wished, but I would not. I watched that night, and I knew that eagle for my father.

The public rites over, we stayed until the fire burned low, and then moved off, carrying the urn, now devoid of Father's spirit entirely, across the river, where we interred it in the great mausoleum of the Antonines, which has housed the emperors' remains since Hadrian constructed it a century ago.

It was done. Father was fully gone and among the gods.

And that meant that Rome now had two emperors, who were brothers.

And who could not bear the sight of one another.

We returned to the Palatine by separate routes and resumed our sullen hatred once more.

A dozen of the least pleasant days followed. We appeared twice in public for our position as joint emperors to be ratified by the senate, and for appropriate rites and ceremonies to take place. On both occasions we did not look at one another and shared not a word.

One thing that was satisfying, even at the start, was the letter I penned and dispatched the first day. Borne by fast ship and held by Praetorians, it would be delivered to a strong, humourless man on the island of Lipari, and within an hour of its arrival, my dreadful wife and her brother, who had been languishing there in exile, would be strangled and finally out of my hair. I had entertained grand plans of making it look as though she had brought the fate upon herself, but with Geta now poised where he was, it was becoming important that I lose one wife and find another. Once I had confirmation she was safely in a jar somewhere I could start looking for a more suitable wife.

Two nights after the interment, Geta's first attempt on my life in the city failed. My Praetorians captured a gladiator in the cellars of the palace, sneaking around with just a curved *sica* blade. He was a brave and strong man, for it took two hours of torture for him to break and name my brother as his master. He was butchered and delivered to my brother's doorstep as a statement. Maximinus tried to persuade me to bring the matter up with my mother, stating that if I did so, I could claim the moral high ground. He was probably right, but now, as far as I was concerned, morality could go hang. I was more interested in blood than morals. As such, I let Geta get away with his attempt, for not drawing attention to it left the game board open for me to make my own move.

I was more direct. I sent a message claiming to be from Mother, asking him to the *aula regia*, the state audience chamber. There, I waited, sword in hand. I knew he would be guarded by Praetorians, and I knew how many he would have, for a *contubernium* of eight men was our usual accompaniment. As such I made sure to have a score of men waiting with me.

Geta's Praetorians opened the door and my men jumped them, overcoming and subduing them swiftly.

The bastard was not there. Somehow he'd either got wind of my ploy or had anticipated it, and had sent soldiers, but not come himself.

Mother was furious with us both when she found out. She told us we were not acting like emperors, or even men. That we would break our oaths was abhorrent. That we would go back on our word to her cut her deeply. We were contrite. Indeed, I was actually truly sorry, not for what I'd done, but for the fact that it had come back to Mother and caused her distress. We were both apologetic.

But we also both knew that would not stop us. Rome was simply too small for us to share. Gods, but the cosmos and everything within and without was too small for *us* to share.

At Mother's urging, the senate voted that sacrifices should be held at the Temple of Concord to the unity of the emperors. It was to be a great public event and would heal the damage done to our reputations by the rumours beginning to spread of our attempts on one another's life. Crowds gathered on the day, the priests and their attendants preparing the sacrificial animals and all the altars and braziers and bowls of water. The consuls arrived, Terentius Gentianus and Pomponius Bassus, to oversee the whole thing. It would have been one of the year's public highlights...

...had either of us attended. The night before, we had bumped into one another in one of the palace's public corridors. Geta had opened the exchange by expressing the wish that the ground would open up and swallow me. I had responded with an opinion that even the ground itself would spit *him* back out. It had quickly devolved into a slanging match, and the moment he had the temerity to remind me that Mother was not my birth mother once more, I went for him. I had no blade, but I managed to get my hands on his throat before the Praetorians managed to drag us apart. In other times a soldier who manhandled his emperor would have been tortured to death for such a thing. These days, Mother's word was more law than any other, and laying a hand upon one of the emperors to prevent him from throttling the other had become nothing unusual.

As such, there was no chance that either of us was going to lower ourselves to attending a sacrifice to our ongoing concord. The very idea was laughable.

I am not the superstitious man my father was. I honour the gods, of course, and I had created enough curse tablets bearing my brother's name that their weight could have sunk a trireme, but I tend to see most of what Father would consider 'signs' as nature or coincidence. Even I, though, could not ignore what happened next.

The rest of that day, after the sacrifices to concord that never happened, was sullen all across the city, the people worried for the state of their emperors. The capitol was still and silent that night, the great temple of Concord rising before it at the head of the forum. The streets were oddly empty, a sense of trouble and foreboding filling Rome.

As such it was a passing group of soldiers from the city watch, the *vigiles*, who were the only witnesses that night. They rounded the corner of the temple of Juno to see the great esplanade overlooking the forum empty of humanity, though not of life. Two wolves skulked in the shadows cast by the Temple of Jupiter, and that alone is almost unheard of. Wolves sometimes come into the city, but to reach the very heart of Rome is amazing. The vigiles, of course, set upon the wolves, driving them away from the capitol. They killed one at the bottom of the steps, right before the temple of Concord. The other was later tracked down somewhere outside the pomerium and dispatched. But the significance of two wolves on the Capitol, and one slain before concord, could hardly be ignored by anyone.

Some took it as a portent.

I took it as a warning.

XXI

Time to Pay the Price

Rome, Summer AD 211

Neither Geta nor I had missed the significance of the wolf omen. We were the wolves, for certain, and one of us was going to die within the city, and soon. We were each determined it would not be us. In truth, that conclusion had been guaranteed now for years, at least since my brother had been made Augustus and interfered with my succession. From that moment on, one of us had a very finite lifespan. What the wolf omen did was step things up.

As Rome continued on its business as always, we began to fight our war on two fronts, one with steel and the other with words. We both felt uncertain of the Praetorians, for there was no guarantee they could not be bought, and so we built up a force of men on whom we could rely. This did involve some Praetorians: those who had been in Geta's retinue throughout Britannia stayed with him, while those who had fought alongside me on the Danubius and felt an affinity with me now guarded my palace. In addition, I brought in a unit of the imperial cavalry guard under Maximinus Thrax, men whom he trusted, and therefore so did I, and the Urban Prefect Cilo, who I knew well, brought in men from his cohorts. Beyond that I had my lictors and a number of solidly partisan mercenaries brought in from the Blue racing faction. My palace was better defended now than any fort in the empire, but Geta had been doing likewise.

That did not stop us making attempts, of course. Blades had been bared now, and the standard set. For months following the wolf incident, every other day some low-life or disaffected soldier would be apprehended in the palace cellars, or lurking around our barricaded corridors, and each time, as they were slowly tortured to death, they revealed the source of their mission to be one or the other of us. We never made any of the attempts public, of course, for to do so would be to tie our own hands in retaliation, and so the attempted killings went on and on, with a regular stream of would-be assassins being sent out broken to the burial pits over the Esquiline Hill.

Moreover, I went through five food tasters in two months, and I suspect Geta suffered as many losses. The most dangerous time was when we were out in the open, which was fairly rare, and even more so when we were both out together. Then, we travelled with a full column of men, those with shields close and ready to leap in front of us. Our routes were checked beforehand, all windows scoured for archers. It was a tense time, and despite our maintaining the fiction that nothing was happening rumour always travels like an arrow, fast and hard to stop. The city seethed with stories of our activity. Somehow Geta managed to twist the rumours about the city to his advantage, often coming off in those stories as an innocent and wronged child, despite the fact that he was twenty-two-years-old, stocky, bearded, and was as busy poisoning and hiring assassins as I. As a consequence, my reputation as an angry and violent man grew. I did nothing to stop that. Sometimes fear is a useful weapon, and I would always rather be thought angry and violent than weak.

However, the growing use of propaganda led to our second war. In this, we began to build webs of clients in Rome that we could trust, a new consilia who would become the court when we finally managed to slip the poisoned mushrooms or the flashing blade past our brother's defences. Essentially, Rome began to experience true polarisation in the form of two emperors and two completely separate courts and imperial bodyguards based in two separate palaces.

My old friend Macrinus the Berber, as *Procurator rei Privatae*, in charge of imperial property, became a close companion, as did Cilo, and a number of other men who knew me for a strong ruler and my brother for not the hero he seemed to the public. I watched with irritation, though, as Geta's council grew, and noted within it a number of people that set my teeth to clenching and my lip to wrinkling. A number of distant family members of the dreaded Plautianus had flocked to Geta's side, driven to it by the news that my wife had finally breathed her last. More irritating was the arrival of Papinian, Mother's friend, one of Rome's greatest lawyers, and the former Praetorian prefect, in Geta's palace. Though he had been staunchly neutral in that role, it seemed that my perfunctory dismissal of the man had sent him running into my brother's arms, and there he could do an immense amount of damage to my reputation. Moreover, Euodus, our former tutor, was now tied to my brother, as well as Castor, Father's chamberlain. It was a formidable group, and my only option was to try and whittle it down before they became too powerful.

The Plautianii were of little concern to me without my wife or her father around, and Papinian was too high-profile, for his removal would draw Mother's undue attention. I set my sights instead on the others, and because I am a direct man, I took a personal interest in them. Euodus travelled everywhere with two slaves, one a clerk with a pen and tablet, the other a bodyguard with a stout oak club. He felt he had little reason to fear anything in the city more than the usual thugs in the streets. He was wrong.

His journey on one Junius day into the city was to be his last. He left Geta's palace that morning with his two slaves and strolled down from the Palatine, across the forum and out to the low land in the shadow of the Capitol, where lies the great Athenaeum of Hadrian, a place of learning and repository of wisdom. I watched him and his companions enter. I was dressed in nondescript military clothes and my usual caracallus, all but unrecognisable. It was early in the morning, and many of its users would not be present yet, dealing with their morning *salutatio* or visiting the baths. I turned to the small entourage I'd brought, ten men chosen from my palace guards – those with the highest skill and the lowest morals, all similarly unadorned with identifying marks. We walked into the doorway of the great building, and I looked around.

Euodus was already deep in conversation with some scholar over by the racks of Geographic knowledge, his slaves standing attentive nearby. At a nod from me, my men began to herd the rest of the occupants from the building, pushing them out of the various doors and closing them after. The scholar talking to my old tutor noted finally that something was happening, and, eyes wide, made excuses and hurried out just before the building's last door was closed.

The tutor turned and frowned at what he saw. Though what was happening should have been clear to anyone, let alone such a clever man, he seemed confused. That emotion only heightened as three men of the Blues faction stomped over at the flick of a finger, and set about beating the club man to death. His screams echoed around the high hall as he fell to the beautiful marble, bones breaking, flesh mangling under the blows of my men. Only when he was gone did they stop and step back, a pool of blood growing around him.

'What is this?' Euodus gasped. 'I have no money. Not riches. I am but a scholar.'

That was when I pulled back the hood of my cloak and he realised who had followed him in.

'Domine, please understand that I hold you in the highest esteem,' he said hurriedly, in a squeaky voice.

'Is that so?' I snapped. I fished from my belt one particular piece of evidence. It was a short poem comparing me to that cursed emperor Caligula, biting satire and vicious rhyme. It had been brought to me a few days earlier, and was one of a number that were currently circulating in the city. The moment I read it I recognised the style and was under no illusion as to who had penned it. I threw it at him. He caught it, awkwardly and looked down at it.

'I don't...'

'Please don't sully this moment with pointless denials. You have been in the camp of Plautianus and Geta since the beginning, and I'm afraid it is now time to pay the price for your lack of foresight.'

As I spoke, my men suddenly slammed blades into the clerk, who let out a short gasp and a gurgle, and then fell to the rich floor beside the bodyguard. Now there was only Euodus and a room full of killers. He backed away towards the scroll racks. I followed, my gleaming eating knife coming out.

'Please,' he begged.

I reached him and thrust out my arm, grabbing him and pulling him away from the wall. He might be a treacherous, oily slanderer, but the knowledge in those scrolls was ancient and priceless and should not be ruined with blood. As he staggered towards me, my blade flashed out. I stabbed him in the throat, and, gripping him tight, pulled the blade across his windpipe and then dropped him. He lay there, gasping, shaking and spraying blood. I turned my back on him and gathered my men. I gestured to four of them.

'We will return to the palace by a circuitous route.' Then to the other six. 'Take the bodies to the Esquiline pits and cast them into the graves of the poor, then return to the palace carefully. I would prefer if Euodus simply disappeared and my brother could not find out what happened to him.'

And that was what occurred. Oh, Geta was sure I had done away with him, and rumour placed the death of Euodus at my door, but there was no proof, and the subtlety of it must have infuriated my brother.

Three days later, the venerable Castor, who I'd never liked anyway, but who had signed his own death warrant with cleaving to Geta, was found in his private baths amid a house full of corpses, floating face down in the warm pool, the water pink, his flesh white.

My third victim was a little more unexpected, but more satisfying than the others, despite the problems it created.

Geta had taken to visiting various gymnasia and wrestling schools, accompanied by his guards and often in the company of a number of his friends from the Green racing faction. We had managed never to meet at the Circus, because the Blues and Greens were not in the habit of training together, and there is a secondary, smaller track near the faction stables they can also use. I had been forewarned of one of my brother's visits on a day of the Green practices.

I had hatched a plan, the latest of many. Over a month of visits to the track, I had managed to have several of the Circus slaves disappear, and replaced them with those drawn from my palace. Slaves are never the most trustworthy of people, for fear is their main motivation, yet there are certain advantages to using them. Firstly, no one really sees them. They can be changed and moved without drawing attention, and are capable of doing things and going places without being noticed. Secondly, other than fear they have one great motivation, and that is freedom. A slave knows better than to run, for when they are caught the result is not worth thinking about, but if they can earn their freedom, the world opens up for them. The most famous example is the baker Eurysaces, a slave in a bakery who earned his freedom and bought his own shop. By the time he died, he owned a string of bakeries across the city and passed on a great wealth to his heirs. Every slave dreams of being a Eurysaces. Consequently, I had set my slaves hidden in the Circus tasks, with the potential reward being their freedom if they succeeded.

The day my brother went to practise with the Greens, the slaves had carefully worked on Geta's favoured chariot and horses. Not content with trusting his demise to one accident, I had four slaves working. One was there to observe and report back to me. One worked with the vehicles, one in the equipment stores, and one with the horses. They were well chosen. That bright Junius morning Geta stepped out to the cheers of his favoured Greens and readied to try a circuit or two with his personal chariot.

The vehicle was a death trap. My spy had worked on the yoke that connected the central two horses to the vehicle, sawing halfway through the timber and then coating the damage with a helping of wax to hide his work. If the vehicle didn't kill my brother, then there was a good chance he would meet his end as he tried to pull free his knife to cut the reins, for the hilt had been loosened in the stores, and likely he would find himself wielding only a hilt, the blade stuck in the sheath. And if those two pieces of work could not be trusted, there was also my most fiendish plot. My other slave had waited until the horses were attached to the vehicle and ready to run out and race and had, at the last moment, tipped a vial of poppy tincture into the mouth of the trace horse and massaged its throat.

The chariot was brought out, and I had all this in a detailed report from my slave spies. Geta stepped towards the chariot. He climbed up onto the platform and prepared to race. All was set. There was precious little chance of my brother making it even along the first straight. He was a dead man walking. Any one of my little surprises should kill him. All three was a guarantee.

He slapped the reins once he was tied in, and the animals began to trot forward towards the line that marked the exercise lap start. He was setting off and about to pick up speed when there was a call. Next moment, he was rolling to a halt as the accursed Euprepes hurried across the sand. He had noticed that the trace horse was looking a little wild in its movement. Apparently he stepped to the drugged horse and examined its eyes, opened its mouth, shook his head, and told Geta to climb down. Then they began to examine the chariot. Soon they found the sabotage. Geta walked away, a little shaky, realising how close he had come to an unpleasant, high-speed death.

All my work undone, and all because of the bastard Euprepes, who should have been our champion in the Blues were it not for my brother's underhand subversion of his loyalties. I think what angered me in particular that day was not my brother's escaping death, for this was only the latest in a long list of attempts he had walked away from. What annoyed me was that it was Euprepes the traitor who had saved him.

I rampaged in my palace that day. No one came near me, such was my foul mood. In fact, while it may have been satisfying, my response was poorly thought through and rather precipitous. I was just too angry for words. That evening, Euprepes, now the greatest racing champion in Roman history and of an age where he should be stopping racing, left the Greens' training and residential complex and went for a drink. He stepped out of their stables and into the Via Euripe, turning and walking happily along the busy street towards the far end and the Via Tecta Porticus, where many of the bars favoured by the factions are to be found. He never knew who jumped him, for before he could even cry out, he'd been barged across to the side of the street where gurgles the Euripe, a long and broad channel that runs from the Aqua Virgo all the way across the Campus Martius to the river. He ended his days face down in the flow, coughing and gagging until his lungs filled with bright, burbling water. It was only when he was finally still that we let go and allowed him to fall back into the street, bloated and discoloured.

Poor decision, for all its satisfaction. I'd let my anger get the better of my judgment. Only rumour connected me to the demise of Euodus and Castor, but this time I had been present and it had all been done in front of witnesses in the street. Admittedly I was covered up, but few men in the capital wear a caracallus, and this time, the men I'd brought could hardly have been mistaken for anything but imperial soldiers. Within hours it was public knowledge that the emperor Antoninus had murdered the champion charioteer of the Greens. Of course, it was put down to jealousy on behalf of my favoured Blues, but it was another blow to my reputation. I straightened and decided that I could live with it. When Geta was mouldering in a jar somewhere, there would be time for me to repair damage to my reputation. Right now it was the good of the empire, and of my own succession, that mattered.

I thought at first that the death of Euprepes had made Mother snap, little knowing the true instigator of what happened next. In a late Junius evening, a slave arrived in my palace, summoning me perfunctorily in Mother's name. With a small entourage, and watchful for hidden assassins, I stepped out and strolled across the Palatine to the old Tiberian palace where Mother now made her home. As always, I was unarmed, for it was not done to enter her presence so, but while moving through the public spaces in between, I was surrounded by blades and shields.

I entered through the grand archway into the huge and decorative atrium dotted with Mother's Praetorians. This old palace was rather outdated and a little austere compared with modern living, but it was not the décor that drew my attention as I stepped inside.

My eyes fell upon my brother, across the room.

'Are you aware that you have gained a reputation as a monster in the city, unlike your beloved brother?' he sneered.

'Not everyone is fooled by the propaganda of your pet poets.'

'Yes, I think Euodus probably knows that now, wherever he is.'

'Is that an accusation?'

'More of a statement,' he replied flatly.

As the argument looked set to erupt into mere name-calling, our attention was drawn by the clearing of a throat. Quintus Marcius Dioga was standing in the doorway with a disarming smile. His smile alone was a talent, for I found myself beginning to calm down.

'Domini, what can we do for you?'

This threw me. Dioga had become one of Mother's more trusted counsellors now, and he would often appear or speak on her behalf. Surely he must be aware that Mother had sent for me. Hadn't she? I thought back on the slave who'd appeared at my door, and it occurred to me that he hadn't worn the plain white of one of the standard palace slaves. What was going on?

The answer, infuriating as it was, came a moment later as Geta took a step forward. 'I summoned *him* in Mother's name. There is something we must discuss, and though it galls me to negotiate with my brother, we have reached a situation where there is no other option.'

I was, I have to admit, intrigued. It sounded a great deal as though he had a plan to end our feud. In earlier days I had sought to do just that, and it had been Geta who had been the impediment to peace. What the sudden change? That made me suspicious, put me on the alert.

'The empress must make time for us,' he said, addressing Dioga.

The soft-spoken man frowned for a moment, as though working through Mother's appointments, and finally nodded. 'The empress will be in the grand triclinium at the moment. Please, Domini, follow me, and I will ask her if she is available,' he said with a bow of the head, and then turned and disappeared into Mother's apartments. We followed. For the first time in ages, Geta and I walked side by side, our entourages following on. Neither of us looked at the other, but at least there was no argument and shoving, through a combination of respect for Dioga and for Mother, whose house this was. We had taken oaths and, while we held to them loosely at best, here in her home they were paramount.

As we walked, I examined Geta's procession. There were new men among his entourage, and they were interesting. I vaguely recognised them as men of Father's consilia from the old days, neither of whom had remained as retainers following his death. One carried a huge rolled up sheet of vellum. What was Geta up to?

We reached the triclinium which had once held the magnificent parties of Caligula and Nero, which overlooked the forum and the Capitol, and there Dioga rapped on the door and slipped inside. He was gone for no more than twenty heartbeats, the conversation within inaudible, and then reappeared with his usual reassuring smile.

'Please, do enter, Domini. I presume there is no call for grand introductions?'

We both shook our head and, as Dioga stepped aside, we entered that great room. Mother was not reclined on a couch as per the norm for a dining-room, but rather seated on a simple curule chair, one inlaid with gold and adorned with purple cushions. I looked about. She was alone. Not only no guards present, but no slaves or servants, and not even the one who should be there serving her wine from the decorative *krater* on the table before her. Two other chairs faced her across the table, and both had been carefully positioned to be slightly lower, perhaps indicating our positions relative to her, certainly informing us of where we stood in this room. How she had managed to set this up within so few moments was impressive.

As we walked towards the chairs, our retinue following, Mother shook her head and thrust out a finger. 'No. You attend alone. No guards or slaves.'

Geta reached out and took the vellum roll from his man before nodding consent for his departure. Dioga then ushered out everyone else, finally bowing to Mother and then stepping outside himself, closing the door behind him and leaving alone the three remaining members of the Severan dynasty.

I opened my mouth and began to speak but Mother, her face like thunder, overrode me immediately.

'No. You do not get to speak. You speak when I tell you. Both of you.'

No one in the empire had the power to speak so to the two of us, yet we sat silent, chastened and obedient at the sheer force of our mother's personality. Geta, though, had an oddly expectant look.

'I have no idea which of you thought to call this meeting, but before you make your case clear, I will take the opportunity to speak my mind. This all has to stop,' Mother said plainly.

I opened my mouth again, and shut it instantly as she glared at me. 'Once upon a time, the word of the Severans was our bond. Your father and your uncle came from obscurity to rule the greatest empire the world has known through their common sense, their plain speaking and their forthright manner. And they always kept their word.'

She reached forwards and dipped her beautiful blue wine glass into the krater, refilling it. Hers was the only glass, I noted.

'You both gave me your word. You would live separate lives, but you would stop this horrid feud, and you would maintain a public façade of peace and concord for the good of the empire. That was your oath to me. You have both broken it so often that your word, I can only assume, means nothing to you.'

I bit my lip, a habit I thought I'd got over in youth.

'I am an old woman,' Mother said. 'In my position, the wives of emperors of old would have retired into happy obscurity once more. I should by now be living in a pleasant seaside villa, with no aspirations to command beyond deciding on an outfit for the day, while my sons rule the empire with grace and wisdom. Instead, I find that my sons are little more than brawling ruffians with purple cloaks, stabbing one another in the back, committing murder in the streets and hiring poisoners. Your uncle would have disowned both of you, and in stronger times your father would have you both over his knee, giving you a good hiding.'

I glanced at Geta. He was clearly waiting to speak, but Mother was not finished yet.

'And so I continue to fulfil the role of your Father, looking after the state while the pair of you fight and argue. You probably have no idea just how many laws I have passed, cases I have read, petitions I have seen and military postings I have granted in your name, because your heads are not where they should be. I am more than disappointed. I am incensed and appalled at the pair of you.'

Now Geta made to speak, but her gaze nailed him to his seat.

'And do not think to play the game that you were born of my womb while your brother's unfortunate mother passed away in the north. I have always held you both in equal esteem. You are both my sons, no matter what, and I made a promise to your father in his later years to look after you *both*. And unlike the pair of you, *my* word *means* something.'

She straightened and took a sip of her wine.

'I have no wish to continue ruling in your name. I want retirement and peace. And I want family and grandchildren. Clearly that is never going to happen in the current situation.'

She subsided, though she was trembling with anger, clearly. Whatever Geta had planned, he was pushing his luck. Mother was clearly in no receptive mood, and I was unlikely to appreciate anything he had to offer.

'Speak, then,' she said, her tone hard. 'Why have you come?'

'I answered a summons I thought from you, Mother,' I said.

Geta nodded. 'I agree that this cannot go on. Rome has two emperors, and neither of us is willing to give up our power, or to share the throne. And while we war, the empire suffers. I would love nothing more than to see that thug,' he said, thumbing in my direction, 'floating down the Tiber with a knife in his back, but as you've often said, Mother, empire has to come first.'

With that, and having captured both our attention, he leaned forward and unfurled the vellum roll on the table beside that great wine krater.

'I propose,' Geta said, 'a partition of the empire. At times such a thing has worked. Marcus Aurelius and Lucius Verus managed it successfully for a time, with Aurelius looking to the war on the northern border and Verus to the east. I see no reason why this could not happen again.'

I stared at the map. I fought down the urge to remind him how the division of empire under Marcus Antonius and his friends had ended up, with fleets at war in the bay of Actium. Something was amiss here. This was too sensible for Geta. He was playing a game, but I didn't know the rules, and that annoyed me.

'It seems to me,' he went on, 'that there is a natural division of the empire along the straits of the Propontic gulf, past Byzantium. On one side, lie the difficult provinces along the Danubius, and Britannia, but also the comfortable ones of Achaea and Hispania, and lucrative Gaul, as well as Italia and Rome itself. On the other side, lie the dangerous Parthian border provinces and the troublesome Judean lands. But they also have the South, which means rich Aegyptus and the grain lands of Africa, as well as the lands of our forefathers. Both of these empires are valuable in equal amounts. A second capital can be set up for a second division. If we cannot share rule of one empire with one capital, then two empires and two capitals seems the natural solution.'

I frowned at the map. The two empires would be more or less equal. It was a neat solution, for certain, and one that could always be undone in future when lines of succession were put in place. After all, after Aurelius and Verus, there was but one emperor again. What was he playing at?

Mother was looking at the map. Her expression was complex. She was at the same time intrigued and horrified.

'I shall have the East and South,' Geta said, leaning back, 'and Marcus the North and West.'

I blinked, snapped suddenly out of the spell. 'What? The North and West to me?'

Geta nodded. 'They are the more restive provinces, which would benefit from a military mind. You are familiar with all the border lands, having campaigned in them all. You are popular with the army, especially in Britannia, Raetia, Pannonia and Dacia. You have a solid foundation in Rome, and Lugdunum, all Gaul, even, prides itself on being the place of your birth. It makes a great deal of sense. And you know I am less familiar in military matters.'

The bastard. It became clear immediately. It was a goad. A perfectly acceptable solution for some, but not with the division as he'd planned.

'Many of the southern and eastern provinces are largely self-administering,' my brother continued. 'With what Father and you did to the Parthians we are unlikely to see any belligerence there in gener-ations. A man with a skill at negotiation and debate could maintain a healthy border there without the need for too much fighting. I am that man. A perfect division. You, a military man, to the wild north, and I, a negotiator, to the complex east.'

The words of my response were fighting for control of my tongue. The bastard.

'I cannot decide whether Alexandria or Antioch would make a better capital,' he murmured, looking at the map. He shot me a sidelong glance, and I saw the corner of his mouth curl up nastily. 'I think probably Alexandria. It has such a kingly heritage.'

'No,' I said.

'Oh?' Geta said in a light tone, a knowing smile on his face. 'It seems to me a fair divide and the solution to our ongoing problem.'

'Of course it fucking does, because you get the empire of Alexander, while I get soggy Caledonia and hairy Germans. No. Give me the East and I will consent.'

And I would. I hated him with a passion, but I would let it all go for the sake of Rome, if he would back down and give me the East. I would be a new Alexander. I would finally take that ancient eastern land and keep it. But I knew that he would never consent. He had no intention of doing so, and, indeed, no intention of this plan succeeding. It was there to make him look good, and me look bad in front of Mother.

Geta adopted an injured look. 'But you know I am of a delicate disposition,' he mewled. 'The warmer lands of the South and East will agree with me so much more. No. I think I would like to retain Alexandria. Perhaps the Parthians will cede to me some of Alexander's lands? Maybe I could even open his tomb again and send Marcus a souvenir?'

I gripped the arms of my chair, fingers whitening. Even with Mother here, I was a hair's breadth from lunging for the bastard and throttling the life from him. Mother gave an exasperated sigh and sat back. I looked across at her and, with a sudden flush of relief, realised that Geta had made an error of judgement. I could see in her gaze the shock and the horror at the very idea of the empire being cut in half. He had thought to provide something she agreed with that I would refuse, but instead what he had proposed she found abhorrent.

'Earth and sea, my children, you have found a way to live divided, with the empire halved and weakened. But what then? When your feud erupts to engulf an empire? Civil war? And what of your mother? How would you parcel her? How am I to be torn apart for the pair of you?'

I nodded at her. 'Mother is right. To divide the empire is to weaken it. And I for one would not be without her. Would you?' I glared at my brother. 'And you will not take Alexander's empire. That is mine to rebuild.' I rose. 'The empire shall not be divided.'

Geta's expression hardened. His ploy had failed badly, and for just a moment, I could see in him that same impetuousness and quick temper

I had inherited from Father. 'But I tell you this,' he said, turning to Mother now, 'by the time the consuls are chosen you will have only one son.'

And with that he turned and stormed out.

I watched him go, remembering the omen of the Capitol. There would be no division and no reconciliation. One wolf would have to die.

XXII

A Weapon of War

Rome, Autumn AD 211

The polarisation of Rome's emperors continued unabated. The forces guarding each palace went from strength to strength as men from various military units flocked to one cause or another, for now any pretence that Rome was ruled with concord had gone. Across the city it was common knowledge that the feud between its emperors had reached its end days, and the empire waited with bated breath to see who would emerge from this contest.

Men from both the civil and military spheres were gradually forced to take sides. Few remained neutral, for to do so was to earn the distrust of both emperors instead of just one, and with the rise of the two opposed factions, even Mother's steadying influence began to wane in the court.

The streets were becoming unsafe, too. The racing factions of the Greens and Blues had never been at peace anyway, but with each supporting a rival emperor, their sporting opposition blossomed into all-out war in the streets, their stables turned into a fortress. Now, no member of the factions was seen in the city without a club or a knife, ready to defend themselves. The Reds and the Whites were drawn into the chaos, one on each side, and because the majority of Romans favour one racing colour or another, gradually, as summer slid to autumn, even the ordinary people in the city streets began to go about armed and take part in the faction clashes.

In short, our feud had long since torn apart the family, but we were now also tearing apart the empire.

Our attempts to remove one another also continued unabated. I managed to subvert one of Geta's cupbearers, who was to present the wine cup to his master tainted with cyanide drawn from peach stones. At the close of that day, the slave's body was delivered to my door, his skin discoloured with the poison he had borne, his eyes wide and sightless, his head almost cut in half with the wide, shallow cup he had carried jammed so far into the mouth it had broken both cheeks and dislocated the jaw.

The next night, my new food taster expired in a shaking heap, and when I had the kitchen staff questioned, a cook was produced who had taken gold from my brother. I had the man crucified outside one of the windows of my brother's palace, where he could not be missed.

And so it went on. I have said before that poison and assassination is not my norm. I prefer a direct approach, and would have loved nothing more than to simply walk up to Geta with a blade and end him in the open, in public. I would even fight him, if he too had a blade. But just as I had drawn around me a *testudo* of protection, so had Geta, and neither of us was going to agree to meet the other now.

The business of empire never sleeps, and so despite our ongoing war, we did what we could to keep Rome running, though even there, we were trouble, I fear. Any appointment by either of us was clearly going to a man from our own faction, and therefore became little more than a playing piece in our deadly game. Every judge handed down opinions based on their bias. Even the plays that were put on to keep the people entertained were carefully chosen by Geta or myself to blacken the reputation of our opponent where possible.

Rome seethed.

So did I. This dreadful stalemate had to end. We were now damaging Rome in our private war, and that could not go on. But I could see no way to bring about a conclusion. We were both so careful, so defensive, and even when we went to see Mother, we did so separately and with a strong armed guard.

In the hope of securing a better line of succession and dynasty, with my dreadful wife now out of the way, I began to look at potential matches in between the to-ing and fro-ing of murderous intent. Unfortunately, our feud had become public enough now that anyone who might have truly made an appropriate empress had left the city with their families, seeking the safety of country estates. When I had brief opportunities to look for a new match, I found the pickings thin, to say the least. I settled with a sigh on the fact that if I could remove Geta from the succession directly, I would have ample time to secure my own dynasty, and so I decided to leave women for now, and concentrate on murder.

At last, on a cold November evening, Mother, at the end of her tether, made a final attempt to bring us together, to try and persuade us to put aside our feud. It was futile, of course, but I understood why she must try, and there was always the faint possibility that some solution lay undiscovered. I left the new palace surrounded by armoured men, with shields held high. We crossed the Palatine by way of the public rooms and state chambers, the old *cryptoporticus*, and arrived at Mother's palace on the far side of the hill without incident. There, in the outer chamber, I left all my retinue with the exception of two men. Maximinus Thrax, that giant Thracian cavalryman, and Macrinus, my old Berber friend with his earrings and African tunic. I walked into the room that Mother still used for audiences, though with the rising polarisation of Rome, such events were fewer and fewer as time went on. She had two guards of her own in attendance, both Praetorians, standing in the rear corners of the room.

I had come wrapped as usual in my caracallus, an eminently practical garment at this time of year when the frost bites into the stones of Rome and the wind carries an icy chill that cuts to the bone. As I stepped into that room, warmed with braziers and lamps, I shrugged out of the cloak and handed it to Macrinus. I was dressed, as usual, in a military tunic with soft, high boots and just a good belt with my usual pouches and accoutrements.

'Marcus,' she greeted me, her tone neutral, giving away nothing.

'Mother,' I replied, and walked across to stand facing her, leaving my men near the door. At least this meeting appeared to be her idea and not another ploy of my brother's. We had no time to exchange more than greetings, however, before the door opened once more and Mother's slave announced my brother.

Geta strode into the room, glanced around, and dismissed all but two of his guards, who entered and then stood watching Macrinus and Maximinus as though they might attack at any moment. All four men had their hands on their sword hilts. The surprise, though, was Geta.

My brother had abandoned his usual rich and bright tunic and had come in a military garment cut much the same as mine. His boots were the hobnailed ones of a soldier, clacking on the marble, and his belt bore the military pairing of sword and dagger. I had never seen him dressed as a soldier, and it felt extremely odd, as though he had tried to mimic me, to steal a part of what I was. Was this some new way to try and counter me?

Clearly his appearance took Mother by surprise, too, for she turned to him and her eyes widened.

'Publius?'

'Mother?'

'What have I done that you would bring a weapon of war into my chambers?'

Geta frowned for a moment, as though he had no idea what she meant, and then looked down at his side. 'This? This is for my safety. Anywhere outside my palace I am at risk from this animal,' he added, jabbing a finger in my direction.

I glared at him, although glaring is more or less my natural expression, I admit. As he looked back at me, I could see him register the fact that I was unarmed, apart from my ubiquitous eating knife. I had never come armed into Mother's presence. Neither of us had, until now. This was new. And he'd made a mistake again, I could see from Mother's face.

'You are safe within these walls, Publius, as is your brother. Surely neither of you would dare to draw blood before me?'

Geta glanced at me again, lip curling. 'I think you underestimate Marcus. He would kill me in the Temple of Peace.'

I would. I would kill him anywhere I could. Anywhere but here. It had simply never occurred to me that either of us would act in Mother's presence. The idea was unthinkable, oddly.

That is where the idea began.

Mother pursed her lips angrily. Geta, wrinkled gimlet eyes locked on me, unfastened his sword belt and held it out. One of his men took it and stepped back once more.

'Now I am defenceless,' he rumbled.

'And I, as always, am similarly unarmed,' I noted, labouring the point for Mother's benefit.

'I have been going through your father's documents,' she said, once we were standing silent and still, her angry eyes still on my brother. 'I hold out that there can be peace between my sons.'

'I have made every effort...' began Geta, eyes wide with feigned innocence, but Mother cut him off with a snappish tone.

'Never think me a fool, Publius Septimius Geta. Just because you are my son does not mean I am blind to your faults. Marcus is a man of violence, and I have long known and come to terms with this. It is in his blood. But at least he bares his blade openly, like a soldier. If you think to tell me that your notion of dividing the empire was anything but an underhanded attempt to goad your brother into some foolish act, think again. And at least Marcus has the good taste not to wear a sword into my apartments.'

Geta looked thoroughly taken aback for a moment, then turned silent, hateful eyes on me.

'It is clear that your father set a precedent in the succession,' Mother went on.

Hope lurched in my heart. I had always thought as much. Perhaps Geta had too, as he was almost vibrating now with anger.

'Marcus was groomed to be his heir,' she went on. 'That much is clear to everyone and always has been. From your father's notes, and from what I know of him and his plans myself, it is clear to me that, initially at least, only Marcus was intended to inherit the throne.'

Now, Geta's lip was twitching. He was furious and could not believe what he was hearing, though it was a balm to me. I had to force myself not to smile. The little shit deserved this, almost as much as he deserved a blade in the gut.

'You cannot mean to...' he spat.

'Hold your tongue,' Mother said. 'You will hear me out, Publius, if not for common decency or in deference to your mother, then at least out of respect for your father's memory.' She paused until she was certain that Geta would stay silent, then went on. 'Your father had intended Marcus, as the firstborn, to succeed the throne. That is natural and there are many precedents for it. You, Publius, had been intended to achieve the rank of Caesar and be a prince of Rome. That would have been a perfect system for the people and the senate, and would have avoided all the ill we have suffered.'

She took a deep breath. 'Your appointment as Augustus and co-emperor, alongside your brother and your father, sprang from two needs. Firstly, the two of you were drifting apart, becoming opponents rather than brothers. Your father tried everything he could think of to prevent that getting worse, and making you equals was his last attempt. The second reason was that since the exile of Marcus' wife, he has shown no interest in pursuing a new match, and the same holds true even now, after her somewhat precipitous execution.' A short glare at me at that point. 'Your father,' she began again, 'as always, had the succession, the peace of the empire and the future of our dynasty in mind, and with no apparent hope for a scion from Marcus, he deemed it prudent to raise you, Publius, in rank. To put it rather crudely, double the manhood, double the chance of an heir. Sadly, it seems that both of you are more intent on your feud than on the future of the family.'

I ground my teeth at that.

'You are both augusti now, both emperors of Rome. Whether that decision was a good one or a poor one is a matter for debate, but the fact remains that both of you now have equal power and the equal right to wield it, by the will of your late father and ratified by the senate. No one can order you to do something you do not wish to do, and so instead of an order, I make this a plea.'

She turned to face Geta directly.

'I ask you, Publius, for the sake of Rome, of the family, and of your wretched mother, to renounce the title of Augustus, and accept with peace and joy the title of Caesar once more. In practise, you will still have the fortune of the treasury, palaces, even military glory, for if there is no conflict between you, then your brother can use your help and your talents.'

Geta's eyes were bulging, but Mother continued in her steady tone.

'You lose nothing that cannot be reclaimed, and in doing so you may save not only the empire, but also your mother and one of her sons. I can ask for nothing more important than that.'

Leaving Geta, furious, mouth flapping soundlessly, she turned to me. 'Marcus, in return I ask that you bury this feud so deep it can never be found, and that you accept that, while you act as the senior heir and direct emperor of Rome, you will not cause harm or fault for your brother, that you will accord him all the respect he deserves and give him the first choice of all important appointments in both the military and civil spheres.'

She leaned back. 'If you will only both accept this, then the family and the empire can be healed. You could be made joint consuls in the new year as a first act of unity.'

I saw my chance dangling before me. I'm sure that Geta and I both knew what this all meant. If we accepted this, it would lower the level of the fire in our feud, but the war had been going on so long now that there was never going to be a happy end to it. It would only ever result in bloodshed. One wolf would die.

But after so many months of my name being bandied about as that of a hateful killer, and Geta being lauded across the city as the golden, peaceful prince, Mother had begun to see the truth of it. She had seen that I came into her presence still a peaceable man, while my brother had begun to arm for war. She had seen how he had forged a plan that would have divided the empire, had it ever been more than an attempt to make me look bad. And now she had finally put forth a peaceful solution that could end it all, while Geta was going puce, shaking and about to start screaming. He had taken half a step to making himself look even worse, and the door had been left open for me to take the other half. I had to be not only accepting, but even magnanimous.

'For my part,' I replied, calmly, 'all I have ever wanted is for the succession to be the way it was intended. The contest between us has driven such a deep wedge. When Plautianus sought a part in it through my brother, I could have nothing of it, but without Plautianus, there is no reason to continue that way.' I could see Geta glaring at me, knowing what I was doing, but he had become so unutterably angry that he couldn't get a word out.

'I would welcome such a decision with open arms,' I went on, almost as though imploring my brother. 'And though there be an order of precedence, we would both be Severan princes of Rome. Publius has lacked the military experience laid upon my shoulders as he himself has noted. As my Caesar, I will make him Rome's most famous general. Together we will conquer the world. And he may take any estate he wishes. Any governorship. Any position. Any role. Consuls we can be, but better still, brothers. A new strength for Rome, me and my Caesar.'

I wondered at the end there whether I'd said 'my Caesar' in too condescending a tone, but the wide smile that crossed Mother's face told me that she had bought my humble plea.

The look in Geta's eye said something very different.

'Never.'

Mother's smile slipped. 'Publius, darling...'

'No. Never. I will never *share* a throne with that animal, let alone be *subservient* to him.'

'Brother,' I said, an imploring voice. I stretched out my hands.

He slapped them aside. 'I know what you're doing, *Caracalla*,' he spat, trying to use my common alias as an insult.

'This could end.'

'You're so right,' he snapped. In a flash, he'd turned to his men and snatched the hilt of the sword the Praetorian held still, fastened to the belt. I suspect I owe my life to his inexperience with weapons. He struggled so to draw the blade that by the time he had it bared, Macrinus and Maximinus were at my side, their own swords out. I almost cheered. He could not have fucked up the meeting better had I scripted it for him. Just to polish the gleam on my reputation, I tapped Macrinus. 'Protect the empress,' I said, and he stepped over to Mother, standing between her and Geta, who now had his sword free and was standing, panting like a wolf, gripping the hilt so tight that his knuckles had gone white.

He could not strike, though. I suspect he would have, if he could, but he would never get past my Thracian giant. The man was like a Titan of old, and very experienced in war. Perhaps if his Praetorians had joined him, Geta could have stood a chance, but the two of them were horrified. To draw a blade against an emperor in the presence of Mother was something even they, allied to Geta as they were, balked at.

In heartbeats the moment passed. The threat was over, though my brother stood there, shaking, breathing heavily with bulging eyes, sword in hand.

'I suggest you leave now,' I said, calmly but with force, 'before you do something you regret.'

He did. He left without another word, his men stomping away behind him. Once we were alone again, I motioned to Macrinus and Maximinus and they both sheathed their swords and stepped back away from Mother and myself.

'I must apologise. I fear that it is my own anger that brings it out in him,' I said to Mother. It was artfully spoken, sounding contrite and reasonable. Mother had ever tried to keep her feelings matched for her two sons, but with the underhand wiles, violent threats and unwillingness to compromise that Geta was now regularly displaying, I could only have started to look more like the golden prince she wanted.

I departed feeling oddly positive. The impasse between the two of us that had held us apart and impotent since the day we returned to Rome seemed to be crumbling, and I had an idea now. In our palaces we were untouchable, that much was clear, and in the open we were too careful and too well protected to get near. The only place our guard was ever remotely down was with Mother, though Geta now seemed to have changed that.

When we returned to my palace, I brought Macrinus and Maximinus into my audience chamber.

'What did you make of that?'

The two men looked at one another. Macrinus shrugged. 'Another pointless attempt to reconcile you, Domine,' he said.

'I don't mean Mother's words, although I would say that this was far from pointless. It allowed me to rise above the matter, while making sure that Publius looked as guilty, petulant and violent as possible. But what I meant was, what did you make of my brother? Of his appearance in particular.'

'A surprise, for sure. And perhaps an admission of fear. I wonder whether he is becoming paranoid.'

Maximinus nodded. 'It does show a new level of wariness.'

I folded my arms. 'But is his armed appearance limited to when he expects to face me, or has it become his norm? Get eyes and ears into Mother's palace. One of the Praetorians perhaps? I want to know how my brother appears and what he says when he is summoned there alone, without expecting to see me.'

I left them to it. The answer came back three days later, and it gave me new hope. Geta had gone to see Mother over the ratification of some decree that he felt sure I would overturn unless it came with the additional influence of the empress' seal. He had entered her chamber alone, leaving his guards outside, but once again he had gone in wearing his sword and dagger. According to my spy, Mother had been cold and angry with him, upbraiding him for his appearance, scorning his need to go about in her palace armed like a common soldier. She had even asked whether he thought he might need a sword to face his own mother.

That was it. That was the time he was most vulnerable, perhaps the *only* time he was vulnerable now: in Mother's presence. Geta's popularity with Mother was waning, while mine was on the rise, and that was starting to show among the court, too, for rumour flies faster and truer than any arrow.

Mother's chambers were where this would end, but everything had to be right. If I was to act in front of Mother, in a manner I had always considered unthinkable, I had to prepare everything so that it appeared that I was only doing what must be done. Geta would have to do something utterly unacceptable and abhorrent, and I would have to look as though I'd had no alternative. More than that, I had to make sure that his bodyguards couldn't save him.

The funny thing about loyalty is that it is a finite thing. Any man might tell you that he would die for his emperor. Any woman might tell you that she would never look further than her fat, balding, violent husband. Any worshipper might promise the world to a god for a small favour. But loyalty should never be called to the test, because every man, and I mean *every* man, has his price. And the baser and more desperate the man, the lower his price.

I had spies start watching my brother's palace. Now, though, they were not looking for weaknesses, nor for malleable slaves. Now they were watching the soldiers who guarded Geta, and they were looking for a certain type of soldier. Over the next few days we found three who matched my criteria perfectly. They were each low-ranking soldiers, two in the Praetorian Guard and one in the urban cohort. They were all grizzled veterans, but they were all jaded and angry, and they were all poor, the reasons for which was uncovered by my spies. Two were gamblers and the other a drunken sex maniac. The former had a habit of blowing their month's pay in the first week, and even after years of service had little to show for it. The latter blew his pay even faster, though he probably had a better time doing it. All were desperate, with little or nothing in the way of career prospects.

The offer was simple.

Change sides. Do me a service, while remaining in the guise of my brother's men. In return I would pay them each a full career's worth of coin for one day's work, along with a promotion to the centurionate, which would see them set for life.

See? Every man has his price, and this was paltry. Of course, for what I had in mind I would never have to live up to the offer.

They told me they would kill him in his bed for me the very first night I bought their dubious loyalty, but I put an end to that notion immediately. I myself made sure never to have less than ten men on duty at my door now, including men whose loyalty was beyond question, and there was no one in the chamber but me, with a sword next to my bed. Any attempt by these three men would fail, I was sure, and then I would have wasted all this time and effort. Besides, I wanted this to look like a necessity, and not a mere murder.

I had three disposable men, a crafty plan, and a location for the deed. All I needed now was the right time.

XXIII

Death in Every Respect

Rome, December AD 211

It took several weeks to plan the murder. Firstly, I had to remove as much suspicion from my brother as possible, so that when the trap was actually sprung, he would be totally unprepared. In my experience, the time when people's guard is down most is when they have just escaped disaster. As such, I sprung two traps that winter, the first with the intention of failure.

I spent a small fortune buying from unwilling spies in my brother's palace the details of his schedule for Saturnalia, which events he would be attending and when, where he would be seated, and so on. I settled on the play he would attend in the Marcellan theatre. Of course, I was not expected to be one of the guests at that event. Neither of us, now, attended anything that the other would be found at. And so Geta felt about as safe as ever he would outside his palace. He arrived at the theatre with a personal bodyguard unit that could have successfully invaded a small country, and they cleared out a full third of the theatre to make sure no one would be anywhere near their master. Geta settled into his seat to watch some mindless comedy – I think it was *The Mother-in-Law* by Terentius – and his men created a safe cordon around him, only his trusted familia allowed close by.

The first of twin blows struck early. As the audience settled into that excited hush, the last preparations being made on stage, the lamps guttering, my paid poisoner struck. Four bearers of treats and sweets were admitted to the imperial presence once they had been checked for weapons. They were made to stand a safe distance from Geta while he decided what he would like, and then the chosen delicacies were ferried across by slaves. Of course, he took almost one or two of everything. These days he was putting on a little weight, partially due to his sweet tooth that led him to eat far too much. However, his food was checked by tasters, of course, just as was mine, and when one barked in shock and threw down a pastry that he had only touched to his tongue, the entire snack array was removed and the servers marched off for interrogation and execution. Geta's eyes played around the theatre, clearly half-expecting to see me looking chagrined. He did not. Not because I wasn't there, though. In fact, I was very much there. I stood in one of the small rooms of the *postscenium*, high up between the rows of columns, above the stage and facing the seats.

I waited until he looked relaxed once more, laughing with that rogue Papinian, who sat close by. His soldiers had checked every room and passage in the theatre, of course, before Geta had even taken his seat. But they had not checked every sheet-covered prop in the storerooms. It was a fairly simple thing, once he was in his seat and comfortable, to slip in past his guards with a couple of my own men, all wearing our hooded cloaks. We found the scorpion bolt-thrower we had 'borrowed' from the Praetorian fortress, removed the dust sheet covering it, and carried it from the prop storeroom to the window with a good view of Geta in his seat.

My two men were expert artillerists, but even artists such as they would be lucky to strike our enemy. To hit a target the size of a seated man some seventy or eighty paces away, at night, in winter, who is constantly moving, is really the province of gods, and not men, no matter what military historians might tell you. Still, we decided we would try. After all, if we could remove him now, while my reputation could take a little hit, I would be rid of him and able to work to regain all. We lined up and took aim, waiting for him to stop writhing and gesticulating. We erred a little to the left, so that if we did miss him, there was at least a chance we might skewer Papinian, which I would also consider a small victory.

We loosed. We only had one shot. If we took time for a second, the theatre would be sealed tighter than a Greek's purse, and we would probably be caught and killed. Or at least the small army I had waiting across the street would be called in and there would be outright war in the theatre. No. One shot and then run. That was the plan.

I cursed as the iron-tipped bolt slammed into the marble seating right between Geta and Papinian, missing both of them by less than a foot. Still, as we pounded down the stairs and out of a small, prepared open door into the street, to the backdrop of a cacophony of panic and fury, I consoled myself that this was all just a decoy, anyway. This was but to *look* like a major attempt to remove my brother.

Mother visited me in my palace two days before the end of Saturnalia, the day after the theatre. She was angry, suspicious and confused. She made veiled accusations, but nothing concrete. She had made enquiries, and all evidence pointed to the fact that I had been in my palace the whole time, and had never left. She felt sure I had been behind the attempt on Geta's life, and I did my level best to play my part down. I pointed out a number of wealthy and influential men my brother had truly pissed off these past few months by appointing his own friends over them, and any number of military units who might decide even spontaneously to do something rash on my behalf, because it was me they cleaved to, and not my brother. I doubt she believed me, though as it was all plausible, and there was no evidence to the contrary, the matter passed. So I had, as far as Geta was concerned, made my next major move. Now he would sit back for a while in that glow of the lucky survivor.

Which would stand me well for what I had planned next.

Saturnalia ended, and I put everything in place. I had my three traitors in Geta's palace contacted at their various gambling dens and brothels and told them to be ready. I hand-picked my own soldiers for the next day, largely from the impressive ranks of the *speculatores*, spies and assassins all, and briefed them carefully, putting them under the combined command of Macrinus and Maximinus, my two most trusted companions. Then, when I believed all was in order, finally, I pulled my trigger. I sent a very gracious message to Mother. I was polite and careful, I regretted what had happened at the theatre and, though I claimed once again to have had no part in it, could only see how it had been done in my name. I believed there was a way we could resolve our differences and prevent any repeat of such things. I also pointed out that there was little chance of Geta answering a summons from me, so I begged Mother to call one final meeting the next day, to see if we could finally resolve matters. I admitted that I doubted we would ever be friends, but I hinted that I would be willing to make a number of sacrifices in the sphere of my power and influence, to make it more acceptable for Geta to accept the title of Caesar. It was all I could now do.

When I had finished my letter, I read it through again and again. It was a masterpiece. It sounded so incredibly sincere. I did not like tricking Mother, but she had to believe there was truly hope, for this to work.

Then I slept. Actually, I slept rather badly. I had a dream in which the spirit of my father, mouldering bones from his tomb held together only by some dark magic, came for me, crying out that I would not kill his other son. In the dream, he pursued me through the halls of the palace until I finally tripped, and fell head first from the highest portico, down three storeys towards the plaza behind his great septizodium monument.

I awoke just before I hit the ground, shaking and soaked with cold sweat.

Consequently, I rose particularly early on that last morning. I felt unsettled by my dream, and it continued to nag at me as I prepared for the day. I tried to relax by using the palace baths. This whole new wing of the palace, built over the foundations of buildings from the times of Nero and Domitian, had been constructed by my father less than twenty years ago, and the baths were the most glorious, modern and efficient across the Palatine. I oiled, scraped, soaked, swam, sweated, swam again, and then lay there as my massage slave pummelled my knotted muscles. An hour or so later I emerged from the baths clean, neatly attired in my usual plain military tunic, and serene in my appearance.

Inside, my gut was churning.

I have said before that I am a prosaic man by nature, not so prone to blind superstition as my father, yet I could not shake the image of his unresting shade pursuing me through the palace, all mouldering bone and eerie spirit. And because it seemed to stay with me long after waking, which is not something I usually find with dreams, I had to at least consider the possibility that there was some deeper meaning to the dream other than mere conscience. After all, had my conscience plagued me over Geta, I would never have come as far as I have.

Still, signs or no signs, dreams or no dreams, I was committed to the act now. Of course, there were plenty of things that could still go wrong, but even if my traitors within Geta's guard decided to change their mind at the last moment, there would be no comeback. The meeting would be held, and we would part in much the same situation as we were in now.

But if it all went right…

I was seriously beginning to wonder whether Mother had changed her mind too. I held myself ready for over an hour, constantly checking the time by the water clock in the sumptuously decorated dining-room, pacing back and forth, going over the plan again and again in my head, trying to anticipate anything that might go wrong.

The summons came. I swallowed the nerves that remained, fluttering in my stomach since the night's terrors. I stepped out of my triclinium and nodded to Macrinus and Maximinus who stood like silent sentinels across the room, Titans in coats of steel. They left the room first, and outside the unit we had carefully chosen for their loyalty and their efficiency snapped to attention, scabbards clattering against iron and leather, chain shirts shushing, metal plates clicking against one another. The morning was chilly, and even in that room of the palace, warmed as it was, our breath plumed frosty, the open windows admitting December's icy breeze.

We marched out past my guards, the door of my private palace, the only entrance to my fortress, opening for what would be the last time. I emerged into the open on the balustraded walkway that overlooked the valley between the Palatine and the Caelian Hill, with its massive temple to the deified Claudius. My eyes fell on that magnificent structure, and I remembered all the stories I had heard of that shuffling clever old bastard. He was a nobody, really, a cruel and shrewd man who rose to the greatest power in the world and was now remembered with one of the most impressive buildings in the city. As I watched the smoke rise from the various offerings burning in temple braziers, I vowed that there would be no such memory of my brother. Geta would have no monuments to keep his name alive on the lips of the people.

A strange determination filled me then, as we marched around that frosty walkway outside my palace and back through a guarded door into the public areas of the complex. Geta's name had to disappear. And not like the damning of emperors in days gone by. I wanted no coins in circulation with his face damaged with dents and scrapes. I wanted nothing to remain. I would damn Geta as no emperor had ever been damned. His name, his image, his very memory would be stripped from Rome forever. Death in every respect.

Across the Domitianic hall and through a series of gardens, colonnades, great halls and finally out and across the great open thoroughfare towards the ancient palace of Tiberius and Caligula, which was now Mother's residence. As we moved out into the open street, my guards spread out and the public were herded back away from the imperial presence. Similarly, Praetorians filed out of the nearest door of that huge complex for which we were bound, and helped secure my access to the place. Moments later I was inside.

We had hurried. I wanted to be the first there. Not that the plan couldn't work any other way, but it made things easier. As we crossed the open entrance hall, it was clear that Geta had yet to turn up, and I smiled grimly to myself. I caught the eyes of several of my men. They had carefully blank expressions. Each and every one knew what they were to do, but such was the paranoia on the Palatine these days that no one dared give anything away, even through an expression. Even the great giant Maximinus looked all business.

We filed into the antechamber and waited while a well-dressed and eloquent slave greeted me with due deference, eyes never rising to meet mine. He entered the room beyond, announced me, and then the doors were drawn back. I strode in, my men following. I was attired as usual, so now that we were out of the worst of the cold, I shrugged off my caracallus and passed it to one of my men. I was now dressed as usual in my straight military tunic and boots, just my normal accoutrements.

As the doors were closed behind me and my men shuffled into position, ready, yet looking slightly bored as always, I bowed my head to Mother.

'So you have offers to make, Marcus? Something that you think might even tempt your brother to relent?'

'I hope so.'

'Would you care to enlighten me?'

I shook my head. 'I would prefer to wait until he is here.'

She nodded her acceptance, and we waited there in silence for just a few moments before I heard the thudding footsteps of the approach of Geta and his entourage. I readied myself. All had to look right.

The door clicked open. First came two burly soldiers. Geta would not even trust me enough to enter at the head of his men. Of course, he was right not to, but this fact registered with Mother, and I could see it in the slight hardening of her jawline, the slight narrowness of her eyes, which only increased as my brother appeared, dressed almost identically to me apart from the cloak, and once more with his sword belt around his midriff. Mother said nothing about it, but her eyes spoke eloquently as she levelled her disapproval at my brother.

'I cannot see that we have anything to discuss,' Geta snapped, glaring at me.

'Father once told me, when he first taught me the basics of rule and of command, that the best war of all is the one you don't have to fight. We have been at war, you and I, for a long time now. Is it not worth exploring all other options?'

Geta sneered. 'You know as well as I that there are no options left. One of us will be dead before the consuls are chosen. And if you cannot do better than you did in the theatre, then I am confident that it will be *me* pissing on *your* ashes this winter.'

Mother flinched at that as though she had been slapped. I tried to contain my glee within my habitual frown. He was walking straight into it. As he and Mother shared a look that held little of their once-close love, I quickly glanced around, noting the position of the three grizzled and desperate soldiers in his entourage who were in my pay. All three answered me with just a flicker of their expressions. All was ready. My gaze darted to Maximinus and Macrinus, and they, too, were prepared. There *was* a small danger to me here. There had to be, but I had to trust in my men. I swallowed down a flicker of doubt and moved. Just a casual step to the side.

'Brother,' I began, facing him, my back to those three men.

Geta spun on his heel, face twisting into a grimace of hate.

'Really? Is that what we are? I think not. I *have* no brother. All I have is an enemy who dropped from the womb of some African whore my father sated himself upon. You are nothing to me, Lucius Septimius Bassianus. Nothing. And soon you will be even less than that.'

It was enough. I knew it for just another blast of hot air, an expression of hate through nebulous threat. But it sounded just enough like a direct warning. It would appear to Mother a declaration of war, and indeed, I could see the fear in her eyes.

My hands, clasped behind my back like a teacher, flickered. A single gesture with finger and thumb.

The trap sprung.

Three of Geta's men suddenly roared, ripped their blades from their sheaths and leapt at me. It was artfully done. I feigned ignorance, turning slowly, eyes widening at what was clearly a brazen attempt on my life by my brother, right in front of our mother. I cried out in shock, as Maximinus the Thracian bellowed a warning, and my men surged forward.

The three soldiers in my pay never stood a chance. I fear I probably owe them for what I did, for I had promised them great things and they had expected to come out of this loyal servants of a sole emperor. Instead, they were cut down in a matter of heartbeats by my men, before they could shout out any accusation of truth. Their bought loyalties died with them.

I did not allow time for anything to settle. The momentum had to keep going. This had to happen now, or it never would.

I roared above the din.

'I am betrayed,' I bellowed, 'in the halls of our mother!'

My men were still moving, but now so were the rest of Geta's. Of course, mine had the initiative, moving first, prepared for what was to happen, ready for it all. Father had been *almost* right. The best war of all is *not* the one you don't have to fight. The best war of all is the one you've won before it begins.

Geta's thugs were outnumbered with the death of the three who'd initiated the fight, and shocked, taken by surprise and slow to react, they stood no chance. My men swarmed over them like a victorious legion storming the ramparts of some Gallic *oppidum*.

I turned to Geta. I fixed him with a look of hate, which was easy to achieve, and took no dissembling.

'You. You would have me cut down in our mother's palace?'

Suddenly, he blinked, shocked. Panic was beginning to take hold of him, and there was a moment of danger. If he collapsed in a blubbering heap and begged, this was all for naught. I could still kill him, but then I would appear little more than a murderer. Or he could find resolve. I could see him struggling to react, panic tearing from him all power of decision.

I had to help nudge him.

'And you call *me* the animal,' I snarled, taking a step towards him. That step was threat. It was provocation. I saw the indecision disappear from his eyes.

Geta tore his blade from his side.

It was all I needed. Macrinus and Maximinus had been watching us carefully, edging closer as this display went on, as the last of Geta's men were overwhelmed and put down.

I could almost have sung or cried with pleasure as I heard my Berber friend's call.

'Protect the emperor!'

And in that moment I saw in my brother's eyes the realisation of what he'd done. In drawing his blade against me, despite thinking to do it for his own protection, he had simply supported the apparent attempt on my life by his men, in continuing that attempt personally. My gaze slipped past my suddenly horrified brother to Mother, sitting on her throne. She had gone white with shock and horror, yet the shock and the horror were not aimed at me, but at my brother.

Geta, her child, who had eschewed his coloured tunics of peace for weapons of war in her presence.

Geta, her son who had changed so, who had refused all attempts at peace.

Geta, who had planned a murder in her own hall.

Geta. A would-be fratricide.

Something passed between us in that moment, even as my men ran to my aid. I could see in his eyes another decision. To strike could cut the bond between he and Mother entirely. But it could also remove me. Backing away and sheathing his blade might preserve the last shred of dignity he could claim, but it risked my men simply butchering him. He was lost. There was nothing he could do.

And that dithering, that indecisiveness and inability to act, cost him everything.

I cried out his name as my Praetorians hurtled past me. I saw the first blow land on my brother. It was Macrinus, his old-fashioned *gladius* slamming into Geta's sword arm, a blow that cut deep and almost broke bone, enough to force my brother to drop the sword. He screamed, but it did not end there, for my great Thracian giant was on him then, the edge of his long cavalry sword slamming into Geta's hip, hard enough to easily break bone. A third blow from one of the others lanced a point into his chest, just below his collar bone.

He was wounded, and backed away, stumbling, burbling, crying. But he was not done for.

He could die from his wounds, but there was always the possibility that he may yet live.

As he fell back, staggering, leg giving way under his damaged hip, a fourth blow struck, and this one caught his neck. The spray of blood told me that he was done for. Unless a medicus got to him in moments, he would bleed out. But I would not have that. This kill was mine to make.

My men backed away, but I did not. I was unarmed, *almost*.

I tore my eating knife from my side – little more than a hand span long, but sharp as a Parthian's tongue, gleaming and ready. I stepped forward as my men fell back. Now there was just Geta and me in the open. He backed towards Mother, mouthing curses, eyes wide. His sword arm hung limp at his side now, empty, and the other hand he'd clamped around his neck, trying to stop the blood, which spurted and bubbled between his chubby fingers. He was defenceless. He could still draw the dagger at his side, but one arm would not work, and if he removed the other from his neck, he would die in mere heartbeats.

He fell, leg giving way beneath damaged hip, and then rose to a stagger once more, backing away, closing on Mother, who sat on her throne in shock and white horror. I kept up my pace, stepping after him, slowly and deliberately. I was the avenging brother now. The wronged prince, dispensing justice on his would-be murderer.

I had actually meant to finish him before he reached Mother, but I had misjudged him. I thought him done, but in that last moment, he seemed to find a reserve of strength and speed, and lurched back fast. Mother's arms went up, and she almost leapt from the seat, but she was too late, and he fell into her lap, blood from his wounds spraying across her, soaking her perfect stola.

'Mother,' he gasped.

Her gaze dropped to him. I could not see what those eyes held in that momentary glance, but when they came back up to meet mine, there was a plea in them that she could not speak, or would not.

'Mother, who bore me, and *me alone*, help me!'

What he perhaps thought was a justification for her aid, however, reached Mother as yet another of his snide attacks on my parentage. With his penultimate words he had just sealed his memory as a man who simply could not compromise or accept who I was.

'I am being murdered,' he gasped.

And he was. Already he was becoming deathly pale, the blood that should be coursing through his veins soaking him and Mother, and growing into a wide pool beneath them both.

I stepped forward. His strength was gone. He had no power to fight back further. I could see in Mother's face that moment of indecision. Perhaps she still clung to a hope that he could be saved, for as I reached them both and my arm lanced out, that wicked short blade dancing forth, her hand came up at the last moment, an attempt to ward off the killing blow.

I drew blood, but from her, not him. The cut across her palm bled free, mingling with that of her son.

I shivered at what I'd done then, but I did not stop. The blade lashed out again, this time slamming into his throat, just beside the clamped hand, severing his windpipe. There was an ugly hiss and then a bloody bubbling.

I stepped back and watched Publius Septimius Geta, emperor of Rome, die in his mother's arms. I stood silent then, bloody knife still in hand. The whole room was silent but for the death throes of my brother, who finally, as the light faded in his eyes, slid from Mother's lap to land in a heap on the floor, splashing up droplets of blood from the pool into which he fell. She tried to stop the fall, reaching out to grab him, hold him up, but her wounded hand prevented her, and he fell anyway. Her eyes rose to meet mine.

There was not hate there, which I might have perhaps expected. Nor was there accusation. My plan had been masterfully executed. I was the wronged emperor, defending myself against an unbending and hateful murderer, even if he was my brother. There was in her, perhaps, regret. There was a loss and a pain that ran deep. I could see the emotion buried within her, but shivering to the surface, rising like water in a well.

'No,' I said.

Her expression shifted. Confusion?

'No. You will not weep for him. You will not mourn him. And you know why.'

It was a hard thing to say to a mother for her dead son, but this was critical. No matter from whose womb I had come forth, Julia Domna was my mother, the wife of my father, and I needed her. I would always need her. And because of that, I had to cut every last tie in the bond between her and my brother.

'He is… was my son.'

'He was an assassin. He was a Caesar who could not accept that fact. His need to take from me everything that I am was what killed him. And because of what he was and what he has done, he will be forgotten, by all the world, forever.'

Her eyes widened. 'Marcus. Please.'

'No. He will not sit with the gods, by Father's side. That is not the place for a murderer.'

A fratricide.

Me.

Her face beseeched me, even though her tongue stayed silent. But she did not cry. She did not mourn.

We stood in silence for a long time. In the end, I waved a hand, a signal to my men. Macrinus and Maximinus stepped forward. 'Take him away and burn him.'

We waited for a time then, Mother and I, with our eyes slightly averted, as my men carried my brother's body from the room.

'You will afford him at least a funeral,' Mother said. Not a question.

My expression did not change. I would rather not, but with what I planned to do, and had told her I would do, I had to compromise and grant her that one thing. I nodded. 'He will have a funeral and a good urn. We will mourn the passing of a son of Severus for one night. He shall depart in glory, and then he shall be forgotten for all time. He will not go into the tomb of emperors. Let him rest in the mausoleum of his ancestors outside the walls, on the Via Appia.'

I could see a flicker then in her eyes. Gratitude. She knew I would have to do what I'd planned. I had given her all I could afford to. He would not be dishonoured. He would rest beside his grandfather's bones, in fact. But he would never be remembered as an emperor of Rome.

'Will you ever love me again?' I asked.

Mother turned those sad, tearless eyes on me. 'I do not hate you. That will have to be enough, for now.'

Epilogue

The aftermath of Geta's demise was a busy time for me, and one that is bitterly remembered in Rome as a time of purging and of blood. A 'terror', they call it. But I could hardly have done less.

I'd spent the night after the killing in the Praetorian camp on the advice of my officers. Despite all precautions, there would still be plenty of Geta's adherents across the Palatine who might wish to strike in revenge, and so it seemed prudent. In return for the loyalty of the Praetorians I praised them and gave them a hefty bonus in coin. After all, it never does any harm to sweeten the pot, does it? That night, as I slept fitfully, my men began to arrest Geta's supporters, gradually decreasing the danger to their new sole emperor, and the next morning I addressed the senate, in the close presence of the Guard.

'I am not unaware that every murder of a kinsman, immediately the deed is known, is despised, and that the name 'kinsman-killer' arouses harsh censure as soon as it falls upon the ear. Pity follows for the victims, hatred for the victors. In such cases it appears that the victim is abused, the victor abusing.'

I went on to remind the senators of the many times I had almost fallen to the wiles of Geta, to describe the attempt on my life that previous day that had triggered the killing, to ask whether any man would do less in defence of his own life. I reminded them of the many fratricides that Rome honoured, from Tiberius and Germanicus right the way back to Romulus and Remus.

I would not say the senators were entirely sold on my innocence, but there were no immediate murmurs of dissent, and I settled for that. The military were largely already mine, and the only revolt I faced was that of the Second Parthica at Albanum, near Rome. They announced they had taken an oath to serve *both* emperors and their conscience would not allow them to change their oath. I soon learned what that oath was worth: five hundred sesterces apiece. As I said before, every man has a price. As for the public, they were easily mollified with Juvenal's old line: bread and circuses. Free food and a few bouts in the arena always buys the man in the street. And so, the senate, the people and the army all being settled, I turned to the removal of my enemies.

Perhaps I could have handled it all better, in truth, and I rushed things somewhat. It was a bloodbath, a 'terror', but I did not want to pause in the work, to be slow and steady, for to do so was to rest, and when I rested I had terrible dreams. Some nights I could sleep easy, but most brought the nightmares. The mouldering spirit of Father continued to hunt me through the halls of the palace, but now sometimes the spirit of Geta was with him, the two of them herding me to my doom like hunters with prey. And as time went on I began to relive in my dreams that last moment of blood and murder in my mother's lap.

Striving to excise the memories along with the threat, I removed anyone I considered the opposition. Everyone who had been a supporter of Geta, who had been an enemy of mine. Every slave, guard, servant and crony who had been locked away in the other palace with Geta for half a year, plotting my demise, met the edge of a blade, almost immediately. They were dumped unceremoniously in the paupers' burial pits outside the city.

Others I took more of a personal interest in. Laetus, who had maintained an oath to support both of us with equal vigour right to the end, I allowed a quiet and distinguished death. I delivered him the poison myself. Then came a steady stream of Geta's consilium. Pompeianus, Sammonicus Serenus, Helvius Pertinax, Cornificia, Julianus Asper, Thrasea Priscus, the list went on. Even our cousin Afer, who had largely stayed out of our feud, but had made a few snide remarks at a dinner, met the executioner's blade. Cilo, formerly my ally, had turned on me since the killing, and in a fit of rage I added his name to the list. I could not remove Geta's memory without sending to Hades all those who would speak his name with pride.

Perhaps the highest profile name on that list was Papinian. In the days following my sole accession, he made numerous barely veiled accusations, despite the fact that the Praetorians had confirmed publicly that there had been a plot to murder me, and that we had acted to save their emperor from a fratricide. Papinian would not accept the change.

I had considered letting him live because of his ties to Mother, but in the end I could not suffer the man any longer, and he was cut down on the steps of the palace with an axe, his body dragged through the streets along with several other dissenters, and left in an unceremonious heap. Perhaps the most personal, though, of all the proscriptions that followed, was that of the Plautianii. My dreadful wife and her family, the brood of that serpent who had sought my fall, all died on their isle of exile.

In a few short months, every man or woman in Rome who Geta had called friend had joined him in the beyond. I reiterate: I do not shy from blood, and cruelty has a place, where it has a purpose. That year its purpose was clear: the excising of my brother from history.

Over the winter, work was carried out all across the empire. Geta's name was chiselled from every inscription, his portraits smashed or refashioned into my likeness, his coins melted down and re-minted. The observance of his birthday was forbidden, and even the speaking of his name became a crime. Geta was systematically wiped from the annals of Rome.

By the time summer came around, Rome was settled and I was secure. I had begun to think about the prospect of a new match and of heirs. Mother repeatedly attempted to persuade me to adopt one of my young cousins in Syria. I declined each time. I had just rid myself of one dynastic opponent, why would I bring another to my bosom? In time I would sire an heir. For now, I had other business to attend to. Much had begun to decline while Geta and I had been at war, and the empire required my attention.

The troublesome tribes of the Danubius pressed us again, and soon I would take the army north and quell them. And after that, my true goal awaited in the East, for I would take that army against Parthia, and add Alexander's empire to my own.

The world awaited me, and I was free of the threat of my brother at last.

If only I could not feel his spectre hovering at the edge of my consciousness, a restive spirit still intent on my doom.

Sword into flesh.

Blood.

Screaming. His. Hers. Mine.

And there... the twin spectres of a father and son, reaching, faces twisting with fury.

I wake in a sweat, the nightmares assailing me even as light streams in through the shutters, forcing me to blink repeatedly, motes of dust dancing before my eyes. I am shivering, despite the summer heat, and the bed sheet is wrapped and twisted into knots, soaked.

Must it be like this?

Must I never rest?

I know that what I have done is unforgivable, and yet could I have done any different?

I rub the sweat from my eyes and focus, the world coalescing around me.

I clench my teeth and pull on the façade of imperium. I will have called out in my sleep, and slaves will be running to check on me, even though they know there is nothing wrong, for this is common to them. I cannot let them see a man hollow. They must not see the murderer.

They must see Marcus Aurelius Antoninus, emperor of Rome.

I straighten.

The good of the Empire comes above all.

Historical Note

As you now know, this novel is not the story of the damned emperor Caracalla. There are reasons for this, the main one being that Caracalla was never actually damned. He may have been an angry, violent man, and at his death he may have been unpopular in sectors of society, but he was, nonetheless, given apotheosis by his successor and allowed to ascend to the gods. This, then, is actually the story of Caracalla and Geta, and the damning of that brother, which remains to this day the most thorough and brutal *damnatio memoriae* of Roman history. The remains of Geta's name scratched out and his portraits obliterated are more numerous and clearer than any other emperor. Other rulers were removed from history generally for political reasons. What remains of Geta's defaced monuments makes it clear that his removal is something more personal and more hateful.

The main theme of this book, of course, is the lifelong feud between the two brothers. History has painted a picture of Caracalla as a vicious monster, and of Geta as the very epitome of Romanitas and gravitas. It may be that Caracalla was vicious, though perhaps not so monstrous, but it seems certain that without the spin of the sources, Geta was more likely to be the epitome of an ass than of gravitas. Caracalla did some impressive and world-changing things in his reign, and while he may well have not been a particularly nice man, he was clearly no monster if one deep-reads the sources. Geta comes down to us as a true prince of Rome, but the simple fact is that when one puts aside the spin, one can see in Caracalla's reactions to him something that triggers them. Geta likely brought upon himself some of the violence.

The simple fact is that two brothers destined to rule rarely see eye-to-eye. Caracalla and Geta were opposed from the very beginning, and no attempt to make them rule together was going to end well. The main thrust of the book aside, I would like to give the history and historiography.

Firstly, I would like to briefly address my characterisation of Caracalla. I am well aware of the prevailing opinion of the emperor, but there are three things to remember. Firstly, that this book barely touches on his actual reign, but is about his youth, competition with, and finally murder and damning of, his brother Geta. Secondly, that people change as they grow, that the Caracalla history remembers is the result of events, and much of this book takes place before and during those events. And thirdly, that emperors were very often biographised by their enemies, and sources are uniformly biased.

And so while you approached this book probably with the image of a brutal, angry, murderous, lecherous fiend who clearly did not know how to smile, remember that everyone was a child once, and that children are more innocent, and please note this rather revealing passage from the *Historia Augusta*: 'He himself in his boyhood was winsome and clever, respectful to his parents and courteous to his parents' friends, beloved by the people, popular with the senate, and well able to further his own interests in winning affection. Never did he seem backward in letters or slow in deeds of kindness, never niggardly in largess or tardy in forgiving – at least while under his parents.'

The question of Caracalla's birth and parentage is a debate that will go on, probably forever. Most historians accept the notion that he was the son of Julia Domna, the same as Geta, born more or less immediately after the parents' marriage in AD 188. Some favour a much earlier date, labelling him the son of Paccia Marciana, Severus' first wife, as early as AD 174. Another date often thrown into the mix is the one I have chosen, 186, and here are my reasons:

If Caracalla had been born in 174, he would have been fifteen years older than Geta, and any real notion of their sharing empire would be less likely. Caracalla would already have been a man and bred for succession before Geta was even born. Moreover, Caracalla is not made Caesar immediately when Severus acquires the purple, which would make sense if he was very young, but would not if he was an adult. Finally, such an early date would mean he would be twenty-seven when he was first married. I have surveyed the initial marriage dates of all emperors from Augustus to Caracalla, and that would mean only five of seventeen would have been older than him.

If he was born in the usually accepted 188, he would have been too young to have been made Caesar, which makes sense, and the only reason I decided against this really was that he would have had to have been fifteen when he was married. That is remarkably young based on the spread of emperors I checked. Of those, the mean first marriage age is twenty-five, and he would be the youngest of all of them, with even the boy emperor Nero being married later than he. It is, therefore, data which led me to choose 186 as his birth year, making him a reasonable and healthy nineteen at his marriage, and still too young to be made Caesar on his father's succession.

That, of course, still made Paccia Marciana his mother, and not Julia Domna. We only know that Paccia died of some unknown natural cause in 186 while Severus was still in Lugdunum, and anyone who has studied ancient Rome will recognise childbirth as a common natural cause in the era. I had my date. And Paccia was not around long enough for Caracalla to have formed an attachment with her. Indeed, it would be Julia Domna still who raised him from his earliest memories. As such, I reject the sensationalist, Daily Mail-esque later reports of him having a steamy affair with Julia, which would only reasonably work if he had been born in 174.

Job done. Caracalla was born in 186 to a mother who died immediately and was raised by a stepmother as her own. On a side-note, there is some suggestion that Severus and Paccia had two daughters some time earlier, but that is neither confirmed nor relevant to our tale as they never appear in the chronology, and so I have omitted them for clarity.

The first scene in this book comes from but a short line in the Historia Augusta: 'While he was in Sicily he was indicted for consulting about the imperial dignity with seers and astrologers, but, because Commodus was now beginning to be detested, he was acquitted by the prefects of the guard to whom he had been handed over for trial, while his accuser was crucified.'

This is actually a relatively minor scene, but carries a lot of weight, for it references the superstition of Severus, which was one of his prime characteristics, his destiny to rule the empire, the fall of Commodus, and the fall of Cleander. We have no details of who led to the accusations against him, but crucifixion was a punishment reserved for slaves and for the lowest of the low, and so Geta's nurse fits the bill nicely. The dreadful Cleander never did anything for anyone that was not in his own self-interest, and so he would be unlikely to have been the prefect that overturned Severus' accusation, but rather one of his successors.

I have largely bypassed the entire rise of Septimius Severus, because this is not a book about him, but about his sons. As such, I have given to the subject what space I could, but focused largely on the introduction of Plautianus, for he is a character of prime importance. The shared history of the man and Paccia Marciana is my own take. The pair, and Severus himself, were all from the same city, and so a shared history is far from impossible. Certainly something important has to be behind the enmity between Caracalla and Plautianus. Though the man marries his daughter to Caracalla in order to gain a toehold in the imperial family, there is no indication that he liked the young Caesar, and certainly we are told in no uncertain terms that Caracalla hates both Plautianus and his daughter. One might have expected, given how Plautianus attempts to use Geta as his banner that he would marry his daughter to Geta, but already Caracalla is relatively young in being married to her at nineteen. Geta would have been sixteen, and perhaps was not on the table yet, and Plautianus was impatient.

The other scene here of import is one that seems rather 'out of left field'. The scene of the young friend of a seven-year-old Caracalla being scourged for adopting the Jewish faith is directly from the Historia Augusta, albeit embellished a little in the telling. It is, along with the amphitheatre scene, which is also taken from the HA, an insight into the young Caracalla that sits heavily at odds with the image of him that history promulgates.

As we move to the east, we see Caracalla in his first real war. The scene in the Taurus mountains is taken directly from sources. We know that Candidus was replaced by Anullinus at around this time, and so I made this event the catalyst, as well as the root of what would become Caracalla's main military theme. We have no idea when the emperor started to wear the cloak that gave him his name down through history, but it is generally assumed that it was when travelling with the army.

Severus was harsh in his treatment of Antioch, far more so than his general dealings after the war, which were largely reasonable. Antioch suffered, and the Historia Augusta tells us that Caracalla overturned his father's policy. Some see this as a later move, but I have chosen to make it all part of the same time in the East. The act does, to some extent, again negate the negative opinion of Caracalla in the sources.

The campaign against Pescennius Niger is well documented. We only know that Candidus was removed from overall command by the time the force secured the Cilician Gates, not why, and so I have tied those two events together and made Anullinus the successful general. The story of the storm clearing the pass is from sources, and something, somewhere along the line, instilled in Caracalla the understanding that a war could be won in better ways than just fighting straight battles. Caracalla's history is replete with instances of him achieving military success with very little actual war involved. I have also made Anullinus the man responsible for the nickname that has carried down through millennia. Something like that had to start somewhere.

Again, the stories of the aftermath of the campaign are all taken from sources, and the speech of Cassius Clemens is not a long way from word-for-word. Caracalla's reaction to the situation is in line with many pictures of him in ancient sources, where even writers who damn him admit that in his youth, he was clever, loving, thoughtful and understanding. This also ties in with his later (after the scope of this book) decision to extend Roman citizenship to the entire empire. Sources tell us about Severus' harshness towards Antioch and Byzantium. The HA says of Caracalla, 'It was at his plea, moreover, that their ancient rights were restored to the citizens of Antioch and Byzantium, with whom Severus had become angry because they had given aid to Niger.' We do not know when this was, and some consider it one of his edicts later as emperor, but the wording suggests that this was almost on the back of Severus' own harsh rules.

We have only scant details for the brief campaigns in the East after the fall of Niger. The fact, however, that they were very much in the ancient conflict zone of Alexander and Darius, and the knowledge that in his adulthood Caracalla was obsessed with the ancient Macedonian, seemed too neat not to pull together. Ancient sources are fairly disparaging about what Severus actually achieved out there, and the fact that he refused a triumph suggests there may be something to that. Whatever the case, they returned to Rome, where, we are told by Cassius Dio, the people were not keen on another war of emperors. The scene in the Circus is from Dio. Whatever the truth of the claims that Severus sent assassins after Albinus, he certainly did strip the man of his title and make Caracalla Caesar, and that seems to have been enough to push the usurper into action.

There is a somewhat unrealistic tale about the Numerianus fellow being a teacher who pretended to be a senator and went to Gaul to raise an army and help Severus. I have commuted that sprawling tale into something a little more likely. Lupus comes off as a bit of a prat in sources, being the first general to face Albinus and losing immediately. I have given him a reason, in the form of diminished troop numbers.

We do not know precisely where the battle of Lugdunum was fought. Most of the surrounding land is fertile fields, and so the terrain would be quite flat. The accounts of the battle are a little strange, and at times confusing. Why Severus and his generals, who were good strategists, let the right wing disappear, chasing fleeing men, is a question to which I would love to hear an answer. I have had them recalled in time to play a part at the end, which at least minimises that loss of control. The battle seems to have gone on a lot longer than was normal in the era, and there seems to have been a lot of to-ing and fro-ing. The left flank change, when it happens, is peculiar. In the sources, the enemy have somehow pre-prepared the trenches in front of them, and run up to them, enticing Severus' army to chase them. There is no indication, though, that Albinus was settled and preparing for a conflict there. If he had such leisure, there are better locations he could have chosen, and so I have tweaked the tale to make the pits part of the actual action during the battle.

Afterwards, I tell the wake of the battle more or less directly from sources. It was not pretty. And then, briefly, the emperor and Caracalla visit Britannia, and Lupus is made governor. Little of note occurs there, and so I have included a scene that presages the importance of Britain to the story, and links in to what was to come.

The campaigns in the East are somewhat confused, when one compares the various sources and finds out how much they disagree. A distillation of them suggests a lengthy failed siege at Hatra, followed by a journey down the Tigris where the army finds the Parthian king wholly unprepared and to have fled. The army proceeds to sack and destroy everything in sight. Babylon is mentioned as one of their targets. During my research for the book where the importance for Caracalla of the Alexander connection began to insist itself, I could hardly help but note that he would be in the city of Alexander's death during the campaign, and so the scene in his palace seems natural.

I read somewhere, and I forget where, a line suggesting that the sacking of Ctesiphon was something of a rite of passage for Roman emperors. Plenty had done it, and plenty more would. And conversely, plenty of Parthian kings had spent their time battering Rome's eastern cities.

Little is said in sources of the following visit to Alexandria. Herodian fails to mention it entirely. Cassius Dio says, 'Thence he sailed to Upper Egypt, passing up the Nile, and viewed the whole country with some few exceptions; for instance, he was unable to pass the frontier of Ethiopia because of a pestilence. He inquired into everything, including things that were very carefully hidden; for he was the kind of person to leave nothing, either human or divine, uninvestigated. Accordingly, he took away from practically all the sanctuaries all the books that he could find containing any secret lore, and he locked up the tomb of Alexander; this was in order that no one in future should either view Alexander's body or read what was written in the above-mentioned books.' And the HA tells us, 'he turned his steps toward Alexandria, and while on his way thither he conferred numerous rights upon the communities of Palestine. He forbade conversion to Judaism under heavy penalties and enacted a similar law in regard to the Christians. [...] In after years Severus himself continually avowed that he had found this journey very enjoyable, because he had taken part in the worship of the god Serapis, had learned something of antiquity, and had seen unfamiliar animals and strange places. For he visited Memphis, Memnon, the Pyramids, and the Labyrinth, and examined them all with great care.'

In his later life, following these events, Severus became almost lame, and weak, and there is a serious suggestion that in Egypt he contracted smallpox, which is the cause of his future problems. The fact that he apparently almost entered a plague zone and that smallpox was rife at times in Africa fits well. Severus' illness, Caracalla's devotion to Serapis and later construction of one of Rome's grandest temples, the connections to Alexander and his generals, are all just too convenient to be coincidence. I have tied all the events in Egypt, which are usually briefly mentioned, into one grand sweep that connects into other parts of the tale. For a short sojourn hardly detailed in sources, Egypt was so important and had such far-reaching effects that I felt it deserved at least a chapter of its own. My description of the tomb of Alexander is from sources. The tomb has never been found. On another Alexandria side-note, sources also claim the taking of the toga virilis for Caracalla in Antioch immediately following the campaign, which would make him eleven, so I moved it to Alexandria, partially because it made a lot more sense in my story, and partially because that allowed him to be a little older and wiser.

We then cover a four-year period in brief. This is the time of Caracalla's real investiture in power, for he is made Pontifex Maximus, one of the Arval Brethren, takes part in his father's triumph, and begins to help take the reins of power. It is also the beginning of the real rise of Plautianus as he uses his position to make himself rich and powerful and inveigle himself more and more into imperial circles. As well as the drama of Plautianus and his fellow prefect, I have focused on the building programs. Septimius Severus is noted as being one of the emperors with a huge architectural impact on Rome. His monuments are well known. The bath house mentioned in the text is actually the baths later finished by and named for Caracalla. Severus also built baths as part of his palace complex on the Palatine. The important monument here, though, is the Serapeum. It is one of the least known and understood of Rome's remains, and yet one of the most important. Outside the church of Santa Maria Maggiore is a monument made from the most immense Roman column. This column is understood to be from the frontage of the great Severan temple of Serapis. Serapis became a central god for Septimius Severus and Caracalla, and given the Alexandrian connection and the results of Severus' disease, that should not be a surprise. Hadrian had apparently commissioned these columns for his rebuild of the Pantheon, but they were simply too big for the temple, and so were used instead for the Serapeum. The temple was one of the most immense in Rome, and though it is not recognised on any tourist itinerary, there are remains to be found other than that solitary column. In the Montecarvallo Gardens can be found substructures and a staircase, while other parts remain to a high standing level in courtyards of the Universita Gregoriana Pontificia. Moreover, the reclining river god statues on the Campidoglio seem to have come from this great monument.

Moving on, we have the campaign against the Garamantes. The entire campaign is poorly recorded, but a minor footnote of history. Herodian and Cassius Dio skip the whole thing. The entire campaign is historically recorded in one line in the Historia Augusta: 'He freed Tripolis, the region of his birth, from fear of attack by crushing sundry warlike tribes.' I have therefore gone to town. It struck me that this was not only a chance for Caracalla and his uncle to bond, but also for him to acquire the connection he will later show with North African cavalry. The campaign as portrayed here, as unrecorded, is entirely my own devising. Some of the details are not. The form of the towns and their water supplies are taken from archaeological evidence. For a long time the Garamantes of the classical era were presumed to be desert nomads. The level of sophistication their empire achieved has only begun to be appreciated following archaeology in the Libyan desert in the 20th century. Still, even now we know so little, and so this campaign is largely fictional in its presented form.

The rise and fall, and fall even further, of Plautianus, occupies only a few short years following the African campaign. It is clear that he had become immensely powerful. Precisely what his attacks on the empress consisted of, we do not know, but they are recorded as happening.

Of this time, Herodian tells us, 'Taking advantage of his authority, Plautianus left no act of violence undone and thus became more feared than any of the prefects before him. Severus united the two families by the marriage of his son to the daughter of Plautianus.' Cassius Dio says, 'So greatly did Plautianus have the mastery in every way over the emperor, that he often treated even Julia Augusta in an outrageous manner; for he cordially detested her and was always abusing her violently to Severus. He used to conduct investigations into her conduct as well as gather evidence against her by torturing women of the nobility. For this reason she began to study philosophy and passed her days in company with sophists,' and later that, 'for a time most of this conduct of Plautianus was not noticed by Severus himself, or, if he did know of it, he pretended not to know.'

The detail of Severus' decennalia celebration is taken from Cassius Dio, or at least the beasts and the banquet are. Later, Dio tells us: 'There took place also during those days a gymnastic contest [...]. And in this contest women took part, vying with one another most fiercely, with the result that jokes were made about other very distinguished women as well. Therefore it was henceforth forbidden for any woman, no matter what her origin, to fight in single combat.' For simple ease, I conflated these events all into the decennalia. Similarly, the banquet is not specifically explained as African, but as being barbarous and involving raw meats and living animals. Having seen some of the things eaten by Saharan tribes first-hand, it was very easy to equate the two.

Of Plautilla and her relationship with Caracalla, all we really know is snippets. Herodian gives us the best of them: 'Caracalla took no pleasure at all in this union, since he had married by compulsion, not by choice. He was exceedingly hostile to the girl, and to her father too, and refused to sleep or even eat with his wife; the truth is that he loathed her and daily promised to kill her and her father as soon as he became sole ruler of the empire.'

His uncle (also called Geta and therefore only ever referred to in this book by his praenomen or simply 'Uncle' to avoid confusion) is not mentioned in sources as being opposed to Plautianus until 204, when Cassius Dio tells us, 'When, however, his brother Geta on his deathbed revealed to him all the facts about Plautianus – for Geta hated the prefect and now no longer feared him.' This is rather telling. The wording is heavily suggestive of an ongoing feud, and we are given no reason for the man's death. It seems to me extremely suspicious that when, at the apex of his power, Plautianus becomes a target, Geta, a man close to the emperor and who hates him, mysteriously dies. That he was poisoned on Plautianus' orders is conjecture, but hardly grasping at the edge of reason. The poison I have used, hellebore, was a known one in ancient Rome, and would be readily available and easy to hide in an acrid spice.

The sign language that I give the brothers at the deathbed is, again, a fiction. No such language is known from Roman sources, but it is again far from impossible, and Socrates, in the 5th century BC, says, 'If we hadn't a voice or a tongue, and wanted to express things to one another, wouldn't we try to make signs by moving our hands, head, and the rest of our body, just as dumb people do at present?'

And so Uncle Geta has initiated the downfall of Plautianus, or the first stage of it, at least.

Caracalla's broken leg is attested in sources, as is the vying of the two brothers in many ways, including racing. It remains unconfirmed whether Geta was responsible for the injury or it was an accident, but in some ways it seems to have been a time of watershed between the two, moving from a cold war into more open hostility. I have been forced by the expediency of telling a story to play a little with the dates here, though not with the facts. The fall of Plautianus is dated to January 22nd 205, while the brothers' vying comes to a head in 206, although much of this timeline is mutable depending on sources, and so I have laid out the events in the most plausible timeline. Whether Caracalla engineered Plautianus' fall or simply announced the facts we will never know, but it seems highly likely that he was at least partially responsible, given the levels of enmity between the two.

Their sojourn in Tibur seems to have been largely uneventful, and so has not graced these pages, and we move on to a conjectural visit to the Danubian border. The histories mention no trouble or visit, yet one piece of tantalising evidence tells a whole different story. The base of a statue found at Gyor in Hungary (Roman Arrabona) is inscribed, 'Victoriae Augustorum nostrorum et legionis I adiutricis piae fidelis Antoninianae Publius Marcius Publi filius Sextianus Epheso pecunia publica decreto decurionum / dedicante Egnatio Victore legato Augustorum propraetore et Claudio Pisone legato legionis V Idus Iunias Apro et Maximo consulibus', which can be translated as, 'Faithful to the victory of our emperor and the 1st Adiutrix Legion Antoniniana, Publius Marcius, son of Publius Sextianus Ephesus set this up with public funds by the decree of the council. Dedicated by Egnatius Victor, imperial propraetorian governor, and Claudius Piso, legate of the 5th legion on the ides of June in the year of the consuls Apro et Maximo.' What this suggests is that historians, probably in demonising Caracalla and ignoring his achievements, fail to tell us of a victory in June 207 on the Danubian border. This is the story I have told.

Indeed, there are signs of reworking of the Danubian frontier in the very early third century, and while they cannot be definitively pinned to Caracalla, the Gyor inscription does suggest his presence there. Moreover, the wealth of statues and devotions to the Severans found in Dacia have usually been attested to a theoretical imperial visit by Caracalla in 213, though his movements in that year would make a visit very short and very difficult. I have therefore had Caracalla pay a visit during his time on the Danube, which makes sense and fills the space if the 213 visit is unlikely.

Of the British campaign, the Historia tells us very little, other than that Severus gained the title Britannicus, and that 'he built a wall across the island of Britain from sea to sea, and thus made the province secure – the crowning glory of his reign.' This is a fascinating point and one long argued by historians. For centuries Hadrian's Wall was thought to have been built by Severus, until evidence unearthed told us otherwise. Clearly Hadrian's Wall and the Antonine Wall both predate Severus. There have been, and still are, arguments that Offa's Dyke along the

Welsh border is the lost wall of Severus. It certainly predates Offa by centuries and bears a marked similarity to the construction style of the Antonine Wall. However, the logic of having walled off Wales, which seems to have been pacified long before, is absent. If that wall is Roman, then it must belong to an era of strife in the region, and therefore not to Severus. The generally agreed answer is that Severus repaired, altered and reinstituted the walls of Hadrian and Antoninus, and that it is the reworking of this to which the Historia alludes. This makes a great deal more sense, and is supported by archaeology. Eutropius tells us that Severus' wall was thirty-two miles long, which is not far short of the Antonine Wall's length, and so it may be that to which we should look.

Despite having the success of Agricola from which to learn, we are told that Severus' first year in Scotland was a horrible, brutal campaign of native guerrilla tactics, Roman suffering, natural obstacles and so on. We are told flatly that Severus pressed for war, even when he didn't have to, and was hungry for this, even though he could hardly walk and was carried for most of it. We are told that he went as far as the 'extremity of the island' where 'he observed most accurately the variation of the sun's motion and the length of the days and the nights in summer and winter respectively.' This cannot realistically have been the north coast of Scotland, and so likely refers to Moray, the extremity to which Agricola had marched a century earlier. Despite this, he is accorded with success against the Caledonii before the winter, only then to face a revolt of the Maetae the following season.

We have no fine detail of the campaign, and so the part I have devised for you, which fits with the sources, follows a push from Stonehaven (which, as a personal conceit I have jokingly named Portus Lapidaria) and the fort at Raedykes, up into the hills, travelling north-west until it reaches the River Dee around Banchory. The line then heads up past Aboyne and to the site of my battle, the unfinished hillfort of Knockargety Hill. All we know from sources is that the natives employed guerrilla warfare and that Rome was brutal in response. Another writer's conceit is my having Severus position forts at the head and foot of Loch Ness, which would effectively secure control of half the highlands, cutting enemy territory in two. The Romans must have been aware of this geographical feature and the element of control it offered cannot have escaped their notice. While there are no confirmed Roman forts in the region, there are tantalising records of what looks like a Roman fort found in the 18th century at the head of Loch Ness but then utterly destroyed during work on the canal. It may be that this was the northernmost fort in the empire, and could have been the work of Severus, if, in fact, it truly existed and was actually Roman. It remains a tempting enigma, and if there was a fort there, then logic would have a fort at the other end of the loch, which may yet one day be located.

The winter that follows in this book contains events drawn from Cassius Dio and from the Historia Augusta. The scene of Caracalla drawing a blade at his father's back is noted by Dio. In the source, it is intimated that this was a genuine attempt on his father's life, and the scene with Papinian and the sword is lifted from that same text. The fact that there is no suggestion that Caracalla had ever coveted his father's throne casts doubt on this. He was co-emperor already and stood to inherit, and his father was old and increasingly infirm. He really had nothing to gain from killing his father, even if he felt like it. Thus, I have manufactured an explanation in the form of the native with a sword. The following scene, with the Ethiopian rider, is from the Historia Augusta, and is taken as one of the omens of the emperor's impending demise. The scene with the persecution of Christians is based on strong suggestions. There were certainly persecutions in 209 in Africa, and it is possible that it was at this time that Saint Alban was executed and martyred, becoming the first British saint. If so, then the blame can be laid squarely at the feet of Geta, for we know that he was essentially running the province for his father that year.

Herodian directly accuses Caracalla of an attempt on his ailing father's life with 'he tried to persuade the physicians to harm the old man in their treatments so that he would be rid of him more quickly', to which we also add his 'he killed the physicians who had refused to obey his orders to hasten the old man's death.' The Historia Augusta, which usually gives us anything juicy about an emperor fails to mention any of this, while Cassius Dio contents himself with carrying on rumour: 'his sickness carried him off on the fourth of February, not without some help, they say, from Antoninus.' Once again, there seems so little reason for this, with Severus already dying, and Caracalla already ruling, and so these rumours are almost certainly fictitious. Still, I have worked them into the story. One interesting fact in support of Caracalla's executions, though, is the case of Galen. That world-famous doctor had been

Septimius Severus' court physician, as well as the emperor's before him, and interestingly his date of death is placed somewhere between AD 199 and 216, and likely after 204, his cause of death not recorded. It is therefore entirely plausible that Galen was one of these victims in 211.

We are told virtually nothing of the end of the British campaign following Severus' death in sources. Herodian tells us he 'signed a treaty with the barbarians, offering them peace and accepting their pledges of good faith. And now he abandoned this alien land.' While Cassius Dio says only, 'With the enemy he came to terms, withdrew from their territory, and abandoned the forts.' Herodian's phrasing suggests a military success that brings supplicative terms, and that is what I have described.

We are told that Caracalla attempted to persuade all that he had the sole right to rule following his father's death, and that when he failed in this he grudgingly accepted joint rule, though never in his heart. That the brothers journeyed back to Rome separately and did not trust one another enough to stay in the same place is noted, as is the division of the palace on their return to Rome. No mention is made of who transported the ashes home. I have made most of the factors preventing internecine bloodshed the work of Julia Domna, which is not expressly said in sources, but is far from unrealistic given her strength, and makes the most sense.

The funeral of Severus back in Rome is taken directly from Herodian, while Cassius Dio furnishes us with the tales of the sacrifice to concord and the wolves on the capitol. On the division of the palaces, we are not given any details. Caracalla's biographer Ilkka Syvanne favours the Severan wing being divided between them, though given the sheer scale of the Palatine palaces, I see it as unlikely that both would squeeze into one corner, and so have given them the two more recent residences on the hill, one each, with the rest to their mother.

The following months are a violent time in the sources. Caracalla is named as the slayer of a number of luminaries, though often the timing is not clear and some may have been either at this time or in the aftermath of Geta's demise. The death of Euprepes is attributed in sources to simple hatred, and the details of the deaths of Castor and Euodus are very brief and uninformative. What is clear is that the relationship between the brothers had by now completely broken down to a mutual loathing and constant near warfare. Herodian is the man who tells us in detail of the plan to divide the empire. That it was Geta's idea and not a mutual one thrown out by their mother makes more sense, when the proposition is that Caracalla gets the East, yet we know from sources just how obsessive he was over Alexander the Great. Hence the argument I have given them that breaks down the meeting. Following that failure, the two emperors were on an unstoppable spiral into bloodshed.

My account of Geta's death follows the lines of what we are told by the historians, though I attempt to make some sense of it. It was clearly Caracalla's intent to kill his brother, but there is something that doesn't quite ring true in the accounts.

The Historia Augusta tells us little of the actual events: 'he went to the Praetorian Camp and complained there to the soldiers that his brother was forming a conspiracy against him. And so he had his brother slain in the Palace, giving orders to burn his body at once. He also said in the Camp that his brother had shown disrespect to their mother.'

Herodian would perhaps have given us a solid account, but for a missing section of text at the crucial moment: 'Since his plotting was unsuccessful, he thought he must try some desperate and dangerous scheme; [a lacuna in the text here, missing the actual murder], his mother dying of grief and his brother from treachery. Mortally wounded, Geta died, drenching his mother's breast with his blood. Having succeeded in the murder, Caracalla ran from the room and rushed throughout the palace, shouting that he had escaped grave danger and had barely managed to save his life.'

And so our most complete account comes from Cassius Dio: 'Antoninus induced his mother to summon them both, unattended, to her apartment, with a view to reconciling them. Thus Geta was persuaded, and went in with him; but when they were inside, some centurions, previously instructed by Antoninus, rushed in a body and struck down Geta, who at sight of them had run to his mother, hung about her neck and clung to her bosom and breasts, lamenting and crying: "Mother that didst bear me, mother that didst bear me, help! I am being murdered." And so she, tricked in this way, saw her son perishing in the most impious fashion in her arms, and received him at his death into the very womb, as it were, whence he had been born; for she was all covered with his blood, so that she took no note of the wound she had received on her hand.'

Later, addressing the senate, Caracalla tells them, 'In his final act of treachery, Geta burst in upon me while I was with my mother, accompanied by swordsmen whom he had obtained for this attempt upon my life.'

There can be little doubt that Geta was hardly an innocent victim at this time. We've been told repeatedly that the brothers had been at one another's throat. We are told by Dio, 'Antoninus wished to murder his brother at the Saturnalia, but was unable to do so; for his evil purpose had already become too manifest to remain concealed, and so there now ensued many sharp encounters between the two, each of whom felt that the other was plotting against him, and many defensive measures were taken on both sides.' And so I have folded the Saturnalia attempt into a longer-term plot which culminates in Geta's death in his mother's arms.

We are told that Julia is prevented from mourning her son, but that does not account for ongoing history. Throughout Caracalla's life as sole emperor, his mother continues to play a central role at court, supporting him. Even in his last days out in the East, Julia helps rule the empire. Her close support of Caracalla for the rest of his years does not speak of an outraged mother and the murderer of her son. That Geta was given a rich funeral and buried with his ancestors says something. There may have been a damnatio memoriae upon his name, and the most complete in Roman history, yet he was not dishonoured in death.

Quite simply the truth of what happened in those final days and the relationships between mother and two sons will undoubtedly never be known. All we can do is interpret what we have and construct a most plausible series of events, causes and relationships.

And so Geta is dead, and with him, the scope of this novel is over, for this was never intended to detail Caracalla's reign. Despite his reputation, he would go on for a number of years, making sweeping changes across the empire, he would build impressive monuments, and campaign on the Danube and then in the East in an attempt to conquer the former empire of his hero, Alexander. He went back to Alexandria in 215, although he is said to have initiated a slaughter there. He would never succeed in adding Alexander's empire to his own, despite attempting to do so through both military and political means, even attempting a match with the Parthian King of Kings' daughter. He would never get to finish his campaign.

Of Geta's damning and of Caracalla's later remorse and bad dreams, we are told the following. By Cassius Dio: 'He exhibited his hatred for his dead brother by abolishing the observance of his birthday, and he vented his anger upon the stones that had supported his statues, and melted down the coinage that displayed his features' and then, 'he was sick not only in body, partly from visible partly from secret ailments, but in mind as well, suffering from certain distressing visions, and often he thought he was being pursued by his father and by his brother, armed with swords. Therefore he called up spirits to find some remedy against them, among others the spirit of his father and that of Commodus. But not one of them spoke a word to him except Commodus; as for Severus, they say that Geta accompanied him, though unsummoned. Yet not even Commodus said anything to help him, but, quite the contrary, so that he terrified him all the more.'

And so ends my tale of Caracalla, and of Geta, the damned emperor, and with it the last of the Damned Emperors novels. In many ways, the attempted absolute removal of Geta from history is the culmination of the damnatio memoriae, and so it seems appropriate to end here.

Simon Turney
September 2022

Septimius Severus
(British Museum)

Caracalla
(Vatican Museum)

Geta
(Palazzo Altemps,
Rome)

Julia Domna
(Vatican Museum)

Inscription from Alba
Iulia in Romania
showing the removal
of Geta's name

The 'Severan Tondo',
showing the Severan
family with Geta's
image defaced
(Berlin Altes Museum)